Her brother walked only a few feet from the steps, until they stepped outside the sphere cast by the exterior light at the entrance. "What is it, Flick?"

"I think you know."

"How could I?"

"Oh, you know."

He grimaced then tried to blank his expression. "It could be a half-dozen things."

"You've never been a good actor, Old Thing."

"You're angry. I don't know the reason. How could I? You've said nothing to give me a clue."

"Clue." That word was choice. "Let's start with the hardest. Did you kill George Webberly? In the bit of time you were gone from the service, did you kill him?"

Portrait with Death
Into Death ~ 3

by
M. A. Lee

WRITERS INK BOOKS

Joy comes with the Dawn

Historical Mysteries from M.A. Lee

Hearts in Hazard
Regency Mysteries with a Dash of Romance

A Game of Secrets
A Game of Spies
A Game of Hearts

The Dangers of Secrets
The Dangers for Spies
The Dangers to Hearts

The Key to Secrets
The Key for Spies
The Key with Hearts

The Hazard of Secrets
The Hazard for Spies
The Hazard with Hearts

Isabella Newcombe's Into Death

Digging into Death
Christmas with Death
Portrait with Death

Contents

Can an artist avoid death when murder paints with blood?

Chapter 1

Wednesday, 31 January 1920

The train whistle blew. Steam clouded the grimy platform. People rushed past, laden with parcels that hadn't gone to freight. Others sauntered along the platform, through the vapor wafting from beneath the engine. Small clutches of people lingered, saying goodbye.

Madoc hoisted his tightly-packed canvas duffle over his shoulder. He gave a shake of his head, to get his black hair out of his eyes. In the months since they'd met, his hair had grown. Isabella thought he had a personal goal to rid himself of anything like the military cut forced on him for years.

The conductor called for boarding, and tears flooded Isabella's eyes. He was leaving. Now. Not weeks, not days. Now. She wouldn't see him for months.

He touched her cheek. "None of that, Bella."

"I wish I were traveling with you, Madoc."

"Not yet. Only two and a half months. Then I will count the days until your ship arrives in Calcutta."

"Seventy-six days, during which I work madly to finish an oil painting and store what we won't need in that box room that Gawen's offering, then I count the days. And try to finish the illustrations for his articles. He hasn't written the last two yet."

"You'll come up with something he can use. You also have those pen-and-ink drawings for Tony Carstairs. London sites."

"I have no worries about the drawings for Tony, but I'm running out of artifacts for your brother." She fretted over the drawings because she dared not fret about his leaving. Married a month, and Madoc was heading to a faraway place. "Madoc, must you work your passage on this cargo ship? I can take a smaller berth or share with someone."

"I need to stay active on this voyage." He had rejected all her ideas for his travel to India, every idea she'd advanced over the past month of their marriage. "Captain Harvey is a cousin of one of my former soldiers. And working my passage will keep me busy. I'll fall into my bunk every night, too worn out to miss you, love."

Isabella clutched his arm. Nightmares no longer plagued him nightly, but they still occurred at odd times, for odd reasons. He'd been demobbed for over a year now. He wouldn't want his new shipmates to know he had any weakness. Madoc made friends easily; he'd win them over—but they would be cautious if nightmares were their introduction to him.

"Besides," he added, "I'm not certain what living arrangements Mr. Tredennit has set up in Calcutta. We won't cross to Australia until July. Our summer is their winter."

"An upside-down world."

"A shake-up of your normal world. It will affect your art." He flicked the golden end of her braided hair. "I'll write letters or send a cable from every port until we reach Calcutta."

The conductor called again.

Madoc bussed her lips with the briefest caress, risking censure for that public affection. Then he was gone, climbing into his compartment. He dropped the window to lean out.

She wanted to climb into that compartment with him.

The train engine groaned then began to pull, wheels squealing on the tracks before they caught and tugged. A man bumped her. A boy dashed between her and the train. When she steadied, the passenger cars were rolling, taking Madoc farther and farther away, faster and faster. He waved. She blew him a kiss. He stretched as if catching it, carried his closed fist to his lips. Then the vapor swirled, the train gained more speed and left the station, heading into the rain and away from her.

She yanked out a handkerchief and blotted her wet cheeks.

"Very touching," said a wry voice behind her. "Shall we have tea before we start back? I know a shop a few streets from the station. They have clotted cream fresh from the countryside."

"Cecilia," Madoc's brother Gawen said to his new wife, in a sigh rather than a quelling tone. "We planned to have tea at home."

Gawen and Cecilia had insisted on joining them on the platform, partly to see Madoc off, partly to give Isabella support.

The two brothers were tight-knit. Gawen also hadn't liked his younger brother working his passage to India and then to Australia. He understood the reason. He posed his arguments. Madoc hadn't listened to him or to Isabella.

Cecilia had insisted on coming to the station for Isabella's sake. She was intent on bolstering her friend. Isabella hadn't moaned to anyone about Madoc's leaving, yet Cess sensed her dismay. She'd tried dozens of distractions in the past fortnight. She had many more planned for the brief days before Isabella left to paint that portrait.

She didn't begrudge the commission for the portrait. It would bring money, a lot of money, money to give her and Madoc a good emergency fund when they set up home in Australia. His job there would take months. Nor was the portrait the chief reason that she had to wait before taking ship to join him. That was the lack of a berth. With the war over and all countries in harmony imposed by treaty, their citizens had eagerly returned to traveling. The first affordable berth that Isabella could book wasn't until April.

Seventy-six days from now.

An oil portrait. Six illustrations for Gawen, based on her remaining sketches from Crete and two artifacts. Ten pen-and-ink drawings for Tony Carstairs. Watercolor landscapes. *Surely those will fill my empty hours without Madoc?*

Cecilia pointed at the railway clock visible on the platform. "It's a half-hour to lunch. Let's eat at a tea shop then go on to St. George's. Gawen, you do need talk to Isabella about your last two articles, and she can see the artifacts that you've picked for illustrations. Then she shall come to the flat for dinner."

"No, I must call a rain check for dinner. I must finish my packing. I want everything almost out of the Kirkgardie Street flat before Filly Malvaise moves into your old room. I still have boxes and boxes."

"I still want you to stay with us." Cecilia looped a hand through Isabella's elbow. Her other hand hooking on her new husband's arm, she steered them off the platform and to the stairs. People coming down the steps had to venture to the side.

"I will not, Cess. You and Gawen married last weekend. You need time alone together."

"We'll have time when you leave."

They emerged onto the street and into a cold rain that spat ice. Isabella popped up her umbrella while Gawen managed one for Cess and him. Cess turned and spoke, but the street traffic drowned her words. Isabella nodded anyway and followed them like a well-trained puppy.

Funny. Last summer I had to fend for myself, and I'll be alone again when I travel to Upper Wellsford for the portrait. Not completely alone, though. Far from her, Madoc was still her husband, and Cess and Gawen were family.

London looked grey and dingy and dreary. Weeks in the countryside as spring emerged would be much better than cooped up in the congested city.

She hoped Madoc found a friend on ship. *He'll make friends quickly. He'll find out their destination and their jobs on board and draw out their life stories.*

That didn't reassure her.

His ability to talk easily to strangers, to manage an unknown crew of workers, and to know work that needed to be done even without a prep for it: those traits had impressed Michael Tredennit. The older man had offered Madoc this chance. The new job had excellent pay and compensation for travel and an opportunity for advancement.

I'm happy for him. I am. I just wish—.

"Isabella, what do you think?"

She came to the present with a jolt and realized they'd passed Gawen's roadster. "Sorry, I was wool-gathering. What did you ask?"

Cess exchanged a knowing look with Gawen then indicated the tea shop across the street. Brightly lit windows offered comfort from the elements. Ice pellets spattered her umbrella. The tea shop's sunny interior, revealed above the bright blue café curtains, promised warmth and welcome. Cecilia launched into a description of a large luncheon.

Isabella listened to little of it. "Of course. Whatever fits with your plans."

She tried to be less distracted as they lunched. The food was excellent and warming. The waitress allowed them to linger. Gawen talked of the last cataloging for the artifacts brought from Crete. Cecilia brimmed with plans for her columns for *Modern Woman* and how her work fit so easily into Gawen's life. She tried a discussion of the new direction in the spring fashion magazines, but Isabella refused to engage in that conversation.

Then Cess began planning visits to four different couturiers, with Isabella needed for quick sketches.

"When are you planning to visit these fashion houses?"

"Next week."

"You forget. I'm leaving for the Midlands in three weeks. I have packing. I have Gawen's illustrations and those drawings for Tony. I can't sketch countless models for you."

"Your trip is a month away."

"Not really. You will want these sketches to be magazine-perfect, won't you?"

"Of course. Just like you do for Gawen."

"That's not enough time. Cess. It's not. Not with everything else I must do."

"Can you not delay your journey? Start the portrait at the end of February? Or in mid-March? Please! A few extra days only."

Isabella cut into the luscious tiramisu, its aroma of coffee and chocolate promising delight. "I shall be at the outer edge of my timeline as it is. I dare not take extra days, or I'll interfere with completing my commission. I won't delay boarding ship." She smiled at her friend, trying to take the sting out of her stubborn stance. "Let me talk to Tony. He may know of a young artist willing to do your fashion sketches."

"Whoever it is," she said glumly, "will want pay for their time."

"Were you not going to pay me?" At Cess's startled look, Isabella laughed.

"I *fully* intended to pay you, Isabella."

"The hole gets deeper," Gawen murmured then hid a smile behind his coffee cup while Cecilia blustered about payment.

The afternoon passed as planned. The ice turned back into rain.

When Isabella called a cab to take her back to the Kirkgardie flat, Cecilia waited with her in the entrance. "Do talk to your Mr. Carstairs. Give him my new address. Will we see you this weekend?"

"With a lorry in tow. I hope to have several boxes packed, ready for storage."

"Stay for dinner. I'd have you visit us every night for dinner before you leave for Upper Slaughter."

Isabella chuckled at the name. "Upper *Wellsford*. Next to *Lower* Wellsford. It has its own rail spur."

"Upper Slaughter," Cess declared firmly. "I predict that your curiosity will be slaughtered within three days of your arrival in that sleepy hamlet. You don't have to stay there the whole time, do you? You can visit us. Every weekend."

"Perhaps not that often. Oil paint sometimes has a mind of its own. I'll ring you if I wish to visit."

"How will you cart that monstrous canvas to Upper Slaughter? Why did the dowager want it nearly life-size?"

"He's her only living grandson and heir to the barony. I'm making a very nice commission, Cess. The canvas and my easel should arrive before I do."

"Oh, bother. That's the cab man. You can manage everything else? If you need anything—."

"I'll see you several times before I go. And I will ask for help if I need it."

"I feel as if my sole fledgling chick is flying the nest. I'll *miss* you, Isabella."

"I'll write daily, Mother."

"Oh, you!"

In this day of bright lipstick, they air-kissed. *Like a posh Bright Young Thing*, Isabella thought as she ran down the steps and slid into the cab.

She understood Cess' strange feeling of loss. It had started for her when a gunshot nearly killed Cess. Madoc's ocean voyage tripled the feeling of deprivation. Life's changes weren't always a blessing.

Cess had no one beyond their little circle. As the youngest daughter of Viscount Salton, she had had a wide circle of acquaintants. Yet she hadn't had friends who became closer than family until the fraught events of last October. The viscount had threatened to cut ties when Cess wanted to marry Gawen. They had married. Maybe the viscount hadn't followed through with his threat.

Isabella was just as alone. She had only an aunt for bloodkin, but that worthy remained in the States. Her marriage to Madoc had barely renewed the feeling of family before his imminent departure loomed. Cecilia and Gawen were her only friends on this side of the Atlantic, and soon Isabella would depart and enter another world where she knew virtually no one.

The cab trundled away, bouncing over pavement that needed repair, the rain pelting the windows and blurring everything around.

Or maybe that was the tears in her eyes.

.~.~.~.

Thursday, 5 February 1920

Flick Sherborne perched on a corner of Alicia Osterley's littered desk and watched as her friend examined the photographic prints she had handed over as soon as she entered.

Blinking owlishly behind the thick round glasses that gave her the nickname of Owl, Alicia closely examined several of the prints. She hadn't commented when Flick had presented her the courier envelope. She merely unwound the string and drew out the prints, spreading them on her desk to see the full range.

That's how Flick knew Alicia would rise in the editing world. Already she had the behavior of Alan Rettleston, managing editor of the *London Daily*. No one had taught Owl the editing job; she came full-fledged with the knowledge. Cold logic about the facts, critical objectivity to judge the audience, emotional reaction held last, after all decisions.

With over two decades in the newspaper world, Alan Rettleston was emotionally stunted. Would Owl become that way? Her boss Lottie Crittenden wasn't. Lottie was a publisher, not a busy editor. *Modern Woman* was her third publication. Where had Lottie gotten her seed money for *Modern Woman*?

Lottie and her nieces Greta Ffoulkes and Tori Malvaise threw fabulous parties filled with London's Bright Young Things and artistic effetes. Flick rarely attended. Even more rarely did she receive an invitation—although the current obligatory invitation was propped on the dining table underneath the kitchen window. Like Owl, she was an employee more than a social equal. When Owl did attend a party, Flick imagined she blinked—well, owlishly at the goings-on in London's high society. Those attending the fast and wickedly daring parties weren't the readership for *Modern Woman*. Owl didn't need to understand wild scavenger hunts and swimming in public fountains and all-night binges driven by white powder.

Owl was a babe in the editing world. Maybe she would escape the jaded cynicism of Alan Rettleston.

The current red-edged invitation came from Greta Ffoulkes, for a Valentine's party. A masquerade The best of young London would be there, eager to celebrate the lives they hadn't risked in the past war. Champagne would flow faster than conversation, and the dancing faster still. Secrets would become public, rumors would start, facts would be forgotten. She might go. In the crowd, no one would look too closely at her reworked black satin. A black mask for her eyes, a red flower pinned to her dark hair, and the Spanish shawl for an artistic touch.

"These are good." Owl slid six prints toward her, the ones of women workers taking a smoke break outside a factory. The women's coveralls hung baggily, with rolled cuffs at wrist and ankle. Their scarves and earrings said *Woman at Work*. The only thing that they shared with the few pictured men were tired faces and slouched bodies leaning against the brick factory walls. "Very good yet not for us. Sorry, Flick. I don't have an article in the next six months that these photos will support. If something changes—."

Sliding off the desk, Flick stacked the photos and tucked them back into the courier envelope she'd swiped from her father's firm. "No worries, Owl. Rettleston will want a few of them. I wanted you to have first pick."

Her friend sighed. "I wish I did have something. So many women will lose their jobs now that the men are demobilized. Perhaps I could commission an article—."

"Not me. I don't write the heavy-hitting. My garden features suit me very well, thank you." Her blue eyes narrowed. "Do you need a break? You look as tired as those workers."

"Perhaps we could do a photo spread. No words. You can tell a narrative without words." She held out her hand for the envelope.

Flick tugged harder at the string that closed it. "You don't get two refusals in one visit, my friend. Alan Rettleston gets second refusal. Besides, a photo spread of working women is not really the audience of *Modern Woman*."

"I know, but the occasional feature—I could argue for it."

"Let Rettleston do his work. Don't worry about me."

Owl pursed her lips as she scrutinized Flick. "You look thinner."

"It's the pants." She tugged at the wide-legged worsted pants made from a man's suiting pin-stripe.

"Are you eating enough?"

Gosh, Owl was determined. She pressed a false humor into action. "Three meals a day. Positively stuffed." She blew out her cheeks.

"Are they square meals?"

"On a round plate. Stop worrying about me, Owl. Or do worry in this way. Would you be interested in a public school garden feature? Boys on a manicured lawn would make fond mothers sigh with contentment. The public school I'm thinking of has clipped topiary. Very photogenic. I have a couple of photos from last October that would work for any publication date, even summer, and the topiary is evergreen."

"Anything you bring us about flowers and gardens we'll take. That's from Mrs. Crittenden herself. We had a flood of letters after your December feature on orchids. It was as if English women had never heard of orchids. Are you thinking of Greavley Abbey where your brother is?"

"Yes. All unexpectedly, too."

"He's not doing well?"

Flick didn't answer that. Owl's fascination with Chauncey was long standing. Chauncey didn't know of it and likely never would. Owl just blinked owlishly at him. "He needs a visitor to take him out of Greek conjugations and Old Guard politics, for which he has little patience."

"When do you leave?"

"A couple of weeks." She slung the strap for her tote over her shoulder. The big bag held her most prize possession, a Kodak Autographic Special camera, bought off a newshound who worked at the *London Daily,* Rettleston's paper. "I must wrap up things here." She grinned, knowing she would look like an eager street imp with her bobbed dark hair and over-sized flight jacket handed down from her brother Allworthy, an ace in the Royal Air Force. "Lottie's party this weekend. The mater's tea before Valentine's Day. A masquerade. Dinner with Rettleston one night."

"You don't have to dine with—."

"Whirlwind shopping with friends. One must have tweed for the country. I might see the rest of winter in Upper Wellsford and bring back more than one article with photos for you."

"I wish I could take those workers," Owl fretted.

"It's not a problem."

"Will you—?" She dropped her eyes and toyed with the fountain pen on her desk. "Please tell Chauncey that I said hello." The bland words didn't match the eagerness that had started her broken-off question.

"I will."

Chauncey might not remember Owl. The petite dark-haired girl with a round face dominated by thick black spectacles would have barely registered on his pre-war scale.

Maybe he had changed. Maybe serving as Greek master at Greavley Abbey School in a sleepy village had changed him for the better.

Shame about the photos, though. Women losing work should be the focus of *Modern Woman*, not flower features.

Chapter 2

Friday, 27 February

Herbert Pollard ran the Hook and Line Pub with a strict hand. From under thatchy brows threaded with more silver than his sandy hair, he stared at the small watercolor easel that Isabella had brought on the train. Beside it on the bar lay her sketchbook, sliding out of her artist's tote, a leather satchel confiscated from Madoc. Isabella fished in her purse for the three envelopes sent from the dowager Lady Malvaise, introductory letters to Mr. Pollard and the prep school's headmaster and young Edward Malvaise, the subject of her portrait.

"We don't approve of the wild goings-on that painters do," Mr. Pollard said heavily. "Specially American painters what call themselves *artistes*."

"We run a nice establishment," his wife interjected from the end of the bar where she worked on ledgers.

The whistle for the departing train blew.

Chilled from the late February wind, Isabella stopped hunting in her purse and turned to the satchel. "Of course not. I mean, I'm reassured that you don't approve of wild goings-on. A woman alone—." She trailed off, letting them complete the sentence with the clichéd responses. Her icy fingers finally felt the three letters forwarded from Lady Malvaise's secretary-companion. She withdrew them and removed the red cord that bound them. Mr. Pollard's letter was on the bottom. Fighting shivers from her walk from the train station, she handed over his. "Did you receive the large easel and canvas and box that I sent? Those were supposed to arrive this morning."

He stared at the letter as if he didn't know what to do with it. "Aye, brought to us this morning they were. I put them in the room you hired."

Isabella winced, thinking of small rooms offered by pubs and the size of the easel and the canvas. The box, the size of a milk crate, had her paints and brushes and turpentine and palette. Would the room hold her?

"What's in this?" He tapped the envelope on the bar.

"Lady Malvaise has promised to pay for my room and board. She writes of the arrangements for you to draw the funds." At least, that was the agreement in her own letter from the secretary. She hadn't opened any letter but her own. "I don't know all the particulars. Will there be a problem with my staying the length of time that I mentioned in my letter of the fifth?"

"No, no problem."

His wife left her stool and came behind the bar to take the letter her husband handed her. "When you wrote, we thought you were a momma worried about her son. His first time away from home and all that. We didn't know you were an artist from America, not until that easel arrived."

"Oh. A momma with a son at Greavley Abbey School. No. I'm not really all the way from America, either. I live in England with my husband. He's Welsh. Madoc Tarrant. The reason that I've come here, to Upper Wellsford, is that Lady Malvaise's grandson attends Greavley Abbey School. It's his portrait that I am to paint."

"The dowager Malvaise?" Mrs. Pollard slanted a look at her husband as she unfolded the letter then dropped her gaze to read. She looked two decades younger than he. Her pale brows pinched in, then she turned to the second page. Whatever she read there turned her incipient frown into a wide smile. "Why, that's fine, then." She turned to her husband. "We'll have no trouble accommodating Mrs. Tarrant. It's as she says. Lady Malvaise will cover any charges for her room and board." She tucked the letter back into the envelope. "And her grandson's at the Abbey School. Has he been there long, Mrs. Tarrant?"

"I think he has attended for several years. I'm not certain, though. I suppose it is too late to introduce myself to Mr. Filmer the headmaster or to Edward Malvaise."

As a bar maid appeared, Mrs. Pollard waved her husband back to his work. She rested an elbow on the bar and watched Isabella tuck the remaining two letters and her sketchbook into the leather satchel. "As to the boy, it's much too late. He'll have Friday Evensong and Compline to attend. Dean Filmer usually comes in after the service. That's late," she added.

Isabella nodded and smiled and murmured her gratitude. Everything they said was helpful. If that meant pretending that she knew nothing about Church of England services, then so be it. Her father had enjoyed what he called "high church liturgy" and the prayers of the canonical hours. A professor of history, he'd relished steeping himself in ritual and music and a setting with a strong weight of centuries.

She missed him terribly sometimes.

Not so much since her marriage to Madoc—although now she missed her husband.

"Will Mr. Filmer come to the pub after ten o'clock?"

"Closer to half-past. You better call him Dean Filmer. That's what he goes by. The dean. The teachers are masters. Some kind of Greavley foolishness, but you know public schools and their traditions."

That reminded Isabella that she'd hadn't seen any women in the pub. "Do you have any policies that I should know about?"

"We have quiet nights here. No ladies in the pub after tea-time unless accompanied by their husbands or sons or a man of the village. Since you wish to meet Dean Filmer, I suppose that gives you permission to be in the pub, but not on a regular basis, Mrs. Tarrant."

"I will keep that in mind. Will I take meals in my room?"

"Bless you, no, Mrs. Tarrant. We have a small sitting room reserved for guests. Mr. Pollard calls it the lounge. We have seating there and tables to serve dinner and breakfast to our paying guests. We keep city hours," she added, sounding proud of that. "Lunch here in the pub, of course. If you're to miss a meal service, be pleased to let us know several hours in advance."

"That suits me perfectly." She and Mrs. Pollard exchanged smiles.

After their original quick judgement, Isabella hadn't expected to like the Pollards. She'd gradually revised her opinion of Mrs. Pollard. The husband remained a mystery.

Isabella slung the strap of Madoc's satchel over her shoulder and gathered up her small easel and purse. Then she bent her knees to pick up her bulky suitcase.

"Sibby!" Mr. Pollard called. "Sibby! That girl!" When no one appeared at the swinging door behind the bar, he pushed it wide, offering a view into a busy kitchen. "Sibby! Get in here."

The bar maid came out, tucking loose strands of hair behind her ears. With her dark hair and trim figure, she would have been pretty, but a scowl marred her sharp features. "What am I to do now?"

Mrs. Pollard rolled her eyes and returned to her ledgers. Mr. Pollard rapped out several sentences about "come when you're called" and "work for me at whatever I say". He finished with "Don't be frowning at me, or you'll be looking for another position."

Sibby kept her gaze on him throughout and nodded or shook her head at the appropriate moments. When Mr. Pollard wound down, she crossed her arms over her bibfront apron. "What's to do?"

"This is Mrs. Tarrant," his wife said calmly from the end of the bar. "Take her suitcase, and show her to the room we've prepared. Freshen the water in her pitcher, and give her extra cloths."

Sibby came around the bar. "This it?" and she reached for the suitcase.

Having lugged it from the station along with her small easel and satchel while the February wind bit through her, Isabella happily relinquished it.

For all her slenderness, Sibby had no trouble with the suitcase on the steep stairs to the first floor. The hall had windows at either end. Light filtered through lacy curtains. The uncarpeted floor looked oiled rather than waxed. Isabella's city pumps clicked on the wood while the bar maid passed more soundlessly in plain brogues.

Sibby stopped at the last room. "This room looks onto the back. You'll like that. Not so noisy as the front." She swung the suitcase onto the bed.

Isabella winced, for the coverlet was a pale printed quilt with interlocked rings in pink and rose and purple. "Do they call that pattern 'wedding ring'?" She peered around the room. The large easel and canvas that she had shipped were just inside the door, leaning against the wall, taking up the scant walk-space on this side of the bed. Madoc had knocked out the easel of rough wood and left it unsanded since it would be freighted. Brown paper wrapped the canvas, protecting it during transport.

"I have no idea. I'm not much for sewing." The bar maid edged around the bed to a square table tucked into the front corner. She claimed a transferware pitcher adorned with a country scene. "I'll get your water, ma'am."

Isabella pressed against the bed to let Sibby pass, then she placed her purse and satchel beside her suitcase. She propped the little easel under the large one.

This room would be her home for the next twelve weeks. *Surely the painting will be done by then!* The little square table for the pitcher and basin took up the corner, with a small round mirror hanging above a shelf. A man who had to shave would devolve to many gyrations to see his face. She stepped over her box of paint supplies, shoved against the foot of the bed. Once around, she found that the other side had much more room. Under the window was a narrow table and a single chair. She switched on the japanned metal lamp, and the room took on a muted glow. Lace curtains half-covered the windows, but there were also heavy drapes pushed aside to reveal the misty landscape. After peering at the twilight-dim back garden, she drew the curtains. She was examining the shelves and hangers of the wardrobe between the bed and the outside wall when Sibby returned.

"Will you have dinner in the lounge or up here, Mrs. Tarrant?"

"Below, please. I intend to start as I mean to go on. Do you think we'll have snow in the morning?" That didn't bode well for her paints. Hopefully, she would soon have her preliminary sketching done, on paper and on the canvas.

"Weather report says Sunday will be warm and sunny, then we're back to cold and rain. There's towels in the bathroom. That's down the hall, right next to the stair. The WC is across from it. Do you think you'll need more cloths for washing?" Sibby had taken to heart Mrs. Pollard's order to give her more cloths, and she crammed the stack onto the little shelf of the triangular corner table.

"Not for a few days."

"I work afternoon and evening. In the morning till afternoon it's Nuala. She'll have your morning tea at 7 sharp. Breakfast a half-hour later. You have a couple of hours before dinner." She nodded abruptly, remembered to smile, then retreated.

With the door shut, Isabella towed her suitcase across the coverlet and set to unpacking. Her few clothes which had crammed the suitcase looked lonesome in the wardrobe. She arranged and re-arranged them then decided to empty the contents of the satchel onto one shelf. Her sketchbook, pencils and eraser, sharpening pen knife and charcoal fit very neatly on the eye-level shelf. A long jacket, two good frocks, and her blouses hung neatly from the short rod. Folded skirts and jumpers and jodphurs filled the other two shelves. Her spare shoes, one pair for walking, the other pair in case of a special dinner, tucked easily onto the bottom shelf. Staring at the empty top shelf, she turned about, wandering what else would fit in the wardrobe and give her more room.

She stubbed her toe on the paint box. In a trice she fit her watercolor paints and brushes and palette, papers and clips neatly onto the top shelf. The small easel fit neatly under the table.

Tomorrow was her first meeting with Edward Malvaise. She also needed to cart to the school the large easel and canvas and paint crate with everything she needed to work with oils. Lady Malvaise had stated positively that the headmaster would provide a room at Greavley Abbey School in which she would work, and the paint crate would store there easily.

Full dark had fallen while she unpacked. Catching the time on her wristwatch. Isabella hurried into a plain taupe frock and tugged on a warm cardigan patterned with gold and bronze overblown roses. She finished her look with eardrops of seed pearls in a gold setting and the single twisted gold strand that Madoc had given her after their marriage. Sliding into a pair of mahogany pumps, she locked her door, slid the key into her purse, then clattered down the narrow stairway and turned down the hall that Mrs. Pollard had indicated with a wave of her hand when she'd mentioned the lounge.

There she encountered Sibby, carrying a tray with covers.

The bar maid gave her a jaundiced look that repulsed any greeting. "Mrs. Pollard says you are to linger over your dinner. You can use the lounge as a sitting room. When Dean Filmer arrives, she'll send him there so you can meet with him."

"That's considerate of her." She held the door then followed Sibby into the room.

The lounge was dim, with only three lamps providing a weak glow. The only welcome was a cheery fire. Three round tables with heavy chairs were set for dinner service. Well away from the fireplace were a settee and two armchairs. The curtains were drawn against the night. They didn't create a cozy ambience. Their dark color absorbed the light, adding to the dimness.

Sibby set the tray on the first table, well away from the fireplace. She removed the covered dishes then departed.

Isabella barely waited for the door to close before she dragged a table closer to the fire and scooted over its chairs. Then she transferred the covered plate and dessert coupe and bread plate. Covers off, she could see the steam rising from the steak and kidney pie. The dessert coupe had an apple crumble that surprised her by being delightful, with cinnamon sprinkled on the custard portion.

When Sibby returned an hour later, Isabella had rearranged the whole room, one table dragged to the window that overlooked the garden with its low wall and view of the trees beyond and the other table relegated to the far end of the room, in front of a set of low shelves, sparse of books yet rich with curios. She'd dragged the settee from the wall. With the deep armchairs across from the settee, she had created a conversation circle on the other side of the fireplace. The circle caught the fire's heat and became cozy. She had claimed the *fauteuil* nearest the fire and was flipping through an old magazine when the door opened.

Sibby stopped short when she saw the changes but said nothing. She gathered the dishes onto her tray. "Will you be wanting coffee now?"

Should I risk coffee in the countryside? American born and raised, she'd acquired a coffee habit early, and English tea didn't quite replace it. Only Middle Eastern restaurants could brew it properly, but sometimes their incarnations of coffee were too strong. "Yes, please, and thank you. My compliments to whoever baked that apple crumble. It was an unexpected joy."

The bar maid smiled, a true smile, not a fake one. "That'll be Mrs. Halsey our cook. I'll tell her you liked it."

"Thank you, Sibby."

"Will you be wanting anything else? Cream and sugar for your coffee?"

"Black, please. I suppose it would be an imposition were you to tell me when the headmaster arrives? I think Mrs. Pollard intended to do so, but I doubt she will bring him immediately."

"He'll be late. Close to eleven. He comes in his auto. Too much trouble to walk from the school. I'll be happy to give you a head's up." She hesitated then, "He likes to be called Dean Filmer."

"Yes, Mrs. Pollard said. I appreciate this, Sibby."

"You'll be here?"

"Yes. I thought I would investigate the books on that shelf."

Sibby lifted the tray, took a step, then paused. "Will I come back to more changes in the room?"

"I hope not. I thought I would leave the sideboard and the shelves where they were."

"Mrs. Pollard may not like it. Is this one of those London room arrangements, furniture out in the room and not against the wall?"

"The dowager Malvaise is paying handsomely for my stay here, for over two months. I would like to have a bit of comfort in the evening. These chairs were too far from the fire."

"You needn't explain to me. I suppose you found cobwebs and dust bunnies."

"I did."

She shrugged. "It's Nuala what cleans this room. You've given her more work of a Saturday morning." Then she walked out the door she'd left ajar and hip-bumped it closed.

Isabella hoped Mrs. Pollard was not too upset with the changes.

How was Madoc enduring his changes? He would be on board his ship by now, with a narrow berth in a cabin shared with other men. A ship mess for his dinner, likely without any sweet dessert.

She tugged out a handkerchief to dab her eyes.

.~.~.~.

Flick didn't like cigarettes, but a cigarette in a lacquered holder was *de rigueur* among the faster crowds. She didn't have to smoke it. If she waved it around, it might stay lit.

Her flatmates had left an hour ago, both in frocks copied from Lanvin's newest creation, thin straps and a deep vee, a dropped waist with a full skirt beneath. Millie paired her rose pink frock with a feathery boa from props while Stefa in yellow threw on the glen plaid throw from the couch, wearing it like an enveloping shawl. They had laughed at Flick's wish they "stay warm". The rain had been spitting ice pellets when Flick arrived back from Fleet Street where she'd gone to sell her photos.

Alan Rettleston ran *London Daily,* and on the 16th he bought every photo that Owl had rejected. As he lit one cigarette off another, he said, "I want more. Men only. Women only. Same style. Same factory if you can work it. Come back in a week with all of them. Do that, and I'll pay a third more."

Flick wasn't a fool; she knew what he was doing. He wanted a narrative: the men gone, women doing their work; men returned, pushing the women out of jobs. Since that was the narrative she'd spotted, she'd follow his instructions.

The money from the photo feature would keep her ahead on funds, an entire quarter ahead.

When she returned to *London Daily* on the next Tuesday at noon, Rettleston set her to work with "Old Pickwick. He's good at crafting a story after the photos come in." While the newspaper's official photographer developed the negatives, she and Pickwick poured over her contact prints, tiny images the same size of the negatives.

This morning Rettleston counted out her payment from his petty cash box. As he handed it over, he talked of a party hosted by Lilibeth Hargreaves.

Lilibeth was a member of the Bright Young Things. At their parties, champagne flowed freely, the music was jazzy or snazzy, and dancers crowded any tiny space. Only the flashiest of London's ton would be on the guest list. Rettleston promised her dinner with dancing before.

Dinner. Dancing. Millie and Stefa had chattered during their morning cuppa that they had a party in the theatre district. Rather than stay alone at the flat or venture alone to a restaurant, Flick agreed to the evening. She immediately worried at Rettleston's grin, more lascivious than she expected. "Would you take me to the Fitzwilliam Victoria Hotel?"

"That old dodge."

"It does lean to the traditional."

"Stuffed shirts and dowdy women," he sneered.

"The food is excellent," she countered, "and they have a chamber orchestra for dancing, not one of the newer brass bands. I met my parents there last month. Dinner, dancing, and Miss Hargreaves' party. That's a wonderful evening."

He let himself be convinced. With dinner in the offing, Flick skipped the late lunch she'd planned and only had tea.

The red dress that she'd bought on a dare from Stefa came off its hanger. A sheath dress, calf-length, demure with its high neck and long sleeves, but the back draped so low it might be called backless. She wore her highest black heels and jet eardrops that she'd picked up at a market stall. The Spanish shawl with its vivid flowers on a black ground was her only concession to warmth. Then she picked up her black beaded purse that held in-case cab fare and ran down the steps to wait for Rettleston in the entrance.

His red roadster surprised her then didn't, for she was discovering he had more than a bit of flash in him. He had the top up against the weather, thank God. She opened the door and slid in before he had a chance to put a hand to his own door latch.

The whole evening whirled. Pre-emptive maneuvering limited the cocktails he pressed on her. Couples crowded the Fitzwilliam Victoria's dance floor, so he didn't request too many dances. Flick spotted a good-looking man staring at her. She winked—yet he didn't see. He looked away just as she did.

He was dining with other couples, the stuffed shirts and dowdy women that Rettleston had decried. One woman was flash, though, glittering rings on her fingers, a spandelle in her marcelled hair, an embroidered dress from a Paris catwalk. Handsome looked younger than the woman, an obvious single in the group, and he looked older than Flick's brother Chauncey but younger than her oldest brother Warren. Her brother Allworthy's age, she guessed. Then Rettleston demanded her attention, and she stopped speculating if Handsome Is was also Handsome Does.

The party at Lilibeth Hargreaves was wilder than she liked but not as wild as the theatre parties that Millie dragged her to. Lilibeth had hired a jazz band on a promotional tour from Louisiana in the States. The dancing was fast, the drinking faster, and Rettleston kept handing her fizzy cocktails. Conversation was impossible, but people talked louder, creating a din that still rang in her ears the next morning.

When Rettleston suggested breakfast, Flick winced. "I have a long drive tomorrow. I need sleep."

"Come with me. You'll sleep after I relax you."

She groaned. "Take me to my flat, please. I've had a wonderful evening, but it has to end. I have to drive. I'm expected."

Flick let him kiss her in the roadster, the gear shift keeping them apart, then she dashed out and up the steps to her flat. She waved from the door. He revved the motor then sped off.

She'd survived the evening.

Now to drive to Upper Wellsford.

Chapter 3

Michael Wainwright did not normally dine with his superior on a Friday evening. A murder investigation solved that very morning, no new case to mull over, he'd been trapped into an affirmative when the chief inspector cornered him to be the spare man at a celebration. Since he liked Chief Inspector Malcolm and had no plans for the evening, he didn't try too hard to winkle out of the invitation.

His tuxedo fit loosely. He hadn't regained the three stone lost in the last years of the war, looking into the fanged maw of hell and surviving only by a screech of talons.

When he woke in the night, darkness surrounding him like a predator monster lurking silent and still, he would forget where he was, when he was. Then an automobile's revving engine would filter from the street below or an ambulance's clangor would peal distantly. He would remember he had returned to London. The next seconds reminded him the Armistice was signed, and most of the soldiers were demobilized. On those nights he thanked God and dropped back to sleep.

Malcolm offered to pick him up, but Michael refused, saying he would make his own way to the Fitzwilliam Victoria Hotel. He hopped a bus and was glad of his overcoat that hid his tuxedo from the workers heading home.

The hotel's marble edifice flew international flags. The Fitzwilliam was beyond his monthly budget except for special occasions, but he had dined there enough to know to walk through the elaborate lobby to the frosted glass doors that led to an atrium and thence to the restaurant with its exclusive dining and dancing. The string orchestra played a foxtrot rather than the international tango gradually replacing it.

Subdued conversations flowed under the strings' harmonies. An occasional flute created a counterpoint. Not for the Fitzwilliam the clarinet and brass.

He was early but recognized by the *maître d'*, a dour man who adopted the mien of a stiff butler.

"Mr. Wainwright, if you will follow me." He walked the fringes of the dance floor to a long table in the corner. "Do you wish a highball or

John Collins to start the evening?"

He avoided the proffered chair that set his back to the room. "Whiskey and soda, please. Forgive me, have we met?"

"On the occasion of a wedding, sir. You dined with the bride and groom. Last autumn, I believe. And Easter last, you escorted an elderly couple. The happy couple also attended that evening."

He had treated his brother and new sister-in-law to a celebratory evening here at the Fitzwilliam. He didn't hide his surprise at the *maître d's* memory. His grandparents were the elderly couple. "You've an excellent memory."

The man allowed a small smile. "Our guests to the Fitzwilliam change rarely, sir." Then he faded away.

While he waited for his superior and the rest of the party, Michael watched the dancers and discretely examined at the other diners. The tables around the dance floor were for couples, with tables for four and six farther back, and larger tables widely spaced behind columns.

A flash of red silhouetted against somber black caught his eye. He watched a couple taking a table behind a column. The woman wore the red, a dress that looked demure until she turned her back and he saw an expanse of pale skin above the draped back. The waiter drew out her chair, sitting her behind the marble column so that he had the barest look at her pretty face and dark hair, bobbed but not crimped as so many women did now. The man looked familiar. Michael caught an edge of trouble associated with his memory of the man.

A waiter delivered his drink. Sipping it, he reminded himself that the day was done, labor ceased. He could shed his role as an investigator. Tonight, his chief had cast him into the role of the charming Spare Man.

Chief Inspector Malcolm arrived, led by the *maître d'*. Malcolm escorted his wife. A lone woman followed then came three other couples, all chattering. He would be Spare Man for the unescorted woman. She wore one of the shapeless styles that were becoming popular, feminized with swirling embroidery that reminded him of India.

Michael stood and greeted them. He bothered to remember last names only, including the single woman's. His job as a detective inspector had built his memory for names. He had to shift down table, away from the couple being celebrated, but that gave him a better view of the woman in red. Attractive rather than beautiful, he judged, her waif look imparted by her bobbed hair. She smiled as she responded to her escort's conversation, smiled when the waiter delivered a sidecar to her and a highball to the man. Yet she kept looking around the dining room, as if she looked for someone.

He needed to focus on his own party, but his subconscious kept watch. He knew the instant the man stood, coming around to draw out the woman's chair. They joined the couples gathering for another foxtrot. The man spoke. Her expression appeared frozen, without its earlier animation.

"Enjoy dancing, Wainwright?" his chief asked.

"Sir, no, sir. Not my thing, especially now."

"No?" the single woman queried. Mrs. Pomphrey. Margaret, Margret, Margot, something like that. A widow. "Did you suffer an injury in the war, Mr. Wainwright? You seem healthy now."

Margot Pomphrey, he remembered. "No injury," he confessed. "I've turned stodgy since the war. My sergeant despairs of me."

"Yet you were watching the dancing. Or the dancers. Has someone caught your eye?"

"Actually, I wondered if the Fitzwilliam had moved into the new decade and would shock us all with the Tango. They've tamed the Foxtrot, I see."

The comment earned muted laughter and turned conversation from him to dancing.

The celebratory couple joined the next dance. Michael felt honorbound to ask Mrs. Pomphrey to dance, and she accepted with an alacrity that kept him distant on the dance floor.

The young woman and her escort had returned to their table. The waiter had presented the entrée. As the evening progressed, the couple received their services more quickly than Michael's table did. Yet the number of times that they danced kept their progress through the dinner at a similar pace.

Mrs. Pomphrey rattled on about after-parties. He listened with half an ear and waited for his glimpses of the dark brunette. He had no hope that he would ever meet her. She would not deign to enter his local pub or dine at the humble restaurants he frequented. He rarely ventured into the society to which the Fitzwilliam Victoria catered.

Their worlds were far apart.

Yet he found himself lingering at the restaurant's entrance as the party dispersed for the evening. The chief expressed his appreciation for Michael playing Spare Man. He clapped Michael on the shoulder. His wife said, "Margot enjoyed the evening. Your idea was brilliant, my dear." Then she patted her husband's chest and clattered through the atrium to the hotel's lobby.

His chief hesitated, as if he knew he needed to say more. Michael quickly said, "Thank you for the invitation and dinner, sir. I will see you on Monday." That put him back in lower status, and Malcolm nodded and followed his wife.

He lingered a few minutes longer, giving the others time to collect their checked evening wraps while their automobiles were brought to the entrance.

The *maître d'* appeared. "Sir. Have you need of anything?"

"A bit of information, if you please. The couple that were seated across the dance floor from us. The table was beside a column. The woman wore a red dress. I have met the man somewhere, but I cannot recall his name." He edged a bob across the lectern.

That last comment and the *doucement* cleared the *maître d'*s expression. "Yes, sir. The gentleman is Alan Rettleston, managing editor of the *London Daily*. We do not see him often. The young lady, however, is well known to us. She has dined several times, usually with her parents of a Sunday, once a quarter, I would say." Then he stopped, waiting for the question that he had guessed prompted the first question.

"Her name?"

"Miss Felicity Sherborne. A photographer, I believe."

"For the *London Daily*?"

"That I do not know, sir."

Michael thanked him and left.

.~.~.~.

Saturday Morning, 28 February

Isabella introduced herself to the maid Nuala then enjoyed her morning tea and poached egg on dry toast.

Mrs. Pollard came into the room when she was refusing marmalade and more toast. Nuala saw the woman and ducked her head before retreating to clear the table now beside the window. Feeling a smidgen of guilt for rearranging the room, Isabella poured the last of the tea into her cup and stirred in another little spoon of sugar.

"Mrs. Tarrant?" The woman placed her hand on the back of a chair. "May I join you?"

"Please do. The sunshine is brilliant this morning. I shall enjoy my walk to Greavley Abbey."

"You spoke with Dean Filmer last evening?"

She nodded as she tapped the spoon then laid it on the saucer. "He will send a man this morning for my easel and canvas and box of supplies. The headmaster has also promised to introduce me to young Mr. Malvaise."

"You haven't met him?"

"The dowager commissioned me. I have her letter of introduction to her grandson."

"I see. You should have no trouble up at the Abbey School then."

Isabella decided to tackle the furniture rearrangement before Mrs. Pollard did. "I hope you don't mind." She swept her hand around to indicate the room. "It's a drastic rearrangement. Last evening the fire hadn't had time to warm the room. I decided to shift my table closer which led to shifting a *fauteuil*, and then I had to balance the room. The more I moved, the more had to be moved. I didn't realize until this morning that this room faces the south and will take advantage of this glorious sunshine. That table by the window will be wonderful on a warm and sunny morning."

"Mrs. Tarrant—."

"February doesn't have many sunny days, I know, but I'll be here through March and into April, and we will definitely have more days like today." There, she'd reminded the woman that she was a long-term guest of the Hook and Line.

Mrs. Pollard grimaced and shifted in her seat. "We have other guests, Mrs. Tarrant. We have three fishermen staying with us. You didn't see them last night because they supped in the pub. This morning they rose early. They didn't quite know where to sit for breakfast."

"I believe I saw them. Three men, young, middle-aged, older. We spoke as they left. Do they each take a different table? I thought they had eaten together this morning."

"They did, this morning, but they don't often do so."

"They chose the window table. That table will be popular, especially this spring. Candlemas was cloudy, wasn't it? We should have an early spring. Did I see crocuses at the gate?"

"You did. Mrs. Tarrant, the fishermen aren't our only guests. Miss Felicity Sherborne arrives today to visit her brother. He's a master at the Abbey School. She plans to stay a fortnight. She will arrive by tea-time, I should think. We have more guests expected next week. Where are they to sit, Mrs. Tarrant? Miss Sherborne cannot retreat to the pub. You will both be vying for the best table and the best seat."

"If we are that crowded, then I hope Miss Sherborne and I can share the same table. It will be lovely to have someone to talk with during meals. Someone new always has a wealth of conversation."

"You have a hopeful view of Miss Sherborne."

"Should I not? What do you know of her? Has she stayed here before?"

"She stays once a season for several days. A long weekend for each of her visits last fall, this time a fortnight, as I said. I believe she's keen on photography."

"I shall enjoy her explanation of photography, I'm certain. I assisted a photographer once." Poor Richard Lamb. Murdered by a colleague at the archaeological dig on Crete. The memory subdued her sparkle. "We will definitely have several conversation starters."

Mrs. Pollard cleared her throat. She compressed her lips, as if she had more to say but wouldn't. She stood and thrust her chair under the table. "I see that you plan to make your rearranging work. Please don't be changing more things without consulting me."

"Nuala didn't have more work, did she?" She pretended not to know that the young woman had had more work. Moving furniture had revealed dust and cobwebs and gravel and bits of leaves hiding under the settee and chairs.

"You said a man from the Abbey School would collect your canvas and easel? Should I admit him to your room to collect them? I assume you'll be at the Abbey all day?"

"Yes, please. And a box. Everything's beside the door. I hope to introduce myself to young Mr. Malvaise before this morning is much advanced."

"The boys play rugby on Saturdays. Preparation for the exhibition games on Founder's Day, the first weekend in April."

"Then I shall definitely need to speak with him early. Thank you for telling me that, Mrs. Pollard. Mr. Filmer didn't mention it."

Her smile looked pinched. "For asking you not to rearrange the room?"

"For giving me the warning about the games today and for telling me about Miss Sherborne."

Mrs. Pollard didn't snort, but she looked as if she wanted to.

The barmaid Nuala came in as Mrs. Pollard left. Staring into her tepid tea, Isabella wondered if Nuala had waited in the hall while Mrs. Pollard delivered her scold … which didn't really come off. She hid a grin and drank the tea, even if it had lost all warmth.

.~.~.~.

"Report's filed, boss." Sgt. Callaway followed Michael into his office. "In triplicate," he added, imitating a nasally corporal. The story of the corporal had entertained Michael over several pints in the first weeks after Callaway returned to work with him.

"Sit down. Tell me we haven't caught another case."

"Not yet, boss. Sunday's still free." Callaway started to lower himself into a chair, then the door behind him opened. He quickly straightened and tucked his hands behind his back, a noncom giving a report to his captain.

Chief Inspector Malcolm barely gave the sergeant a glance. "Closed your case?"

"The sergeant filed the papers earlier."

"Good then. You two will have the rest of the weekend free."

"We hope so, sir."

"I have a commission from my wife." He acted as if the sergeant wasn't there. The chief was probably used to servants standing around. "My wife and I hope you are free for dinner Saturday next. Just the four of us. Margot Pomphrey enjoyed last evening."

He saw Callaway's eyes roll. The sergeant would relish that bit of information and ruthlessly tease Michael. "If no case arises, sir. I must insist on paying my way, however."

"Nonsense. This will be a favor to us. Evening attire, I would think, though we do not plan to attend a party afterward. Plans do change, however. Best to prepared." He waited expectantly then, and Michael was forced to thank him for the invitation. His chief then turned to Callaway. "How is Mrs. Callaway, sergeant?"

"My mother is doing well, sir. Thank you for asking."

The door shut behind Malcolm. "You're doing better, Callaway," Michael praised. "You gave no hint that you knew he'd forgotten you aren't married."

"He'll never remember that, boss."

"Not until you rise in the ranks."

"That's not likely to occur."

"The world's changing."

"And you're having dinner with him, boss. Again. The world's staying the same. People find their levels and stay there. Like him and his wife setting you up with that Pomphrey woman. Again."

"Then we'll have to hope a case will interfere. That reminds me. We had a man in our station some months back. I cannot remember the case. Alan Rettleston. Editor on Fleet Street. *London Daily*. Do you remember?"

"Not our case, boss."

"No. Just here in the station."

"I can ask around, quiet-like."

"Do that. I'm curious."

"Trouble, boss?"

"No. Not even a hint of it. Just my curiosity."

"You know what curiosity did. A case right up our alley. I'll see." He faded back and shut the door just as quietly.

Michael worked through paperwork until he reached an old file from months back, the weeks immediately after he'd returned to police work. He hadn't thought the war had returned home with him until he came on that crime scene. Unsolved still. He rarely had time to review the case, but he kept the file on his desk for spare moments like this. He leaned back and started through the documents, reading each one individually, trying to shift them around, like puzzle pieces that fit in multiple spots. A new angle? Missing facts? Different kinds of interviews? He'd thought at first that his newness as a detective inspector hampered him. He no longer thought that.

Callaway knocked then poked his head around the doorframe.

"Come in." Michael closed the file. "I need the interruption."

"MacBride case, boss?"

"How did you know?"

"Still worries me, too. We'll get to the answer, boss, never you doubt it."

"In this year, I hope. Already a half-year has passed, and we're still no closer. What do you need?"

"That man, boss, Alan Rettleston. He was in the station. Charges never brought." He touched his nose.

That nose-touch meant that Rettleston had paid his way out of the charge. "What brought him to us?"

"Assaulted a Jane at a Mott Shop. Broken bones the worst of it. Re-arranged her face for her. Surgery needed there. The Jane was willing to charge, but nothing doing. You have anything we can use?"

"No. I just recognized him. He was at the Fitzwilliam Victoria."

"Was he? That nice place? With who?"

"Whom. A pretty lady in a red dress."

"She'll need to be warned."

"Unfortunately, she might not view me as creditable. You know these new things. They don't automatically accept everything the police says."

"No one should do that. But a word of caution ...."

"Anything else, sergeant?" He drew the file back toward him.

"No, boss."

"Then we'll plan to have a normal Sunday, shall we? We might manage some interviews on this before a new case crops up."

.~.~.~.

The walk to Greavley Abbey did not take long. Few vehicles passed on the road. Isabella took to the wide verges whenever she heard a motor, but the macadam was easier walking. The road was bitumen in Upper Wellsford itself, but it changed to the crushed gravel mixture once she passed the last village cottage. Trees grew along the grassy verge. The forest looked cleared of undergrowth although deep within the old-growth trees were tangles of bushes. The understory along the verge looked to be flowering trees, drinking up the sunshine that didn't penetrate the oaken canopy. Driving the road in spring would be a celebration of color.

When a brick wall began running alongside the road, she knew the Abbey was near. The wall seemed to die away deeper into the forest. She wondered the reason for its building.

She hadn't searched for Greavley Abbey's history. Lacking a cathedral or an influential monastic order, the abbey had escaped Henry VIII's deprivations, and the village had built its own church, a plain grey-stone building with a Palladium style front and an octagonal bell tower at the back.

Her sole source at the London Library in the Pall Mall had claimed Greavley Abbey had a checkered past. The monastery, still Catholic yet its influence greatly reduced, survived until Henry VIII and then Oliver Cromwell. In the Jacobean Glorious Revolution, the monastic order was forced to remove. A wealthy merchant purchased the whole, Abbey Church and dormitory and extensive grounds. The merchant's heirs grew wealthier in successive monarchies. Yet while the family accumulated wealth, the blood was not as prolific. By the 1780s, the last merchant had no direct or collateral heir to name. He fastened upon the idea to form a school and spent his last three decades doing so.

Isabella reached the grand entrance with its round spheres topping the supports for the open ironwork gates. She stopped to catch her breath. Distant shouts let her know the boys already were at play. She saw no one moving about the front. The Abbey Church stood to her right, medieval in shape with stained glass windows and a high bell tower that reminded her of Notre Dame in Paris. Before her was a manor house, Palladium style, and she wondered if the childless merchant had built both manor house and village church.

In the narrow opening between church and manor she could see through to a building of grey stone, much like the church. That must be the monks' dormitory. She saw the barest corner of a further building and wondered at it. The manor was of a warm brick with grey stone quoins. The house rose three stories, taller than the church and its dormitory, although the crenallated bell tower ran a story higher. The manor's architect must have sought symmetry with the church buildings rather than an imitation of the earlier buildings.

Trees grew, old and strong, to her left. Along that side of the house was a boxwood hedge. She wondered if that was the approach to the maze that had fascinated the librarian.

The church and the manor formed two sides of a square. The librarian had spoken of a cloister walk and three other buildings, one for administration, the second for teaching, and the third for the teachers' lodgings. Only they didn't call them teachers, Isabella remembered. Mr. Filmer had called them masters, and he was the headmaster, but she was to refer to him as Dean Filmer.

Surely in this great place would be a lockable room for her painting. The headmaster had said that she could leave her work without worry. Yet her late father had taught at public schools, in America and here in Britain. Boys easily became imps.

Chapter 4

Saturday Mid-Morning

As she crossed the graveled parking, Isabella peered into the courtyard, now visible through the opening between church and manor. She saw nothing of the maze the librarian had gushed over.

Isabella slowly climbed the steps of the manor. The distant shouts rang louder, briefly, as she used the shining brass bell beside the oaken door.

The door swung open. The butler who appeared was prematurely grey, stiff with importance rather than age. "Yes?"

"Mrs. Madoc Tarrant, to see Mr. Filmer. He is expecting me."

His eyebrows raised, but he stepped back, admitting her to the house.

The entrance was a lovely Regency-style, with papered walls and light furniture. The sun shone through the fan window above the door and re-created the fan pattern on the long run of darkly-stained flooring. A celadon ginger jar centered a sideboard. One door opened to a shadowed room; the other door was closed.

He paused, obviously expecting her coat. Isabella tucked her iris scarf into a pocket and slid off the heavy wool. He stepped through an open door into a shadowed room. She nearly followed, but he returned immediately, without her coat. "May I take your purse, Mrs. Tarrant?"

"This is my artist's satchel. I'll keep it, please."

"Then follow me, ma'am." He led her under the flight of stairs, past a portrait of a Renaissance gentlemen and then a pair of portraits in Roundhead dress, staring across at each other. They reached a hall that bisected the house, but he continued past it. The walls weren't papered here but painted panels. She peeked down the bisecting hall and saw several doors, all closed. They passed two more doors, then they reached a door centered on the wall ahead.

When he opened that door, she saw greenery and felt a waft of humidity. Sunshine flooded the room. Greenery, ironwork, and glass. They entered a convervatory.

The butler descended four steps then led the way around an elephant-leaved plant and a thickly-fronded palm.

"Mrs. Filmer, the artist has arrived." He gestured to a path winding between green leaves.

Once Isabella circled the great plants, she saw a woman standing to meet her. She smiled a welcome. The woman bent her head to accept it, and Isabella hid an inner eye roll.

Mrs. Filmer wore silk and pearls with her country tweed skirt and jacket. Her heels were stylish pumps, and her strawberry blonde hair was neatly dressed in a rolled chignon above her collar. Her walk in the wind and cold had left Isabella blown and tousled, far beneath the smooth elegance of this woman.

She retook her seat, crossing her ankles and sitting upright. "Dodges, have my husband notified. Bring tea. I am certain Mrs. Tarrant will want refreshment after her walk."

"Tea would be lovely, thank you."

"Do have a seat, Mrs. Tarrant."

She took the chair gratefully. It was ironwork, like a garden bench, but a cushion kept the seat from becoming hard. She looked around, at the plants, at the iron-framed construction. The blurred scene beyond the windows looked like a formal garden with pyramids of evergreens. A tall box hedge backed the garden. The area was empty, devoid of shouting boys at their games. "This is a lovely conservatory."

"A later addition to the house. You will see that it overlooks the formal garden. The building to the right is the Prior's House."

The blurred Prior's House still revealed its flamboyant architecture. She could see other buildings as well, a long dormitory-like building and a square three-storied structure beyond it, neither like the church or the Prior's House or the manor but like plain boxes. "I understand the school's library and offices are in the Prior's House. Does Dean Filmer have his office there?"

"Yes. Only the Prior's House and this house have been fully modernized. The boys' dormitory does not even have electricity. My husband believes it strengthens the boys' characters to face physical hardship, and since it was good enough for the monks—well. Should you need a telephone during your time with us—."

"There's a telephone at the pub." She didn't want to begin by imposing.

"That open call box has little privacy. Should you need to ring anyone, you may convey a message to Gilchrist, the major domo at the Prior's House. The administration building for the Abbey School," she clarified. "If the telephone there is unavailable, Gilchrist will arrange with Dodges for your use of ours."

"I do not anticipate such a need, but I shall certainly remember your kind offer, Mrs. Filmer. My husband is traveling abroad. He shipped a couple of weeks ago for India, where he will meet his immediate superior and plan for the coming months. I will travel during May to join him."

"You have an incentive, then, to finish your portrait."

"I am eager to start the portrait, yes."

"I am surprised the family did not have this portrait done at the holiday break."

"I believe Edward was on holiday with a friend, not with the family."

"So his education is to be interfered with at the whim of his grandmother?"

Isabella re-folded her hands on her lap.

"Have you and Mr. Tarrant been together long?"

"Actually—." The conservatory door opened, interrupting with the arrival of tea, brought on a tray by the butler. She heard the china rattle as he disappeared from sight, then a great clatter occurred, and he wheeled a hand-trolley around the bushy palm. He rolled it to a stop beside Mrs. Filmer.

"This is Dodges, our butler. He has nothing to do with the school. Gilchrist answers directly to my husband. Should you wish to speak with me, Gilchrist will convey your wish to Dodges. That will be all." She lifted the teapot and seemed not to notice the butler's abbreviated bow before he left on silent feet. "Sugar and cream, Mrs. Tarrant?"

"Cream only, thank you."

"I am glad for your interruption of my day. Saturdays are for the school's athletics. My husband and the other masters—indeed, the whole of the school staff are busy at the field. The dean even confiscates my own secretary. His secretary has commitments throughout the weekend."

Mrs. Filmer did not seem perturbed by the loss, but Isabella didn't trust that judgment. She had taken two reads on the woman, the first welcoming and inclined to assist while the second seemed haughty and careful to draw strict lines between the manor and the school propre, an uncrossable line.

They finished the tea with commonplace observations about the late winter weather and the state of the gardens. Isabella was recounting the London librarian's instruction that she explore the maze when a glass exterior door opened. Cold air rushed into the conservatory.

Dean Filmer came in, removing knitted gloves. Behind him was a youth who had achieved a gangly height. Wind and cold had reddened his cheeks and nose. Sweaty hair was matted to his head, and he held a knitted cap in one hand. His hair might be as fair as his sister Victoria if it were not so sweaty. She knew better than to voice that resemblance, especially as he had already passed the dean's height.

As they unwound their scarves, Isabella stood to meet them.

Dodges appeared from around the palm.

"No, no." The dean waved the butler away. "We will not linger." He chafed his hands to warm them. "We have competitions to return to."

Out of the dean's sight, the boy lifted his eyes heaven-ward, and Isabella bit back a chuckle. Edward Malvaise seemed to have the opinion of youths everywhere about older men claiming to be involved in competition when they merely rooted from the sidelines.

The youth murmured politely at the introduction, and Isabella quickly produced his grandmother's letter of introduction. He stared at the seal. "Dean Filmer said I'm to have my portrait painted."

"That is the plan. The dowager explains in her letter."

He turned it over, looking again at his name scrawled in a spidery hand across the front of the envelope. "Portraits take a lot of time. I remember my sister Alexa's portrait. She had to sit for hours."

"I'm not certain your grandmother mentions it in her letter. We discussed potential scenes, and she mentioned that you were fond of rowing."

"Fond? I suppose she would say that."

"I thought you could wear your rowing whites and stand with an oar?" At that, his glance was quick and wary, and she hastened to add. "I should warn you. I don't work like other portraitists." Isabella didn't explain that he was her first official portrait. "I will take a lot of preliminary drawings. I will need you quite a bit on our first days together, working out colors and hues and your stance, then not so much the next week. Once I start the portrait, we must work at the oils' schedule, not mine. Perhaps five weeks? Three or four hours every day? Once I finish, I will varnish the painting before I deliver it to your grandmother."

"Lady Malvaise says all that in here?" He again turned the envelope he still hadn't cracked open.

"I do not know what she wrote. I am not privy to that."

"Where will this painting be?" He glanced at Dean Filmer. "Am I to go to the village?"

"No. The dean has offered—."

"I thought one of the unoccupied rooms at the Prior's House, Malvaise."

"The canvas is rather large. Almost life-size," and Isabella really hoped someone had picked it up and was bringing it to the school. "The dean is very kind with his offer. He assures me that the room's floor will not be damaged by paint droplets."

"It's a wonder what carpets can cover," his wife murmured.

"I don't see how—with my studies—."

Isabella didn't think his studies were Edward Malvaise's objection.

"The dowager Malvaise's wishes must be met," the dean said firmly, and Isabella wondered what the old lady had promised for allowing this favor. "Your athletics will continue as required. Sundays will remain the Lord's Day." He shot that statement at Isabella. "The first sitting will be Monday."

"He'll be standing, my dear," Mrs. Filmer commented, "not sitting. He'll become tired."

"Yes, yes. We can easily accommodate the dowager's wishes. Let's see, Mrs. Tarrant. Malvaise will come to you instead of morning chapel for an hour. He will also be free at 11 o'clock; he has an open hour then. And everyday between 3 and 5 in the afternoon he is free."

"Sir, that doesn't give me time to drill my lessons."

"Should you fall behind, the master will provide tutoring in the evening. Do those working hours suit you, Mrs. Tarrant?"

Isabella winced at the eight o'clock start. That meant an early rising and cold walking to the school, but the dean had managed to clear four hours each day. If she worked diligently with young Malvaise during each of those hours and on the background and oars and sculls while he was gone, she should finish the portrait a few days early, not later.

"On the oils' schedule, of course."

Mrs. Filmer rang the bell.

"If adjustments to those times are necessary—."

"We shall see," the dean finished for her. "Very well, on Monday, Malvaise, you start with Mrs. Tarrant."

"I am to find her at the Prior's House, sir?"

"We will meet at the Prior's House entrance, shall we?" Isabella smiled at him, still uncertain how he was accepting this portrait. "You will not need to wear your whites for the first day."

Malvaise nodded. "Thank you, sir. Ma'am. Mrs. Filmer." He left through the glazed door.

Dodges appeared. "Gilchrist," Mrs. Filmer said, that name becoming an order, and the man left as soundlessly as he'd arrived.

"I must return to the grounds." The dean began rewinding his scarf.

"Do you foresee any difficulties, Mrs. Tarrant?"

"No, sir. You are most obliging. I understand your reason for banning work on the Lord's Day."

His wife folded her hands on her tweedy lap. "I should think so."

"And I would not wish to remove Mr. Malvaise from his sports on Saturday, sir. I would like to see the room in the Prior's House that you have assigned to this endeavor."

"Gilchrist will show you. I ordered that earlier. I hope you will have a spare hour here and there to speak about painting with some of the boys who express an interest. Once the news spreads of this portrait, and the news will spread, others will certainly be interested."

Is he warning me? "I understand. Perhaps between the chapel hour and the forenoon hour that Malvaise has free? Ten o'clock?"

"Consult with my secretary the day prior. He will organize the boys and see them notified. Now, my dear, I will have a late luncheon with the boys as usual. Dinner at eight."

"The cook prepares it for nine," Mrs. Filmer returned without any inflection.

"That's acceptable, dear. Mrs. Tarrant, good day."

Her estimation of the dean had risen as he managed the times for her to work with Edward Malvaise. If she could coax the youth into working with a good humor, this commission would not seem a drudgery.

Chapter 5

Saturday Mid-Morning

The butler appeared with another man, older, his silvered hair a swept-back mane. He wore the same livery, but he had on knitted gloves, not the white cloth ones that Dodges wore.

"Gilchrist. This is Mrs. Tarrant, the portraitist," Mrs. Filmer explained. "Please show her the room set aside for her use. The dean informed you this morning."

"Yes, ma'am. Immediately, ma'am. Mrs. Tarrant, if you will come with me."

"A moment, if you will, Gilchrist. Mrs. Tarrant, I will not see you again today. Should you have need of anything from the manor, Dodges will assist you or my secretary, Miss Collinsworth."

"Would it be possible, Mrs. Filmer, to explore the maze and the garden during my time here?"

"You mean other than today? I suppose. If the garden and maze are in use, Dodges will inform you. You may wish to follow the river walk back to the village. It leads directly to the Hook and Line. It is certainly more interesting than following the road, and I am informed reliably that it is much shorter."

"I shall definitely explore that. Thank you for the refreshment."

"The French say *pas de quoi*. I believe that is the correct answer."

Not a thing. Was that a backhanded way for Mrs. Filmer to say she'd done nothing? She needed a third revision to her view of the woman.

Isabella followed Gilchrist out of the conservatory, to the front entrance, and then outside. They returned to the gravel park then stepped onto a flagstone path to go between the manor and church. It accessed a wide open area, with pebbled paths intersecting across the grass.

"This is the Crossing, ma'am, a common area. That building with the cloister walk is the boys' dormitory. You will have no reason to venture there." He didn't mention the blockish buildings further along. "This is the Prior's House before us. You notice that it utilizes the flamboyant gothic style."

The building did not repeat the grey stone of the church but used a red brick, explaining the manor architect's use of brick. Narrow arch windows looked through stained glass onto the Crossing. The tracery at the top of the ribbed windows formed a netlike design set with blue glass. The pointed arch above the thick-boarded door was topped by a fleuron with a guardian angel brandishing a sword. "A medieval cathedral in miniature. It is charming."

"Ma'am."

She heard a truck motor behind the dormitory. Hopefully, that was her easel, canvas, and paint supplies. She saw it through the lancet archways where the cloister connected the Prior's House to the dormitory. The truck puttered past then rolled behind the administration building.

The dormitory was forbidden to her. She wondered how much of the church's interior had survived. Perhaps she could investigate on Monday.

Gilchrist unlocked the massive door. Iron braced the heavy oak planks. The iron was scrolled as elaborately as the tracery above the stained glass windows. The building's interior was lit by modern lamps, a jarring note that said electricity had trumped design aesthetic in the renovation.

"Please wait here," the man ordered. He confirmed she'd stopped then walked along the wide hallway to a back corridor.

Isabella slowly turned on her heel, taking in the vaulting of ancient wood and the aged armorial banners that graced the walls of the entrance.

Gilchrist returned with a man carrying her box of paints, and a flutter of eagerness surprised Isabella. Since the moment she'd received the commission, she'd viewed it as something to be done, not something to enjoy. She'd dreaded it since the dowager contracted with her, but she'd accepted for the money she would earn. Now, she had a gentle flurry of excitement which promised she would enjoy this opportunity.

.~.~.~.

Saturday Afternoon

Frozen by the drive up from London, Flick motored to the Hook and Line Pub. Under her wheels the surface changed from bitumen to loose gravel. As she switched off the engine of her late model green Calcott, a young man appeared from the converted stable. He wiped his hands on a grease-stained cloth.

She lowered the muffler that had kept her nose and chin from freezing, and stretched her stiffened arms, then reached for the handle that opened the door.

"Miss Sherborne, welcome back." He opened the door wide. "You drive all the way from London?"

"More fool me," she muttered then flashed a smile as she thrust out one trousered leg, hoping she could stand after hours on the road. She'd stopped only for fuel breaks. "I didn't know if I would arrive before sundown, but I have, thank God."

"You're in time for tea."

"Another thank God." Now that she was standing, she stretched again then twisted from the waist. Chauncey's old jacket moved easily, the reason she wore it for driving.

"Is Mrs. Pollard expecting you?"

"I telephoned early this morning."

He retrieved her train case and suitcase from the backseat. She lifted her tote which served for her purse, notebooks, and the all-important camera. The Kodak Autographic had never let her down, and she babied it so it would continue to work.

"I'll carry this up to your room."

"Thanks. Tell Mrs. Pollard that I will be in shortly. You will need to fill the tank before you garage the Calcott. Then you can bring in the box in the back."

He peered through the window at the crate stuffed with developing equipment and fluids. "You need all that?"

"I do indeed."

She waited until the pub's half-glass door shut behind him before she tried her first steps around the Calcott. As she tottered forward, she kept a hand gliding on the tire fender, as if she loved the feel of the green metal rather than needed it for balance. By the time she rounded the front, though, she was walking normally, her toes prickling and her feet no longer numb. As much as she loved the freedom that the Calcott afforded her, the thinly cushioned seats over an iron frame were not intended for hours of continuous support.

The pub was ill-lit and smoky. Most of the light was directed at the long bar with its gleaming taps at front and glittering bottles of liquor behind, shelved in front of a mirror. The bar itself was a polished wooden plank, and brass fittings glistened with gold. As Flick approached the bar, Mr. Pollard pulled a glass pint from a rack behind him and began filling it, careful to develop a foam. She almost wished she had arrived after tea, but these days she preferred a cocktail to a pint.

She gently lowered her camera tote and straddled it to protect her investment. "Mr. Pollard, I have finally arrived." She saw movement off to her right and realized someone sat at the end of the bar. The column support had hidden them. "Hello, Sibby."

"Miss Sherborne."

"M'wife's seeing to the tea and dinner, Miz Sherborne."

"May I use your telephone?"

"Public, idn't it?"

"Are you calling your brother, Miss?" The barmaid slid off her stool. "He's here." She pointed to the far corner.

The high-backed bench facing the bar was empty, but Flick accepted Sibby's word. Camera hoisted and the strap back on her shoulder, she walked to the booth. As she passed tables, she spotted a couple of the Old Guard, as Chauncey called them, teaching masters at Greavley Abbey. She smiled brightly and nodded a greeting, putting on her best society air. Her purpose here was to cheer up Chauncey. Nothing else mattered.

She peered around the bench. "Surprise!"

She startled him. He jumped then looked up. "Flick! What are you doing here?"

"Come to see you, Old Thing." She advanced her bag in then slid onto the bench, hiding a wince from sore flesh. His pint of ale had foam at the bottom. He'd drunk it down quickly then. Never a good sign. "I was desperate to escape London," she lied, "and here I am. Are you happily surprised? Do say you are. Or will I be treated to 'Good Lord, the little sister is bugging me again'?"

"That was always Warren's complaint, never mine or Darton's." At mention of their late brother, an early casualty of the war, his smile died. Then he forced it back in place. Since the second smile looked much like the first one, she knew it had been forced as well, another bad sign. "I am glad to see you. Very surprised." He leaned over the scarred tabletop. "And suspicious."

"Suspect all you want," she claimed airily. "I'm after an article on topiary, and I remembered Greavley Abbey has topiaries in that formal garden. Unless Mr. MacAlphin has gone crochety and chopped them down."

"No. Still there."

"Excellent. I hope to work the maze into that article, too."

"You should have called, left me a message that you were coming."

"I wanted to surprise you. Surprise!"

Sibby arrived at the table with an unasked-for pint, a third bad sign. Flick flashed an upward look, but the bar maid didn't meet her eyes as she exchanged the full glass of stout for the empty. She started to turn away.

"Sibby!" Flick didn't ask for a pint, even if her dry throat wanted a light beer. She had risked Mrs. Pollard's ire with her trousers. "My brother will join me for dinner."

"Flick—."

"I won't take no, Chauncey. You need fattening up, all bones and skin."

He grimaced. "I'm not dressed for dinner."

"You have time to finish that ale, walk back and clean up, put on a tuxedo, then come back for dinner. You can drive my auto."

"Good Lord, you drove from London?"

"This is not the Antipodes, you goof. Yes, my body is complaining. Let's not discuss it."

Sibby headed for the bar. Chauncey scowled and drank his stout.

He *was* skin and bones, a fourth bad sign. His skin stretched over his cheekbones. His eyes and cheeks were sunken, his Adam's apple clearly visible in his thinned throat. He'd looked worse when he'd been demobbed, but she didn't like seeing him retreating to that gaunt look. She gauged him based on the day when he'd appeared at her door, wanting nothing but to sleep and sleep. With his dark hair spilling over his brow, his skin as pale as hers, refusing to take a tan even though he'd served in Italy, he looked like a spectre come to haunt.

As he was haunted.

She'd hoped time and the normalcy of life would restore him, and they had. They just hadn't delivered the complete miracle that she'd prayed for.

"Well then, what can you tell me about the topiary?"

"What can you tell me about London's high life?"

"Dancing. New music called jazz."

"You were supposed to say *nothing*, Flick! You should know *nothing* about London high life."

"After last evening, I may know more than is healthy for me." She regaled him with her evening, drolly reciting only the humorous events. Chauncey asked questions, laughed at the right places, and drank his stout slowly. Memories hadn't choked all of him. Maybe time and normalcy were working.

When they parted, she offered her auto for his return to the Abbey School. He refused. "The walk will do me good. I'll go by the river path. As for dinner—." Something flashed across his gaunt face. "I may bring a friend. Miles Farrell."

"Your friend now?"

"School medic," he said, as if that explained it. "Although he's usually engaged on Saturday evening, he's at loose ends tonight. He asked me earlier about dinner. Do you mind?"

She didn't know Mr. Farrell. "Are you trying to avoid my conversation?" she teased.

"No. Never!"

"Ha! I don't believe you. Bring him. I'll rustle up someone. There's bound to be a visitor to the pub, even in this cold weather. We'll make up a four or five. Maybe a fisherman."

"No, no, no. All we'll hear is bait and tackle." Then his smile vanished. The spectre reclaimed his face. "Flick, you shouldn't have—."

"Don't say it, or I'll know you want to be rid of your little sister."

"Never that."

She liked his fervent tone. "You better go, Old Thing. It's already twilight."

She walked with him to the back door, which was down a hall from the pub, beside the kitchen. The door stood open, and Flick peeked in, hoping to get an idea about the meal. Mrs. Halsey was clattering pots and pans, and her two helpers were trying to keep up with her.

Chauncey vaulted over the low stone wall that surrounded the garden then waved at her. She watched him disappear under the trees.

Something burdened him. Some worry. Not the nightmares. Those were horrid enough. He'd recovered from those enough to engage with her. Perhaps the vivid memories only haunted his sleep and had retreated from his daylight hours.

Yet something else had fastened upon him, leeching life. Even in his worst days, when he'd first come home, Chauncey hadn't missed a retort when she teased him.

He'd missed a retort this afternoon, when she teased him about escaping her conversation.

What worried Chauncey?

. ~ . ~ . ~ .

"Hello there!"

Isabella looked up from her sketch of sculls and oars mounted on the wall of the rowing shed. Approaching her was a man in baggy clothes, a creel on one hip, a fishing rod in his hand, a stick in the other, providing balance. He was limping. He lifted the hand holding the fishing rod and waved it. She hesitated then returned a tentative wave.

He came along the path she'd taken from the garden. The path started behind the maze, and she'd happened upon it by chance, as she circled around the maze, wondering if there was another entrance. The path wound under oaks with thick underbrush. At the river, the path began its trail beside the water. The oaks gave way to willows. In summer the willows must drift their tendrils into the water. With winter holding sway for a month longer, the path had winter mire and leaf litter, dead leaves clung to the oak branches, and the willows were denuded of their graceful tendrils.

The man hobbled. The limp slowed his advance. He looked familiar. Was he one of the fishermen that she had spotted at the Hook and Line?

She wondered what he had been doing at Greavley Abbey? Did he want to see someone at the School? Or at the Manor?

If he'd been at the School, though, he would have followed the gravel road. It came straight to the Rowing Shed. Perhaps he had explored the garden. It had disappointed her. No doubt with spring blossoms on the shrubs and flowering transplants from the greenhouse, the garden would be a glorious display. This deep into winter, with the land barely lifting its groggy head, only the stark topiaries offered visual interest. She hadn't explored the boxwood maze. That needed a later excursion.

Isabella finished a last area of her drawing then closed the sketchbook as the man neared. She stowed everything into her satchel and slung the strap crosswise.

"Good afternoon," he called. "You're at the Hook and Line, aren't you? You came last evening."

"That's me," she said ungrammatically and very American. Now that he was within a few yards she saw his waxy skin, the deep-set eyes of someone long ill. His clothes were baggy because he had no weight to him; his jawline and hands looked like flesh stretched over raw bones. Once he'd gained the cleated ramp to the shed and dock, she saw his stick was one used in golf, a driver turned to use as a cane. "You're there, too, aren't you? Mr. Edward—No, Mr. Elwen, isn't it? Does the river have good fishing?"

He grimaced. "I lack the patience that I once had. Mrs. Pollard said we had an artist among us. And a photographer to come."

"Were you up at the School? The topiaries are rather fine."

"I'm not much for gardens. Are you headed back to the pub? I hoped we could walk together."

Does he not trust his balance? Has he done too much today? "I should. I daresay, with all my explorations and sketching, I've likely missed tea."

In common consent, they took the path alongside the river. They had gone about 10 feet, Mr. Elwen managing to stay abreast with her by speeding up, when he asked, "Will we see the Hook and Line turned into a charming sketch to be pinned to the pub wall?"

"I hadn't considered … but the pub would make a good sketch. It has a charm, doesn't it? Greystone like the cottages. I wish it were thatched. That would be charming."

"Bugs coming through the thatch. No, thank you."

She chuckled. "What's a few bugs for a picturesque sketch! I would have to take poetic license—."

"Artist's license."

"Yes, indeed. I could definitely put in the thatched roof then. And give it a prettier setting, perhaps beside the river rather than a walk away through the woods. Thank you for coming with me, by the way. Mrs. Pollard told me the path was shorter than the road and very easy to follow, but I didn't trust the way. Locals have a different view of how things work and often leave out important parts of directions."

"You have traveled much."

"I was fortunate to do so when I worked as a governess. All the way to Crete."

"I'm impressed."

"So was I," she said drolly and was pleased by his laugh.

"We will likely see Nelson and Sandhurst. They're much more serious than I. If you see them, be quiet."

"So as not to scare the fish. I know."

The path was well-trodden but uneven. Isabella managed it in her brogues, but Mr. Elwen began to flag. She guessed war injuries, physical ones while her husband Madoc's were of the soul. The golf driver steadied his steps, but his progress had definitely slowed.

They left the willows. "That's the end of Abbey grounds," he puffed.

Unmown grass lay shaggily on its side as the river banks rose a little. The old abbey must have been selected because it was near a ford.

"Imagine this in another month." Puffing, Mr. Elwen stopped and swept his rod out to indicate the whole river and the ground they'd covered. "Beyond the pub, you can see the gentle banks of the river, all along the village, well past the bridge. Perfect for watching the rowing. The crowd cheering. The sculls skimming over the glittering water, surging ahead with each stroke of the oars. The coxswain calling the strokes. The boys grunting with effort. Colored flags greeting them as they near the finish. That's what you should sketch. Not the pub with a thatched roof."

"Were you a rower?"

"Once. Never again."

"It's early days yet."

He didn't look at her. He began walking, a heavy step on his good leg, swinging the bad one forward with the driver holding part of his weight. "It's been months. It doesn't get better."

"When were you released from hospital?" she dared to ask, intruding more than he'd opened the door to admit.

"October."

October. She was in Crete then. She had attached herself to Gawen's archaeological dig and been convincing him that he needed an artist to record the dig itself. There she met Madoc, and her world changed, no longer alone, no longer friendless in a foreign country, in love and loved. And two men murdered while happiness brought sunshine to her heart.

Now she and Madoc were married and turning to the next adventure, their first venture together. Months from now, she would be in India then in Australia. And after—who knew?

"That's only four months ago. Not really that long."

"You sound like the doctors. Give it time, they say. Build back the muscle that was shredded. Look. There's Sandhurst."

Sandhurst had already packed up. He dragged his fishing creel from the river then turned and saluted them as they drew even with him. The silver on his temples glinted when he doffed his slouch hat and swept a deep bow. He moved like a young man, but his clean-shaven face had sagging jowls like a basset hound. He climbed the bank in long, easy strides and joined them on the hard path.

Entertained by Mr. Sandhurst's self-deprecating fishing jokes, they continued on. Very soon she saw the pub through the trees. Its smoking chimney promised warm fires. The river walk continued past the pub, fading away as it reached the gentle slopes before the village.

Sandhurst sat on the low pierced brick wall that created a curtilage of the garden and swung over. "Taking my catch to the cook. I've a fancy for trout with my dinner. Shall I take yours, Elwen?"

"I didn't catch anything."

"I've an extra trout."

"I don't need charity," the young man flared.

Sandhurst deflected Elwen's anger with a shrug. "I doubt Nelson caught anything. Probably scared the fish with his whiskers. A trout on your plate will twist his nose for him."

"It can't get uglier," Elwen grumped, but this time no anger colored his words. "My thanks, Sandhurst."

The man waved off the gratitude as he strode away.

Isabella found herself like Mr. Sandhurst, for making Mr. Elwen laugh and trying to build up the young man with extra protein.

Chapter 6

Saturday evening

On her way to the lounge, Isabella passed Mrs. Pollard drifting along the hall. Her lace-trimmed olive dress with its shawl collar and mutton-chop sleeves had been fashionable during the war. Her auburn hair looked soft and lovely in an updo with marcel waves, and Isabella wondered who'd earned the extra effort.

White tablecloths, china plates, silver flatware, and crystal goblets had transformed the lounge from everyday to a special evening.

The table away from the fire was occupied by a middle-aged couple that she'd not yet met. The man had a dog collar. Clergyman and wife, already engaged in an oxtail soup. The three fishermen had joined at the window table. They looked smart in dark suits and crisply linen shirts. Isabella nodded to Mr. Elwen and Mr. Sandhurst.

They called her over to meet Randall Nelson, middle-aged with a wavy Garibaldi beard and mustache. "Cod we be friends? That would be fin-tastic." His table partners groaned at his puns, but Isabella chuckled.

A young woman, stylish with bobbed hair and a silk column dress, had claimed her table. She rose from her chair as Isabella turned from the fishermen. "Mrs. Tarrant?" She smiled as she extended her hand. "Forgive my boldness. I'm Flick Sherborne. Mrs. Pollard mentioned that you are an artist at work and alone, like me. May I presume to ask you to join my table? Especially since Sibby tells me that I've confiscated yours."

"It's a pleasure to meet you, Mrs. Sherborne."

"It's Miss, and I give you leave to call me Flick." She shifted a vivid shawl on a black ground on the back of the tulip chair, but she waited to sit until Isabella did.

"Four settings?"

"Yes, that's right. Sibby didn't get it wrong. My brother will join us. He said a colleague would also come. Miles Farrell."

"I don't wish to intrude."

"I guarantee that you are not. Chauncey would rather his little sister did not pester him, and he'll look upon you as a boon. *I* consider you a boon since you're saving me from an evening regaled with the exploits of boys and the trials of teaching. Both my brother and Mr. Farrell are at Greavley Abbey School. They wouldn't dare descend to those depths with you, a pretty stranger, at our table. I'm just family and more easily put-upon. With you here, I will escape a boring evening."

"I'm convinced. I will also escape a boring evening, Miss Sher— Flick," she amended, seeing the young woman prepare to correct her.

After serving soup to the fishermen, Sibby had approached their table, and Flick gave the maid a brilliant smile. "See? I told you that Mrs. Tarrant would agree."

"I never said Mrs. Tarrant weren't agreeable," the maid shot back. "Would you like anything special to drink, ma'am?"

"No, Sibby, thank you. What does Mrs. Halsey have for us?"

"Four courses, with oxtail soup for starters and a lemon chiffon for enders."

"Not the steamed pudding?" Flick sounded disappointed. Having relished the dessert last evening, Isabella understood.

"Lemon chiffon. It's a new recipe." Sibby nodded sharply, checked the other two tables, then hurried out.

"My brother should arrive momentarily." She tugged at her dark hair, as if the bob cut was new and bothered her. "Chauncey is prompt.

He's always been early to anything … except for those years he couldn't be dragged down for breakfast. When my mother refused to indulge him on school holidays, he returned to being on time. I would hope Mr. Farrell has the same promptness. He works at Greavley with my brother. Chauncey has the Greek courses. Mrs. Pollard said you're an artist?"

Does Flick always dash from topic to topic? Maybe it was nerves. Isabella blinked at the change then explained her commission, ending with "My first true portrait. I've done several in oils before, part of my instruction years ago, but I prefer watercolors to oils and landscapes to people. Tony—Tony Carstairs, who has a gallery in London—."

"*The* Tony Carstairs?"

"I guess? He's a *The*?"

"I should say so." Reverence rounded her vowels. "His gallery is highly respected in the art community. He was wonderful artists, including those in the avant garde. I'm not sure he ever descended to Dadaism."

"De-descended?" she sputtered. "No."

"Is your work at his gallery? Lucky you."

"Luck indeed. My friend Cecilia introduced us. I had no idea—. He always wants more of my watercolors and sketches, but I thought that was because I'm such a slow artist."

"You must make a tidy pocket."

"It's a *tiny* pocket. He sells my works at the low end. I *have* heard outrageous prices for large canvases," she whispered.

"Then your commission for Lady Malvaise will increase the demand for your works."

"I don't think—."

"I'm serious." Flick looked serious, her China blue gaze steady, the smile vanished from her face. She even nodded. "Even if the portrait is only seen by visitors to Emberley, the commission alone will add to your reputation. That's if it's any good. Will it be good?"

"It won't be a Rossetti or a Millais, but Lady Malvaise will be pleased. That I'm sure of."

"See? She'll show it off, word will get out, and before you can clap your hands, you'll have more commissions and a growing reputation. Mr. Carstairs will quadruple his prices on your landscapes and sketches, and he'll be extraordinarily pleased, for that will increase his commission."

"No, I won't have more commissions." She said it without regret. "I'm leaving England in a few weeks. I'm to join my husband in India and then a month after, we'll cross to Australia. He has work there."

Flick wasn't dampened. "Then your reputation will gradually grow, and Mr. Carstairs will more slowly raise his prices. But you have opportunity!"

The last word gained a wealth of meaning, and Isabella wondered if Flick were talking of reputation and gold. She didn't paint for either of those reasons.

Her new acquaintance toyed with one of the crystal goblets. Her level gaze from bright blue eyes no longer pinned Isabella but focused inward. "You're not a war widow. I'm grateful for that." She took a deep breath. "My brother had a difficult time in the war. He avoids all talk of it. If the conversation turns to the war, he will likely leave the room. I didn't think to ask until after I'd imposed myself on you. But you're happily married, thank God," she flashed that bright smile, "and soon to travel to exotic locales. We shall have plenty to counter school masters' talk. Here they are."

Two young gentlemen had entered the lounge. The first had golden hair; the second was dark like Flick. The first looked around as if he owned the room and merely decided where to hold court. The second stood straight, but his thin frame seemed braced against the world.

Isabella caught that impression only briefly, then the two were coming toward their table. The first man led the way, making Isabella doubt her identification. It was the second man, though, he with clear blue eyes shadowed above his hollowed cheeks, who bussed Flick's cheek.

"Hello, Young Thing."

"Hello, Old Thing. Hello, Mr. Webberly. May I introduce you to Mrs. Madoc Tarrant? She's an artist. Isabella, this is my brother Chauncey, the despair of the Sherbornes. He disappointed our grandparents by not taking to the dog collar or the robed periwig."

"The periwig was our brothers' choice. I had no interest in pontificating to a congregation. Are you the artist who is painting a portrait of one of our students?"

"The same." She offered a calm greeting and a small smile.

"Brave girl," the gilded man said.

"Do you think so? I do not." Her refusal to take the compliment surprised that gilded man. Isabella was a little confused. Hadn't Flick said the fourth would be a Miles Farrell? This was a George Webberly, and already she disliked him.

"My sister's an intrepid photographer. I doubt you know that," Chauncey sank into his chair as if weary of the day. He still gave a bright smile, but it looked at odds with his shadowed eyes. "She's probably pestered you with questions about your life." He picked up the carafe of red wine and began filling his goblet. Then he passed it to Isabella.

"I am not intrepid. Orchids are hardly dangerous."

"I beg to differ. You are definitely intrepid, sister mine. I've ridden with you in that auto. What is it? A Calcott? Webberly has a Crossley."

They'd barely sat down, and Isabella knew that she'd have to stay focused. Sister and brother liked to jump from topic to topic, and she would need to keep up.

"If Webberly hadn't driven, well—I didn't want to walk in these togs. By the way, Mrs. Tarrant, this is George Webberly, fellow black-robe at Greavley Abbey School. I roped him in at the last minute."

"Once he told me that I would dine with beautiful young ladies, I was eager to drive him." Webberly's attention stayed on Isabella, and she thought *uh oh*.

Flick saw his interest in Isabella and turned to her brother. "I thought you said you would bring Mr. Farrell."

"He couldn't make it. Emergency with one of the boys. He's our medic," he told Isabella. "Different kind of call for his services now. You're here without your husband?"

"He's on his way to India. I'll join him, after I finish this portrait for the dowager. Dealing with her is what makes me intrepid."

He grinned. "*The* grande dame?" Chauncey Sherborne's blue eyes sparkled with humor, and she revised her opinion of a sad young man.

"Very much so."

"You'll need it, to brave Filmer. He won't be pleased if you draw the Malvaise boy from his classes. Nothing interferes with instruction."

"Truly? Dean Filmer was most accommodating when we spoke on Friday and Saturday. He's assigned me a room in the Prior's House for the sittings."

Webberly leaned close, encroaching on her space, not difficult to do at a square table but unnecessary. "He wants to oversee your work."

"Is there a reason he should not oversee my work?"

The man drew back. "No, no, not at all. I thought artists were very tempermental about works in progress."

Her response must have sounded a little hostile. Isabella gave a winning smile even as she leaned back in her chair, a double message of friendliness matched with hands-off. "I suppose I am tempermental when the paintings are my own. This is a commission. That's different, somehow. Are you temperamental, Flick, about your photographs?"

"The city scenes, yes. Not the garden shots. Those are the bread and butter."

Sibby interrupted them, bringing the soup. The conversation turned thrice over before the maid returned to remove the soup. The clergy couple were already past the entrée. The fishermen had just received theirs. Isabella craned a little to see if trout shared Mr. Elwen's plate with the beef Wellington.

Webberly had focused on Flick's description of a London party. He quizzed her about the hostess and the other guests, the dancing and the music.

Chauncey's brother was not listening. His eyes had dulled dark again. Isabella missed their sparkle. "Flick said something about your being the Greek master, Mr. Sherborne. I suppose, since you may have had some theological courses, you were reading Greek for the New Testament."

"Have to do classical Greek here."

"Cambridge or Oxford?" She shot the question rapidly.

His eyes gleamed. "Oxford," he shot back.

"What do you like best about classical Greek? The myths? The drama? Sophocles and Aeschylus? Or history? Herodotus?"

Those blue eyes took a little life. "You credit me with more wit than I have. It is drama. Euripides. I'm working on a new translation of *Medea*."

"The baby killer?"

"That's not really accurate. She's—." He shook his head and chuckled. "If I start explaining Greek myths, my sister will have my hide for boring her friend."

"I did ask." He lifted a single shoulder. Isabella tried again. "Why Euripides? Why not Sophocles? I suppose too many scholars focus on Sophocles and Aeschylus. Is it because his plays are about the downtrodden? I mean, Jason abandoned his wife and children. And he wrote about the Trojan women."

"Don't blame me, Flick. I didn't start it." He leaned back for Sibby to place the beef Wellington before him. Roasted potatoes and asparagus spears were placed artfully on the pink Primrose china plate.

"I'm to blame," Isabella confessed. "My father taught classical and medieval history. He preferred Euripides, too. This smells wonderful, Sibby."

"I'm still upset about the steamed pudding." Flick pouted like a toddler. "Maybe Mrs. Halsey will repeat it in the fortnight I'm here. Will she, Sibby?"

"This Friday. Mrs. Halsey says to tell you the asparagus comes from the Greavley greenhouses." She placed a gravy boat on the table. "A red wine reduction, but if you're partial to a stronger sauce, Mrs. Halsey has mustard."

"I'll have the mustard," Mr. Webberly said.

"Surely not." Flick apparently had firm views on food. "Mrs. Halsey has a reason for producing the red wine sauce."

"I like mustard with my beef."

Flick sat back with a huff.

"I'll bring it in a moment, sir." Sibby offered another decanted carafe of red wine before she retreated again.

"You're staying a fortnight?" Her brother resumed the topic. He frowned a little, as if Flick's extended stay worried him. "I thought you came for the weekend."

"I'm a working girl, Chauncey. I'm planning an article on the Greavley gardens. The topiaries. Perhaps a planting cycle, if your gardener doesn't keep hiding from me."

Webberly laughed. "You'll have to walk fast to keep up with old MacAlphin."

"Or rise early. He sits on the docks in the early morning, drinking tea from a vacuum flask. Shocked me, the first time. He was still as stone, steam rising from his tea and fog rising from the river."

"I can see that picture. I could paint it."

"And I could take a photograph! How did you see him so early, Chauncey?"

"I see him on my morning run."

"Morning run? You remember when you were a slugabed."

"I find it commendable," Isabella interjected. "My husband occasionally runs, but the past month he spent more time boxing. Do you run far? Madoc had a loop."

The twinkle had definitely returned. "Along the river, to the road and around, to my start at the Rowing Shed. That's where I see MacAlphin, every morning."

"I think highly of you, brother, never doubt that I do. But why running?"

"Too much sitting at my desk, grading tests and writings and my translation work."

"What are you translating?" Much of the conversation had flown too rapidly for Webberly to interject, but he managed now. "Do you have a contract with a publisher? You have not mentioned it."

"I wouldn't, especially not around the Old Guard."

"God, no!" Webberly scowled. "Dried sticks and stuffed grumps, the lot of them. They're not happy unless they're lording it over us or poking holes in our comments. And Westbrook Neville won't let things lie."

"More trouble with him?"

"Constant trouble."

"What trouble?" Flick looked genuinely curious. Recalling her father's talk about the petty grudges that teachers would hold, Isabella wasn't encouraging.

"Tricks. Spiteful ones. Mixing up my graded papers with the

ungraded ones. Fouling my test questions so that the secretary types them up incorrectly. Spilling ink bottles all over my plans. Undermining me with the boys. What *hasn't* he done? I saw them in the pub, you know. Did you, Sherby? Neville and his evil twin Reynard Trumble. They're always plotting. And Titus Bellamy as well, at a table. He had that chessboard out. You've seen it, Sherby."

"I have. That's all Bellamy talks about. He's Maths," he explained to the women. "Tries to turn everything into a formula."

"I'll serve them yet for that last trick," Webberly vowed. "You didn't say what you were translating."

Chauncey's face flushed. "Nothing with a pay chit at the end of it, Webberly. Don't fret. I'll pay you in good time."

"Just wondering, old chap."

Flick jumped in before the conversation flew away again. "I want a photograph of that gardener. With his tea, by the river."

"A photograph of MacAlphin? Whatever for?"

"It would be a wonderful scene," Isabella commented, supporting Flick's turn of the conversation. "The fog rising from the river, the steaming teacup, everything hazy except the man in his workclothes."

Flick smiled. "Yes. You see what I mean."

"The artist's eye," Webberly intoned in a mocking voice.

Flick glared at him then turned back to Isabella. "Different perspectives in different media would be interesting. Your eyes and mine, your painting and my photography. Would you use watercolors? To capture that haziness?"

"Oi!" Chauncey interrupted. "Webberly and I aren't talking shop. You can't either."

Isabella ignored him. "I'll go with you to this MacAlphin gardener. I walked around the gardens yesterday. Seeing it through his eyes would be interesting."

"Will you have time?"

"I'm afraid that I will have an abundance of time. Oils have to dry before you can paint more, and I am restricted on the times that Edward Malvaise will come for his sittings. Or standings, actually. His grandmother wants him in rowing whites. White oil paint definitely has to dry, or other colors will smear into it. I planned to do some landscapes of the garden and the river."

Sibby removed their empty plates then distributed the salad service, a *chaudfroid d'oeuf.* She collected the salads from the fishermen before carrying out her laden tray.

Flick's back was toward the three men while Isabella had a clear view of them. Their conversation had died as they consumed the entrée and had never recovered. Mr. Sandhurst had tried several comments, but neither Mr. Nelson or Mr. Elwen had replied to his sallies. During the salad course, Mr. Sandhurst launched into an involved story that required gesturing with his fork and spreading his arms wide.

"Mrs. Tarrant? Mrs. Tarrant?"

Isabella offered a ready smile. "My apologies. I was ruminating on the river and its riparian delights." Chauncey sputtered, and she liked him even more. Webberly was back to being bored. "What is it, Flick?"

"I would like to take some photos while you're painting. The artist at work. I do photo features and articles for *Modern Woman*. You may know it? It's published by Lottie Crittenden. She's sister to Sir Reginald Malvaise."

"I know the magazine, through my friend ... and new sister-in-law," she remembered with delight, "Cecilia Tarrant. She just married my husband's brother. She serves as a creative consultant. You work for *Modern Woman*?"

"Freelance. They just turned me down for a story, but *London Daily* picked it up. I've met your Cecilia Tarrant. Alicia Osterley introduced us."

"Owl? Owl's at this magazine?"

"Yes, Chauncey." Flick peered at her brother, looking for something in his face. "Why do you want to know?"

He'd blanked his expression. "Oh, you lose track of people. You know how it is. What does she do there?"

"Do? Virtually everything. She deserves the title of managing editor, but she's only an associate editor. They probably think she's too young for that." She paused, but Chauncey didn't respond. She turned back to Isabella. "Your friend has some excellent ideas for the magazine. It's been a little scattered with its coverage since Lottie no longer plans the issues. Owl's been frustrated about that." Her gaze flicked to Chauncey, but he was drinking wine. "Isabella, would you allow me to photograph you?"

"Edward Malvaise may be a little disconcerted by a camera."

"Oh, I wasn't thinking during the sittings. Or standings." She grinned at the emendment. "I can see how some ladies might be interested in the development of a portrait. I meant the sketches and watercolors of the garden. Gardens are my specialty. My article on orchids was a recent favorite."

"*You* wrote about the orchids article for *Modern Woman*? *And* took those beautiful photos? That was a wonderful article. I would be honored to have you photograph my work."

"Can you sketch by the river? We could run both the sketch and the photo in the magazine? That would be a treat."

Conversation turned general. Chauncey demanded no more talk

about art or photographs and asked about Isabella's upcoming voyage. Mr. Webberly continued his abrupt pronouncements. Sibby brought white wine then their lemon chiffon cake, a tartly sweet ending to the dinner. Once Isabella realized how wonderful the cake was, she made her thin slice last as long as possible. Flick did as well. The men finished quickly, but only Mr. Webberly kept looking at his watch.

Chauncey gave a great sigh. "If you have somewhere to be, Webberly, I can walk back."

"You won't need to walk," Flick said then savored the lemon icing on her fork. "We'll take rugs and put the top down and enjoy the moonlight. Winter's almost over, and I cannot wait for spring."

"A moonlight drive sounds like a great plan," Webberly said. "You up for a drive, Isabella?"

Her eyes opened wide. "A drive?"

"She's coming with Chauncey and me. Go on, do, Mr. Webberly. Don't let us keep you any longer from your appointment. I did not know you had scheduled a later appointment."

"How could you know? I didn't mention it. Sherby, I need that soon."

"I'll give you a paper." He reached again for the carafe of wine.

"Not good enough. I need it."

"I'll add a surety. Not now, though. Tomorrow."

"Look, Sherby—."

"Stop calling me that name. Tomorrow, I said. Tomorrow, I mean."

Webberly's hand tightened on the back of the chair. Then he straightened and sent a general smile around the table. It looked amiable and entirely fake. "Ladies, I enjoyed lingering over dinner. Wonderful to meet you, Isabella. Perhaps we can get together again."

He waited, and she realized that he intended her to respond. "Nice to meet you, too."

Webberly checked his cuffs then strode out.

The fishermen had already left. The clergyman's wife looked up as Webberly left, but he didn't look around or pause. At the door, he nearly collided with Sibby.

Flick finished her cake and mused over her coffee until her brother huffed. "I thought we had a midnight drive."

"We do. I regret jumping in, Isabella. If you wanted a drive with him—."

"I did not." She said it firmly then ruined it by giggling. That set Flick off, and every time her brother asked "what's so funny?", they only giggled more.

Chauncey stopped to speak with the clergy couple. When he rejoined them, he had his hands in his pockets, treating the tuxedo as if it were a sport coat and corduroys. "That's the vicar. Leverett. His younger brother has the lower forms for history. He's giving the service at the Abbey Church tomorrow. The vicar, not the brother. You should come. The church's one claim to fame is the Altar Screen. Thirteenth century carving. Managed to survive Henry the VIII and Cromwell. That alone is a miracle. Will you come? We can tour the gardens after. If it's warm enough, we should have a picnic by the river."

They tripped into the hall and turned to the pub.

Isabella glanced toward the kitchen. In the dim lighting she saw a man and a woman outside the kitchen door. Wearing an olive-green dress, she leaned against the wall, hands planted to the wainscoting. The man in a tuxedo leaned over her, an arm braced on the other side of her head, her auburn waves catching a halo of light. The dim bulb on the hall gilded his hair. They didn't touch except at their lips.

George Webberly and Imogene Pollard. The appointment he had to keep? Distaste banished the aromatic coffee from her mouth.

Chauncey held open the swinging door. He saw the couple but didn't react. His gaze shifted to Isabella. When she passed, he let the door flap closed behind them.

Saturday evening had packed the pub. Mr. Pollard held court behind his bar, his jacket shed, collar open, and sleeves rolled up. Under yellow braces his shirt looked rumpled.

Flick had stopped at the end of the bar to speak with a freckle-faced youth. She turned away as they reached her and led them to the door while the youth picked up a tray of foam-topped beer. "That's Willard. He gassed my auto. I've rugs in the back. A minute to fix the top, and we'll be on our drive."

"How will we get back in? Won't Mr. Pollard lock the doors at closing?"

"The pub should still be open, and if not—well, I know where Mrs. Halsey keeps a spare key to the kitchen hall door."

"Because you've used it before," her brother alleged.

"Guilty. Run me in. Oh wait, we're going to run *about*."

Isabella giggled, then they all were laughing, excited as children allowed to run wild.

Chapter 7

Sunday Morning, 29 February 1920

The jangling alarm of Flick's clock sounded. She fumbled from under the bedcovers, grabbed the clock and slid up the lever that stopped it. Then she tugged the covers over her bed and huddled under them, keeping warm.

The morning had come too early, for their drive last night was too late. Well worth it, though. Isabella Tarrant was a good egg. She'd made Chauncey laugh several times, and he had relaxed around her enough to use her first name. Something was bothering him, though. Not sleeplessness from nightmares and memories of the war. Maybe that was finally receding. Maybe that punishing morning run he'd described worked a healing. With both mind and body totally engaged, his soul could concentrate on healing.

He was probably starting one of those morning runs right now.

Flick groaned and sat up, keeping the covers over her shoulder. Yawning, she wound her clock then slid up the other lever to prevent the alarm from sounding later. Then she edged from under the warm covers and slipped into her robe. She hurried to the hearth to add more coal. The fire had died down overnight, but when she stirred the coals, she found little flames that happily licked over the new fuel. Waiting for the room to warm, she retreated to the window and peeked around the curtain.

Dawn had brightened the sky, but the light by the back door to the kitchen hall spread a golden glow into the garden, all the way to the back wall, where the oak trees stood sentinel. And where an additional light cast erratically over the garden wall. A round sphere of light, darting about, up to the naked branches, over the trunks, into the distance, then back. Projecting from a bulky shadow at the low wall.

Then the bulk separated into two people. Two heads, both blonde, gold and flaxen. A man and a woman. And Flick realized the darting light came from the torch that the man held. He helped the woman over the low brick wall. The torch had darted about as they had embraced.

He retreated, the torch guiding his path. The woman hurried from the wall to the pub. The light from the back door revealed pale hair and a blue skirt longer than her thick coat. She reached for the key that Mrs. Halsey hid in the niche above the shutter. The woman disappeared. A great wave of light spilled into the garden from the open door. Then Flick saw her dart back to the niche to replace the key. The light shut off with the door's shutting.

The only pale blonde she knew who would also be privy to Mrs.

Halsey's hiding place was the morning maid Nuala.

And that golden hair could be George Webberly.

What would Imogene Pollard think about Webberly with her maid?

Had Isabella seen Mrs. Pollard and Webberly kissing last night? Chauncey had. He said nothing, but she could read his face.

Did Herbert Pollard know about his wife's new interest?

A love triangle with four sides. The situation was ripe for mischief. *I rarely find a use for clichés, but that one certainly fit.* She smirked as she let the curtain drop into place and went to scrounge her sponge bag from the wardrobe.

I wouldn't want to be George Webberly.

. ~ . ~ . ~ .

Mrs. Pollard brought the toast tray to the sideboard. She dusted off her hands then came to Isabella's table. "Good morning, Mrs. Tarrant. May I join you?"

"Please, do."

"Did you enjoy last evening's dinner?"

"I did. Everything was superb, especially the cake. I sent my compliments through Sibby to Mrs. Halsey. Miss Sherborne tells me that such wonderful dinners are commonplace here. You have a jewel in your cook."

"As long as Halsey controls the kitchen. She's threatened to leave us. Every month or so she claims that she's going to get a cottage in the Lake District. I doubt she will, though. She'll probably die as she's rolling out pastry for a savory pie. Nevertheless, I'm traveling to London today to visit several placement agencies for another cook."

"Ah, you think lightening Mrs. Halsey's kitchen duties will make her happier? I should hate to never again taste her cooking." *Why is she telling me this? Why is she telling me about going to London?* "How long will you be in London? Are you going by train?"

"The morning train, yes. I expect to return late Tuesday."

"Then I hope you will have an enjoyable trip." She picked up the little dish that held marmalade and used the tiny spoon to ladle out a serving for her dry toast.

Bracing a hand on the table, Mrs. Pollard rose. "Sibby will help you with any difficulties. You should address any problems to her rather than my husband or Nuala."

Ah. That was the reason. "I have found Sibby very helpful."

"Good. Excellent." She patted the table then left, rearranging the flatware on the window table, shifting a couple of plates on the sideboard. As she left, Mr. Elwen and Mr. Sandhurst came in. Before the lounge door shut, Mrs. Pollard spoke sharply to someone in the hall. "If you don't improve—." The rest of it was lost with the shutting of the door.

Seconds passed, then the hall door opened again, and Nuala entered with a covered platter. She looked waxy pale, as colorless as her flaxen hair, her blue dress hanging on her and almost reaching her ankles.

The two fishermen shifted over to allow her to set down the platter. She removed the lid, releasing the aromas of bacon and sausages.

"More tea, Nuala," Mr. Sandhurst ordered, "nice and dark." He laded his plate with an offering from each dish on the sideboard. Mr. Elwen followed suit, the golf driver tucked under his arm so he could fill his plate. Then both came to her table. "May we join you? You look bright-eyed this morning after your late-night drive." He saw her surprise. "We saw you leave."

She lifted her cup. "The wonders of coffee, bringing me back to life. My husband swears by it, dark roasted and strong. I think he picked up the habit when he was stationed in Turkey and afterwards in Crete. Were you in the pub when we left?"

"Saw that green auto. Flashy ride."

"And lots of fun. Miss Sherborne's a great driver."

"How late did you stay out? You hadn't come back when Pollard closed down the pub."

"How did you find a way in?" Mr. Elwen asked.

"Sh-h. It's a secret."

Nuala hurried in with a large teapot which she set beside Mr. Sandhurst. "There, sir. Anything else? Blackberry jam? Apple? Do you want anything, Mrs. Tarrant? Mr. Elwen?" When no one asked for anything, she hurried out.

Mr. Sandhurst waited until the door shut, then he shook his head. "That girl. She'll tumble down ere long."

"I beg your pardon?"

"My room looks over the back. I saw her coming in this morning, escorted by George Webberly. Webberly isn't one to do the honorable."

"I didn't know you were acquainted with Mr. Webberly. You didn't speak to him last evening, at dinner."

Mr. Sandhurst crunched his bacon. "There's people who you want to meet, people you'd rather not meet, and people who want to ignore you. That's the way of it, isn't it, Elwen? Elwen knows him, too, don't you? He's the kind of acquaintance you cut from your life." He mixed the rest of his bacon with his eggs and scooped up a bite.

With Isabella's blue eyes turned his way, Kenneth Elwen stuttered, "I'm not—I can't—I didn't—. I've heard unsavory things since—. In the war he—. He's a worthless—. I'd rather not discuss it."

She found herself grateful that he hadn't said what he so clearly wanted to. "I believe I would prefer that as well. It's Sunday and a day for grace. If you don't mind." Mr. Elwen shook his head. Sandhurst grunted when she looked at him. "Do you fish on Sunday? Or will you attend the service here in the village?"

Mr. Elwen pushed the food around on his plate. Sandhurst cut into his sausages. "I find God more easily in the world He made, Mrs. Tarrant, rather than in a man-made building. During my sixty years I've had a surfeit of the evils men can do."

"I suppose that rules out the Sunday service." The conversation was its own minefield—*and I shouldn't think of it that way.*

Flick saved her, bustling in with too much cheerfulness. She'd dressed in a pale pink twin set with only pearls as adornment and a brown tweed skirt hemmed demurely. Like Isabella, she served herself eggs and dry toast. "Marmalade on the table? Good. I will probably regret it, after last evening's cake." She took the fourth seat. "My brother's idea of a picnic includes bread and butter and a jam pot, and Mrs. Halsey will doubtless have another sweet that I must finish entirely. Keep this up, and this skirt won't fit next Sunday."

"I expect to gain a stone if every day's cooking is like Friday and Saturday."

"Isabella, we cannot let that happen." Flick salted and peppered her eggs. "Is that tea?"

"Coffee. Mr. Sandhurst has the tea."

Without hesitation, he handed over the large pot.

Flick thanked him and continued talking as she poured and added cream. "Mrs. Halsey takes Monday and Tuesday off, and we get whatever eggs and soup and bread that Mrs. Pollard devises." She shifted the salt and pepper out of the center of the table then set the teapot in the place she'd made.

"Not this Monday and Tuesday. Mrs. Pollard is going to London."

"Is she?" Her first sip of tea downed, she looked at the men. "Hello. I'm Flick Sherborne. Who are you?"

Mr. Sandhurst laughed. "You're one of those new Young Things, aren't you?" He introduced himself and Mr. Elwen. Flick put a hand over the table, and each man solemnly shook it. "What's this about Mrs. Pollard and London?" he asked Isabella.

"She told me this morning. She wants another cook because Mrs. Halsey threatens to retire."

"Mrs. Halsey is the best reason to stay here," Flick said. "Surely they don't mean to push her out?"

"I think it's the other way 'round. They want to keep her here by lightening her load."

She drank more tea, ate more eggs, then asked for the marmalade. "We may have time before the morning service to explore the church, especially that altar screen Chauncey mentioned. That's my brother," she told the men. "He's a master at the Abbey School. We're going to the Abbey Church for the service. Would you gentlemen care to join us?"

Both declined although Mr. Elwen asked, "Are the masters required to attend the service?"

"I don't think so," Flick said. "On my previous visits, when I didn't attend a service, I've seen a couple of the masters out and about."

"How many times have you visited Upper Wellsford?" Mr. Sandhurst asked. He drained the teapot into his cup.

"This is my third. I come to visit my brother. Does that make me a regular? I'm staying longer this time. I plan to take photographs of the topiaries at the Abbey. Have either of you gentlemen seen the topiaries? And there's a maze, too, in excellent repair. Although it's hard to appreciate a photograph of a maze when all you can depict is the hedge wall."

When Flick began describing the dark room she'd set up in the closet in her room, the men excused themselves. She kept talking until the door shut, then she leaned back and took a deep breath.

"Why are you talking so much?"

"You looked a little overwhelmed when I came in."

She remembered Mr. Elwen's reaction when Mr. Sandhurst had talked of George Webberly. "One bit was awkward."

"Flick to the rescue! I'm being silly. I promise I won't talk your ears off. I want to bring my camera with us. I won't take photographs during the service, I promise, but on the picnic I might take a few snaps. Chauncey translates well in black and white, and the two of you on a picnic blanket, sun shining and the wind howling behind you. I'm looking for visual interest."

"How on earth would you show the wind howling?"

The morning remained bright and windless, a rare gift in late February. With the hood fastened on the Calcott, the drive to Greavley Abbey was enjoyable—although Isabella cheated by throwing a rug over her knees.

She had dressed as sedately as Flick yet with less flair, only a peony scarf doubled around her neck to set off her dark suit. Mindful of the picnic, she'd worn the flats reserved for long days of painting.

As they drove through the gates, an ache for Madoc struck her like a physical blow. *Where is he? Has he reached the Mediteranean yet?* He had promised to wire or post a letter in every port. What was he doing this Sunday morning? She wanted him so much—and she had months before she'd see him.

Boys tall and short streamed from the dormitory to the church, entering by the road-facing portal or running around to the front doors with their pointed ribbed arches and carved bosses. In their dark suits with the yellow-edged collars, tri-point handkerchiefs peeking from the yellow-banded chest pockets, and ruthlessly combed and pomaded hair, they looked as natty as any London dandy skewered by P.G. Wodehouse. They certainly weren't the ruddy-faced, robust scrappers that Isabella had seen roaming the Abbey grounds on Saturday.

A few masters stood in their robes at the doors, "taking count," Flick murmured as they walked from the graveled forecourt of the Georgian manor to the medieval church.

A black-robed man separated from the others and lifted a hand. The sun burnished his dark hair, giving it strands of spun gold.

Another automobile parked beside the church as Chauncey met his sister and Isabella. The passenger door opened as the brake was set, and the vicar sprang out, moving with a younger man's agility. Bible in hand, he jogged to the side door. A middle-aged man emerged from the driver side. He opened the rear door and offered a hand to the hatted lady in the back. A black veil half-covered her face. Her dress and long jacket were of black and cream swirls, and she carried a black purse that matched her black shoes. Then the man climbed back into the auto and backed to the other side of the forecourt. He drove away in a spurt of gravel.

"Good morning, good morning," the vicar's wife called and waved as they reached the flagstone path alongside the church. 'Is it not a glorious day? Would you care to join me?"

"Thank you, Mrs. Leverett, but my brother has a place for us at the back, where he must stand. He's beadle today. Chauncey," she muttered, "tell me you can find us a back pew?"

"Done, Young Thing. Even if I have to move some boys."

"My hero."

They had time to examine the age-darkened altar screen with its twelve apostles before the service. Above the apostles were creatures tame and wild, a draught horse beside a cow and her calf opposed with a hart and a doe and fawn, a sheep with twin lambs and hunting dogs after a wolf, birds atop bushes and chickens with a proud rooster.

"Where's Judas?" Flick hissed.

"They replaced him with St. Matthias" Isabella whispered. "He's the one with the axe and the book."

Then the vicar was standing at the altar rail and beginning his welcome, and they hurried to their pew. Isabella spotted the Dean and

Mrs. Filmer in the first pew on the right. The stained glass window there depicted a wild-bearded man with a sword in one hand and a plow-share in the other. Gilchrist and Dodges sat together partway back. The former looked haggard, as if he hadn't slept. The manor butler looked waxy pale, as if he'd been sick.

Or seen a ghost.

The boys slid down to give the two young women places on the aisle, and Chauncey stood behind them in his duty as beadle.

During the sermon Isabella stared at the stained glass. On the vicar's left were Noah and his ark, Abraham and Isaac and the ram, Moses with his tablets, Nehemiah atop the walls of Jerusalem, the tumbling walls of Jericho. To the right were Paul composing his letters, Peter fishing, Philip in the Ethiopian's chariot, John writing his letters above the fiery cauldron. The vicar spoke of the parable of the sower and how some people's lives were harder than others. During the communion she noticed that Mrs. Filmer had not returned to her seat, but she returned by the end of rite. Then the vicar gave the benediction, and they returned to the sunshine, so radiant that the day had warmed to spring.

"Give me fifteen minutes." Chauncey already had his robe off. "I need to stow this and collect our picnic. I'll meet you in the garden. Have you seen it, Mrs. Tarrant? The maze is considered fine."

"I haven't explored the maze as much as I wished. I thought you were going to call me Isabella."

"Hurry," Flick said, hoisting the strap of her tote with the camera higher onto her shoulder . "No doubt we have a hike before us to reach your perfect picnic spot."

"It's only a little bit upriver," he vowed, but Isabella decided her flat heels were a wise decision.

The two young women strolled through the Crossing and took the steps that descended to the formal garden.

"Have you truly not explored the maze, Isabella?"

"I ventured to the third turn, but I worried I would become lost. I didn't have a lot of time. Perhaps tomorrow."

"We can quickly walk it and be finished before Chauncey is here. Once you know the secret, it's not difficult. Three by two by three by two, alternating. We begin to the left. Most people start to the right. Did you do that?"

Isabella chuckled. "Yes, I did. I would have been soon stuck, wouldn't I?"

"A definite dead end. Look, a hawk."

They watched the raptor swirl on the updrafts before following the side path of the long rectangular garden. The plan followed the *jardin à la francaise* with stacked circular wheels at each corner, spiraling pyramids of topiaries creating a center line, symmetrical center beds within flowing arches, raised beds at either end with boxwoods kept dwarfed, and a serpentine boxwood wall around the exterior.

"The focus for your article?"

"Yes. A feature for each design and then instructions on how to develop and maintain the simplest design. I think the readers of *Modern Women* will enjoy it. Not as much as the orchids."

"We women do love flowers."

They bridged the entrance to the maze, a grassy verge between the gravel path that surrounded the edge of the garden. With the gravel no longer crunching beneath their feet, they could hear voices, a man and another voice, too soft to determine.

They paused. "Should we go on?" Isabella murmured. "Someone's before us."

The man's voice lifted a little, enough to distinguish that he spoke with a lilt. Irish.

Flick caught Isabella's arm.

"As if I can!" That was the woman, voice crisp with emphasis, the words bursting out as she forgot the need for privacy. The man murmured, his words still too soft to hear. The woman spoke over him. "I hate this place! It will never change! The same people, the same things to do, day after day after day. I hate this place, and I hate him! I want to leave."

"And where will you go?"

Isabella towed Flick back a step, but the young woman lifted a finger for 'one minute more'.

"I have *nowhere* to go," the hidden woman complained loudly. "No family. No home. He convinced me to drop my friends, forget about my aunts and uncle. My family was too lower class, and we needed to hide that connection. As if it made a difference! Everyone still treats me like dirt on the bottom of their shoes, scraped off at the door. My aunts, my friends, they won't take me back. I gave them up for him. And now I'm trapped."

Flick's eyes widened. "Do you know who she is?"

Isabella shook her head. She tried another step away, but Flick didn't budge. She wanted another minute.

The man's response was too low. The woman didn't moderate her voice, no longer strident but still carrying. "I thought I'd found a way to cope."

"An *affaire*," that was clear enough, and the man's censure was equally clear, "is not a way to cope."

"It gave me something he couldn't control. That's all I cared about.

You don't know how he has to make every decision a drawn-out discussion. Then he ignores what I think and makes the decision he wanted to. Or he tells me over and again how my wishes are wrong."

"Then do something else. In the village. You were his secretary before the war."

"I hated that. He was only too happy to replace me. It's boring. Nothing to do all day but type and file and answer the telephone."

"You have skills. You can find employment with a lawyer, with the doctor. Even the magistrate might have a position for you. Something with more people coming in. Not boys. Or take the bus to the factory in Lower Wellsford. They need office staff, I'm certain."

"Take the bus?"

"It's better than involving yourself in an *affaire*. That was a temporary solution … not last. From … courting …."

"Look at you! So righteous!"

Isabella finally recognized the woman. That snide tone could only belong to Verna Filmer. The dean's wife, complaining of her marriage. Complaining of her life in a manor, with servants for every task. Bored with her life. And bored with her life when she'd been secretary to her husband. Bored before then, too?

"… not judging, Verna … my advice. I wish … weeks … entangled yourself … George…." Only a few words came clear, enough to decipher that the man was judging Verna Filmer, who had entangled herself in an *affaire* rather than asking for help. Then he said, "You were content earlier this week. What happened?"

"… involved with that maid at the pub."

"Nuala," Flick hissed, and Isabella wondered how she knew.

" … every woman," he said.

"I expected that. He's so handsome. But—." She stopped abruptly, then she wept, and her sobs were soon muffled, as if she'd flung herself on the man.

Or he'd taken her into his arms.

Flick dragged Isabella away, along the grassy verge that bordered the boxwood wall of the maze. They had to return to the crunchy gravel to gain the steps out of the sunken garden. At the corner of the maze, they stopped.

"Well, that was an earful!"

"An earful I didn't want to hear." Isabella wished she could unhear it.

"Did you figure out who the woman was?"

"Mrs. Filmer."

"Verna Bryant Filmer, who lords it over everyone in the village, even the vicar's wife, and Mrs. Leverett is granddaughter of a marquis.

Did you know the man? No? Miles Farrell."

"I haven't met him."

"I haven't either, but he's the only Irishman around. He came to Greavley in September, with the other new masters. He replaced the nurse. Farrell was a medic during the war. I think Dean Filmer hired him for that very reason. Chauncey says he's easy to talk to—."

"Obviously."

"And he gives excellent advice."

"If people ask for advice before they entangle themselves in an *affaire*."

"That's not quite the thing people contemplate beforehand, Isabella. They're just ... there."

"Will you think badly of me if I say she was looking for an *affaire*?"

"I had the same impression. She wanted to stick it to her husband. To the dean. I wonder if Chauncey knows."

"Don't let's talk about this. It's horrid."

"You're in the honeymoon stage of marriage."

"And I want to stay that way as long as possible, Flick."

"You saw him last evening, didn't you? With Mrs. Pollard. This morning I saw him with Nuala."

They fell silent, absorbing everything they'd heard and seen about George Webberly. Isabella found she couldn't cast that conversation in the maze out of her head.

Chauncey crossed the lawn to them. He wore tweeds and carried a box with a rolled blanket on top. "Ready?"

"Ready and more," his sister said. "I'm starving. What have you brought us? I hope it's more than bread and butter and a jam pot."

"Cold beef sliced thin and cheese and apples and yeast rolls. That satisfy you?"

"A feast! You did well, Old Thing."

He tossed the blanket to his sister. "Carry this, Young Thing. It's two. One for under us, one for cover if the wind picks up. It may. We're by the water. Did you enjoy the maze, Isabella?"

"We didn't go into the maze. It was occupied."

"Miles Farrell," Flick said, "counseling someone. They were quite upset. We heard more than we wanted."

"Then I'm glad you didn't interrupt." He led them along the boxwood hedge and to the woods behind it.

"I came this way yesterday," Isabella said, disliking the silence that kept asking them to gossip. "The path's easy from the river to the pub. A little mucky here where the sun never shines."

On the path ahead, a crow lifted off a humped thing.

Flick, in the lead, stopped abruptly. "Dear God."

A dead man lay face down on the path. His tweed suit looked untouched. Bright blood covered his head. The gilded hair in the gory mass was unmistakable.

George Webberly.

Chapter 8

Sunday Afternoon

Chauncey stepped between them and the body. "Don't look. Flick! Don't look. Give me a blanket." He draped it over the body. "Go back to the Prior's House and telephone the constable and a doctor."

"He doesn't need a doctor."

"Then an ambulance."

"And who should we tell? Where will we find them?" Flick stared at the blanketed body and remembered the blood. "Time is a necessity in a murder, isn't it? Chauncey, you know where people will be. You should go."

"How do you know that about time?"

"I live in London, Old Thing, and a daily rag buys my photographs. I've a lot of newshounds in my circle. Now, off you go."

"Isabella—."

"Do go." She was determinedly looking away from the covered body. "I won't have hysterics. This is not the first violent death I've encountered. Flick is right. You should hurry."

He left the picnic basket on the path, but neither Flick nor Isabella wanted to think about food.

For quite a few minutes, longer than she liked, Flick couldn't think of anything to say. Her first thought was unfortunate, for she blurted it out, eager to end the silence. "Where have you encountered violent death? Oh. Were you at that horrid holiday party at the Malvaise country estate?"

"We found the body." She resolutely faced away from Mr. Webberly and looked back toward the Abbey. She must have hated the silence, too, for she added, "I was on that archaeological dig, too, where a man was murdered and artifacts were stolen."

"Really?" Not lucky at all. She understood the newshounds' gory acquaintance with murder.

"It's when I met my husband. And Cess Arkwright. Tarrant now."

"Wait. Arkwright. That Arkwright? The archaeologist who stole from his own dig and wound up in that foreign prison? That dig? Didn't another man die?"

"Yes. A worker."

"I read about that. But—if Cecilia Arkwright … Tarrant, if her husband is in prison, how did she--?"

"Nigel Arkwright died in that prison."

This was awkward. Flick didn't have the right words, only the wrong ones. "She didn't wait a year's mourning, did she?"

"Well, she'd already hired lawyers so she could divorce Nigel. She decided in October, before his role in the thefts was discovered and he was imprisoned. She's very happy now, with Gawen."

Flick's brain finally worked out the connections. "Your husband's brother is Gawen Tarrant, the archaeologist. Is your husband an archaeologist?"

"No. Currently, he's off to build a road. He likes the physical work."

"Like Chauncey's running." Flick suspected that Madoc Tarrant had lingering problems like Chauncey.

The trees hid any view of the school. In the distance, a train whistle blew. The tote strap dug into her shoulder. Flick lowered the tote to the ground then hugged herself. The twin-set and tweed had looked perfectly warm for a sunny day. Here beneath the great oaks with their multitude of branches, the sun peeked through but without the warming radiance of church-side. She shivered and wrapped her arms tighter, wishing the tote held something warm instead ….

…Of her camera.

The newshounds talked of forensic photographs documenting crime scenes.

She hauled the camera out of the tote.

"What are you doing? I mean, what—why do you need to take photographs?"

Thank God that Isabella Tarrant wasn't an idiot. Flick fiddled with the lens setting, trying to judge what she'd need underneath the trees. "Chauncey will call the local constable who will report the murder to the local magistrate—. That's the squire, I think. They'll move the body—."

"Wait. With a murder, the body is not supposed to be moved."

"How many murders do you think they have in Upper Wellsford? Or in Lower Wellsford? The crime scene will be lost before they decide to call Scotland Yard."

"You can document the scene," she said with dawning understanding. "How will you develop the photographs?"

"My room has a closet that I've turned into a darkroom. Do you remember my talking about it at breakfast?"

"Yes. On and on."

"Well, all I need to develop the film into negatives is tape around the door and someone to watch that no one opens it. Nuala ruined a whole roll of film last autumn. Even with my sign posted not to open the door."

"I can guard the door if you'll give me a magazine or a novel to read."

"I have the newest issue of *Modern Woman* and three photography magazines. Oh, and a newshound at the *London Daily* gave me an American publication called *Photo Era*. My issue of the *Photograph Journal* is old. It has an article about a new camera, a prototype much smaller than this." She hefted the Kodak Autographic. "Be careful with that issue."

"I will guard it carefully."

"Then, the only thing I'll need for photographs is an enlarger. It's too bulky and huge to transport. I'll have to borrow one. If Wellsford Upper or Lower doesn't have a camera shop with an enlarger, I'll go farther afield. And you can tell the detective inspector who comes that he'll soon have photographs of the scene."

"That's smart thinking, Flick. If a detective inspector comes."

"Oh, one will. There's too many suspects."

Isabella's face turned toward the body, then she quickly looked away. "You think so?"

"I can count three women. Who knows how many men?"

"We could just convince the constable not to move the body."

"Do you think any man will listen to women telling him his job? *Exactly*," she said at Isabella's grimace. "Besides, the constable won't want to leave Webberly out here overnight. I don't see anyone coming from Scotland Yard until tomorrow."

"What do you want me to do?"

"Hold the blanket back. You don't have to look."

"I'd rather not. His head's a mess." Isabella carefully stepped to the body. She crouched and gingerly pinched fingersful of the blanket. Then she stood, the blanket lifting with her.

"He was clearly bludgeoned. Ready?"

"Are you? You'll have to focus and hold steady for the photograph."

Flick swallowed. Then she aimed the camera and focused on the head's position. And she was very glad breakfast was hours ago.

She took the head-shots first, then full body, then the area around. She caught two images of Isabella holding the blanket, clearly looking away as she held the blanket up. She even took photos of the picnic basket. "Does that look like something in his hand?"

Isabella lowered the blanket enough to peer over. "Which hand?"

Flick pointed then squatted to focus on the glint in Webberly's right hand. "It looks like a gold chain, not a coin."

"There's something in his jacket pocket. This side."

"I see." A crumpled paper had stuck a corner out. Webberly hadn't shoved it deeply enough into the pocket. She snapped several images, including his near-side jacket pocket which lay flat and looked empty. Then she lowered the camera. "You can cover him again."

Isabella carefully draped the blanket. Flick took photos of that. The sequence of the negatives would maintain a record of what they had done, when and how. She twitched a corner of the blanket to cover his hand then straightened. "Do you see anything that could be construed a weapon?"

"No branches. No rocks. It would have to be a stout stick, to do that damage." She closed her eyes. "I'll be seeing that for a while. When do you think it happened?"

Flick was still searching the path, toward the river. "Just before we left the church. There's blood here, beside the path."

In all, she counted six patches of blood, leading toward the river, away from the body, all on the right side of the path, spaced about a foot apart.

"During the service," Isabella mused. "Giving several people an alibi. And whoever did this, they could have taken the weapon with them. Flung it into the river. Your brother is taking a long time."

Flick checked her watch. Chauncey had left over a half-hour ago. What was he doing? She shook out the second blanket. "We'll share." Once Isabella took a corner, Flick stowed the camera in her tote then took her side of the blanket and twisted until it was over her shoulders.

They huddled together, facing away from the body, waiting for Chauncey's return.

He had no apology as he jogged along the path. "The constable is coming. He's waiting on the magistrate and the doctor."

"Who is the magistrate here?"

"Sir Robert Goodkind. And before you ask, Young Thing, I don't know anything about him. I don't know anything about anyone in Wellsford, Upper or Lower. Dean Filmer said that you should wait at the manor. The Prior's House is locked, and he doesn't intend to open it. He's sent word to Dodges to expect you."

"We'll leave you the blanket," Isabella offered. "It's cold here, under the trees."

"And colder still, back to freezing before sunset, I'd think. Wind's picking up, and clouds are moving in fast."

"I don't like leaving you here alone," Flick fretted.

"I'm not afraid of dead men. It's the living who have the power to destroy. The dead hold no terrors." He glanced at the blanketed body. "Especially George Webberly. Not now."

Flick and Isabella hurried back to the Abbey propre. The trees cleared to reveal the green hedge of the maze and above it the warm brick of the manor house. The grey quarried stone of the Masters' Lodgings and teaching hall stood stalwart.

They started around the hedge, following the grassy path. "Who do you think did it?" Flick whispered.

"I have no idea. Someone not at the service."

"I didn't count heads, did you?"

"I didn't see Webberly there, either. They didn't have to be at the service. They could have come from the river, not the Abbey School. They could have come from anywhere."

"At least we have firm alibis."

"Yes. And the vicar and his wife. All the boys. None of them left during the service. And Dean Filmer. Gilchrist and Dodges." She stopped abruptly.

"There was an awful lot of comings and goings, weren't there? Mrs. Filmer. A couple of the masters came in and out." Flick didn't mention Chauncey. He'd stood at the back. She couldn't say for certain that he'd stayed for the entire service. *Not Chauncey.* Yet he'd said that about Webberly, that he no longer held any terrors for Chauncey, *not now.* Last night, before he left them, Webberly had asked for something of Chauncey. She had dismissed it then, but *I'll give you a paper*, he'd said, and *add a surety.* Had he owed Webberly money?

No terrors. Not now.

They'd reached the formal gardens. Two of the older masters stood at the far steps that descended to the formal garden. The men were watching the school buildings and the Crossing, not the woods side. They stood, in the same crossed-arm stance, a barricade for any nosy boys. Flick and Isabella continued walking along the grassy verge. Their approach surprised the men who'd heard nothing behind them.

"Where did you come from?"

"The river path through the woods."

"Here, you were not supposed to—."

"We were with my brother Chauncey when he found the body," Flick said, short of patience. "We maintained the scene while he alerted the authorities. Now we're going to the manor. As ordered."

"A body? We weren't told there was a body. Is someone dead?"

"What did Dean Filmer tell you?"

"That there was an incident and to keep the boys from wandering into the woods and down to the river. We are to direct whoever comes to the river path."

"George Webberly's been murdered," she said baldly.

"Murdered?"

"George Webberly! Wonder if Neville—."

"He wouldn't."

"He hated the man."

"Still—."

Flick lost her fragment of patience, the most of it broken when she took the photographs, the rest of it gone when they stood shivering under the blanket, a dead body within five feet of them. "The constable is coming. You need to direct him to the river path behind the maze. We're going to the manor."

"Wait! How do you know he was murdered? He could have drowned. We should send them by the road that stops at the Rowing Shed."

"He's not in the water. He's on the path."

"He was bludgeoned," Isabella added. Flick felt a trickle of satisfaction at the men's shock.

And she was appalled at herself.

"We should tell Neville. And Bellamy."

"You must wait here together," Isabella said, "as the dean ordered. Come, Flick." She started walking with the words, surprising Flick with the speed of her stride. When they were past and entering the empty Crossing, Isabella stopped and pressed her hands to her face. "I shouldn't have told them that."

"They'll discover it soon enough."

Her reply was a grimace.

The manor's side door to the Crossing opened as they passed the recessed steps. "Ladies." Dodges stood there, rigid and proper in his dark livery, still white-faced. *Had he heard the news?* "The dean sent word to expect you. If you will come this way."

Sickness? Or something else? Isabella was right, Flick realized. The suspect list would be large.

Inside, the hall of the manor was chilly. The butler paced ahead on silent shoes. They passed six closed doors, three per side. The painted wall panels were a cream that reflected the weak wintry light. Between each door were paintings, Cavalier and Renaissance style, wide lace collars or stiff ruching. The dark eyes of the portraits followed their passage.

A climbing staircase featured the oval entrance hall. Two portraits dominated, both recent. Dean Filmer, life-size before his hair greyed, wore black robes and colors. One hand rested on a stack of thick and weathered books. A globe was positioned at his feet. Moorland rose behind him. The other was Mrs. Filmer, young and beautiful, with a draped lace bodice to her ruby gown, and a silver chain about her throat. She stood beside a column with sapphire curtains behind her.

"Miss Sherborne," the butler said, a soft reminder that she wasn't here to tour the house. She thought it significant, especially in light of that overheard conversation in the maze, that the dean's portrait was larger than his wife's. Every day of their wedded life the woman must look at the two portraits and know her husband had begrudged her the three extra feet that would match their portraits in size.

Dodges stood beside an open door. Isabella had already entered. Flick could hear her, expressing gratitude that the dean had offered them the comfort of the house while they waited for the authorities.

"What has occurred?" Verna Filmer looked at Flick as she entered, but her gaze quickly returned to Isabella. "My husband said only that there'd been an incident."

Isabella looked at Flick and waited.

The two Old Guard knew now and would quickly tell, as soon as they were released from their duty. What was the point of secrecy? "We stumbled upon George Webberly. He'd been—." *Should I say killed? Murdered?* She settled for "—struck down. Probably from behind."

Dodges choked and retreated from the door, leaving it open.

"Struck down? Is he greatly injured? I know the doctor is sent for."

The sound of a motor interrupted her. They all looked out the tall window.

A black automobile had turned into the gate. A truck came behind it.

"That's Sir Robert Goodkind's automobile. Why is he—? That isn't an ambulance. If Mr. Webberly is injured—."

"He's not," and Flick thrust obscurity away. "He's dead. Someone murdered him."

"What? George is—George is *dead*? I don't believe you."

Flick and Isabella exchanged a brief look.

"I talked with him. Not two hours ago. He was here. In the garden, I mean. He said—. He—." She pressed fingers to her brightly painted mouth. "Murdered?"

"We found him," Isabella said gently.

"Was he injured? We must help him."

Isabella flung a silent request for help to Flick, but Flick had used up her politeness. Mrs. Filmer was already shocked. *Is that a sign that she didn't commit the murder?* "He's quite dead, ma'am. Murdered."

Mrs. Filmer dropped her hand. Her lipstick was smeared, a garish parody of a smile. "Tell me."

"On the river path behind the maze."

That firm fact shook her. "On the—behind the—. We used to meet there. I-I—." Movement caught her attention. She stared at the door, and Flick turned to see the butler returned.

"Shall I bring refreshments, ma'am? Or tell the cook to set back the luncheon?"

"I can't—." She sprang up and raced from the room. Dodges nipped out of her way. They heard her rush up the stairs.

The butler's mouth was a set grimace. "Will the magistrate and the constable be coming here or going to the Prior's House? The dean did not see fit to inform us of his will. You need not answer, ladies. I shall be ready, whatever occurs. Please, be seated. I shall bring tea."

.~.~.~.

Michael Wainwright clicked off the telephone then re-connected to the operator. He revealed none of his roiling emotions as he emotionlessly gave the number to reach his sergeant.

After a few rings, the operator came back to the line. "My apologies, sir, but the party is not accepting the connection."

"This is Detective Inspector Michael Wainwright of the Metropolitan Police. I wish to speak to my sergeant Trevor Callaway about an urgent police matter."

"Shall I attempt to re-connect, sir?"

"Do so, every fifteen minutes, for the next two hours, please. The Metropolitan Police is grateful for your assistance. Ring twice here when you have connected to him."

"Oh, sir, yes, sir." Excitement replaced the operator's efficient astringency. "Two short rings, sir."

He hauled out a recent ordnance map for the Midlands, fixing the location of Upper Wellsford. He perused the village's environs and then those of Greavley Abbey. He noted the country lanes as well as the railroad line. Yet the train schedule revealed that only a spur reached the village. An automobile would be faster travel and enable them to move without impediment around the area. He found little information about the village itself. Callaway would take over that task, to con what he could then relay it as they drove up.

Michael rang the department to requisition an automobile. The chief inspector was before him and had ordered it a half-hour ago. He must be familiar with the area around Wellsford.

He drew out a pocket-sized notebook and reviewed what his chief had related. *George Webberly. Teaching don at Greavley Abbey School—only they called the dons masters at the Abbey School. Repeated blows to the head. Killed in woods behind Greavley Manor.* He checked the ordnance map again. *No suspects. Constable Amsley would take preliminary statements.*

He packed, kit and clothes, wellies to stow in the boot. Today was unseasonably warm, a guarantee that the weather would soon turn sharp.

The telephone rang at the 45-minute mark.

His sergeant sounded out of breath. "The operator says it's a police matter, boss?"

"Pack up, Callaway. We have a case in the Midlands. We'll leave before dawn and make good time on the main roads. By my calculations, we should arrive before afternoon."

"Midlands? Do you expect to return soon? Only, I've a box of fresh groceries, boss."

"Pass them off to a neighbor and ask for a couple of meals on your return. I need you to consult your network. Upper Wellsford and Greavley Abbey School. We may arrive before the press, for once. The villagers may not think to notify the rags. The local magistrate and constable certainly won't. Nor will you, Miss Operator."

"Cor!" she breathed. "How did you know I were listening? Is it a murder? Jewelry theft? Both?"

"You have your orders, sergeant. I'll see you outside my flat at half-past four. You'll have to change your plans for the evening."

Callaway sighed. "She was a red-head, boss."

"Explain sweetly, and she'll cook you dinner when you return."

"Do you think we'll have a resolution by next weekend? Only I'm thinking of your next Saturday evening plans with the chief."

"I have no plans, sergeant. Will your red-head wait?"

"That I don't know. Not sure of her yet, boss."

"Promise her the details," the operator put in. "She'll wait for you."

"You ought'n't to listen to police matters, miss," Callaway said before Michael did. "Half-past four, boss. Out with the dairy men."

Michael rang off.

He had hoped to spend the next week sniffing out information about Miss Felicity Sherborne, her work, her play, the little ins and outs of her life. If he could meet her, seemingly by chance—. If they sparked—.

He shrugged. Should Fate intend for them to meet, the ball was already rolling, Sisyphus-style, flattening everything in its way. No path he paved would re-direct that ball.

Michael wished he weren't so fatalistic. The Presbyterian streak ran too strongly.

He had his own informant to consult about the case. A friend in the War Office Records Department kept Sunday evening hours to cope with the overload of work since demobilization. He claimed the filing would slow down soon. When they'd met for a drink at the local, he hadn't said how soon that would be. Shadwell would happily break away from his work to answer his old colonel's inquiry.

Chapter 9

Sunday Afternoon

Dodges' tea was an elaborate serving of savory pastries and elegant sandwiches with sweet confections and a fruity cake.

Is Dodges celebrating? Or is this the kind of tea they have here at the manor? His behavior was as rigidly proper as ever. Isabella couldn't decide.

Flick filled up a plate. "I feel guilty for indulging, but that's not going to stop me."

Isabella creamed her tea. "It does seem heartless, doesn't it? But how can we refuse?"

"It looks like a celebration. Or a wake. An Irish wake. Have you ever been to one?" She began describing one that she had attended before the war, "when I was in my awkward teens."

They had polished off their plates and sipped the last of the tea when the door opened. Dodges ushered in a nondescript man in old tweed. "Sir Robert Goodkind, the local magistrate."

"Hot tea, if you would, my man. Ladies." The magistrate picked up a plate and laded it with the remaining savory pastries and fruited cake. "Forgive me, ladies. I haven't eaten since breakfast. Cook will have dinner when I return, but that will be some hours yet. Now, which one of you is Miss Sherborne? Ah, then you must be Mrs. Tarrant. I didn't anticipate that Mrs. Filmer would leave visitors to her house unattended."

Since Flick had just sipped tea, Isabella answered. "Mrs. Filmer was greatly shocked by Mr. Webberly's death. She retired for privacy."

"Hmph. I daresay no more shocked than you three were." He frowned at a savory pastry then took a bite, chewing slowly. Once he'd swallowed, he glanced up from the plate, his eyes a mossy brown as nondescript as his clothes. "Mr. Sherborne says that he left both of you with the body while he contacted us."

"That's correct. We covered the body—." Isabella stopped, thinking of evidence and wondering if she was walking into trouble. At Christmas she hadn't mistrusted Detective Inspector Wainwright, but too easily she recalled the smooth questions from the Greek inspector last October, looking for the murderer of Richard Lamb and suspecting everyone, including her.

"Then we uncovered it," Flick took up the account. "The blood stains on the blanket probably won't match. We uncovered it so that I could take photographs. A gory sight it was, and not one I'm eager to repeat. You'll be wondering the reason," she rushed on, guessing the question that Sir Robert had opened his mouth to ask. "I'm a professional photographer. We thought it best to make a record of the scene as we found it. We weren't certain how much it would be disturbed. I hope you don't think Isabella and I are gory gawkers."

"Hmph. Gory gawkers. That's good. No, no, I'm glad someone took photographs. I would have called for our local photographer, but he's out of the area for the day. My constable's made notes of the scene, but it's not the same as seeing it. We'll have to move the body, you see. Not the best situation. Scotland Yard's man should see the body *in situ*, as it were, but that can't be helped. We'll have rain by evening, definitely tonight, the way the clouds are streaming in. Weather's changing. Photos are good, good. My thanks, Miss Sherborne. How many did you take?"

"Quite a number, including the area around the body and several feet along the path either way."

He finished his plate and returned to claim the remaining sandwiches and sweet pastries. For a wispy man, Isabella didn't know where he put the calories. "How soon can you have the photos available?"

"I can develop the film this evening, sir, but I'll need an enlarger to make suitable prints for the police."

"Good, good. We have a camera shop in the village. Owned by Nigel Roberts. He's gone to some exhibition, his wife says. Not expected back until evening. I called. I knew we'd need photos. Scotland Yard won't arrive until tomorrow."

"You've already called them?

"As soon as Constable Amsley said he'd never investigated a murder without a clear suspect. Hmph. Not quite the thing 'round here, you see. Amsley's currently taking your brother's statement, Miss Sherborne, over at the Masters' Lodgings. Will you ladies wish to speak with him there or here?"

"Speak with my brother?"

"No, miss. My apologies. The constable. He must take your statements. Preliminary, of course. The inspector who's coming will want to take a more formal statement, but I think it best to have a few things in motion for them. After your shock, this is a much more accommodating place. Nice fire. Comfortable chairs." He gazed at them expectantly.

Dodges entered with another pot of tea. He glanced over the empty tea service. "Do you wish more sandwiches and—ah, cake, sir? Cook will have them in a trice."

"No, no, I shouldn't. Well, perhaps a sandwich or two. And another slice of that cake. Jolly good it was."

"Of course, sir." He bowed then left, as silently as he'd entered.

"Now. Where were we? Ah, yes. My constable expects to interview you here. Shall I send word that he must expect you at the Lodgings?"

Isabella exchanged a look with Flick. "We thought to drive back to the Hook and Line, sir. I have my auto here, you see."

"Good, good. I'll tell him to find you there. And whoever comes from Scotland Yard will find you there?"

Isabella lifted her hand. "Sir. I may be here. I'm painting a portrait, and I was to begin tomorrow morning. In the Prior's House."

"And, of course, I'll be using the enlarger at Mr. Robert's store."

"Good, good. I'll ensure he expects you. Now, Mrs. Tarrant, you are a portraitist. Who is your subject?"

"A student. Edward Malvaise. His—."

"Yes, yes, I know. Dean Filmer keeps me apprised of the … well, I am aware the Malvaise boy attends here. Who sent you?"

Why does he ask that? "The dowager Lady Malvaise. She contracted the commission at the holidays."

"She did not wish to wait until the summer break?"

"Lady Malvaise determined the arrangements, sir. I do not remember her exact words, but she informed me that the war had deprived her of two grandsons, and she had no way to remember them. I am surprised they were not photographed, but—."

"Lady Malvaise determined the arrangements? With the dean?"

"I believe her secretary booked my room at the Hook and Line. I brought three letters of introduction with me, one for her grandson, one for Dean Filmer, and the other for Mr. Pollard. Her arrangements suited mine, so I followed them."

"Did you know Mr. Webberly?"

"We met Saturday evening. Flick's—Miss Sherborne's brother brought him to dine with us."

"You had not met him prior?"

"No, we hadn't met. I had never seen him before Saturday evening. I did walk around the Abbey grounds on Saturday, after I met with the dean and Edward Malvaise, but I didn't encounter anyone who belonged to the school."

"When did you arrive here in Upper Wellsford?"

"Late Friday afternoon. This is my first visit here."

"American?"

"I've been here in England a few years. My father came over, before the war, to teach in one of the public schools, and I came with him. I served as a governess for Lady Baskille's daughter and before that for the son of Dr. Lionel Ivers." It wouldn't hurt to drop a couple of powerful names.

"Baskille? Sir Clive Baskille?"

"Yes, although Lady Myrtice Baskille was my direct employer. I taught her daughter Zenobia. We spent our entire time in London."

"Good, good. Zenobia would be twelve now, wouldn't she? And Dr. Ivers, you tutored his son? In what?"

When would Sir Robert notice that she'd omitted two crucial years, employed by Gareth Harcourt-Smythe, who illegally stole then traded archaeological artifacts? He'd escaped arrest on Crete. Isabella didn't think it wise to bring up his name. "I taught Clarence the basics of Latin and Greek grammar and quite a number of the myths. Clarence is now at Harrow."

"Greek!" Flick exclaimed. "You and Chauncey can natter along together."

Isabella smiled but shook her head. "I'm certainly not at your brother's level."

"Hmph." Sir Robert regained control of the conversation—only to Isabella it seemed more like a polite interrogation over tea. "What do you think of our village, Mrs. Tarrant?"

"Charming. I haven't really formed an opinion of the villagers. I expect, in the weeks that I'm here, that I will meet several people. I look forward to that."

"Good, good. These are just preliminary questions, you understand. To gain a picture of you. Ha, picture, with you a portraitist. And you a photographer, Miss Sherborne. You're strangers to us here, and I'd like to have somewhat of an idea for Scotland Yard. Now, Miss Sherborne, what is your business in Upper Wellsford?"

"I'm visiting my brother. Oh, and I'm writing a photo article with a feature on the topiaries in the garden. They're a curiosity, don't you think?"

"Your brother is the Greek master? Yes, he did say that. When did Dean Filmer employ him?"

"Before the autumn term began."

"Has he ever served as a teacher before?"

Flick frowned. Nor could Isabella understand the reason for that question. "Chauncey was among the first to enlist, straight out of his college at Oxford. This is his first position. I believe his tutor at Oxford gave glowing references to the dean."

"Since the beginning of the term, how many times have you visited?"

"October. Late November. This is my third visit."

"Three times within five months. Did you see him at holiday break?"

"Of course. He stayed at my flat before we drove to my parents."

"Good, good. I believe you said you were a professional photographer."

"I *am*. I have photo features in magazines and newspapers. In this coming week you should see one of my photo features in *London Daily*, about women dismissed from their jobs since men are hiring back."

At the mention of the newspaper, he frowned. "Do you have a radical bent, Miss Sherborne?"

"I beg your pardon?"

"*London Daily* is on the left."

She flashed a smile. "I would love for my photographs to appear in the *Times*. Not yet. And if wishing women weren't losing employment that makes them independent wage-earners is considered radical, then I am, Sir Robert."

"I suppose you were happy with the Representation of the People Act."

"I am not. I still cannot vote. I do not own property, and I am not thirty years of age. However, I do agree that the Act is a step forward."

He still frowned, and those mossy brown eyes lost their glint and looked hard. Isabella shifted uncomfortably. She wished she had a witty comment that could break the tension that had developed during Flick's last words. Flick glanced at her, and Isabella gave a little shake of her head.

"I have more photo features about flowers and gardens. I said, didn't I, that I was here for an article on the topiaries? I had a recent feature in *Modern Woman*. Is your wife a subscriber? She may have read my article on orchids. That was very popular."

"Hmph. That orchids screed was yours? You started her obsession with orchids. She wants a greenhouse now, so she can attempt them."

"Guilty as charged."

"Topiaries are next," Isabella reminded. "Lady Goodkind may wish to trim the boxwoods. Unless you hide that issue."

"I cannot recommend that," Flick chimed in. "My readership is important."

Humor twinkled, replacing the hardness. "I believe I can intervene to save the boxwoods." Then his twinkle vanished. "Your third visit, I believe you said, Miss Sherborne. Had you met Mr. Webberly previous to this visit?"

"I had. Briefly. I spent only a few minutes in his company. Saturday, at dinner, is the most time that I have spent with him. Mrs. Halsey had beef Wellington and lemon chiffon cake. I was disappointed that she hadn't made steamed pudding. Have you tasted her steamed pudding? It is divine. She could serve it every night, and I would not tire of it. Have you had dinner there?"

"Only shepherd's pie or a plowman's lunch."

"Then I urge you to bring Lady Goodkind on a Saturday when Mrs. Halsey is determined to impress. Or perhaps not. You would steal her from us lesser mortals."

The door opened. Dodges admitted a navy-suited man, clearly a uniform. He brushed crumbs from his double-breasted wool. "Sir, the doctor wishes to speak with you."

The magistrate stood. He slid his plate onto the now-empty tea table. "Ladies, I leave you with Constable Amsley. He will take a brief statement, then you may return to the Hook and Line."

"I would like to speak with my brother before we leave."

"Of course. Did I say that you should not? You three are not suspects. You attended the church service."

Isabella waited for Flick to mention the minutes that Chauncey had left, but perhaps she didn't know her brother had stepped out. He'd missed a good portion of the homily.

Had Chauncey admitted his quarter-hour departure to Constable Amsley?

She remembered the crumpled paper and the gold chain. She remembered Webberly's hissed comment of last evening, to which Chauncey promised a paper and a surety. "Not good enough," Webberly had said firmly.

Paper and a gold chain. Chauncey's written word and his surety.

Was Flick protecting her brother?

Did she need to protect him?

Did Flick *know* she needed to protect him?

.~.~.~.

Report of George Webberly's death had reached the Hook and Line before their return. The conversation buzzed as they passed through to the stairs.

Flick ran up to her room, muttering about fixing the dark room. Isabella remembered that she had agreed to serve as guard. After the magistrate's close questioning and the constable's careful transcription, she supposed Flick had forgotten.

Isabella had waited in the auto, the motor chugging loudly, while Flick ran into the Masters' Lodgings to speak with Chauncey. What had sister said to brother? Nothing much, for her return was mere minutes. She'd scowled, her brow crinkled and her mouth downturned. She'd related nothing, just released the handbrake, found first gear, and revved off. Flick's distraction on the drive back had nearly caused an encounter with three boys crossing the road from the Abbey woods to the scrub trees on the other side. Isabella hadn't thought it wise to pester her with questions.

Surely Chauncey couldn't have killed George Webberly? In a quarter-hour?

Who had a motive? Mrs. Filmer. Nuala. Mrs. Pollard—but she was on a train to London. Dean Filmer, jealous about his wife and Webberly. Mr. Pollard.

All of them seemed inadequate as suspects.

I don't know enough. More people than those five must have motives.

He'd complained of his fellow masters and their grudges. Who had he mentioned? Someone named Neville. Webberly's life beyond Upper Wellsford should definitely be reckoned. No one sprang whole-cloth from the wind. His past had to be woven into the fabric. Isabella did not envy whoever came from Scotland Yard.

She shed her coat then sat down to look out her window.

Flick had a view of the back garden and the woods that obscured the river. Isabella's view was the Abbey Church's bell tower, higher than the surrounding trees.

Why had Sir Robert asked Flick about meeting Webberly? Did he suspect Chauncey? Should he suspect him?

I can't dwell on this. I don't know enough.

Flinging a scarf around her shoulders, Isabella tromped downstairs. The pub was crowded. Mindful of Mrs. Pollard's request, she headed for the lounge, hoping for quiet.

The room was warm, with a fire burning cheerily. The three fishermen were there, claiming the settee and *fauteuils*. The cheerful Mr. Sandhurst rose at her appearance and motioned to his chair. "Mrs. Tarrant, please sit here."

"That's quite alright. I'll sit—."

"I insist. I must get away from the fire." He tugged at his collar. "It's too cozy. I may drop off to sleep. Elwen and Nelson and I are just nattering over the day?"

Nelson half-rose then subsided onto the settee. "Do you want tea? Elwen, ring the bell," but it was Mr. Sandhurst who tugged the bell rope.

"Tea or coffee, Mrs. Tarrant?" Mr. Sandhurst sank onto the other end of the settee and picked up his glass. "For myself, a good stout. Tell Sibby you want sandwiches."

"I do not, but I'm guessing that you do."

"Hoping it holds us to dinner. Sibby, what will Mrs. Halsey give us for dinner?"

The maid's sharp features looked pinched. "Pea soup, ham and greens, and a bread pudding."

"Fishing holiday, but I'll return a stone heavier," Mr. Nelson said gloomily. "I shouldn't look forward to my dinner more than I look forward to flinging the rod."

When the door shut behind Sibby, Mr. Sandhurst leaned forward, propping elbows on his knees. "Is it true one of the masters was murdered? Heard you and Miss Sherborne found him."

"We did. Along with Miss Sherborne's brother."

"How was he killed?" the old man asked. "Forgive my nosiness," he added when she hesitated. "I retired from police work a few years ago."

Nelson exclaimed while Elwen paused before continuing to drink from his flask.

"Nothing grand." Sandhurst looked embarrassed. "I worked the desk. Never solved a case. I wouldn't know how to go about putting all the clues together. Half of evidence is memory of what people said and what they said they did, and clever ways of looking at evidence. I miss the knowing, though, of things when they happen. There's an atmosphere in the station, like a buzz of electricity, when the inspector's about to make an arrest. Now that's a fine thing. Lived for days on that energy."

"So we're not morbid," Nelson said, letting his raw-boned hands dangle. "Just curious. Is the news accurate? You found the body?"

Isabella saw no harm in a few snippets. "Yes. He was struck down on the path behind the maze, the one to the river."

"Coming to the Abbey or leaving?"

"How can one tell?"

"Direction he fell," Sandhurst said. "If he fell toward the river, he was heading that way. Ergo, toward the maze and garden, then he was coming from the river."

"Or he stopped to talk," Nelson said, "turned about during the talk. You know how some people pace. Could have been struck then."

Heading toward the river, but that didn't mean he'd come from the Abbey. A gold chain in his hand. A paper crumpled and thrust into his jacket pocket. "I didn't think of that." Isabella tried to slide around their questions. "I'm very glad that I don't have to solve this case."

Sibby returned with a tray bearing teapot and cups and a small plate of sandwiches. "Mrs. Halsey says tea's been served, but she reckons as you need this, Mrs. Tarrant. *Not* the gentlemen."

"Thank you." She gratefully poured the tea, added cream, then leaned back, sipping it. "Have the sandwiches before Sibby returns," she offered.

Nelson scooped up the plate and passed it around.

"Do you think that constable has a hope of solving the murder?" Elwen rubbed at his brow.

"Sir Robert Goodkind, the magistrate, telephoned Scotland Yard. He expects their arrival tomorrow."

"Scotland Yard?" Sandhurst said around his sandwich. "The big boys. Must be expecting a difficult time of it."

"That constable's probably offering up his thanks to the gods," Nelson chuckled. "I wouldn't want to be the one to find the clues and sort the suspects."

"Who would you think was a suspect?" she asked curiously.

"All of us," Sandhurst said, his bite now swallowed. "Even me with my years on the force. That's how a detective inspector works. Draw the widest circle then whittle it down. Alibis first. Where people were and when. How that can be checked. Unless he finds lies and inconsistencies that will send him straight to the culprit. Should he not, he'll look for discrepancies. That's where the best ones operate, in the discrepancies. Like Elwen here, without his stick this afternoon."

"My leg needs strengthening. I can't rely on the stick, the doctors say, not and expect it to improve. I thought I wouldn't need it." He shrugged. "I was wrong."

"Still think you need a better cane," Nelson said.

"Leave it," Elwen gritted and unstoppered his flask.

"How long have you been out of hospital?" Sandhurst asked.

"October, after two years in."

"And the leg no better." He frowned at the offending limb.

"The surgeon had to rebuild muscles and bones. The knee was shattered. It's mostly tin." He knocked his knee as if expecting to hear the metal ring.

"A miracle that you're walking."

Elwen barked. "I'd rather the field surgeon worked his miracle on my unit. We were wiped out by a damned acting lieutenant's order."

"Forgive the language, Mrs. Tarrant," Mr. Nelson hurriedly said.

"I do." The war killed so many, decimating a generation. And it shattered the survivors. Mr. Elwen, young, healthy—except for his leg. Madoc and Chauncey Sherborne, haunted by battlefields.

"Do we have to talk of this? I'd rather hear about Webberly, not me." Elwen shifted, muscles stiff. "Scotland Yard will have plenty of suspects. I talked with that Miles Farrell from the school. He told me Webberly had an unsavory character. A real blighter. Dean Filmer contemplated severing his employment now, not waiting for the end of term."

"Farrell said that? When?" Nelson straightened in his seat and reached for his pint.

"Last night. Here. We fell into conversation and re-acquainted ourselves. I hardly remembered Farrell. We met—two, three years ago. I didn't know he'd left his work at hospital."

"Small world," Sandhurst said, finishing off the last sandwich.

"Very small when you travel," Nelson said. "We English tend to congregate together."

"Where have you traveled?" Isabella asked. She wanted a conversation well away from death of any sorts. "I had the good fortune to travel abroad with my employers. France. Italy. Greece. I met my husband on the isle of Crete."

"Hail, fellow traveler, well met. Spain? Morocco? Given a choice, you should travel there."

"After my commission here is complete, I travel to India to rejoin my husband."

"Ah, travel," Mr. Sandhurst leaned back and clasped his hands over his stomach. "Did I ever tell you of my fishing trip to Scotland?"

"Another fishing story?" Elwen complained.

"Well, it's a choice, old chap. We continue to make Mrs. Tarrant uncomfortable with our questions about today, or we make you uncomfortable with stories about fishing. I'd rather be gallant to ladies."

Chapter 10

Sunday Evening

Flick opened the door to the hall and began fanning the smell of chemicals from her room with the newest *Photograph Journal*. She had opened the window as well, even though the cold night air rushed into the room, displacing the fire's warmth.

Isabella Tarrant came up the steps.

"Here's my watcher."

"Oh. Are you ready for me?"

Flick didn't have the heart to say she'd been ready over an hour ago. She hadn't, not really. Isabella might have wanted to talk, and Flick didn't want to, not after Chauncey refused to tell her what George Webberly was pestering him about on Saturday evening. Paper and surety: a crumpled paper and a gold chain. Her brother had a gold chain for the medallion Great Uncle Tristan had given him. *What if—? No. Chauncey would never.*

A little whisper taunted her. *The war changes people.*

Not that much, she told the voice and hoped it would stop pestering her.

"I've developed the film. In a half-hour I want to make small prints then pick the best for enlarging." She checked her watch. "We should have a good three hours before dinner."

"Pea soup, ham and greens, and a bread pudding, Sibby says."

"Bread pudding? Isabella, you're in for a definite treat. I don't know what Mrs. Halsey does. I doubt she'll ever give up her recipes, but that is one I'd love to have. Cinnamon sticky wonder. What have you been doing?"

"Talking with our fishermen and keeping the conversation away from George Webberly. They did ask about finding him, then they very nicely didn't ask anymore. Mr. Sandhurst talked about fishing in Scotland, and Mr. Nelson had an interesting story about mistaken identities in Morocco. It's ice cold in here."

"I had to air the room out. Developing chemicals, you know."

"It smells like vinegar. We can't sit in here. Come to my room."

Flick left the window open but shut the door then followed Isabella to a much nicer-smelling room. Isabella offered her the chair at the window while she climbed onto the high mattress. Before she'd settled comfortably, Flick said, "Listen. When I came upstairs, Nuala was up here, crying her eyes out."

"About George Webberly? You did say that you saw them yesterday morning. That makes two women apparently heart-broken about his death." She carefully put her feet on the quilt and leaned against her pillow.

"Three if we consider how Mrs. Pollard will react."

"But could a woman have the strength to do that damage?"

Flick grimaced. She feared the images she'd squared into the camera's viewfinder would haunt her. "Never discount a motivated woman. The first blow would stun him, rendering him too weak to defend himself."

"I know of two men who didn't think highly of him. Didn't he complain that an older teaching master harassed him with petty tricks?"

"Two men, and my brother is one of them." Isabella started to disagree, and Flick talked over her, intent on getting the haunting voice into the open. "You heard, as easily as I did, their conversation about paper and a surety. Chauncey has put himself in a bad light. I'm certain he'd never commit murder—or even think about it. Belief, though, is not facts, and whoever comes from Scotland Yard is bound to look very closely at my brother as a suspect."

"You know your brother best. You're certain. That's enough for me. We won't consider him. Who's the second man?"

"Miles Farrell."

"The medic? The one we heard with Mrs. Filmer? He certainly didn't *sound* like a friend of George Webberly. Oh, that makes sense. Mr. Elwen, before we managed to turn the conversation away from the murder, he said that Miles Farrell said that Mr. Webberly was an unsavory character and that Dean Filmer intended to fire him. Soon. Before the end of the term."

"Really? I might add Dean Filmer to our list of those who had problems with Webberly, but does it give them a motive for murder? Greed. Obsession. Which is lust by another name. Hate. Who you are. What you are. How you are."

"That's smart. You've thought about people's motives for murder?"

"I devour murder mysteries. I enjoy the puzzle and the psychology."

"I like mysteries, too. Loveday Brooke."

"Lady Molly," Flick countered, and they smiled at each other, breaking the tension that had tried to build itself into a wall.

"So, lust is probably the second oldest motivator in the Good Book, with jealousy being the first. Cain and Abel. Envy in the official seven deadly sins. Hate, wrath, is the third. I can't see anyone killing another person because of sloth or gluttony."

Flick grinned. "Unless it's over control of Mrs. Halsey's cooking." She checked her watch for the time on the photographic negatives. "I may have to overexpose a few photographs. Those negatives appear dim. You don't have to serve as watchdog and brave the chemical smell and the cold."

"I won't shirk my promised duty," Isabella declared. "I'll prop a chair outside your door. And you promised me those magazines."

When the bell rang for dinner, Flick had the bulk of the tiny prints finished and hanging to dry. Only three photos so far were useless. She retained the prints, more for the detective inspector than because he'd learn anything from them. With Chauncey in the mix of suspects, she didn't want any question raised about her evidence, especially that she might have attempted to hide it. That would be more suspicious.

Mrs. Halsey's bread pudding earned accolades all around, including from the vicar and his wife, who once again came for dinner. They joined Flick and Isabella at request.

Mrs. Leverett revealed herself as a chatterbox. "The vicar insists that I have the weekends free of toil. He rests on Monday, when the parish will let him, poor man. They can never understand why he takes a day off when everyone is free on Sunday. We're here every weekend unless we're invited to the baron's on Sunday."

Isabella buttered a roll as she asked her innocuous question. "Do you ever dine at Greavley Abbey?"

"We are invited to High Table, which is the first Sunday of a term. I must admit, though, those London chefs that the dean hired, they're not a patch on Mrs. Halsey. She's the real treasure of Upper Wellsford. The Pollards can charge higher prices because of her, and once people taste her cooking—well, Miss Sherborne, you can testify to that, can you not?"

"I would pay twice over for every day that Mrs. Halsey cooks. I would soon bankrupt myself."

"The Pollards lucked in when they hired her, after they bought the pub. Upper Wellsford is *not* an attraction, and Lower Wellsford is just ... sad."

"Mrs. Leverett," her husband cautioned.

The vicar need not have worried her words would carry beyond the room. The three fishermen—minus Mr. Elwen—had adjourned to the pub to share a smoke. Mr. Elwen had pleaded his injury and retired to his room.

"Cigars," Mrs. Leverett said in a whisper as the door shut behind the men. "Nasty things."

They tried to winkle an additional serving of bread pudding from Sibby. "It's not on," the maid declared. "It's not there."

Mrs. Leverett raised her eyebrows at Sibby's forthright statement then fell to gossiping about the Abbey School and Upper Wellsford, yet the woman firmly refused to talk of George Webberly. "We must not speak of evil on the Lord's Day. You must tell me of London. What are your favorite shops? Where do you buy your tweed, Miss Sherborne?"

After another hour of this, Flick pleaded more negatives to develop. She waved off Isabella's offer to help. She hurried to her room, remembering her first stay here at the pub when Nuala opened the closet door while Flick was working. That had ruined a whole roll of film. When she realized the catatrophic result of simply trying to discover what the sound was in the closet, the maid was horrified. Both maids had been very careful on Flick's second visit.

Still, her heart raced before she opened the closet. The prints were still there, clipped to a string to dry. She counted twice, then rolled up her sleeves and donned an apron. Then she set to work finishing her self-appointed task.

. ~ . ~ . ~ .

After the Leveretts left, Isabella sat alone in the lounge. She watched the flames, mesmerized by the heat dancing over the coals.

And she turned over everything of the day.

Flick worried about her brother. That was expected … but to that extreme?

Sibby came to clear the last cups. Seeing Isabella and no one else, she stopped abruptly then perched in the other *fauteuil*. "Well, I was of two minds to say anything, but here you are and here I am. Mrs. Halsey says I should say nothing."

Isabella winced at that opener. Opportunity and a warning-off never boded well for any conversation. "I will talk with you, Sibby, but do you not think you should wait a day or two? Especially if you are unsure."

The maid continued to sit bolt upright, her hands flat on her apron-covered knees. "I'm not unsure about any of it. I know what I know. It's about that George Webberly."

"Then the constable would be the appropriate person to speak to."

"I'm not going to tell a man. He's got no understanding of women. And this is important. Well, it could be important. That's not for me to judge. Someone better than me needs to decide."

"I don't think—."

"I've been thinking about it all day, more than all day. The news of his death, that just decided me to say something. My question was who to tell. And here you are. You found the body. You'll have to speak to that constable and to whoever comes from Lunnon. Tell them what you know. Tell Scotland Yard." She shivered dramatically. "I'm not the one to decide what happens then. Up to them, and you can tell them that for me."

"Um, my relating your evidence would be hearsay, I think, Sibby. They may first hear of it from me, but they would need your words of what you know, not mine. I cannot testify for you, should it come to that."

"It will come to that."

What can it possibly be? "Tell me then. I'll convey it to the right person, and they can decide. But you should expect to see them."

"Exactly. You'll know how to tell them and how much. I'd just blather along and tell them more than they need to hear and confuse them. That wouldn't do Nuala any good."

"This is about Nuala then?" Nuala, whom Flick had seen with George Webberly.

"It needs to be told, but not to that high-and-mighty constable. He won't care at all about Nuala. She's in love, you see. He'll run right over that and set her to crying."

"Nuala and Mr. Webberly?"

"He had her all sixes and sevens. He wanted her to go with him for the weekend, and Nuala—I had to convince her to work this weekend. She needs this job, Mrs. Tarrant. She fits here. She wouldn't stand an office or a job in a factory. She's plenty smart—except about that Webberly. He talked such a smooth line to her. She would have figured him out, soon enough, when Mrs. Pollard made him throw her over. Mistress and maid can't be—well, not the same man."

"Indeed. Miss Sherborne and I had discovered their connection to Mr. Webberly, both Nuala and Mrs. Pollard. Mrs. Filmer, too. And if we discovered that he was playing three women in only two days—well."

"Her, too? He was good at fishing for hearts, weren't he?"

Lust and obsession were definitely motives for murder. Jealousy and hate would be stronger motives. Isabella could see all three women roiling with those base emotions. Did one of them kill Webberly, though? Flick wouldn't have her dismiss women as suspects. Recalling the bludgeoning Webberly endured, rage drove the murder. Yet rage had many original motives. "If you wish me to tell Constable Amsley about their relationship—."

"It's not just that. Did you know Mrs. Pollard threatened to fire

Nuala?" The maid gave a serious nod. Here was the heart of Sibby's worry. "She can't do that. Where's Nuala going to work? Where will people look after her? A factory in Lower Wellsford? The brewery? That's all fine and good, but they will replace her quick enough when a man needs to work. She ain't fit for office work, even if she managed to get some bloke with eyes in his head to hire her. She wouldn't last a week. They ain't going to let her just answer the telephone and file her nails. If she worked as house-help, they would take advantage of her. No, she needs to keep her job here."

"I am convinced, Sibby. What do you need from me?"

"If you tell that constable or a mighty detective from Lunnon, then you tell about all Webberly's women, not just Nuala."

"I would anyway."

"Nuala loved him. Mrs. Pollard—and likely that Mrs. Filmer, they were just playing. He chased skirts, that's obvious, and he was good-looking enough to convince most skirts to give him a go. He had a good patter, too. I nearly fell for it—until Nuala recited his patter to me, like it was brand new. That stopped me cold. I'm not on a string. And me and Nuala, we're friends. I look after her."

Isabella wondered how far George Webberly's patter had gotten him with Sibby. If Nuala hadn't shared his line, would the friends have turned into competitors?

Why were some men such selfish rotters? Never caring what lives they destroyed as long as they got theirs. Thank God she knew men who weren't that way, or she'd think the whole gender blighted.

"How long has Nuala been involved with Mr. Webberly?"

"Not long after he came here. Early in autumn, when term started. Nuala didn't get all starry-eyed until late October. She was a veritable grump when school broke for the holidays."

"How long has Mrs. Pollard been irritated with Nuala?"

"Since January. Wasn't until three weeks ago that she started giving Nuala real trouble three weeks ago. She'd took a weekend trip to the seaside and came back all grumpy. Mr. Webberly happened to be gone that weekend, too. Guess we know where."

George Webberly and Mrs. Pollard had a weekend together. He must have let certain things slip. Foolish man. "You didn't know of his involvement with Mrs. Filmer?"

"No. Nuala must have known. She was talking desperate. 'I have to keep him,' she'd say, and 'I'll do anything.' Tell that to some man, though, and they'll think she's so desperate she killed him herself. Fell into a rage and picked up a stick and bashed his head in. Nuala would never do that."

Would she not? No one understood their own depths. How can they understand anyone else? How can Sibby understand Nuala if she'd never faced those depths herself?

Sibby had certainly described the method of murder. How did she know that?

Isabella hated murder. Unchecked hatred that killed. Everyone became a suspect. The police viewed every word, every fact with skepticism. Neighbors and colleagues, hosts and fellow guests, friends—they became wary as well.

She *knew* Flick hadn't killed Webberly—but had Flick's brother Chauncey?

Sibby had continued speculating, looking for anyone to blame other than her friend. "Should we tell that detective inspector who could have killed him? Like Mrs. Pollard?"

"She couldn't have done so. She was on the train for London."

The maid huffed. "Not her. I saw her in the village at noon. She was talking to the curate's wife after the service. She must have taken the later train."

Which returned Mrs. Pollard to the column of suspects.

Along with Sibby and Nuala and Mrs. Filmer.

And Chauncey Sherborne.

And a dozen unknowns and more.

"I see the dilemma you're in, Sibby. I will speak to the constable when next I see him as well as to whoever comes from Scotland Yard. They will wish to speak with you."

Sibby stood, brushed down her apron, and began collecting tea cups and saucers. "They can get the particulars from you. I'll be happy to give them specifics. I didn't feel right, not telling what I knew, but I didn't want to blurt it out to that uppity constable."

Isabella hadn't found Constable Amsley uppity. He behaved differently around Sir Robert Goodkind and while in Mrs. Filmer's drawing room. *How did he behave around Sibby? Uppity? Prideful? Arrogant?* She didn't see that in him. "When he took our statements, mine and Miss Sherborne's, the constable was not arrogant."

That gave Sibby pause as she reached across a table. Then she firmly shook her head. "No. Uppity is the right word. He won't hardly talk to a body, not even to say 'It's a fine day' or 'Beg your pardon'."

Isabella suspected hidden motives to Sibby's unhappiness with the constable.

The maid had a good heart. She was occasionally abrupt but always willing. Loyal to her friend.

Amsley was scrupulously polite when he noted their statements.

She eyed Sibby. She and Constable Amsley were a similar age, past their first blush. Most of their friends would be married with a child or two.

Sibby was not pretty in the young-blooming way of Nuala. Freckles spattered her sharp features. Her eyes of a pale green looked colorless in candlelight. She scraped her straw-colored hair into a tight bun. Amsley was a robust man of ruddy cheeks and vivid coloring, dark hair and bright blue eyes. He could blow Sibby down with a single huff and puff.

They would be a good match.

"Maybe he's shy," Isabella proposed.

The maid stopped. The china rattled on the tray. "I didn't think of that."

"Does he talk to other people? Or is he quiet, off to himself?"

"He comes into the pub every night, late, before Mr. Pollard locks up, even when it's late on the weekends. He never talks to no one, only when they talk to him. Just drinks his cider and leaves when the door's locked."

"Well, that could be two things. He could be at the pub when it closes so Mr. Pollard never has trouble from anyone wanting to drink more. Or—."

Sibby bit. She slid her china-laden tray onto a table. "Or what?"

"Or he wants to walk you home."

"I only live a step away. I don't *need*—oh."

"Exactly."

"But how—what—I've always refused."

"He's offered to walk you home?"

"He hasn't, not for a long while."

Isabella couldn't believe she was giving relationship advice, but the poor girl obviously needed it. She'd missed the earlier clues. Hopefully, the constable was eager for his next chance. "Then when you take him his pint tonight, you ask if he'll kindly see you home, that the murder has you rattled."

"A woman shouldn't do the running. My mama always said that. I shouldn't have to ask him, not if he's interested."

"He has asked before, and you rebuffed him. Probably with 'it's just a step'. He must be sitting there, trying to think of another reason to be alone with you."

"I don't know," she said slowly. "He could see me home just because he thinks it's part of his job."

"You can try. It doesn't hurt to try. It's a simple request."

"Then what? He walks me home, and we shake hands on the doorstep. He leaves, and that's that, done, with no other chance."

"You ask him if he wants a cuppa. It will be a cold night, and he'll likely have rounds. Once he's sitting at your kitchen table, you get him to talk."

"About what?"

Good Lord, this was a lot of advice. *Am I a bleeding hearts column?* "Ask him about himself. Not being a constable. Ask about who he is."

"I can't ask that. 'Who are you?' He'll think me mad."

"If you want to know if he's interested, Sibby, you'll find a way to talk to him. Or you won't, and you'll always wonder."

"Is that what you did with your husband? Asked him who he was?"

"I believe he noticed very early that I was interested in him. He saw my sketches of him. Luckily, he was also interested." She smiled, remembering those early days, before a proper courtship. Drawn together, an irresistible force, from their first moments together.

"I'll try," Sibby said sturdily.

"I'll cross my fingers. I'm going up now. I've a long day tomorrow, my first day working with my subject."

"Good luck to you, Mrs. Tarrant. Those school boys can be right— well, I won't say the words."

"And good luck to you, Sibby."

Isn't it strange? Isabella climbed between cold bedcoverings and reflected that life always presented opposites. *Murder happens. Love blooms. The scale balances.*

Chapter 11

Monday Morning, 1 March 1920

Mindful of her trek to the Abbey, Isabella rose early. A loose flannel skirt and a tan sweater would make it easy to move, and thick tights would keep her warm. As she prepared her artist's satchel, she considered how she would begin the portrait. Loose sketches of Edward Malvaise, standing in various poses. The youth might have a preference, but a good composition would have him on the riverbank, scull and oars beside him. Perhaps he could hold an oar? In went her pencil roll, eraser pouch, and a pen knife to sharpen the pencils.

She added her travel clock. The chapel hour would fly by. Setting an alarm would prevent her from such deep absorption that she wouldn't lose all track of time. Her watch would do for the hours between her allotted time with Edward Malvaise.

The canvas would have to be prepped.

Her sketchbook went into Madoc's old satchel. She had Saturday's drawings, of the Rowing Shed, sculls, and oars as well as a few sketches for the watercolors she planned. Flick had mentioned an illustrative map of the garden. She needed to begin that. Memory would serve for a sketch but not a draft, and eventually she would need an exact map of plantings. And the route in the maze.

Dean Filmer mentioned bringing some boys to discuss her process.

The day and her satchel had filled before she started.

Mr. Nelson and Mr. Elwen were before her in the lounge. Both looked blurred, as if they'd made inroads last evening. Mr. Sandhurst came behind her, with a cheery hello and a springing step that belied his extra decades.

Sibby brought a teapot for the men then stopped beside Isabella's table.

"You're early in." Isabella commented. The maid had said she worked afternoons and evenings while Nuala had morning and the noon luncheon time.

"When Mrs. Pollard isn't here, Nuala needs extra help. Once the day is started, I'll take off home and have a nap. You're to breakfast earlier than we expected. We were going to bring tea upstairs in a half-hour."

"I suppose only fishermen rise at such an early hour." She nodded at the three men at the window table. Mr. Nelson was announcing his plan for the day.

"A lady like you, yes."

"I have an early start at the Abbey. Dean Filmer has graciously offered the chapel hour to work on the portrait. Every day. I do work for my living, Sibby."

"Not the same work, is it?" The maid's gaze skittered to the men, now discussing the best spots along the riverbank. She lowered her voice, scarcely above a whisper. "I did want to say, Mrs. Tarrant. You were right. Exactly right." Her sudden smile brightened her freckled face, giving it prettiness.

Isabella had to think quicky before she remembered their conversation after dinner. "He walked you home?" She used no names. Sibby didn't need teasing.

"And came in for a cuppa. We talked past the tea getting cold in our cups, even with a top up."

"I'm happy for you. Will he walk you home this evening?"

"He asked to do so every evening." Her pale green eyes glowed.

"He said he'd like to have tea and talk for hours."

"That's wonderful."

They shared pleased smiles, then Sibby straightened. "What's for you this morning?"

"Eggs, toast, and tea, please. I must walk to the Abbey."

"You'll have more than that. Mrs. Eccles comes in when Mrs. Pollard is away, Mondays and Tuesdays. She's started the ham and bacon. These men want a good start to their day, and adding a bit more for you is no bother."

"Can the ham and some cheese go into a bun for a sandwich at lunchtime?"

"I'll wrap it so you can keep it in your bag. Would you like an apple? Last autumn's crop. And I'll tell Mrs. Eccles to plan for you every Monday and Tuesday. When Mrs. Halsey comes on Wednesday, I'll let her know, too. Will Miss Sherborne be early up, do you think?"

"Our directions are different this morning. She's off to the local camera shop to use their—." Isabella stopped as Flick entered. She wore an elongated persimmon dress that displayed her slender figure. The color set off her dark hair dramatically. "But here is she."

"Good morning, Miss Sherborne." Sibby drew out the chair across from Isabella. "Tea? The full breakfast, or just toast? I remember you're partial to Mrs. Halsey's marmalade."

"I am. Eggs, too, however they're offered this morning." She placed a courier envelope beside her place setting and looked a question at Isabella.

"I didn't expect to see you so early," she said promptly.

"I intend to march over to that camera shop as soon as possible. Before he opens."

"With full armor?"

Flick grinned. "The best method of attack when you're imposing." She tilted her head at the door through which Sibby had gone. "Well?"

"With Mrs. Pollard gone, apparently Nuala needs assistance. Sibby was updating me on improvements in the prospect for love."

Her dark brows rose at Isabella's obscure comment. Then she glanced at the three fishermen, all silent and staring out the window—and likely listening in case they heard anything of yesterday's horror from the two chief witnesses to the scene. "Was prospecting occurring?"

"A certain blockage needed to be dug out."

Sibby returned with Flick's tea, coming to the table at the end of their obscure conversation. "You'll remember, Mrs. Tarrant, what I told you last night to tell—?" She nodded rather than add her own obvious comment.

Isabella nodded. "Of course. I'll mention it as soon as I have opportunity. Do you think I can have some of Mrs. Halsey's famous marmalade?" Sibby would not have discussed any of her worries about Nuala with Constable Amsley. After she'd bridged the awkwardness between her and the constable, the young woman wouldn't want to send his mind spinning away from the two of them.

Once Flick had the tea to her liking, she tapped the courier envelope. "I brought the prints down. I'd rather not make photo prints of the whole roll. Will you help me sort out the worst? I won't enlarge those."

"I'm on a bit of a tight schedule, Flick. I have to be at the Prior's House by eight o'clock."

"Then we'll start now."

She was surprised at the tiny size of the prints, several to a single sheet, rather erratically aligned. It was difficult to see them properly, but by the end of breakfast and a second cup of tea, they had the photos down to twenty for enlargement.

Flick slid everything back into the envelope and wrapped the red string about the button. "The detective inspector will receive everything, of course. Negatives and these prints as well as the enlargements. I didn't want to waste our local photographer's time and photographic paper with unnecessary work. I doubt anyone will think to reimburse him for the use of his equipment and developing fluids and special paper. That's the primary reason that I want to reach his shop before the business day starts."

"You'll need reimbursed as well, for that roll of film and the time you've expended."

She shrugged. "I'm not pressed for cash right now. Not like Chauncey," she murmured, so low that Isabella wasn't certain she was supposed to hear or respond to that addition. Flick set down her teacup with a clatter. "If you see that brother of mine while you're at the Abbey, tell him that he and I need to talk. Privately. That wasn't possible last evening."

"I doubt I shall see him. I won't be anywhere near the teaching hall or the Masters' Lodgings. Do you still want that illustration of the garden? Will you want the maze?"

"Certainly. When do you leave this afternoon?"

"After the boys have a scheduled hour of free time, which is after five o'clock, I believe. I will do the sketch of the garden for that hour."

"We can work out the drawing of the maze then. And after that hour, which I will spend with my brother, we'll drive back. A nice slow drive after you've no doubt been standing most of the day." She glanced at her wristwatch. "This afternoon, then," and she hurried out of the room.

Isabella followed more slowly, with a half-hour to walk the mile to the Abbey grounds, more than enough time. She donned her overcoat, scarf, and gloves for her brisk walk. When she came downstairs, Mr. Pollard pointed to her sandwich and apple on the bar. She stowed them in her satchel and set off.

No traffic passed her until a milk-truck trundled past. The driver whistled, but she ignored him. She wondered about Madoc. Missing him was a dull ache in her breast. *What is he doing? Where is his cargo ship now?* Eventually, she reached the Abbey wall, but she kept to the macadam for walking. Frosty dew slicked the grassy verge.

As she entered the Abbey gate, the church bell began tolling the hour. Two black-robed masters already waited at the front of the church; one stood by the side door. Lights shone through the ground-floor windows of the manor, but the curtains remained closed in the upper floors. The double-door of the front had a wreath of yew tied with black ribbons. *For George Webberly?* She wondered who had commissioned that memorial? The dean or his grieving wife? The school would have to observe the passing of its Latin master, even if his death were a scandalous murder.

Isabella had crossed the forecourt when the boys began to clatter out of their dormitory. Talking and laughing, they headed for the church, becoming subdued as they encountered the masters who hurried them inside. She veered away from the boys.

She spotted Chauncey Sherborne talking with an older master. He looked right at her, seemed surprised when he identified her, then deliberately avoided her gaze. *What is he expecting?*

Dean Filmer sailed from the manor by the side door. He wore full regalia: black robe with flying sleeves, a colored stole that flapped from his speed, and a beribboned beret. He held a scrolled sheaf of papers and saluted her but didn't pause. She wondered if he would read a homily for George Webberly in chapel.

Dodges stood in the open door. Isabella almost waved at him. She did smile and nod. Stiffly correct, he merely bent his head before closing the manor's side door.

The Prior's House had a single mourning wreath.

The door opened before she knocked, and the uniformed figure of Gilchrist blocked the threshold. He wordlessly stepped back. Remembering his sickly pale look of yesterday, Isabella looked closely today, for he stood in the pool of light cast by the overhead fixture. He remained pale, and a distant gaze contemplated something far beyond physical walls and windows.

He walked before her and unlocked the door to her assigned room.

Then he handed her a key from his fob pocket. "For safekeeping, ma'am. In these early stages, we need not concern ourselves with mischief. Once your work has started—."

"Certain boys are tricksters?" He didn't respond, so she added, "Precautions are always wise."

After he left, she started positioning the easel for the best light through the tall windows, clear glass here on the lane-side of the building.

Gilchrist hadn't confirmed that the boys were mischief-makers, and she couldn't help wondering if an adult was responsible. *And for what? Petty vandalism?* Willful destruction of property was her only concern.

George Webberly had complained of petty tricks. When he hadn't charmed her, he had tried to gain her sympathy. Modeling herself on Flick, Isabella had given him short shrift. She knew what a teacher did in his work. Her father had been a don before his death. Webberly hadn't impressed her, either as a teacher or as a man. Poor man, she measured him against Madoc. Of course he fell short.

Trivial tricks like missing chalk, a window of his rooms opened so that loose papers blew around, those were minor irritants to a day. Marked translations disappearing. Charted plans ripped to shreds. Those were more than simple tricks. Whoever had replaced his typed test questions must have known Latin, and Webberly blamed Westbrook Neville, who had taught that subject as well as *belle lettres*. Yet Chauncey pointed out a flaw, for multiple masters had more than the rudiments of Latin.

Had the trickster begun with petty tricks that escalated to serious damage ... and then to murder?

The door opened, and she hurriedly straightened from kneeling beside her paints box.

Gilchrist appeared. "The dean, ma'am. He thought it best, from today forward, to admit you through the side door that opens at the Cloister Walk. That would be at the end of this hall. Do you need anything for your morning session?"

"A pitcher of water and two glasses would be very nice."

"Very good, ma'am."

He gave the impression of bowing.

The canvas tried to overbalance as she maneuvered it to the easel. Light footsteps hurried across and took the weight of it from her.

"Where to, ma'am? The easel?"

"Yes, please. Gently. Up a little. There. Thank you."

Edward Malvaise set it gingerly on the easel ledge then stepped back. "A bit large for you, ma'am."

"Perhaps. I'll find a stool. Or a sturdy chair. My husband built this easel, for large canvases like this one. Good morning to you. Are you unhappy to miss chapel?" When he looked quizzical, she added, "The dean will likely talk about George Webberly's death."

"As a lesson to us. No real information. You can give me that." He grinned openly. "Didn't you find the body?"

"I believe whoever comes from Scotland Yard will frown upon my telling all and sundry."

"Maybe I can charm it out of you. Or offer to lift more heavy things." He didn't look abashed, merely cheerful.

Isabella happily took this Edward Malvaise over the stiff youth from Saturday. He seemed helpful and friendly. She wondered if his father had never been so. Escaping an hour sitting silent on a hard pew had won her a little grace, and Sunday's murder had given her more.

They were sitting on a cushioned bench underneath the tall windows, discussing potential poses when Gilchrist returned. The butler set his tray on a table near the door, poured two glasses from a glass pitcher, then left, all wordlessly.

"You've managed to win over Gilchrist, I see."

"How? I find him rather rigid."

"He didn't freeze you with a stare, and he brought that pretty quickly. I saw him leave, remember? You did ask for water?"

"Yes." Gossip about Gilchrist was as out-of-bounds as the murder. "Now. We could have the river in the background. We could put the scull in the water."

"The only place you can see the scull from the riverbank would be the dock at the Rowing Shed. The dock is low enough. All along the riverbank it's steep."

"I can always take artistic license."

"Is that like poetic license? Changing things from reality?"

"Would that bother you?"

"I imagine that I'll stare at this portrait every day of my life. Unless it's bad." He grinned again, that easy smile that sparkled in his eyes. "Then I'll demand the portrait be consigned to the attics as soon as Lady Malvaise leaves us."

"I don't *think* it will be bad."

"I reserve judgement." The grin edged into a smirk, but the twinkle belied any ridicule. "I like the idea of standing with the oars."

"Not rowing?"

"I might prefer that, but I do not believe Lady Malvaise intends that kind of portrait. Active, you know. She wants to see me," he added, the words lacking vanity. "She wanted to see my brothers. They died in the war, you know."

"Yes. So. Standing. Oars. The scull in the water at the dock." She wondered that he called his grandmother *Lady Malvaise*. Recalling the woman's strict behavior at Christmastide, Isabella supposed she rarely unbent even for her family.

"Another scull on the dock."

"That would add color." She quickly sketched loose lines to show the extra scull.

The hourly bell tolled before she had a standing pose that pleased her. Yet they'd accomplished good work, and she had hopes for the forenoon hour. A distant train whistle echoed the nine o'clock bells as the train for London drew into Upper Wellsford's station.

As he shrugged into his jacket, Isabella drew out the key Gilchrist had bestowed from an inner pocket of the satchel. She dropped in her travel clock then followed Edward into the hall. He watched her lock the door.

"The dean's request," she explained.

"Wise. I know my friends and their pranks. What will you do now? I didn't think, when the dean outlined his schedule, but you've hours with nothing to do."

"Not so! I have the canvas to prep and the background to paint. I need more detailed sketches of the sculls and oars. That sounds strange to say. I've a friend in London who wants any watercolors and another friend who wants two illustrations of the garden, for a magazine. What do you have next?"

"Maths. If I'm late, old Bellamy will roar. I'll blame you," he added without embarrassment. "You are the adult. You should have released me before the hour."

She sighed audibly.

"If I run, I won't be late."

"No, don't explain, Mr. Malvaise. I remember the lives of school boys. My father taught at one. The boys against the teachers or masters, as you say here. And I will happily take the blame as long as you do not take advantage. I *should* have stopped before the hour. I brought my travel clock, but I neglected to set it."

"I will not take *too* much advantage." He held open the side door, and they descended to the Cloister Walk. Boys jogged or scurried past. "You know your way from here? You have only to follow the road. It dead-ends at the Shed."

"Not a picturesque walk."

"I wouldn't think you'd want to go through the woods. Not after yesterday. I've been good, not asking anything, haven't I? Will you answer one question? Was his head all pulpy from the bludgeoning?"

"No! Good Lord! What kind of gossip have you heard? Besides, I tried not to see the details."

"Did you faint? Did Miss Sherborne faint?"

"We did not. She took photos. She's a professional photographer."

"I doubt she takes photos of dead bodies."

A passing youth bumped Edward's shoulder. The youth walked backwards to say, "Better move it, Counter. Old Bellamy spent the morning roaring at the fourth form."

Edward gave that curious shrug and head-tilt that youths had perfected to mean *sorry, but*, then he ran to catch his friend.

Isabella already had questions for the forenoon hour. How did Edward come to be called *Counter*? What had he heard about George Webberly's death? Who was the trickster who had pestered Mr. Webberly? A master or a school boy?

The boys would know. Male or female, that age always knew.

Chapter 12

Monday Morning

Nigel Roberts had a long nose to match his long face, long limbs, and long torso. *Spindleshanks*, Flick thought as soon as he unlocked and opened the shop door. "Miss Sherborne?" he confirmed.

"Yes. Mr. Roberts?"

"Come in, do." He stood back to admit her to his shop. She looked around as he relocked the door. "There. We shouldn't be disturbed until time for opening."

A woman stood before the curtained doorway to the back of the shop. "Mrs. Roberts?" Flick guessed.

She nodded but said nothing.

The shop itself was tiny, one side given over to display, the other to take photos, with the counter beside the door on the display side. Brownie cameras and boxes of film were widely spaced on the top shelves. Before the window was a set-up for simple photos, a chair before a backdrop, an ornate carpet, curtains pushed against the wall. The window display had frames of various sizes, promoting the photos that a camera would take.

Mr. Roberts went behind the glass-fronted counter. Expensive cameras were locked in the case along with more boxes of film and satchels designed for the larger cameras. Beside the cash register was a notebook. "Sir Robert Goodkind called me last evening, after I arrived back. A tragic business, very tragic. And you unlucky enough to have to take the photos."

That wasn't quite how Flick would have worded what she'd done, but it worked without delving too deeply into motivations. "That's correct. I used contact prints to select which photos would need enlargement. I have about twenty of those."

"Sir Robert didn't know how experienced you were with development of photo prints."

"I have a dark room in my flat, and I've developed my own film into negatives and created contact prints since '14. I didn't really start taking photographs as my work until '17. Is three years sufficient time to develop experience?"

"How often have you created photographic prints from your negatives?"

"Since '17, as I said. I take photographs of gardens and plants as well as candid street photos. Once I started working professionally, I needed to develop my own negatives and photo prints."

He stared at her a moment, as if assessing her credibility. Did he not think a woman capable of professional photographic work? "You have a fully equipped darkroom?"

"I wish. I have everything but an enlarger. For that, I rent time at a London shop and use their enlarger. Purchasing an enlarger is not an expense I can afford. Nor would I have room for equipment of that size in my tiny flat. You need not worry that I will tug you away from your own work, Mr. Roberts, so that you can develop my film for the police. I'm quite experienced."

"Hmph," he said, reminding her of Sir Robert. "This is my wife Matilda."

"Hello," Flick said politely. Her opinion of Mr. Roberts remained low. He should have introduced his wife first, not checked her experience before he turned her loose with his equipment.

He focused on the bulging tote hanging off her shoulder. "You have your camera with you?"

"Do you wish to see it? It's a Kodak Autographic. I bought it second-hand from a newshound who works for the *London Daily*." She reached for the strap.

"No, no. You have friends in the newspaper business?"

"Photographer friends." She thought of Alan Rettleston, but the editor wasn't really a friend. Many of her newspaper friends kept their shops open by contracting with *London Daily* and other newspapers. A few resorted to more sordid means to pay their bills. "I freelance for a woman's magazine, *Modern Woman*. Perhaps you've seen it? I do articles about gardens and flowers for them. That's one of the reasons I am here in Upper Wellsford. I'm working on an article about topiaries at Greavley Abbey manor." *Do you have enough information for gossip, you gormless noddy?*

"Ah, you work freelance. I didn't think you would be a photographer for a newspaper. Just a woman's magazine. Gardens and flowers. Hmm. My wife belongs to the Wellsford Garden Society. They have a competition in May."

That *just a woman's magazine* confirmed he was both gormless and a noddypoll. Misogynist, probably. Flick pitied his wife. "You should cover the garden competition for your regional newspaper. *London Daily* purchases some of the photo features that I dream up. I receive credit for every photo. F. Sherborne," she added, bolstering her credentials. "I know Sir Robert volunteered your equipment and supplies without your permission, but Scotland Yard is expected today. These photographs are crucial to their understanding of the crime scene. Sir Robert explained that it was impossible to maintain the crime scene, didn't he? With photographs in hand, whoever comes from Scotland Yard can start their investigation immediately. May I start work, please?"

He looked doubtful. "May I see what you have?"

"I only have contact prints for you to view. You can look at those while I work. If you have more questions, I am certain Sir Robert will answer them."

"Hmph."

He stared at her, and Flick stared back. She'd said everything she needed to and more. If he delayed her work or refused to allow her to work, she would make sure he received all the blame.

Mr. Roberts didn't outlast her. He came from behind the counter. His wife vanished quickly through the curtain. He led her that way more slowly.

Past the curtain was a little hall, with a staircase to their living quarters above the shop and descending to a cellar below. A door on the opposite side stood open. Flick saw a desk, chairs, more shelving, and filing cabinets. Another door beyond it remained closed. Then they were into a larger room with a table, a more elaborate set-up for portrait, and a side room with a red light above the door: the dark room.

Mrs. Roberts stood beside the table. "Should I make tea, Nigel?"

"Not yet, dear. We have work to do. While we wait for the photos to dry will be the time for tea. We may have to delay opening the shop. Perhaps you can prepare a sign to place in the window? And turn off the shop lights. Now, Miss Sherborne, here is my dark room." He opened the door and switched on the red light. He had to step inside to pull the cord for the overhead light, a bare incandescent bulb. "I have the solutions prepared for you."

"Thank you. That's a kindness."

The dark room had table-height shelving on both sides and no window, making it *light tight* once the incandescent light was off.

To the left on the bench were tubs of fluids, the wet side. She asked about the order of the fluids as she examined the wire strung along that wall. His order matched the proper sequence. She counted his clips for hanging the photo prints to dry. He had more than enough. Beneath that bench were bottles of the various developing fluids. The bottom of the squared-U was a sink with taps. Predominant on the bench of the dry side was the enlarger. She checked that she could turn the knobs to adjust the size and focus the enlarger. Storage shelves above seemed to hold boxes of photo print paper while general storage seemed reserved for below the bench.

Another cord dangled from the ceiling, near the enlarger. She glanced up and saw another red light bulb, the working light.

The room was an excellent work space, not like her cramped dark room, adapted from an old scullery. For a half-second she envied Nigel Roberts, then she shoved the envy of that man away from her. He wasn't worthy of envy.

She would get the dark room she wanted, eventually.

Lifting her tote to the dry-side bench, Flick laid out the courier envelope then took out the bulky Kodak Autographic. She set it beside the tote. The first money she had and the first time technology adapted the camera into something smaller but better than a Brownie, she would purchase that, even before an enlarger.

"That's a good camera," he remarked.

"Fiddly to focus, especially with close range. The man who sold it gave me lessons, especially on close-ups. I anticipated that close-ups of flowers would be my main focus."

"Flowers are a suitable subject for a female photographer."

She tried to ignore his comment. "The Autographic is heavy to tote around. You have a nice set-up here and a good studio at the front. Camera on tripod. Extra lighting. Do you take a lot of portraits? Have you used any special filters?"

"Some. Are those your negatives?" He reached for the courier envelope.

"Negatives, contact prints." She slid the envelope from beneath his hand, unwrapped the string, then reached in for the sheets of contact prints. "Here. Take a look at these. I didn't try to line them up properly. I just needed to see which negatives would be best to develop."

He lifted the prints, stared closely at the tiny images for seconds, then hurriedly lowered them. "What are these dark splotches on the grass?"

"Blood."

"That's a little too detailed."

"I'll have to expose those areas additionally. Finicky work."

"Tricky." Then, his voice grudging, he added, "You do good work, Miss Sherborne. What I could tell. Of course, a good Autographic makes camera work almost simple."

Several of her newshound friends would disagree with him on that. She held out her hand for the contact prints.

"You plan to develop all of these?"

"Only about 20 of them."

He handed her an apron and hovered while she donned it. His gloves were thick and bulky, made for large hands. She would fumble a lot.

She found the tongs, found the other equipment she would need, laid everything out, then reached for the first negatives. Mr. Roberts continued to hover.

"Did you know Mr. Webberly?" she asked for something to break the silence. "Had you met him?"

"No, we never met. He's a master at Greavley Abbey School."

"Yes. That doesn't elevate him above you. Indeed, someone's brought him down."

"Miss Sherborne!"

She had scandalized him, but he didn't leave.

Nigel Roberts hovered at her elbow through the next three hours. She worked in parallel, one print moving ahead of another which moved ahead of the next. He watched so closely that she often had to ask him to move. As always, the process fascinated her, from a blank paper receiving the enlargement, then the image appearing on the blank paper, then to the fixing bath, and finally to the rinse. The magic made up for the smell of the chemicals, like over-burnt sulfur.

When she clipped the last photo print to the strung wire to let it dry, he opened the door to admit good air and natural light. Cool rushed in, displacing the warmth built up in the tiny scullery.

"Tea, Maltilda."

"I'll just sit for a bit," Flick said, "then I'll clean up."

"*I* will clean up," he offered. "I have my equipment a certain way, you see," and she was tired enough to let him.

She hadn't slept much last night, nor had Mr. Elwen across the hall from her. Nightmares had troubled him. George Webberly's body through the camera viewfinder haunted her. Tonight might also be lost to her. Focusing on the results of his bludgeoning had burned the image onto her brain, as fixed as the print on the photo paper. No wonder Isabella had refused to look. Flick had thought she didn't want to offend her artist's eye. Now she knew Isabella hadn't wanted to risk obsessing over gory details and the fragility of life.

She drank the tea, two cups, both with cream and sugar. She needed the pep.

When she stood to leave, photo prints, contact prints, and negatives returned to her courier envelope—counting three times to be certain— she thanked Mr. Roberts for the use of his equipment.

"Whatever is necessary to catch that madman." He grimaced, and she wondered if the image of Webberly's bloody head would disturb his sleep.

"Yes, that is the goal. Do submit an invoice to Constable Amsley for the photo paper and the chemical fluids that were used. The constable will direct it to the proper authorities so you will receive reimbursement. Thank you, again, Mr. Roberts. It was nice to meet you, Mrs. Roberts."

Flick didn't draw a deep breath until she was outside in the brisk air and sliding behind the wheel of her Calcott. She motored away until she was out of sight of Roberts' Photography. Then she pulled to the side and opened the courier envelope. She'd barely looked at the prints except to check for clarity of detail. If she'd pored over the photos as she wanted, both Mr. and Mrs. Roberts would call her mad—or murderous.

She didn't study the gruesome photos. The others were sharply depicted, even to the splotches of blood beside the path and the glint of the gold chain in Webberly's hand.

Then she stowed the envelope. Maybe an hour or two more, then she could put this horrible murder behind her.

.~.~.~.`

Isabella showed Edward Malvaise her sketches of the sculls and oars. "Now we must concentrate on you. I found this pole—."

"The beadle's mace."

"It can stand in for an oar."

"We should walk to the Rowing Shed. Use a real oar and scull."

"Later, when we're firming up the pose. You will soon grow weary of the number of sketches I require. You will think that we will never have any progress toward the canvas."

He shrugged.

Isabella balanced the beadle's mace along his arm, the top leaning back, behind his head. *Three sketches*. That would give an excellent idea of the composition. "Have you attended Greavley since you were a first former?"

"Like my brothers and father and grandfather and great-grandfather."

"Your family might as well be called founders." She adjusted his hold and the angle of the pole then stepped well back. "Where will you attend university? Oxford? Cambridge?"

"Oxford. Family tradition, you know. My sister, the youngest—."

"Alexa."

"That's right. She wanted to attend one of the women's colleges there. That idea was soon nixed."

"Indeed?" The sketch was coming rapidly, as if the pencil had a divine hand directing it, not hers.

"Aunt Lottie's the only bookish one."

Isabella surfaced enough to reflect that Lottie Crittenden wasn't bookish. Having a name on the masthead of a magazine might qualify, but the woman delegated most of her duties. She remembered Alicia Osterley from the Christmastide party. That young woman had seemed more responsible than her employer.

Flick had said that her friend Owl did the work of a managing editor.

"She has a magazine. *Modern Woman*."

"I remember." She shifted her stance and glanced up to find his keen eyes on her. "My friend Flick—Felicity Sherborne—does photographic features for *Modern Woman*. We spoke of the magazine last Saturday evening." Really, she couldn't have eased into the conversation on her own without seeming obvious. "When we dined with her brother Master Chauncey Sherborne as well as George Webberly." She tried a test. "Poor Mr. Webberly."

Edward Malvaise obliged her with a snort. "Not so poor. He wins money off his fellow masters. Poker. Or he did. Picked it up in the trenches. He boasted about it. He said he held a lot of vowels on one master."

"Did he boast much?"

"Daily."

"Do you know who owed him money?"

"And who would want to kill him because of it?" the youth said, revealing a canny mind. "That went out with duels, didn't it? I've heard tales."

"Do tell." She lowered her sketchbook. "Let's try a different stance. Would you ever hold the oar across your shoulders?"

"No," he scoffed.

"Propped in the crook of your arm?"

"That, yes."

That pose seemed more active, more natural. Her pencil flew over the paper. "How did you come by the nickname Counter?"

"Still counting on my fingers when I entered here. Ridicule from the master didn't stop the habit. He gave me the nickname. After that, with everyone saying that name, I stopped on my own."

Wisdom. Taking something intended bad and turning it to good. "What did you think about George Webberly?"

"Not one of us," he said promptly, revealing class arrogance. She waved her pencil for him to continue and devoted herself to the wrinkles in his sleeve so he would think she was too involved in the drawing and wanted him to fill the air. "Webby wanted us to think he was gentry, but he wasn't. Too many slip-ups. Sherry thought he remade himself in the war. At the first of term, he boasted of gaining a field commission to lieutenant. He stopped talking about it when he realized that only flew with first formers."

"I'm not one of your class," she pointed out. She switched to another pencil, a softer lead that would shade more easily.

"You're American." He chuckled. "In every word you say. I telephoned about you. To my grandmother."

"Oh. When?" She glanced up, met his gaze, then returned to the sketch.

"Sunday evening when we are allowed to call home if we wish. She said you married a Tarrant. Welsh family. One's an archaeologist and a professor at St. George's University in London."

"Which is definitely not Oxford or Cambridge." Isabella refused to glance up, just concentrated on shading the first sketch.

"Squint's brother knows a Tarrant, from the war. Says he's a good man. Good officer. Shot in the leg, toward the end."

"That would be my brother-in-law, the professor. I married the younger brother. He's not of a scholarly bent—although I think he had planned for that, before the war. Quite a number of young men changed their plans when they came back."

"Like George Webberly becoming a Latin master at a boy's school."

Isabella shrugged and returned to the second sketch. Maintaining a casual conversation was difficult. She wanted to pester Edward with questions. "My husband is on a freighter bound for the South Seas. He's going to build a road in Australia. I believe Chauncey Sherborne was headed for a religious vocation. He's now teaching Greek. What do you think Mr. Webberly had planned before the war interrupted?"

"His Latin's good. Law? He wouldn't have stuck it … or he would have gone shyster with it. We heard rumors that he wasn't—. It wasn't that he was decidedly bourgeois, Mrs. Tarrant." *How like his sisters he sounded.* "Squint's brother wouldn't say, only that it was bad, hushed up. He couldn't discover more, and he nosed around for it. Got in trouble with his superior. That we know."

"That sounds nefarious. A spy? A criminal?"

"He served in the trenches. He hated the cold rain, but he played rugby every Saturday."

"I think we should change poses." She dropped the sketchbook and carried over a chair. "Put a foot up there. I think we'll keep the pole in the crook of your arm. Yes, that's the pose exactly." She picked up her sketchbook, studied the nib of her pencil, then turned to a new page. "This may be it."

"We never stand this way with the oars. The deck doesn't have anything to prop your foot on."

"Let's try it. Look up. Turn your head a little. To the left. Yes. Hold that, please. What were we talking of?"

"You were asking about Master Webberly," and when she looked up, he smirked. Her subterfuge hadn't worked at all.

She gave an abashed smile. "Very well. I'll stop pretending then. What was his time at Greavley like? Was he a good Latin master?"

"He knew Latin. He used to poke at the Old Guard. Said they had lost their will to live. 'Sans teeth, sans eyes, sans taste, sans everything,'" he quoted Shakespeare. "Webby didn't need a text. He assigned texts to translate, but he didn't use them in the classroom. He would spout Latin off the top of his head. Master Sherborne can do that in Greek. Boffo said it was *The Iliad.* Something about wrath or rage."

"'Sing'," she recited the opening, "'the anger of Achilles, son of Peleus, that brought countless ills upon the Achaeans. Many a brave soul did it send hurrying down to Hades, and many a hero did it yield a prey to dogs and vultures.'" Then she rolled it out in ancient Greek and hoped he missed her stumble.

His surprise was obvious. "That's swell."

"Don't think I can do more. My father taught Greek and classical history. He loved the former and tolerated the latter. Hesiod and Herodotus, you know. Which of the Old Guard did Mr. Webberly poke most often?"

"Westbrook Neville. He taught Latin when my oldest brother was here. Probably when my father was here. But Neville, he was book-bound. Couldn't say anything without opening a book. Nevvy likely expected to continue teaching Latin, but the headmaster hired Webby for this term."

She'd heard most of that once already, sometimes twice. "Did you think this Westbrook Neville was the one who provoked Mr. Webberly to wrath?"

"Playing tricks?"

"Mr. Webberly complained of it at dinner."

"You *dined* with him?"

"Apparently, he was a last minute addition, as was I. Miss Sherborne, the photographer I mentioned, invited me. Her brother invited Mr. Webberly—who complained. A lot. Do you think Mr. Neville would have killed Mr. Webberly?" Rather than answer, he grimaced, so Isabella prodded harder. "Come, you know something. The boys always know before the masters do. Or was a boy tricking Mr. Webberly and making him think it was Mr. Neville?"

"Not Chevington."

"One of your mates? Like Squint and Boffo?"

"He's a sixth former, well ahead of me. Word is that he had it in for Webby. Never heard the reason." He broke stance. Isabella scowled and waved her pencil, and he quickly resumed the pose, off only a little. "Chevvy didn't play those kinds of tricks. He likes it direct. He took it out of Webby every Saturday. Rugby."

"Who is Chevington?"

Edward pretended that she hadn't spoken. Since he was volunteering the information, she decided not to pester him. "Could be old Nevvy acting up. Or Filmer paying him back for every flirtatious conversation with his wife. Or someone else." He grinned broadly. "Webby wasn't liked. That clock says five minutes to the hour." He propped the mace against the wall. "May I leave?"

She displayed the last sketch, finished except for his feet. "We've greatly advanced this hour. You need not return this afternoon. Shall we meet in the afternoon hour tomorrow? I will need to consider several things before we move forward."

"No morning chapel or forenoon?"

"No. Use that time to ensure your rowing whites are in order. I will want you to wear them on Wednesday, especially for our forenoon and last hour. And a brightly colored kerchief. I haven't decided a Windsor knot or a simple Ascot. Four-in-hand might bridge that nicely. Bring three ties, in case we wrinkle them."

"Brightly colored. I have yellow, for the school, and red. And black in case I have to attend a funeral."

"Yes, those three."

"Black."

"I am an artist. I can make it any color we decide. Like cerulean. Blue with a bit of green."

"I thought it meant heavenly."

"That, too."

"I have a school tie. We can do the school colors. Gold and black. Are you ready to start the portrait?"

"Not quite. We're close. I will decide colors, accent colors like the tie, your whites which will not be truly white, and the background colors, the water, the scull and oars, the bit of the Rowing Shed that may be there. Once we decide that, we can launch onto the canvas."

"This is a lot of work for an artist. I thought you would start painting immediately."

"That way can lead to disaster. If I were painting for myself, I would do that, but this is a commission."

"Right-O." He paused. "Mrs. Tarrant, I want a favor. Don't tell the dean about Chevington. Or any of the masters, not even Master Sherborne."

"I shan't. I would like to have Chevington's first name."

He grinned, the impish one, not the smug smirk. "Tomorrow afternoon, Mrs. Tarrant."

Isabella stowed the mace in an obvious spot then replaced the chair, straightened a few other things, then picked up Madoc's satchel.

She wished he were here instead of muddling through information on her own. She would definitely tell Flick everything that she'd learned, especially about Westbrook Neville and Chevington.

She hadn't decided what to tell Scotland Yard's representatives. She would need to meet the detective inspector first.

Chapter 13

Monday Noon

Isabella perched on the top step to the church's side door, partially out of the chilling wind, beginning to bluster as clouds packed into the sky. The slaty clouds had covered over the blue, but they were high. Nightfall might bring more rain, though. It was good fortune that she'd delayed the next meeting with Edward Malvaise until tomorrow afternoon. And she was very glad that Flick had offered her a ride back to the village. Sunday's warmth had merely been a peek at spring, not a promise.

Her view gave her the graveled forecourt, the gates, and the drive. Centering the circular drive was a planting of ornamental evergreens, blue spruce and weeping spruce that she recognized along with that curious platter-like conifer and a goldy green bush growing like a pyramid above a ground-clinging juniper. Flick likely knew the common and scientific names of the five plants. When people drove through the gates, the manor would dominate, for the Abbey Church and school buildings were off to the side, balanced by a large stand of old oaks on the other side, stretching from the road-side wall to past the manor. If Isabella leaned forward, she could see the entrance to the Crossing, between the manor and the angled church.

No boys had come this way in her half-hour of sitting with her sandwich and apple. The dormitory kept them directed away from the front buildings. The Prior's House, the teaching hall, and the Masters' Lodging were even further back, out of sight.

She bit into her apple, sharp and aromatic, and considered what next to do. She needed to find the gardener, whose name she did not remember.

The church side door behind her opened. She scooted over to give more room to whomever passed.

The black master's robe made identification difficult. As he dropped down the steps, that dark hair and the broad set of shoulders made her guess Flick's brother. "Mr. Sherborne. Good afternoon."

He checked. "Mrs. Tarrant, how do you do today?"

"Very well. I have an excellent apple. Is there a noontime service? I didn't hear singing or the pipe organ."

He looked quizzical. "No?"

"He met with me." A man of an age with Chauncey Sherborne came down the steps. Instead of the master's robe, he wore a tweed jacket and flannels. "Introduce us, Sherborne."

"Mrs. Madoc Tarrant, this is Miles Farrell. He serves as medic for Greavley. Forgive me." He backed up even as he spoke. "I must run on."

"Of course," but he hadn't waited for her acceptance. His long strides had already carried him to the Crossing's entrance.

"Always in a rush is our Master Sherborne."

She looked curiously at Miles Farrell. Vivid in memory was overhearing his talk with Mrs. Filmer. The Irish brogue was muted now. Emotions had likely increased it to yesterday's level.

Which meant that yesterday, before they stumbled upon George Webberly, Miles Farrell's emotions had run strongly.

Someone had mentioned—who was that? Chauncey? Mr. Webberly?—that Farrell tended to the boys' physical and emotional hurts. Was that it? She also heard a faint echo of someone saying Mr. Farrell had served near the front during the war—or was that her invention? *No wonder I can't remember. I've talked to too many people with whom I'm barely acquainted.* "He said you're Greavley's medic?"

"In the war I was a medic. They call me that here rather than *nurse*. I'm not the matronly, motherly sort that the former nurse was."

That tallied. She leaned against the cold brick of the entrance arch, the better to look up at him. "Where did you serve? In a hospital where the men recovered? Or in a field hospital near the front? Or were you stationed with a line unit?"

"Field hospital although the occasional assignment sent me to the front. Whenever a big push was expected. Eventually, they moved me to a recovery hospital. They probably thought I'd seen too much death. Whoever they are." He had a charming smile, and he used it with a one-shouldered shrug that created nonchalance.

She didn't think he was nonchalant about his war service. Who could be?

"Here at Greavley I'm a step below their old nurse. I can manage the small hurts. No major ones, here."

"I am surprised another trained nurse was not hired."

"Ask the dean. I've never bothered." Again he gave that one-shouldered shrug. It imitated Edward Malvaise's, but she didn't think it carried the same meaning. "Filmer mentioned that the old nurse mollycoddled the boys. I imagine he wanted to bring in a more manly regimen to the school. He hired Sherborne there and Webberly as the language masters and another young master still green in the gills to assist with maths. He brought in a younger games master and replaced the matron with me. Filmer never explained what he was doing, just threw us into the masters' common room and expected us to thrive. The Old Guard didn't give any help." He came down the steps. Shoving his hands into his pockets, he tilted his face to the sunshine, looking young and hale and trouble-free.

"Someone, I'm not certain who, told me that you have counseling sessions with the boys and others."

Mr. Farrell lowered his head and gave that charming smile. *A mask,* Isabella decided. "One can say that, Mrs. Tarrant. The boys would say that I talk their heads off. Habit, developed when I worked in hospitals. Part of my work there. Tend to physical wounds, allay the emotional ones. Psychological ones, I should say. That's the new term. I don't limit my counseling to the boys. Anyone that asks has my ear. Even you. Oftentimes, people only need someone to listen."

"Like Mr. Sherborne? I'm surprised you met with him in the church."

"My office is wherever people find me."

"Is he—Mr. Sherborne—is he greatly upset by our finding Mr. Webberly's body? I didn't see him, not after. I know his sister is concerned. I believe his service was traumatic to him. I know it was for my husband."

"It wasn't his service. His conscience is pricking him, I daresay. He's acquired a couple of things that he shouldn't have. They're preying on him now."

She considered bringing up his meeting with Mrs. Filmer in the maze, but she couldn't find the words to introduce that. Somehow, that seemed more difficult than asking "Did Mr. Webberly seek your counsel?"

"Now why would you ask that?"

"Curiosity,"

"Killed the cat, Mrs. Tarrant."

"He had secrets, I am certain. Everyone does."

Mr. Farrell propped a foot on the step and braced an elbow on his lifted knee. "Secrets. Troubles past and present. We do all have them, even a pretty lady like you. Webby, poor man, was not the best fit for Greavley. Disrespected by the boys. Resented by a couple of his colleagues. He didn't improve those situations."

"On Saturday evening, when he dined with Miss Sherborne and her brother and me, Mr. Webberly complained of someone playing tricks. I thought a student, but Edward Malvaise—you know that I am painting him? Edward disagreed. He said that a master had descended to tricks, a petty revenge. And I remember Mr. Webberly said, quite distinctly, that he would 'get his own back'."

"His very words?" The Irish came out strong on those R's. "I will admit that a few shouts did disrupt the peace of our lodgings after we came in from the games. My attempts at intervention were useless. I escaped." The wind ruffled his dark hair. Were it longer, he would have a curly-top. "The Old Guard thinks me an interloper."

"Along with Mr. Webberly and Mr. Sherborne and … the games master?"

"Sherborne and Alexander didn't replace one of the Old Guard."

"Nor did you."

"Matron Berrycloth was well liked, especially by our contumacious Old Guard. I have these three strikes. In American baseball, they would call me out. See, I know a bit about America." He smiled, still trying the charm. "First strike: I'm Irish. Second strike: I'm solidly middle-class, the hidebound bourgeois, while Greavley prides itself on its gentry masters and students."

"I believe the school's founder was a merchant rather than gentry."

She wrapped her apple core in the wax paper that had wrapped her sandwich before shoving it deep into her satchel.

"He was wealthy. Money makes a lot of sins acceptable, doesn't it? Isn't money the determiner of the ruling class in America?"

Why is he trying to show me how much he knows about America?
"I believe Mr. Sherborne is neither gentry nor wealthy."

"He's on the fringes. Close enough to be acceptable."

"What's your third strike?"

"I'm something of a radical for a free Ireland. We have a lot of political disagreements in the Common Room."

"I thought you served in the British Army. Mr. Kenneth Elwen told me that. He's a fisherman staying at the Hook and Like."

"White feathers. Didn't want one of those." He shifted then crossed his arms. He kept his foot braced on a higher step and eased back and forth, back and forth, a slow rock. "I remember Kenneth Elwen. One of the tough cases. It's a miracle he's walking. The rest of his unit isn't. The surgeon had to rebuild bone and muscle tissue. Here's a curious coincidence. Gilchrist and Dodges also know Elwen. Their sons were in the same unit. Dodges' son died. Gilchrist's son— well, he can work at trimming bushes and thinning seedlings."

"What happened to that unit?"

"Hushed up after is all I know. We're lucky we're on this side of the war and still breathing." He straightened. "Now, Mrs. Tarrant, may I escort you anywhere? I've a free hour before the boys start pouring in with excuses to miss evening chapel or tomorrow's test."

She nudged her satchel. "I'm going to the formal garden. Between here and there is not enough of a distance for me to get lost. Miss Sherborne is coming later. She's promised to show me the secret to the maze. I hope to find the head gardener and ask a few questions. What is his name?"

"MacAlphin. Let's find him." Miles Farrell offered his arm. Isabella didn't want to be rude, so she dusted off her hands then accepted his offer.

The route Mr. Farrell chose wasn't the Crossing. He angled over the forecourt before the manor then headed around the winter-dead lawn on the other side. Steps took them down to the bare-branched oaks. A few leaves swirled in the wind, and Isabella caught at her hair before the wind buffeted it free.

They followed a path between the trees and a short retaining wall, manor-side. The lawn had narrowed as it came around.

"I understand this was a rose garden," he reminded, his tone easy. "The headmaster before Filmer removed the roses. He wanted a croquet lawn."

"Can one play croquet in such a narrow space? I would strike a ball over this wall. It would be lost in the trees. Or someone would strike it away for me. Croquet can be rather ruthless."

"That is a question. The former headmaster must have intended the wall as a handicap."

"Or did he play a merciless game and declare everything beyond the wall as in-bounds?"

He laughed. "That would be cruel, not just merciless."

"I should find the Great Lawn as well. Do they play cricket there or just rugby?" She felt his look but preferred not to acknowledge. She craned her neck to see around the manor's corner.

"For a visitor to Greavley, you are acquainted with our games."

"Edward Malvaise talked of athletics during our session this morning. Models often do so. There's not much for them to do while an artist requires them to hold a pose."

"Did he?" He sounded distant, and Isabella realized he had looked up, at a first-story window.

When she looked up, she saw the flutter of a lace curtain and nothing more.

Mr. Farrell glanced at his wristwatch. "I have forgotten an appointment. Do forgive my absent mind, Mrs. Tarrant." He stopped at the steps that broke the length of retaining wall. They climbed to the formal garden. Directly across the garden were the steps descending from the narrow lawn beyond the Crossing. "I leave you here. One of the scholarship boys will soon find you, and you can request MacAlphin. He'll know where the old man is. The maze is MacAlphin's pride. You should ask him to escort you."

"If the maze is his pride, he would not appreciate my attempts to recreate it for a magazine illustration. Mazes should be puzzles."

"Printing the key to the maze would certainly destroy the puzzle for everyone. People should have to memorize it, as the rest of us did."

"Perhaps I can convince Mrs. Filmer to serve as my guide." There, that was neat. *But how do I say we overheard them yesterday?*

"Mrs. Filmer?" His laugh sounded genuine. "She has lived here for over a decade, but I had to teach her the maze's key. She is still not certain of her way. MacAlphin is the better choice."

"Did you escort her through the maze on Sunday?"

"We were not together on Sunday."

Her eyes opened wide at his lie. "My apologies. I must have misheard."

"I went to the village on Sunday."

"After the service?"

Those merry blue eyes took a flinty glint. "Before the service. I didn't return here until the hullaballoo was in full cry."

"That's right. You were not at the service."

"And you were."

"Miss Sherborne and I attended with her brother. The altar screen is rather extraordinary."

His eyes had narrowed, warrior fixed upon his foe, and she wondered if he'd spent his summer fighting for a free Ireland. "And you three found the body after the service. I hope you were not greatly upset, Mrs. Tarrant?"

"It was upsetting and unsettling." As was his lie.

Why does he not want to admit he was in the maze with Mrs. Filmer? Why does he not want to admit being close to the scene and time of the murder? Well, actually, that question was her answer.

Did Miles Farrell have a motive to kill George Webberly? Was he protecting Mrs. Filmer?

Lies would protect no one when Scotland Yard arrived.

"I will not delay you longer. Appointments are important." She held out her hand. "I thank you for the escort."

He held her hand rather than shaking it. His hand was warm, hers cold. "Don't stay too long in this wind. It has the bite of winter. Frost in the morning, I would expect."

"I believe those tall boxwoods will give shelter to the garden and the maze? Is there a statuette in the center? Or a bench?"

"A small fountain. Turned off to keep the pipes from freezing. You should see it and hear it in the blaze of summer."

"Did you not come here in September? I wasn't aware that it was still hot here at that time."

"I first c-came here just after Midsummer. I c-came for an interview and ex-explored afterward."

Not once had he stuttered over his words, but he did now, and Isabella suspected another lie. Had he met Mrs. Filmer then? Perhaps something grew between them, more than the acquaintance of headmaster's wife and the counselor to the school.

Perhaps George Webberly's conquest of Mrs. Filmer had angered Mr. Farrell.

Perhaps I am too suspicious. People can have secrets without being murderers.

He touched his fingers to his brow, mimicry of a salute. "Good day to you, Mrs. Tarrant." He headed back to the front of the manor.

Would Dodges admit him? Or would Mrs. Filmer do so?

The flutter of the lace curtain had to be her. He hadn't remembered his appointment until then.

She had liked Miles Farrell, but most of what he'd said could not be trusted.

.~.~.~.

Dr. Woolsey might prefer a country practice, but the wounds to the deceased hadn't fazed him. "Boer War," he'd said, as if that explained his *sangfroid* to Michael and Callaway. The doctor had then pointed out the stunning blow at the crown of the head followed by four blows delivered to the side of the head. A heavy stick of some sort landed the blows. "No impression of splinters or any pattern from wood. I doubt it was a branch. Swinging blows, I believe, directly and accurately applied, with the force concentrated to this area behind the temple. The blows cracked the skull then fragmented the bone."

Minutes ago, the train whistle for departure had blown. Now they heard the grinding squeal as the steam engine began pulling the passenger and freight cars.

"Type of stick?" Callaway asked, scribbling rapidly.

"A finished piece of wood or something heavy. Weighted to increase the impact. I discern no pattern. Heavy, to be certain. I'd say metal, but it's not the usual shape."

"Weighted tool with unusually shaped end. Could a woman wield that kind of skull-cracking force?"

"Easily if they had the proper swing." He reached to the bench and lifted a file. "List of my findings and the contents of his pockets and items found around the body. I have retained the items in cold storage. Would you like to see them?"

Michael followed his sergeant who followed the doctor down to the cellar. They examined the items: wristwatch, wallet, handkerchief, automobile key, two door keys, key to a small lock, loose change, a couple of collar tabs. Flannel pants, corduroy jacket, shirt with bib front—as if he hadn't bothered to change from his shirt when he changed from a tuxedo, undershirt, small clothes.

As the doctor relocked the cabinet, he said, "Sir Robert Goodkind will appoint an inquest within a few days."

"I hope to have my investigation finalized before then, Doctor. Time of death?"

"Constable Amsley will have that. I concurred in my report."

"Constable's meeting us at the magistrate's, boss."

Michael bent his head to acknowledge his sergeant's mutter.

Yet when they arrived at Sir Robert Goodkind's stately Georgian manor, the constable was absent.

A stiffly correct butler did not make them wait in the wood-paneled entrance. He led them to a back hall where a footman waited outside a room. The footman hurriedly opened the door, and the butler preceded them with a droning "Detective Inspector Michael Wainwright and his assistant, sir, from Scotland Yard."

They entered a book-lined room with the curtains partially drawn against the rising wind. A large desk dominated the room. Behind it was a middle-aged man who looked weary of the day. Grey had tinged his soft brown hair. He was slope-shouldered, and the desk seemed too large for his frame. He finished signing a document then looked up. His long face and sagging jowls gave him the appearance of a basset hound. "Gentlemen. Welcome." He stood and offered his hand over the desk.

Michael stepped forward and shook his hand, firm and single in its shake. Callaway did as well then stepped back and readied his notebook and pencil.

"Would you prefer tea or coffee?"

"Coffee, sir. Sgt. Callaway prefers tea, well sugared."

Sir Robert gave the order to the waiting butler. Then he shuffled the papers before him and weighted them with an unusually shaped rock at the corner of his desk. He waved at the *fauteuils*, those deep French armchairs in a semi-circle before the hearth. "Join me." He sank into the deep armchair.

Michael followed suit. Callaway took the one furthest from the fireplace.

"Have you seen Dr. Woolsey?"

"We've had his report and examined the evidence he had for us, sir."

"Good man, Woolsey. Knows his business. Constable Amsley will be admitted once he arrives. We have attempted to leave the investigation to you. The constable has taken a few preliminary statements at my direction. He will provide those at your request. Amsley is eager to work with you. He's a country soul, at heart, for all that he walked a beat in Liverpool for several years before coming here."

The door to the study opened, and the butler returned, trailed by a maid with a large silver tray holding two pots as well as cups and saucers. She placed the tray at his direction on a side table then hurried out. He served Michael first, then Callaway, then the baron before retreating.

After an obligatory sip, Michael set his coffee on a side table then leaned forward. "What can you tell me, Sir Robert? As an objective person on the scene, your observations are crucial."

The man's eyelids flickered in surprise, then he nodded and set aside his own coffee. "Constable Amsley and I arrived together. Dean Filmer, headmaster of Greavley Abbey School, he directed us to the river path through the woods. He did not himself enter the woods. He believed that he could best serve by directing the doctor and the ambulance when they arrived. He also informed us that he had confined the boys to their dormitories and would provide us with a list of those boys on the premises at that point."

"Is there a reason for that list?"

"An abundance of caution. The boys' routine is highly scheduled except for a couple of hours daily. Amsley will tell you more. He will also have the list. I believe he collected a check-in for the church service and is matching that to the school's roster. I followed the constable into the woods where we encountered Mr. Sherborne standing watch. He covered the body with a blanket before he telephoned us."

The name Sherborne struck Michael, shifting his focus. Yet Sherborne was not an unusual name. This man probably did not know of a Felicity Sherborne. He pulled his attention to where it belonged. "This Sherborne left the body alone while he telephoned?"

"No. His sister and her friend waited there while he telephoned."

Sister. "They just happened to have a blanket with them?"

"They had planned a picnic on the riverbank. A rare day, almost like spring."

"What was your impression of them, Mr. Sherborne and his sister and her friend?"

"Mr. Sherborne was eager to leave the scene which I allowed. He did not, however, return to the two ladies. They had taken refuge in the manor."

"He left them for several minutes with the body."

"Close to half an hour."

'Then he avoids them by going to his rooms? He ignores whatever emotional upset they have? That is strange. Where did he go?"

"The Masters' Lodgings, where he has rooms. The Lodgings are the second building behind the Prior's House. He gave the excuse of translations to mark. That is in his statement."

"And the women?"

"The sister and her friend waited for my arrival in the manor, as I said. We spoke briefly, then Constable Amsley took their statements. I allowed them to return to the pub, the Hook and Line."

"Where we're staying," Callaway murmured.

"You will definitely want to speak with them. You may find both of them at Greavley Abbey today. The artist is painting a portrait of one of the students, a commission she received a couple of months ago from the Malvaise family."

Michael brightened. An artist and the Malvaise family. Could that be—? Callaway beat him to the question. "Is that Mrs. Madoc Tarrant, Sir Robert?"

"You two are familiar with her?"

"We've met. At Christmastide," Michael felt more than saw Callaway's sharp look. The impression he created was that they'd met at a holiday party, not that she had been attacked, twice, because of a murder at Emberley. He didn't want to detail the circumstances. That case had nearly had three murders. "It's a strange coincidence to encounter her again. She is recently married to one of my captains."

Callaway wouldn't correct him, but the sergeant cleared his throat and lifted his pencil, ready for more notes in his atrocious scrawl. They both liked Isabella Tarrant. His burly sergeant had gone all brotherly with her since her honesty had nearly incriminated her. Only a strong alibi kept her out of the suspect list.

And here she was again.

"Should Mrs. Tarrant be removed from the constable's list of suspects?"

"We need to know more before we eliminate anyone." That was standard procedure. Callaway cleared his throat again, so Michael wouldn't miss his displeasure.

Chapter 14

Monday

"And Mr. Sherborne's sister?"

"Miss Felicity Sherborne," the magistrate said. Even expecting the name, Michael felt like he dropped a hundred feet. "A professional photographer, she informs me." Sir Robert's tone made evident that he didn't quite believe her claim. "We shall see when she provides us photo prints of the murder scene."

Fate had definitely set its Sisyphean ball rolling. Michael again encountered Felicity Sherborne, this time with murder between them. He preferred a dance floor and Alan Rettleston's antagonism as obstacles. That bottomless feeling let him know trouble was coming. God help him. First, Isabella Tarrant, involved closely in another murder, and now Felicity Sherborne.

At least Callaway didn't know about his boss's interest in Miss Sherborne.

Then Michael heard what Sir Robert had said. "Photo prints of the murder scene? I understand that you needed to remove the body, but you brought this Miss Sherborne in to take photographs of the scene?"

"I did not. She took it upon herself while waiting for her brother's return from notifying us." His words had become clipped, almost curt. Sir Robert didn't approve. "While Mrs. Tarrant held up the blanket, Miss Sherborne took photographs. They tell me that they thought it necessary to record the scene. I do not think either lady had a high expectation for an investigation in a rural area run by a young constable and a magistrate who normally deal with drunks and poachers. Miss Sherborne informed me that she would develop and enlarge the photographs before your arrival then turn the prints and the negatives over to you. They said they were eager to help."

Sir Robert hadn't wanted their help but needed it. Having to accept what he didn't want must be like drinking bitters for the magistrate. Michael understood that feeling. It burned his throat and bothered him for days.

"Yet her brother was eager to return to his rooms," he commented. "Quite a difference."

Before Sir Robert replied, the door opened. The butler didn't quite step into the room. "Sir, Constable Amsley waits in the morning room. Because of his tardiness, sir, he says he should not delay you."

"Excellent." Sir Robert stood, and Michael and Callaway did also. "If you need anything, Detective Inspector, the constable will answer your questions. You will wish to examine the case in detail, I know. Make use of the morning room. I will be absent for several hours. Chesterton will provide what you need. If you have an emergency, he will contact me. Chesterton."

"The automobile is waiting, sir."

"My wife?"

"James has informed her of your imminent departure. Inspector, sergeant, come with me, please."

In the morning room the constable was sorting papers on a round piecrust table. The flowered bowl that must have decorated the table had been placed on a low table before a settee. When Michael entered, the man straightened and stood at attention. He looked young, but Callaway's information said he'd served in Liverpool before coming to the Wellsford district. His appearance should belie his experience. From the bulky folder in his hand and the number of papers on the table beside him, he wanted to impress.

"Scotland Yard." Awe rounded his voice.

Callaway snorted. "We're not gods."

"Aye, sir. I know that, sir. But—Scotland Yard."

"Aspirations to the Met Police?" Michael had reached the table. He surveyed the documents, stacked in order he saw, for there was Chauncey Sherborne's statement, the name typed at the top with paragraphs below, and a list topped another stack, and a death certificate form rested atop a third. The constable had used clothes pegs to keep the stacks together.

"No, sir. Not at all, sir. I like Wellsford, sir. Quiet. Peaceful. After the trenches—." He stopped and swallowed.

"I thought you came here from Liverpool."

"That's right."

"Where did you serve? When?"

"Ypres. '14 to '16, sir. Wounded. Not gas, thank God. Knew some boys, though. Went back to Liverpool then, but—well, a country district suits me better, sir."

"I see," and Michael did, unfortunately. Rain. Mud. Flooding. Assaults. Shelling. Gunfire. Flares every night. Gas. Filthy men crowded in muddy trenches together. A country district would have suited him better as well, but that wasn't the job he received. He wound up in hot and dry Turkey, and for three weeks he had thought it better. Only later had his unit transferred to entrenched Europe. "Nice to meet you, Constable Amsley." He introduced himself then the sergeant. "Callaway was at the Somme."

"Cor," Amsley breathed, and his burly sergeant's ears turned red.

Expecting Amsley to want to know about his service, Michael preempted him. "Walk us through the case, Constable. These look like statements, reports, and what are these lists?"

"Suspects, sir, based on what connection to the victim that I can discern."

"Let's just call him Webberly, shall we?" He reached for the statements with Sherborne at the top. "Do we start here?"

"Best place, I think," the constable said, "These are statements from the people who found the victim. Mr. Webberly, sir."

Callaway picked up another stack and removed the clothes peg. "Remind me, Amsley, to have a conversation about office supplies. What are these? Death certificates and what else?"

"Doctor's findings. Ambulance drivers' statements."

"Thorough."

"I try to be, Detective Inspector Wainwright."

"Just say *boss*," Callaway said. "Trips right off the tongue."

. ~ . ~ , ~ .

Greavley Abbey's gardener had aged last century. In the last two decades, he had only become more weathered, blue eyes washed clearer than a pale sky, gnarled fingers knobby like oaks, body as thin as a wintry twig but agile with withy growth. He had an iron spade's strength that controlled his workers, the four scholarship boys and the four undergardeners, the men destroyed by the Great War, who wanted only to trim hedges and thin seedlings in the greenhouse. MacAlphin gave them orders they could take and suggestions they could ignore.

Chauncey had told Flick about the old gardener, but she hadn't quite believed him, not until she saw him give a man a quarter his age instructions for an espaliered pear tree then clambered himself up a ladder to cut out the winter damage to a tall boxwood.

After introductions, MacAlphin came down the ladder and led her around the current work, stopping at a veteran working at a serpentine wall. The man had mortar to repoint the bricks. Flick indicated her camera, and when the old head gardener said nothing, she snapped several photos.

"I never realized," she said, "how much work in a garden never touches growing plants. The hardscape is as important as the flowers and shrubs and trees."

"You want to see the kitchen garden? Or the greenhouse?"

"Tomorrow. You have given me a whole article's worth of information, and we haven't touched on the topiaries. A kitchen garden, though—. That's something I would want to know, and I'm sure my readers would as well. We might do seasonal updates? Do you have a coldframe method for the early vegetables? The lettuces? Radishes? Carrots? Turnips?"

"Leeks. Parsnips. Onions."

"I've never cooked with parsnips."

"They take on the flavor of the meat they're cooked with." He stared at the sky with its breaking clouds after the night's rain. "Tomorrow for the greenhouse. You'll want sunshine. 'Twill be warm in there."

"Do you maintain the manor's conservatory?"

"Aye."

"That may be another article. I'm at the Hook and Line for a fortnight. I thought I might run out of things to do, but I think I will have more than I can crowd in. Topiary. Hardscape. Greenscape. Kitchen garden. Conservatory." She dug out her notebook and pencil. She would need to turn her brief code into better notes and begin sketching ideas. Spry Mr. MacAlphin would not hide his disgust with her inability to remember. "Tell me, please, the name of the undergardener who is repointing those bricks. I need it for the photo caption."

"Robby Gilchrist."

"Gilchrist? Like the majordomo at the Prior's House?"

"Son." He tossed a stray leaf into a nearby wheel barrow then drew her away from the wall. "All set to clerk for a London solicitor till he was conscripted."

"Was he injured?"

He tapped his forehead. "Shell shock."

"I see." The image of Mr. Gilchrist at the Sunday service imposed itself on his son's face. "Does he reside with his father?"

"Aye, they're in the old carriage house. Gilchrist wanted the change from the Masters' Lodgings, where he had a efficiency. They'd lived there since Robby came home, early in '19. Back in November, Gilchrist said their rooms weren't working. He wanted to move. We managed it before December."

"Not working? They had several months there. Why would the rooms suddenly not work?"

"Bad memories was all he said, that and not wanting to disturb the masters. Me, I think someone was bothering his son. Needed away from him."

"That's not right! Our veterans are important! Did Mr. Gilchrist inform the dean?"

"We took care of it quiet. No good disturbing the masters. Their wishes come before servants. Persnickety lot."

"That's how my brother describes the Old Guard, persnickety. My brother has his own troubles from the war. He's taken up running, he says, to clear his thoughts."

"Aye. See him of the morning, when I'm having my tea on the dock. I hear good things of Master Sherborne from my boys." He nodded at one of the scholarship boys grubbing dead leaves from under a holly.

"That's great. He was another who didn't aim for his current profession. He was angling for the church, but when he was demobbed, all he told us—my parents and me—was that he couldn't stick that idea." She dropped the notebook into her tote and the pencil into a pocket of her jodhpurs. "I must be getting on. I promised to meet Mrs. Tarrant at the maze and show her the secret."

"That the artist who shipped her painting and that wood contraption? Bigger than her, the jobber was saying."

"Yes. That wood contraption is an easel to hold the canvas while she paints. I believe she said her husband built it. She began work today with young Mr. Malvaise."

"Student?" When she nodded, he snorted. "Him I don't know. My boys haven't mentioned him, and he never comes around."

The scholarship boys might be another potential story. Bright boys able to better their education and win a chance for a university. More along the lines of *London Daily* than *Modern Woman*, although if she pushed the idea of scholarship endowments—. She mused over the idea. Letters to other public schools were needed. Interviews with personable boys and their parents, with headmasters and tutors. That article sounded like too much work for the time she currently had available. "Mr. MacAlphin, I thank you for your kindness today. You have amazed me. I look forward to our time together tomorrow. In the afternoon? I want to spend the morning developing the film of today's photos. How may I find you?"

He gave directions for the work he had planned for Tuesday. She confirmed a couple of points then headed for the manor and formal garden. A quick glance at her watch spurred her on. Isabella would be waiting, hopefully sketching the garden as a map.

What would Isabella say when Flick added Robby Gilchrist to the suspect list?

He might have an alibi.

She recalled Mr. Gilchrist's sickly face, Dodges equally wan and waxy.

Robby Gilchrist could have a completely innocent reason for not attending the service with his father.

Yet he'd wanted to leave the Masters' Lodgings well into the autumn term. The only change from early in the school term to November was the arrival of the new employees, Chauncey, George Webberly, Miles Farrell, the games master whose name she could never remember, and another master whose name she couldn't recall. *Barely a beard*, Chauncey had said.

I should ask Chauncey about Robby Gilchrist.

She knew her brother wasn't the cause of the younger Gilchrist's upset. Miles Farrell had been a medic. He had an even temper. She couldn't see him causing an upset. That left George Webberly and the games masters.

She would lay money on Webberly creating problems.

. ~ . ~ . ~ .

Constable Amsley spread out the originals of his statements like a winning poker hand. Erasure smudges and little correction marks dotted the pages. Michael stood back, hands in trouser pockets, while Callaway read the typescripts. He finally rolled off seven names. "Dean Filmer. Verna Filmer. N.W. Dodges. Robert Gilchrist Sr. Nuala Rice. Sibby Waycroft. Herbert Pollard. Who are these?" The sergeant began scribbling.

"Headmaster. His wife. Butler for the manor." The constable touched each statement in sequence, going slowly for Callaway's writing. "Majordomo for the school. Next two are bar maids at the Hook and Line. Man who owns it."

"What does a majordomo do?"

"Same thing a butler does, I'm guessing, plus porter and other things."

"And the list?"

"Servants for the manor. MacAlphin, here, this column," he pointed to the list of names running down the right side of the sheet, "these are the outside staff. MacAlphin is head gardener. These names at the bottom, those are his scholarship boys. They see their tutors— what they call masters here—four hours and give MacAlphin four hours."

"And these statements?" Callaway touched the three set off to one side, near the medical reports. "Chauncey Sherborne, he has Greek. Mrs. Madoc Tarrant, she's the artist. Miss Felicity Sherborne, sister to Chauncey."

Michael's head came up at the last name. He tried to stop it and couldn't. He hid the betraying look by going to the window and looking out at Sir Robert's expansive lawn.

Callaway would have noticed. Nothing slipped his sergeant. "They found Webberly."

"That's right. Watched over the victim, you could say, until we got there with the doctor."

"These look like basic statements. We'll have to interview them again. Sir?" Callaway resorted to the official *sir* rather than his usual *boss* when he wanted to impress.

Michael turned. His sergeant's expression was carefully impassive. He came back to the table and scanned a couple of statements. "As Sir Robert said, these are for immediate impressions."

"A starting point, sir," Amsley offered.

He replaced the papers, careful of their stacks. "You've done good work, Constable."

Amsley permitted himself a smile. "Doing my duty, sir, from what I remember they talked about doing in Liverpool." He pulled two more typescripts from under the medical report. "This lists everything the victim, Mr. Webberly, had on him. This is everything I found within a twenty-five-foot radius of the scene."

"Was Webberly killed elsewhere?"

"No. Doctor Woolsey said he was killed at the scene."

Callaway took possession of the lists. "Anything more?" Michael asked, wanting to move forward.

The constable grimaced. From his pocket he took a little notebook like Callaway's. "I made a list of suspects. I won't claim it's accurate, but it gives a bit of direction, some people you might not consider."

Callaway peered at the scrawl without taking the notebook. "Chauncey Sherborne? The one who found the body?"

"That's right, sergeant. The medic what helped the doctor, he said Master Sherborne and the victim, Mr. Webberly, didn't get along. Gambling debts and such."

Another strike by Fate. Michael would need a close interview of Felicity Sherborne, one that included accusing questions about her brother. Fate had brought them together even as it conspired against them.

"Got another master here." Amsley pointed at a name further down the notebook page. "MacAlphin, that's the gardener, heard the victim and him arguing in the maze. Westbrook Neville. This happened the morning of, before most people were out and about. This here," he touched the bottom of the list, "is a scholarship student. He and the vic—Mr. Webberly were crosswise, according to the gardeners."

"MacAlphin appears to be an excellent source," Michael said dryly.

"Giving us the names of his workers, overhearing the victim argue with—."

"Westbrook Neville. He's a master, too."

"And pointing out a boy who was crosswise with Webberly."

"He didn't mention one name. Robert Gilchrist."

Callaway looked up. "The majordomo?"

Amsley shook his head. "His son. I know for a fact that Robby Gilchrist works with MacAlphin, but he's not on the list. Gilchrist Younger had his problems with the vic—Webberly. I've broke up fights in the pub between them. And I got my ear filled when I walked Gilchrist home after he drank too much to see his way. Been months since a fistfight, but—."

"How many months?" Callaway poised his pencil.

"Before Christmas. No, before December started. I thought it settled between them. Now I'm not sure. There's extra reasons for the trouble between them. They both knew the same girl in London. Gilchrist Younger won that round, but Webberly won at cards. He was in debt to Webberly. The main thing, though, I never got that out of him. He clammed up. Said he'd spend a night in jail before he talked of it."

"What?"

"Something bad from the war. They were in the same unit."

Michael's War Office source had said Webberly ordered his unit up and over into certain death while he hung back to watch from the trench. A fool exercise that he'd volunteered his unit for. Nothing gained, not even for a diversion. Afterwards, emotions ran so high on the line that Webberly had to be recalled, then he was transferred to another brigade in a different field of operations.

Definition of a fatal mistake, his source said.

Callaway had chuffed at that report saying *Fatal for his men but not for Webberly*.

Had someone decide to wreak revenge now?

Michael doubted an action in the war had caused a death years later, but he would keep that motive in mind. "Who else do you suspect, Constable?"

"You've scratched out names," Callaway accused. "Why?"

"Before the doctor's findings, I added in women. Webberly was a lady's man. Dr. Woolsey said the blows came from a heavy stick. I don't reckon a woman could do that kind of damage."

"Depends on the stick," Callaway said. "Give us the names. Verna Filmer. What for?"

"She was having an *affaire* with the—Webberly. Public secret. I think only her husband didn't know."

"Is he on your list? He might have known and kept quiet about it. Saving face until he could take action."

"Murder?" Michael asked. "That's extreme."

Callaway shrugged. "I've seen it, sir," and Michael bowed to his sergeant's longer experience with violent deaths.

"Imogene Pollard, wife of Herbert Pollard of the Hook and Line. He's on my list because of her. The bar maid Nuala Rice. Now, I don't think it's her. Mrs. Pollard, though, I can't tell. I don't like her much. She's uppity and no cause for it. Just started her *affaire* with Webberly. They went away for a weekend in February."

"Valentine's Day tryst?"

"Maybe. I didn't think of that. Poor Nuala thinks she's in love with Webberly. I don't know what Mrs. Pollard thinks about his death. She's off to London. Not expected back until Wednesday."

"Pollard because of his wife, same as Filmer. Anyone else?" Callaway seemed determined to mine the constable before they viewed the scene. The sergeant kept the opinion that a bobby on a beat knew better than anyone else who'd done murder. To him, constables were rural bobbies.

"Well, sir." For the first time, Amsley looked reluctant. "We have no official photos of the scene."

"I understand that photos were taken by Miss Sherborne."

"That's right, sir, but not official ones. We got a photographer in Upper Wellsford, Mr. Roberts, but he was gone for the weekend. Didn't come back till eleven last night. His wife helps him in the shop, but she didn't come out to the scene. Said she didn't know how to use the camera he had left. I don't know—." He blew air up to his forehead. "Well, sir, Miss Sherborne's a problem. Her brother's a suspect."

Callaway snorted. "Then the photos are useless to us."

Michael shook his head. "I think we should wait to see Miss Sherborne's photos before we judge. Does Mr. Roberts have her photo prints?"

"No, sir. I had hoped he did. He did say that she developed a score or more this very morning, before you arrived. He thought she had double that number of negatives."

"Where are the prints now?"

"I don't know, sir. She didn't leave them with Mr. Roberts."

"Miss Sherborne still has them?"

"Unless she destroyed them because they incriminate her brother or a friend, like Miles Farrell."

"I want those photographs, Constable. And the negatives. All of them."

"Yes, sir. She's staying at the Hook and Line, sir."

"Go there now."

Amsley looked miserable. "Miss Sherborne's not there, sir. I asked when you arrived. She drove out of the village after she left Mr. Roberts. She headed in the direction of Greavley Abbey. Said she was going to meet her brother and Mrs. Tarrant."

"Then we shall follow her. We need to see the scene of the crime before we start interrogations. You will ride with us, Constable."

Callaway gave him a jaundiced look as he stowed his notebook in an inner pocket. Michael and he discussed cases as the sergeant drove, yet neither would offer any ideas, stir up motives, or review evidence when someone else rode in the auto.

"Early days, Callaway. Early days." Not even the chief inspector would expect a solution on the day they arrived.

Chapter 15

Monday

Isabella emerged from the maze and saw Flick taking photographs of a spiraling topiary. The head gardener stood beyond the half-wall, on a lower path as he raked the pristine lawn.

Flick let the camera dangle from a strap around her neck then bent to the tote at her feet and withdrew a notebook. A quick notation, then the notebook returned to the tote, and she came to meet Isabella. "How did your wander through the maze go?"

"I found the way on my own, starting left, as you said." She nodded in the direction of the gardener. Since Flick was now closer, she lowered her voice. "Have you ever seen the gardener without a tool?"

Flick laughed. "It is his job. Did you start the illustration of the garden?"

"It's very rough. I'll create a much better illustration for printing later."

"Nothing elaborate. Details can be lost."

"Yes. I've done several illustrations from the dig on Crete for my brother-in-law. I finished the last few before I came up. Three illustrations per article, for ten articles. Fortunately, I started them in Crete. You may have seen them. They're not in an academic journal.

All Britain, I think he said."

"Your brother-in-law. That's the professor, isn't it? Prof. Tarrant of St. George's University in London. I'll have to look for his articles. How long will they run? Ten articles?" Even as she accepted the sketch, her focus remained on the head gardener. "Garden tools. I'd didn't realize—," she murmured.

"What is it?" Isabella glanced at the old gardener. How could he find anything to rake up? The lawn looked pristine to her.

"Garden tools have metal heads, don't they? The rake. The spade. The mattock. The hoe."

Isabella hadn't wanted to remember the gory damage to George Webberly's head. She did now as well as a tool creating that damage.

At her gasp, Flick looked at her. "My apologies. Let's look at what you've drawn. This is the maze."

"Very rough."

She turned the sketchbook to horizontal, back to vertical. "This is good. Rough, as you say, but very good. Boxwoods for the maze walls, the fountain. You should have MacAlphin describe the fountain for you."

"He's the head gardener."

"And knows everyone who would have access to garden tools."

They shared a look.

"Horizontal or vertical for the garden plan?" Flick asked.

Isabella told her then waited while she examined the formal garden with its arched beddings. "I don't know what will be planted in the center beds. Flowers to give color but which ones? Annuals? Perennials? The sides have room for border plantings. Have you ever seen what was planted there?"

"Only autumn colors, gradually removed as the garden turned to winter. Another reason to talk with MacAlphin. He'll give you the plan for this year, I imagine, and may even escort you through the greenhouse. This will be quite a bit of work for you. I didn't realize. Did I mention compensation? How much did Prof. Tarrant pay you?"

"He didn't pay me; the magazine did. He just funneled the money to me." She named the sum. "That's for three illustrations. That's not how your contract with *Modern Woman* runs, is it? You're freelance, paid by them on delivery. Why don't we divide by three then take off about fifteen percent? Does that sound reasonable? Can you pay me on delivery? That's how I worked for the professor."

"I can and will. That amount sounds right. Since I'm bringing illustrations as well as photographs, Owl might weasel out more money for me. Alicia Osterley, I mean. You remember, my friend at *Modern Woman*?"

"I remember that we talked about her. I met her at Christmastide, at Emberley." Again Isabella didn't say what she'd thought of the young woman. Surrounded by strangers, her employer demanding one thing after another, Miss Osterley might not have been at her best. She had definitely been awed by Lottie Crittenden and the whole Malvaise family. Isabella turned to recite her day. "I saw your brother in passing, hurrying from the church to the teaching hall."

"At chapel?"

"At half-past noon. I had tucked into the alcove of the side door, eating my apple."

"What on earth was he doing there?"

"Meeting Miles Farrell."

"The medic?" In her surprise, Flick stopped walking, then she skipped a step to resume her place beside Isabella. "I know he's not a medic anymore, but that's how Chauncey refers to him. What did Chauncey say?"

"He barely had time to acknowledge me. I think he must have been late. Mr. Farrell talked a few minutes."

"Why was Chauncey meeting him?"

She hesitated, but Flick had turned her head, her eyebrows arched as she waited for an answer. "I gathered the impression that Mr. Farrell was counseling your brother. Does your brother have many nightmares about the war? My husband," she rushed to add, "still has them, and he's been demobbed for over a year. I believe it's a common ailment. Part of shell shock."

"Ailment? I would describe it more as a debilitating malaise. Early on, he had more than nightmares. Couldn't eat, didn't even want to climb out of bed in the early days. Least little noise from the street, and the shakes would seize him for hours. And the nightmares. He refused to mention anything to our father who was in the Boer War. Father never talked of his service. Chauncey had to talk with me. That was the only way he could get back to sleep. Talk and talk and talk, never about his experiences, from the time he woke until morning tea. We mostly reminisced about our childhood. Then he stretched out on the sofa while I had to head to work. I had regular work as a mannequin then. I'm very happy to be rid of that job. Time eased Chauncey's nightmares. I had hoped they'd vanished entirely. If he's talking with Miles Farrell, that can only be good. Last night, in the wee hours, I heard one of our fishermen calling out."

"That would have to be Mr. Elwen." Isabella thought she remembered that his room was across from Flick's. "I didn't realize that nightmares still haunted him."

"How could they not? I read the reports of battle. I've heard descriptions. I had a friend who worked at a field hospital, and he said—. Well, no one needs to hear that. Doubtless, my imagination is far below reality. Please, let's talk of something else." They had reached the graveled parking beside the church. "How was your time with the privileged heir of Emberley?"

"He surprised me by being amiable. And very forthcoming, especially in our forenoon hour. Apparently, the boys' dormitory is rife with speculation about George Webberly's death. I imagine they're finding it difficult to concentrate on their studies. My father—he was a don at a public school in the Lake District—."

"Really? You've been in England for several years then?"

"We came over before the war." She didn't want to talk of that. She wanted to pursue what Edward Malvaise had shared.

Yet that was not to be. A dark automobile pulled in, the wheels crunching loudly over the gravel and drowning normal conversation. Three men sat in the auto. *Was that—?* Before Isabella decided, the driver had parked beside Flick's green Calcott and killed the motor.

The automobile's doors opened, and the three men emerged. The burly driver spoke over the hood to his passenger, a tall man without a hat. The wind caught in his dark hair. The sun lighted his face, burnished as her husband's still was from years in the Mediterranean sun.

Flick had lifted a hand to shield her eyes from the weak sunlight that reflected off the automobiles. "Who is that? The tall one? I've seen him in London."

"That," Isabella said with an inner glow of satisfaction, "is Detective Inspector Michael Wainwright and his sergeant Mr. Callaway. Scotland Yard has sent their best."

. ~ . ~ . ~ .

The man she'd seen last Friday evening at the Fitzwilliam Victoria was a detective inspector?

With Scotland Yard.

And there Flick had been, dining with Alan Rettleston, who liked to walk the edge of respectability and brazen his way out of any trouble.

Flick's steps slowed while Isabella's had increased, rapidly crossing to meet the men when they were only a few steps from their auto. She stopped, wondering how Isabella knew men from the Metropolitan Police Force.

The third man, exiting the back seat, wore a navy uniform. The local constable, she guessed.

As she watched Isabella shake hands, Flick remembered the scandal at Christmastide, murder at Emberley and the public arrest of a financier's wife. Owl had talked about it once then refused, even after the arrest in London and reports of the guilty plea died from the newspapers.

Isabella must have met the men there, at the same time that she picked up her portrait commission from the dowager Malvaise.

It was a small world. Made smaller by Flick's own near meeting with this detective inspector only three evenings ago.

Isabella led the three men to her. The burly sergeant looked at her with open curiosity. The constable was preparing to use his notebook. The detective inspector—Yes, it was him!—had moderated his smile, congenial rather than broad.

Ah, yes, I'm a suspect now.

Flick had hoped to see him again, to meet him and see if attraction sparked.

The detective inspector had the looks and slow movements that she liked. Dark hair without a pomade, sharp dark eyes, a lean tanned face with its long nose. A decided chin above his firm mouth. From her surreptitious spying last Friday, she knew his movements were measured, not quick and flighty; decisive and confident, rather than jerky. He hadn't worn flashy tie pins with his tuxedo, and its shiny fabric gleamed with age. A detective's salary likely didn't stretch to flash or a pristine new tuxedo.

His grey flannel coat was good, his shirt points crisp although he and his sergeant must have driven from London today. Hours in the auto. She knew too well what that was like.

They had reached her. Flick lowered her tote to the ground. Deciding to imitate Isabella's American welcome, she stuck out her hand.

"Flick." Isabella gave a chuckle. "Or should I say Miss Felicity Sherborne? May I introduce Michael Wainwright, a detective inspector with Scotland Yard? Although we met only in January, I feel as if I've known him for years. He commanded my husband's unit. And this is his sergeant, Trevor Callaway, epitome of the cheerful policeman."

"Now, Mrs. Tarrant," the sergeant said, "you're taking away my thunder, and we've barely started this case. Next thing, you'll be telling us how you must be a suspect."

The detective inspector said nothing, merely shook her hand then fell back a step, hands behind his back. At rest, she remembered from Chauncey's descriptions of military stances, before actual service in the war killed his enthusiasm.

"But I am a suspect!" Isabella cried. "I found the body. Rather, we did. Along with Flick's brother, who is a master here."

"I'll not believe you did the deed," the sergeant protested. "Not with those lily-white hands."

"These, sergeant," she waved her cold-tipped fingers in the air, "are well smudged from my pencil."

The detective inspector continued silent, his gaze flashing around their group. When the banter ended, he fixed on her. The amber lights in his dark eyes surprised her. "Miss Sherborne. Constable Amsley here gave us to understand that you have photos of the scene. You did not leave them with Mr. Nigel Roberts. I believe you developed them at his shop."

None of that was either question or command, merely statement, but his keen gaze pricked her conscience. She didn't claim a mistrust of Mr. Roberts. That sounded defensive, the impression she did not want to give. Instead, she bent and searched her tote. "Heavens, yes. I have the photographs here, safe with me. As well as the negatives. All the negatives," she thought it wise to add. She straightened and handed over the courier envelope. The inspector took it from her, but he didn't unwrap the string and look inside. "I printed the photographs at Mr. Roberts' shop. I developed the negatives in the dark room I created out of a closet in my room at the pub. Will you want to examine that?"

"We need all of the negatives, for a proper sequence of evidence."

"Flick said that exact thing," Isabella exclaimed.

"Why did you believe it necessary to take photos?" Callaway asked.

Flick wondered how many suspects were fooled into thinking they were safe when that sergeant asked his questions so soft and gentle. She glanced briefly at Isabella who was friends with Scotland Yard's best. Flick would use that to her advantage. "We didn't quite trust the investigative skills of the local constable. My apologies, Constable. I am certain you are a fine fellow."

The constable grinned. "At drunks and burglary, Miss, not murder. I agree with you there."

Isabella chimed in. "Flick had her camera. We had a long, long time before her brother returned from notifying the headmaster and the constable. I can't take credit for the idea, but I thought it best, especially when we realized they would remove the body before anyone from Scotland Yard came—if they were intelligent enough to call Scotland Yard. And they were. Flick made good use of the time."

"Did *you*, Mrs. Tarrant? Make good use of your time?"

The sergeant's question sounded so odd that Flick gave him a quizzical look, but the answer came from his superior.

"A map of the murder scene? Or your impression of it, the position of the body?" which was another odd question.

"I didn't look," Isabella said baldly. "Once we spotted Mr. Webberly and realized—what had happened, I didn't look. I held the blanket while Flick—."

"The blanket?"

"We covered Mr. Webberly with a picnic blanket. I held it while Flick took photos, then we draped it back over him."

It was Isabella's explanation, but all three men looked at Flick.

"Mr. Webberly's state didn't bother you, Miss Sherborne? You are enured to such scenes?"

"No, Inspector, I am not enured. The photographs bothered me much more than I realized. I had trouble sleeping last night. I expect I will again today, after spending the morning working on the prints. I don't—I take photos of orchids and topiaries. I'm not a newshound. But these photos, they seemed a necessity."

"And necessity drives," Isabella said while the sergeant nodded and the inspector stared at the courier envelope. "Will that be all, gentlemen?" she asked, and Flick thanked God that Isabella wanted this meeting over. "I'm cold. We were heading back to the pub."

"We can find you at the Hook and Line this evening? We will have more questions about yesterday, I'm afraid."

"We gave statements to the constable after Sir Robert Goodkind interrogated us."

"Flick, it was hardly an interrogation."

She didn't choose to apologize. She watched the inspector.

He gave a small smile, directed to Isabella although he turned the last of it on Flick. "I know you would rather commit yesterday to the past, over and done with, but I don't let other people run my investigations. The constable took quite a number of preliminary statements yesterday. The sergeant and I must repeat all of them. I'll let you ladies return to the pub and warm yourselves by the fire and sip a hot toddy. We have a crime scene and evidence," he lifted the courier envelope, "to review. Until the evening, Mrs. Tarrant, Miss Sherborne."

The sergeant touched a finger to his hat. Constable Amsley nodded.

Then the three men strode past, the constable giving directions as he hastened to keep up with the other men's longer strides.

Flick refused to watch them enter the Crossing, but something in her drove her to glance at the men as she stowed her tote in the back floorboard.

They had stopped at the first steps descending to the formal garden. The headmaster had met them. Standing just in view, as if he'd come from the Prior's House, was Gilchrist.

Flick slid behind the steering wheel. Neither woman spoke until the auto exited the gates and turned onto the narrow road. Only then did she cleared her throat. "Are they always like that?"

"Like what?"

An artist saw in minute detail what people wanted to hide. She tried to keep her face composed, her voice steady—but her fingers trembled where they gripped the steering wheel. "Like that. They started friendly. That sergeant teased you. Then their questions became probing."

"They do have an investigation, Flick. We *are* suspects. At this point, everyone is. *We* know we didn't do it. You need to get over your fear of being a suspect and decide to help. I thought that was the reason you took the photos, to help the investigation."

"I did. I do want to." Yet an unknown fear clutched her throat, like a wild animal in the fanged clutch of a wolf.

"You're not used to being in a murder investigation."

"Of course not."

"Few people are. This is my third."

"Third?" She glanced over before she could stop herself and quickly looked back at the road. The days had started lengthening, but twilight still came rapidly in late February. She couldn't see Isabella's face. She watched the passing trees, the macadam stretching before the Calcott's hood. Then she remembered everything she knew of Isabella and her husband and their backgrounds and felt foolish. "Oh, you mean the murder at Emberley and the one at the archaeological dig. Were you a suspect in those investigations?"

"Yes and no," and as Isabella explained, they reached the village.

Flick left her auto standing in the courtyard and followed Isabella into the pub.

Isabella was obviously not a suspect in the minds of the inspector and the sergeant. And she was Flick's alibi for the time of the murder.

Yet that wolf still had her by the throat, waiting to bite down.

.~.~.~.

As he led the way to the path behind the maze, the headmaster introduced himself as Dean Filmer and talked rapidly—nervously, Michael judged—about Greavley Abbey's history and the school. When they arrived at the river path, he refused to trod a step off the grassy verge that surrounded the maze, the ground associated with the woods contaminated in his mind. "The constable accompanies you. Surely you no longer need my guidance. Our games master has attempted to intercept any boys wandering into the woods. He has directed them to use the road if they wish to walk along the river.

MacAlphin has also placed one of his older men at the approach from the river. The site should be as the constable left it."

"The path goes to the river?"

"Intersects with the river path," the constable hastened to say. "Many people use that path rather than the road. It's quicker."

"To where does it lead?"

"To the village, at the Hook and Line, then it broadens out, becomes part of the village green. 'T'other way it just meanders, connecting all the farms."

"Thank you, Constable," Filmer said, as if he were in charge. "I have traversed these paths myself but not in recent days. Last summer, I would think was the last time, walking to the pub on a fine moonlit evening. One has to return, you know. I usually drive."

"Are there other pubs in the village?"

Again Filmer answered. "Not in Upper Wellsford. Lower Wellsford has several uncouth establishments. If you have no more need of my guidance—." With the words he turned away.

"In your statement," Michael said, which stopped the dean's retreat, "you said that you did not see George Webberly on Sunday."

"I rarely see any of the teaching masters after the Sunday service. They have their appointed rotation of duties given to them after the Saturday games. One tries to be fair. My secretary, Mr. Dunley, will have a copy of the rotation through February. After four o'clock on Saturday, unless a master has a Sunday duty, they are free until morning chapel on Monday."

"Webberly was free?" He waited until Filmer bent enough to give a nod. "And he did not attend the Sunday service?"

"As I said."

"Did you observe any other teaching masters absent from the service?"

"Mr. Alexander, the games master, was absent, but he had injured his knee during the final match on Saturday. He does not habitually attend since he is agnostic. Everyone assigned a duty was present. As I said, my secretary will have the roster for the month."

"Is it possible for any one to leave the service?"

The dean sighed heavily. "A few masters have a smoke outside during the service, but they return to finish their duty."

"Would you know if any one of them absented himself for longer? Or returned mere minutes before the end of the service?"

Filmer frowned, obviously perturbed by the continued questions. "My attention is on the sermon. The beadle will know that answer."

"The beadle?" Callaway asked. He hadn't taken any notes, but at that he flipped open his notebook. "Now who would that be?"

"The man would be on the roster."

"You don't remember."

"I believe Master Sherborne served as beadle, but I would not swear to it. I do know the boys were well behaved. Sherborne can quell outbreaks with a glare. He's turned into a good master."

"You sound surprised."

"We are fortunate in his employment. He intended for the church, you know. The war derailed that."

"You are surprised Mr. Sherborne became a good master. Why is that?"

"Webberly wasn't. Alexander had a few problems at the beginning. Mr. Farrell settled in quickly, but some of the boys didn't want to interact with an Irishman. They had to be spoken to. I believe they knew of family members harmed by Free Staters. They questioned if Mr. Farrell had participated in the conflict there. He reassured them that he had only recently been demobbed and that he had served as a medic during the late war. One does not expect political unrest to reach into the forms."

He wondered the reason that Filmer told so much about this man Farrell and avoided Webberly and Alexander. "How would you describe Webberly as a master?"

"Late with starting classes. Late with marking translations. Often absent or neglectful when he monitors the boys at their conning information and practice drills. He knew his subject—he was our Latin master—but he didn't use the prescribed translation. He claimed that answers to the documents used previous to his arrival had been handed down from the older boys. He wanted all new texts to assess what the boys had actually learned, an investment of money that I deemed excessive. Webberly implied that the previous Latin master had not realized the fault and advanced boys not capable of a higher level."

"That had to cause dissension with the former Latin master. If that person is still employed."

"Westbrook Neville now has the sole responsibility of letters."

A neat sidestep about dissension. "Did arguments occur between Webberly and any other master?" Michael pressed.

Filmer didn't want to answer. His mouth primmed, like an old prune. His gaze darted away. He crossed his arms. Callaway kept his pencil poised. Constable Amsley stood at rest, but his whole attention was on the dean.

"Dean Filmer? Would you answer my question?"

"Arguments occurred, in the common room and in planning sessions in my office."

"What stance did you take?"

"We will not demote any boy approved for a higher form. Webberly did not like that stance. Master Neville approved. That increased the dissension in the common room."

"Have any other teaching masters had arguments with Webberly?"

"None have come to my attention."

Which didn't mean that no arguments had occurred. "I would like to interview this Westbrook Neville." Michael addressed Callaway, who would already have noted the name. He knew his sergeant. He said it mainly for Dean Filmer, so the headmaster would not interfere.

"Greavley Abbey School is at the service of Scotland Yard. Now, Inspector, Mr. Webberly must be quickly replaced. I have many letters to compose to teaching agencies. You must excuse me." Dean Filmer strode away, the sleeves of his black gown and the ends of his colors flapping in the rising breeze.

"He avoided answering your questions." The constable looked concerned. "Sir, you should have pressed him to answer."

"Callaway will have noted the questions Filmer avoided."

"*And* the ones that he pretended to answer but didn't," his sergeant added. He flipped his notebook closed and stored his pencil. "That Webberly sounds like a right piece of work. Think we'll find evidence of more arguments between him and this Neville and other masters?"

Michael shrugged. "What I think is that this Neville and Webberly may have come to blows, and that's how Filmer became involved. He would have avoided any involvement unless pressed into action."

"I didn't think the upper crust resorted to blows." The constable sounded unsure. Michael hoped the young man had realized those first statements didn't contain enough information.

"Masters of the cut direct," Callaway said, repeating something Michael had said a couple of months ago. "You going to contact your War Office source for information about this Irishman Farrell?"

"If necessary. I'll ask about this man Alexander and Mr. Sherborne at the same time. I want to wait, to see if any other veterans' names arise."

Callaway grunted. "Where's this crime scene, Amsley?"

Deep under the trees, the dried grass and vines along the path were trampled, no doubt by Amsley, Sir Robert Goodkind, the doctor, and the ambulance men.

After a close inspection of the ground, marked unnecessarily by a handkerchief tied to a stiff bramble cane, Callaway straightened. "Blood stains not washed by the rain. Soaked into the ground. So much that last night's rain didn't wash it all away. Can't see the patches along the path that you noted, Constable."

He had gone past them and pointed at a couple of areas. "Rain got rid of it, sir. Made like a trail, getting fainter and fainter, heading for the river. It was quite clear yesterday."

"Webberly? Staggering after he got hit?"

"Stay here, Constable. Callaway, with me."

They walked the path to the river and stood on the bank, looking at the longer trail that the path intersected, studying along the riverbanks. Sweeps of grass just above the waterline gave evidence of the rain-swollen river, abated now. Farther along, toward the village, a man stood on the bank, a fishing line trailing into the water.

"That river's convenient. Whatever got used," Callaway said heavily, "it'll be at the bottom of the river. Reckon the murder was planned?"

"Premeditated?" Michael clenched the fists he'd shoved into his overcoat pockets. "Fits. A meeting in the woods, far enough in that no one can see. A weapon at hand, easily disposed of. No one to see Webberly go into the woods and not come out. No one to see our murderer, either. Nothing that points to the murderer, Callaway."

"We may need luck, boss."

Chapter 16

Monday Afternoon

Michael stared at the woodbine and weeds that choked the riverbanks. "Callaway, we need to check along the riverbanks."

"I'll see it done, boss. Both sides?"

"I think we do not need to worry about the far side. Or anywhere close to the village."

"Do you think we need to drag the river, boss?" Callaway was watching the current speed toward the village. "I can call for a team."

"We'll wait on that, sergeant. Any stick with a weighted head would sink immediately. If the murderer threw the weapon in, it's not going anywhere. Our problem is determining if the weapon is in the river and where. If we head into next week without any result, then we'll consider dragging the river."

He watched the river's flow, increased after last night's rain, then looked downriver. The bridge that crossed at the village was out of sight, behind the stand of willows leaning over the water.

He hadn't expected a straight-forward case. Even when he discovered the murderer quickly, he needed to untangle all motives that kept the Crown prosecutor willing to pursue conviction. The only straightforward case Michael had encountered involved a robbery turned deadly, and that was in the first months as bagman for the detective inspector who'd trained him, before the war changed the world.

Michael sent Constable Amsley to search upriver before he turned back and followed the river path to the village. He would meet them at the pub. Michael and Callaway walked downriver until they encountered the Rowing Shed.

A crew of boys stood on the dock, oars in hand as they listened to a man about Michael's age. Sculls tugged at the lines, wanting to go with the water. The games master noticed them but kept talking to the boys. As they neared, the man gave instructions about the speed of the river as well as stopping before the bridge. He set them to their sculls, four boys to each scull, then turned to meet them.

"I say, you must be the Scotland Yard men." He greeted them chin tilted up, emphasizing his square jaw. The wind ruffled his brown hair, lightened at the tips but showing brown at the winter-grown roots.

"And you must be Master Alexander."

A splash drew his gaze. He watched a boy retrieving his oar. "That one will never learn balance. Coach Alexander, yes." He glanced at them. "And you are?"

"This is Detective Inspector Wainwright. I'm his sergeant, Callaway. This is your first year at Greavley Abbey?"

"First year, yes."

"What did you do before?"

The man grimaced. "War."

"And before that, sir?"

"I coached at Cambridge. We won the Boat Race in '14."

"When were you demobbed?"

"June last year. Filmer hired me in August."

"Prior to your hiring, did you know anyone here? Did you discover a common connection after your arrival?"

Alexander set his arms akimbo, hands against the ribbed band of his navy cardigan. "No and no. Everyone was new to me."

"Where did you serve in the war?"

He looked uncomfortable. "I flew a Bristol F.2 then a S.E.5."

"RAF?" Michael asked, taking charge of the questions. "You saw heavy fighting then."

"Don't like to talk about it."

"We don't need your war experiences. What relationship did you have with George Webberly?"

"Relationship? None. We weren't friendly." He glanced at the rowers who struggled to direct their sculls in the rapidly moving river. The first two boats were already out of sight. "I didn't like Webberly. I'm not saying he was a lie factory, but he'd pulled the wool over Filmer's eyes. Neville said he'd be gone before the term ended. That might be because Neville did him in. I don't know. I'm not interested in arguments in the common room. I'm not often there."

He described a deliberately lonely life. "What are you interested in, Mr. Alexander? How do you spend your free time?"

"I have correspondence."

"You have a wide range of friends that you write to every evening?"

"If you must know, I'm writing a memoir cum history cum guidebook."

"Of your war experiences?"

"Of sculling. Is that all? I need to gather the boys who landed in the village."

"One more question. Where were you during the church service yesterday?"

"I'm agnostic," he said quickly, as if that answered the question. Michael waited. Alexander added, "I don't attend the service. I only attend the feast-day services when Filmer demands that we all attend."

"That doesn't answer my question."

"I was rowing. I row every evening and three times on Sunday, morning, early afternoon, late afternoon. I'm games master. It's impossible to row on Saturday. I hope to compete at the Regatta and the Summer Olympics in Belgium. Single rower."

"Intense," Callaway muttered when they had released the games master and headed on the graveled road back to the Abbey School. "No wonder he's rail-thin."

They came to the Masters' Lodgings, and both checked the distance to the maze. Close, very close. Not three minutes' walk. The teaching hall came next, three storied with tall windows, interrupted at the floors. The building didn't match the Gothic construction of the Masters' Lodgings, echoed in the manor and in its first iteration in the church and its attached dormitory. At the doors, stone carvers had attempted the flamboyant style of the Prior's House, but the windows were narrow and unadorned, depending on symmetrical repetition of a plain style.

The church's bell tolled the hour. In a bare minute boys flooded out of the teaching hall, heading for their dormitory, chattering loudly as they scurried along.

"I'm thinking we need a schedule for the weekday and an idea of the weekend activites. We also need that roster of boys at the service and the masters' duties at the church service. What was the name of that secretary?" Callaway flipped open his notebook, not pocketed after their interview of Alexander. "Dunley," he answered himself.

As they mounted the steps to the carved door of the Prior's House, it opened and the major domo filled the threshold. "Gentlemen." He didn't move.

Michael stopped, letting Callaway do the work. "We're Scotland Yard," the sergeant said. "D.I. Wainwright. I'm Sgt. Callaway."

"Sir." The man looked straight at Michael.

"The headmaster gave us to understand that we could conduct interviews here."

"If the dean wishes it so, then it shall be so." Yet he still didn't move.

"We sent notification to Westbrook Neville and Chauncey Sherborne that we wished to speak with them. Have they arrived?"

"Both masters have made themselves available for the requested interviews. They await you in the library."

"We would need to interview them separately." Callaway dropped his geniality whenever he grew impatient. When that stony voice emerged, he harked to the brawler that Michael suspected he'd been before he entered the force.

"A moment." Michael gestured downward, a sign for the sergeant. He mounted a step, and Callaway slid over, ceding it to him. "Mr. Gilchrist, isn't it? Do you have something to tell us?" With the barest hesitation, he added, "How well did you know George Webberly?"

"Sir. I was not acquainted with him. Before yesterday, I personally knew only his position here at Greavley." He spoke precisely, slowly, each word given its significance.

"As Latin Master. Which Dean Filmer admitted caused dissension with the former Latin master, Westbrook Neville."

"As you say, sir. I am not privy to any altercation between them."

"But you know of it. May we enter?"

Gilchrist fell back. Once they stood in the parqueted hall, he swept the door closed. Turning to them, his face impassive, he droned, "Complaints do not funnel through me to the headmaster. The proper procedure routes complaints through his secretary, Frederick Dunley."

"Is he available?"

"Mr. Dunley has not yet left for the day. He is assisted this afternoon by Miss Collinsworth, personal secretary to Mrs. Filmer. As Mr. Dunley traveled to Bath for the weekend, Miss Collinsworth assisted Dean Filmer on Saturday and Sunday."

"We would wish to speak to Miss Collinsworth."

"Not Mr. Dunley?"

"Tomorrow, perhaps. He has an alibi for the weekend. Would you convey our request to her? And to him?"

"When she has finished her consultation with Mr. Dunley, she will wish to leave. Her day ended at four o'clock. I will, however, inform her of your wish."

"Don't use the word *wish*, Gilchrist. She *will* see us today."

His silver-crowned head bent in assent. "I will inform her that she must speak with you before she leaves."

"You didn't see or hear any disagreements in the Masters' Lodgings. What did you know about them?" Refusing to let the majordomo hide behind words, Callaway was ready to write in his notebook.

"The general impression, sirs, is that Mr. Webberly enjoyed causing disruption in the masters' common area. He often interfered with discipline, one of the numerous ways he would undermine what he called the Old Guard. He was known for rudeness, often snoring loudly when one of the Old Guard would speak of plans or lessons."

Callaway wrote, touched the nib of his pencil to his tongue, then wrote again. "Who did he put in this Old Guard?"

"Any teaching master on staff prior to the war, sir. Mr. Dunley, even Miss Collinsworth would provide you with that list."

Gilchrist should be escorting them to the library, where Westbrook Neville and Chauncey Sherborne waited, but he continued to linger in the entrance. *Have we missed something?* Michael wondered. The major domo had carefully worded every answer, saying exactly what he intended, no more and no less. *Have we missed some point that this stiff man won't bring into the conversation but considers vital to convey? If only we knew the question he wanted us to ask.*

"Did Webberly enjoy causing dissension? Who else did he pester?"

Callaway had a bulldog persistence once he latched onto an idea, worrying information until he'd uncovered all the meat to be consumed.

The major domo never looked away from Michael. "I know Masters Sherborne and Neville had disagreements with Master Webberly."

Disagreements. Not altercations, the stronger word. Michael reckoned Gilchrist didn't think either Sherborne or Neville the murderer. "Anyone else?"

"Dodges detested him."

Detest. A much stronger word than dissension or argument.

"Dodges. That is the butler at the manor. Why did Dodges detest him?

"Mr. Farrell has that answer, sir."

"Who is Mr. Farrell?" He couldn't recall. Callaway was flipping back in his notebook. The name had also escaped his recall.

"Mr. Miles Farrell is the school's medical officer. Mr. Farrell started with Greavley Abbey School in September. He replaced our former nurse, Matron Berrycloth, who was greatly admired. The boys were not hesitant to see her for their little ills."

"You call this Farrell the medical officer."

"He is not Board qualified as a nurse. He served as a medic for his army service. An orderly who received additional training to attach to a trench unit. I have not heard specifics of such a position, sir. I do know that at other times, Mr. Farrell served in field hospitals."

"Is Miles Farrell available for an interview?"

"I shall see, sir."

Between dragging information out question by question and answering obscurely rather than directly, the major domo had tried Callaway's patience. He snapped his notebook shut but managed to reserve whatever words he wanted to snap out. Michael intervened. "Mr. Gilchrist, we need to have our interviews now. Which way is the library?"

Gilchrist slowly stepped back. He turned on his heel and led them down a side hall. Several doors opened to the left. To the right, the front side, one door centered the long wall while another door opened very close to the exterior door ahead.

Did we continue to miss the question that Gilchrist wanted asked? Or is his manner commonly so reserved and slow?

As the major domo opened the door, revealing a room with tall bookcases, they heard heels click on the parqueted floor. "That will be Miss Collinsworth, sir, leaving for the day. I trust you will make your own introductions to Masters Neville and Sherborne while I convey your wish for an interview to Miss Collinsworth."

"And send for Miles Farrell. They can wait outside the library."

The tall shelving under the windows were filled with spine-faded books. Stained glass quotations topped the individual windows, and the last of the sunlight cast pretty colors about the room. Scattered about the open space were long tables, each with three chairs, all facing the door. Beside the door was an elevated desk with a three-drawer cabinet, holding the various accouterments, file cards, stamps and a metal tin for an inked pad, no less than three pencil cups, and four stacks of thick books, not high but definitely worthy of scholarship. Wrapping the three interior walls, a balcony ran along the upper shelves, those books' spines not weathered and therefore newer. Two spiral staircases, one each side of the door, gave access to the balcony.

The sight of the library, the smell of old books and new ones, the faint odor of ink used and pencils sharpened, transported Michael back to his school days.

Westbrook Neville and Chauncey Sherborne sat with a chair between at the table immediately facing the door. Neville had a glistening mane of white air. He had folded his arms across his chest, a classic defense to close himself off. One knee jigged up and down constantly. The young man betrayed his nerves with fists on his knees, only visible as they came into the room. He had the same dark hair and pale Celtic skin as his sister Felicity Sherborne. Although their faces matched, the young man's had a stark angular cast, emphasizing his masculine structure while hers was a little more rounded.

Michael crossed to the table, Callaway at his elbow. The sergeant detoured to fetch two chairs from another table. "Gentlemen, I am Detective Inspector Michael Wainwright, and—."

"We know who you are," the older man interrupted. "Why are we here?"

"We wish to interview you."

"What direction will your questions take?"

Chauncey Sherborne snorted. "You know that, too, Neville. Of everyone here at Greavley, we two had the most grievances against Webberly."

The older man leaned back. "He was merely a colleague. We had differences of opinion, nothing more. You owed him money, Sherborne. Gambling with him, weren't you?"

Neville had thrown Sherborne under the bus. Why had he? Distraction, certainly. What more? Michael studied the older man.

"Those were friendly games." Sherborne smiled as Michael took one chair and Callaway plopped onto the other, his notebook already out, his pencil already scribbling. Michael might have believed that calm explanation if he hadn't seen those clenched fists. "Poker," Sherborne added. "Picked it up in the trenches."

"You served with Webberly?"

"No. He was in Italy, wasn't he? I was in North France. We did not meet until our arrival here. Our service gave us a connection, that's all."

Michael had intended to question them separately. He still would, *later, when I know more about this whole situation.* "Yet you had altercations?"

Sherborne shrugged, a stiff movement rather than one with ease. "He wanted paid. We draw our pay once a month. I ran a little short last month and this one, too. Unexpected expenses over the holidays. We settled our differences, though. We had dinner together with my sister and another lady on Saturday night, at the Hook and Line."

"Was the other lady Mrs. Madoc Tarrant?"

"It was. I don't really know her. Nice lady, though. She ignored Webberly's attempts to flirt."

"Did Webberly do that often? Flirt with the ladies?" He was glad to hear that his former captain's bride had ignored Webberly.

"He fancied himself a ladies' man."

"Did he flirt with your sister?"

Sherborne grimaced. He glanced at Neville. Scooting his chair more inches from the table, he crossed his legs. "He tried, the first time she visited. Flick wasn't interested. She's no fool, for all she's five years younger."

Michael wasn't successful at hiding his own grimace. Chauncey Sherborne called his sister no fool, yet she'd gone to dinner and dancing with Alan Rettleston. He wondered if they'd attended a party after. Rettleston crowed about his acquaintance with the racier of the young Blue Bloods in London. The man would *look* for a decadent party to attend.

He shook his head to cast those ideas out of his head. The case needed his focus. One question about Felicity Sherborne crept in. "When did your sister first visit?"

"October." He uncrossed his legs and leaned forward, casting a look at Callaway with his notetaking before glaring at Wainwright, his protective instincts about his sister riled. "Look, dangle whatever idea you've got about Flick. She didn't have anything to do with knocking off Webberly. I invited Webberly to dinner, partly to use his auto, partly because he was pressing me for the money I owed. I knew Flick didn't like him. She didn't kill him." He leaned back, tapping his fingertips on the library table. "She couldn't. She and Mrs. Tarrant and I were at the church service when Webberly was murdered."

"You three can alibi each other?"

"I served as beadle. Ask the vicar. Look at Filmer's damned rotation of duties. I stood behind all the pews to keep watch on the boys. Flick was always with Mrs. Tarrant."

"From your description, it sounds like only at the back of the church would someone be able to alibi you."

"Because I served as beadle," he repeated, the words so curt that Michael wondered how easily the young man would lose patience. "I was there from the opening prayer to the bitter benediction."

"And you, Mr. Neville?"

"I attended the church service."

"You had no duties? Were you present for the entire service?" The man merely nodded. Michael wanted a spoken answer. He decided to press his chief point. "You and Mr. Webberly had many altercations. About the money you owed? About the arguments he caused in the common room?"

Chauncey Sherborne had scooted his chair away from the table. He obviously considered his interview ended. He had re-crossed one leg over the other, and the crossed foot swung easily, a vivid argyle pattern revealed. Westbrook Neville shifted uneasily, but he kept his gaze dropped. "George Webberly lorded it over us that he now taught all the Latin classes."

"I understand that he implied your instruction of Latin was lacking."

That angered the senior master. His head came up. His smile was no smile, more a sneer. "Webberly liked to create problems. He was good at that. When you have interviewed enough people, Inspector, you will discover that I also have an alibi. Everyone saw me at the church service. I sat directly behind Dean Filmer and his wife. You should interview her. Verna Filmer left the service, for a good half-hour. The entirety of communion. I doubt her discomfort had more to the do with pablum rather than the vicar's topic."

"Does Mrs. Filmer often leave the church service?"

"She does not."

"Did you see her leave, Mr. Sherborne?"

"No. I had to deal with an issue. I saw her return."

"Had you seen her earlier? Before the service?"

"She didn't acknowledge me." The young man gave a cheerful grin. "I'm low in the hierarchy, not worthy of her notice."

"Did you see her earlier?" Michael repeated patiently.

"Over an hour before the service started. I was returning from my run. I had a late start this morning. We—my sister and Mrs. Tarrant and I—we were out late Saturday night, driving around."

"Did you notice anything about her appearance?"

"I didn't notice. I needed to clean up."

"Her hair was mussed," Neville interjected, "when she returned. I stared at it long enough, before she left the service and after her return. Like her hat had fallen off, and she replaced it without a mirror." He looked smug. "By that, I surmised she hadn't returned to the manor. She has mirrors in every room. Sherborne, do you think she would have killed Webberly?" He asked the question before Michael could intervene, and he ran with the idea. "They had argued earlier. I heard them on my morning constitutional, which I do every Sunday an hour before the service. She was angry with him. I heard someone bludgeoned Webberly. Could Verna Filmer have murdered him?"

"I'm asking the questions, Mr. Neville," Michael said calmly. "Please allow me to do so. You and Mr. Sherborne may speculate later."

Sherborne didn't look like he wanted to speculate with Neville.

The door opened behind him. "Sir." That was Gilchrist. *What does he have for us?*

"Gentlemen, our first interview is concluded. I will wish you to answer more questions. You should remain available for interview, here at Greavley or in the village."

"Are we suspects?" Neville huffed.

"For the moment, you are witnesses. Thank you for your cooperation."

The older man stood, his chair scraping back on the wood flooring. "*Witnesses*. I can name a half-dozen who should be suspects." He stalked around the table and headed for the door, Sherborne at his heel.

Callaway looked up from his notes. "Interview with the vicar, boss?"

"Yes, that will be necessary. I also want to discover who else knew about the argument and Mrs. Filmer's departure from the service." Callaway wrote as Michael turned to the major domo. "Are Miss Collinsworth and Mr. Farrell available?"

"She awaits, sir. He has not yet arrived."

"Show her in."

"As you wish, sir."

The woman who entered wore a fawn flannel jacket buttoned over a white ruffled blouse and a tweed skirt of a length acceptable before the war. The black T-strap heels clicked on the flooring, successfully drawing eyes, and Michael gauged their height and the stocking seams. The secretary disguised herself as demure, but those shoes revealed an inner flash. He raised his gaze to her plain hat with its vibrant tri-color braid as she seated herself. She'd dressed her hair in a plain bun, but its brassy color wasn't natural. She was well past her first bloom. His age, he reckoned, and fighting it.

He and Callaway resumed their chairs. The sergeant gave Michael a narrow look, as if to say, *See what we've got here.*

Michael studied her as Callaway took her particulars of age and employment and address.

"Are you from this area originally?" Callaway asked. She stared. He looked up from his notebook. "Miss Collinsworth?"

"London, originally and recently."

"Which area?"

"I moved about."

"How did you come to Upper Wellsford?"

"Dean Filmer hired me from an agency. I stayed because I like the work. Is this an interrogation?" she demanded. "I do not come to the school at all on Sundays. In no way do I have any information about this scandalous murder."

Her choice of *scandalous* intrigued him. If the press appeared, would she be a source for them? "When did you last see Mr. Webberly?"

"Saturday. He participated in the games against the older boys. One of them kept knocking him down. Targeting him, Dean Filmer said, but he didn't intervene. You should question that boy."

"Who was it?"

"How should I know? I am employed by Mrs. Filmer. I do not interact with the students."

"Never?"

Mouth compressed, Miss Collinsworth glared at the single word that questioned her statement. She glanced at Callaway, watching her rather than taking notes, then turned her baleful gaze back on Michael. "I might encounter a boy when Mrs. Filmer sends me here with a message or when the dean chooses to enlist my time in his office, whenever Mr. Dunley is not present."

"Do you stand in for Mr. Dunley often?"

"No. He does not often press for days off, and he is rarely sick. I had to replace him for a couple of weeks last autumn, when he was sick, but he quickly recovered." Her Received Pronunciation accent faltered a little, revealing a London clip that had nothing to do with the upper class. She quickly controlled it. Her words became sharp, clear, exact. "Mrs. Filmer was displeased that her husband required my services. I was displeased with the smelly boys who came to his office. Mr. Farrell should not have sent them."

"Then you have had occasion to interact with students?"

"If I am substituting for Mr. Dunley. I would not call any of those times an *interaction*. I take their names. I send them into the dean when he buzzes."

"For what reason do the boys come to the dean's office?" He had never seen his old headmaster in his office.

"Discipline. The masters will send them."

"Like Mr. Farrell?"

She leaned back. Her hostility lessened. "I do know that he intervenes between the boys and the masters. The boys often seek him out before they reach the headmaster's office."

"Had Mr. Farrell intervened in the discipline of the boy who knocked Mr. Webberly down during the games?"

She frowned at him, at Callaway. Her eyes rolled heavenward.

"Lord, how should I know that?"

"Did Webberly speak to the dean about the boy after the match ended?"

Her look became pitying. "Are you desperate for suspects, to be asking me that? I would have no idea. I didn't remain for the end of the match. I returned to the office and locked up for the day. The dean said he would make any necessary notes later."

"Did you like Webberly?"

The question's sudden turn didn't faze her. He wondered how much experience Miss Collinsworth had with police grilling. She certainly had no fear and little respect for either him or Callaway.

"No. He did not like me. He liked them young or with money."

"Like Mrs. Filmer?"

"You said it, not I."

"Mrs. Pollard?"

She shrugged.

"Who else? Without money?"

"The maid at the bar. The one who works mornings so she's free for him at night. I'm waiting to hear about the catfight when Mrs. Pollard decides to draw her boundary lines."

"Mrs. Pollard and Mrs. Filmer? Or Mrs. Pollard and the bar maid?"

"Either. Both." She gave a little smile, more of a smirk. "Are these the only questions you have of me? I have a long walk to my home. Nightfall comes early, and I don't like walking the road at night."

"Do you live in Upper Wellsford?"

"I do not. I'm in the opposite direction. May I leave?"

"A few more questions, Miss Collinsworth. We can see to your transport to your home."

"I'd rather walk than ride with you bulls. No offense intended."

Michael bowed his head. "None taken."

Callaway coughed his disagreement.

"We were told that complaints were filed against Webberly."

"I told you that I don't work in the headmaster's office. I'm employed by his wife."

"I think you would have kept your ears open for any gossip. Tell us what you know."

She sighed. "You were talking to the man who filed the most of the complaints."

"Westbrook Neville."

"Of course."

"Why of course?"

She gave a look that questioned Michael's intelligence. "Mr. Webberly showed him up as a Latin master. He didn't care who knew it. He liked his little digs. Mr. Neville retaliated with tricks, just like a boy, and it escalated from there."

"Tricks?"

"I'll be missing my tea," she complained before she answered. "Mr. Neville turned an uncapped ink bottle upside down on Mr. Webberly's plans. He opened the windows in his rooms and let the wind blow everything around. He did it again when it was raining. Hid test papers, marked or unmarked. Put tacks in his chair. That sort of thing. Mr. Dunley said either Mr. Webberly or Mr. Neville filed a complaint every week we were in session. You should talk to Mr. Dunley, not me."

"Where were you yesterday?"

"Visiting my parents in Chalmsley. I took the late train on Saturday. I returned on the last train Sunday. The station master will remember. Now are we finished?"

"One more question, Miss Collinsworth. The reason that you are hostile to the police?"

"I'm not."

"You certainly give that impression," and Callaway humphed in agreement.

"I do not like my life interfered with. This is an interference. I would be home by now."

His sergeant leaned back, giving her the fish eye, Michael figured. "You may leave, Miss Collinsworth. We would not discommode you further."

"Right-O," Callaway said and grinned at the woman.

She sniffed, opened her mouth then shut it, then stood up and walked quickly, clickingly, to the door.

His sergeant waited until she passed through the door then murmured, "She's not going to walk home, not in those heels. You want I should see who picks her up?"

"If you can."

Chapter 17

Monday Afternoon

As Callaway hustled out, the major domo appeared. "Sir, Mr. Farrell has gone to the village."

"Do you know when he left?"

"I believe a half-hour ago. Shall I ring Mr. Pollard at the Hook and Line and inform him that you wish to interview Mr. Farrell?"

"You think Farrell's gone to the Hook and Line?"

"He often visits that pub. The ones in Lower Wellsford are distant."

"We'll locate him ourselves when we return to the pub. Your assistance is appreciated." Especially after Miss Collinsworth.

Gilchrist hesitated at the door, but when Michael looked a question, expecting more, the major domo gave that regal incline of his head and retreated.

Michael didn't wait for Callaway at the Prior's House but left the building and slowly walked to the forecourt. Boys moved past, angling across the quadrant, walking slowly along the cloister, leaning together against the dormitory.

He met his sergeant at the auto.

"She hopped a lorry that was waiting for her past the gates, near the bend."

"Waiting for her?"

"Stopped on the verge. Revved the engine a bit when I got past the gate, but he didn't engage gear until she slammed the door on the cab."

"Do you think they saw you watching?"

"She didn't look 'round. I wasn't in view of his mirrors, or I would have seen his face." He paused. When Michael didn't ask more, he offered, "Bit of a minute to ring headquarters, boss. I can put in an inquiry for a brassy-haired woman in her thirties, missing from London since the autumn. Any arrests under the name Collinsworth. Or variants, like Collins or Worth, Lindsworth or Longsworth."

"Do you think that she may have a convicted family member? Is that the reason for her hostility?" Michael considered it, but then he considered the time wasted on the search. "No. It's an interesting question, but we would waste valuable time and resources pursuing that question. Miss Collinsworth is not a suspect. She can produce an alibi. I doubt someone came to the Abbey with the specific intent of murdering Webberly."

"You know those London gangs, boss. Some of 'em don't need a reason for mayhem. We know they've got a long reach outside London."

"At first look, Callaway, this isn't a London job. The motive is here. The murderer is here."

"At the Abbey School? In the village?"

"We've barely considered what we have, and already we have several good suspects. I'd like to explore their motives. Ask more questions. Find more answers here before we reach for a farflung perpetrator."

"Right-O. Where to, then? The Masters' Lodgings? Or back to the Hook and Line, to talk to this Miles Farrell?"

"We need a statement from the vicar. We'll have that before we go to the pub and see Farrell." He lifted the courier envelope. "Then we'll look at these photographs. Find out what they tell us."

. ~ . ~ . ~ .

Flick ran upstairs to her room, desperate to shed the weighty camera before supper.

Isabella ventured through the pub, not as crowded this evening. In rolled shirt sleeves and suspenders, Mr. Pollard leaned on the bar, talking to Mr. Sandhurst. She paused to greet them before she pushed wide the swinging door.

Her appearance surprised a man and woman in intimate conversation. She halted. A mental flash reminded her of Mrs. Pollard and George Webberly … but she was in London and he was dead.

And this woman wore a sunny yellow dress covered by a white apron.

Before she could retreat, the man straightened, and she recognized Constable Amsley. He'd shed his official helmet, but his navy coat was still double-buttoned. "Mrs. Tarrant."

"Constable. Sibby," she added, now that she saw the maid's face.

"Did you see the detective inspector?" Sibby wanted to know. Her hand had dropped from the constable's chest to entwine with his. *Claiming her territory.*

"I did, and I know him. He's my husband's former commander. Sibby, do you think a spot of tea is possible? I'm chilled."

"It's that cold, I'm surprised you're not over all ice. Go into the lounge. I lit the fire earlier. The room should have warmed. I'll bring the tea in a moment."

"And a cup for Miss Sherborne as well, please. Good evening, Constable."

Two men had claimed the *fauteuils* near the fire. They stopped talking when she entered. "My apologies if I have interrupted." Only as she approached did she recognize Miles Farrell.

He had partly risen but sagged back into his seat when the other man made no effort to rise.

That man was Kenneth Elwen, sunk into the chair, still wearing his shabby coat and baggy trousers for fishing. "Mrs. Tarrant. How goes the painting?"

"No painting today, Mr. Elwen, just sketches, but the day went very well. My subject is more amiable than I expected. I'll think we'll manage a friendly relationship for this portrait. Sitting for a portrait can become tedious." She didn't try the joke about 'standing for a portrait'. "How was the fishing today?"

"No success. I should horn in on Sandhurst's spot tomorrow. He caught three today." He hauled himself up, using the chair arm for leverage and support. "I must change before dinner." He touched a finger to his forehead and hobbled out.

Mr. Farrell watched him with a measuring eye. His expression wasn't quite perplexity, wasn't quite a frown, but a melding of the two. Then he looked at Isabella, and he became all smiles. "I thought I saw you sketching the garden this afternoon."

"You did. Miss Sherborne has hired me to illustrate one of her garden articles. The plans of the formal garden and the maze."

"And you said the portrait is progressing?"

"Sketches for the pose and the background. Preliminary steps, of course, but I will prep the canvas tomorrow, and I may touch paint to it by Thursday, days ahead of my expectations. Mr. Malvaise and I settled on a plan much more quickly than I anticipated, and my sketches at the Rowing Shed will only need notes about sizes of oars and sculls."

"You said young Malvaise was amenable to the portrait." His comment was intended to sound interested, but his thoughts were clearly elsewhere.

On George Webberly's death? On Verna Filmer? Or on something else?

"Amiable. He is an amiable young man." She caught his flashing frown, quickly gone. "That surprises you?"

"I do not really know Edward Malvaise. He's in an upper form and doesn't come to me with complaints. I'm glad to hear that he behaved well."

Silence fell. Awkward silence. To break it, Isabella lunged into a tried-and-true conversation. "Have you had tea yet? Sibby is bringing a light one."

He stood. *Driven out by my attempt at conversation?* "My apologies for abandoning you, Mrs. Tarrant, but I'm in need of a pint. Multiple schoolboy ailments, and while I played nursemaid, I craved a strong ale."

Sibby passed him as she brought tea and a plate of biscuits and savory tarts. She poured a cup then passed it to Isabella. "There. That will warm you from the inside." She perched on the edge of a straight-backed chair that had somehow been left in the semicircle before the fire.

"You have news," Isabella guessed then sipped, closed her eyes in thankfulness, and sipped more, wanting to hold the cup close to bask in the steam. "You and the constable have certainly progressed."

Sibby's glow shone as bright as her dress under the serviceable apron that swallowed her thin form. "I have, all because of your advice. He walked me home, last night, and he came in for tea."

"Do tell." An ache for Madoc struck her breast. For a long second it hurt to breathe, then the ache died. *I should have gone with him. I miss him. Would it be possible to exchange my ticket for an earlier berth?* That was the best motivation for working diligently on the portrait. She already had an excellent start. Isabella reached for a biscuit and rested it on her saucer. "How long did he stay?"

"We talked for an hour!" she caroled, then reality thumped down. "Mind you, it was hard to get the first words out of him."

"How did you manage that?"

"I asked where he grew up. He's not from the Wellsford area, you know. He's only been here for two years, after the old constable died. The squire hired him. From Liverpool, of all places."

"Two years? Well before Armistice, then. Did he not serve?"

"Early on. He was wounded, and they disabled him. He never said what kind of wound it was, but he looks healthy to me. Healthy enough to wade into that fight at the brewery and take on men twice his size."

"A fight at the brewery? When did this happen?"

"Last spring. That's when I first noticed Freddy."

"Freddy? Constable Amsley?" *Freddy* didn't sound like a man that would wade into a fight. "Were you at the brewery?"

Sibby nodded. "Mr. Pollard pays better. Besides, now the men are coming back, the women are losing their jobs."

"More trouble coming for the brewery?"

"Freddy says not."

"Well. Sibby, you have certainly crossed the first hurdle. And perhaps the second and third since Constable Amsley came to see you here, long before the pub's closing time."

"Oh, he didn't come to see me." Sibby spoke guilelessly, too happy with results to think about slanting the truth. "He came to ask when Mrs. Pollard would return. He thinks that detective from Scotland Yard will want to question her. Along with Nuala."

Both women were involved with George Webberly. Would Michael Wainwright want to question Mrs. Filmer, too? "When *is* Mrs. Pollard expected? I don't remember, just that she went to London."

"Tomorrow afternoon." The maid stood and brushed her hands down the apron.

The lounge door opened, and Flick swept in with her long strides in those wide-legged trousers. "Tea? Perfect. I'm frozen."

Sibby clambered to her feet. "Will you want another pot of tea?"

"I think so," Isabella judged. "What do we have for tonight, without Mrs. Halsey?"

"Cottage pie."

"No sweet?" Flick sounded disappointed. "That may be good. Else, I shall get fat. Thank you, Sibby."

"I might find more biscuits," she hinted as she left.

Flick added coal to the fire then collapsed into a *fauteuil*. "I don't remember walking miles and miles, but I am exhausted. How did your time with Malvaise the Younger go?"

"Better than I wish. Flick, he clued me in to some Abbey School gossip. Did you know Webberly and a youth named Chevington were on the outs?"

"Another suspect? We already have Mesdames Filmer and Pollard, their husbands, and Nuala in addition to a harassing member of the Old Guard, and persons unknown. Do you think a woman could have struck those blows?"

" 'Hell hath no fury'," she quoted.

The door opened. Miles Farrell appeared. He carried his pint of ale and dropped into the other *fauteuil*. "Ladies. I have it on good word that you will soon have tea."

Isabella waved at the single savory tart that remained on the tea tray. He claimed it then leaned back, nibbling the crust.

Flick frowned, and Isabella wondered if she'd had her eye on the savory pastry. "Will you not miss Table at the school, Mr. Farrell?"

"Even without Mrs. Halsey, the pub fare is better than bangers and mash. That's on Table every Monday evening. We have cheese pudding on Tuesday," he stopped to groan dramatically, "cottage pie or shepherd's pie on Wednesdays—that's a treat, toad in the hole as the Thursday treat—which it's not, and a good stew on Saturday. The cooks surprise us for High Table. What brings you back to us, Miss Sherborne? Another visit with your brother?"

"Partly. I have a couple of garden features to write."

He sputtered. "What can you find in a garden in wintertime?"

"Topiaries," she said promptly.

"So you come to your brother's workplace and pester him while you're about your work."

"I say!" Flick sounded more hurt than angry. "Chauncey and I are close. He was gone for over five years. I'd like to re-connect with my brother, please."

"Didn't he stay with you in London, after he was demobbed? Before he came here? I would have thought you re-connected then."

She gave an inelegant snort. "He was scarcely interesting in re-connecting with family in those first weeks."

"I would think," Isabella said cautiously. Mr. Farrell's questions were like an interrogation, "that Flick's brother wanted to celebrate life in his first weeks in London. Evenings with his friends or parties with drinking and dancing, finding a girl to embrace against the cold dark."

Flick jerked. "Owl," she whispered, as if she saw a reason she hadn't seen before.

"I can see that," Mr. Farrell agreed. "That would re-integrate him."

A curious comment. "Do you know anyone who didn't re-integrate?"

"Not specifically, no."

"You served, Mr. Farrell? I didn't know that." Flick slung a leg over her knee and swung her leg. "Did you find it difficult to *re-integrate*?"

He swallowed ale. "I didn't really encounter what the men in the trenches did."

"What do you consider signs of a difficulty with re-integration?" Flick was terse. Miles Farrell had pinned a concern of hers, and Isabella remembered the little she'd let slip about Chauncey's problems.

"Nightmares," he answered promptly. "A lack of resumed friendships."

"Hard to do when those friends died," Flick murmured.

"True, some did, but not all of them. Former acquaintances may find themselves thrust into the friendship role. Drinking to excess. Abuse of medication to drown memories more than to escape pain. The drinking and the drugs will worsen the nightmares. Gambling to excess, beyond an ability to pay."

The door had opened as he enumerated his list. As he reached the end, Isabella realized the people had paused within the doorway, as if they didn't wish to disturb the conversation. She looked their way and saw Michael Wainwright and Sgt. Callaway. When she smiled a greeting, the sergeant returned her smile. Mr. Wainwright, however, was focused on Miles Farrell.

"My brother didn't gamble to excess," Flick defended. She hadn't noticed the investigators behind her. Nor had Mr. Farrell. "After everything he experienced, his nightmares are understandable. They lessened dramatically in the weeks that he stayed with me. Are you claiming he drinks to excess? Mr. Farrell, are you?"

"I did not specifically intend to catalog your brother's symptoms,

Miss Sherborne." He drank then said, "Sherby is not the only man of my acquaintance who has more than one of those symptoms." He saw Isabella's attention focused behind him and turned.

Flick had her call to arms for her brother. "I know that Chauncey enjoys the odd game of poker—."

Mr. Farrell's gaze returned to her. "He lost heavily to Webby."

"He always covered his debt."

"Not in the last month. I counseled him about that reckless disregard for the money he lost."

"In your meetings?" Isabella thought it wise to warn Flick. "Inspector, Sergeant, come join us. The bar maid Sibby promised to bring more tea and biscuits. If you're staying here, the cost of tea is included in your stay. I hope you remain until Wednesday, for Mrs. Halsey will return then. You must experience her excellent cooking."

Michael Wainwright joined her on the settee while Callaway took the straight-backed chair. "We are staying here. Tea will be most welcome. Sir, are you Miles Farrell of Greavley Abbey School?"

"I am," and he drank more ale.

"I am Detective Inspector Michael Wainwright of the Metropolitan Police. My sergeant, Trevor Callaway. We have questions for you, Mr. Farrell."

"Ask away." He seemed unconcerned, sipping at his ale then finishing the savory pasty. Isabella handed him a napkin. He took his time cleaning his crumbly fingers. Then he folded the napkin and held it. "Do you wish to ask your questions in private?"

"I think privacy is not necessary," the inspector said. "We have confirmed your whereabouts at the time of death. That's our chief concern."

Isabella rose. "I should prepare for dinner."

Michael smiled at her. "You need not leave on our account, Mrs. Tarrant."

When Sgt. Callaway glanced at his boss, Isabella realized his surprise at the comment. A strange undercurrent flooded over her. Michael Wainwright wanted her to stay.

Or he wanted Flick to stay.

But why?

He still carried the courier envelope that Flick had given him. No doubt he had questions.

Isabella settled back and folded her hands on her lap, composing herself to wait.

Chapter 18

Monday, Late Afternoon

Flick had prepared to leave with Isabella, but she had to lean back in her chair when Isabella resumed her seat. Why did the inspector want them to remain for his interview of Miles Farrell?

Maybe for the photographs.

He held the courier envelope with the photographs that she'd printed this morning. Hard work with Nigel Roberts leaning over her shoulder, monitoring her use of his equipment, the whole dark room familiar yet not familiar to her.

Miles Farrell had frowned. "Look here, inspector, how do you know where I was at the time of Webberly's death?"

"The vicar informed us that you attended the service at Abbey Church. You sat on the right, about the middle, on the outside aisle. He also said that you did not leave during the service."

"That's right." He rested his half-empty glass on the thick upholstery arm of the *fauteuil*. "I wasn't on duty for once, but I decided to stay at the School rather than venture abroad. Warm day. Good for spending it by the river."

"Did you have another reason to attend the service?"

The man's eyes flared. "Another reason?"

"I understand from the vicar that you do not attend unless you have a duty, nor do you take communion."

"I'm Catholic."

"So you wouldn't take communion in an Anglican church. Do you always go tramping?"

"Unless it's too cold."

"I understand other people had planned a picnic. Did you plan anything with anyone?"

Flick startled. *He's talking about us, Chauncey and Isabella and me.*

"No, but I didn't know the weather would be fine on Saturday evening. I plan my tramps then. I'd spent the day on the games field in the shivering cold. I didn't consider a hike at all."

"Perhaps another reason motivated you to attend the service on Sunday."

Farrell grimaced. "All right, I did. Someone wanted to talk with me. They told me minutes before the service. We bumped into each other in the forecourt." He gave a half-laugh that had no humor. "I'm known for my talks with people who have problems. Just today, in fact." He gestured to Isabella. "Mrs. Tarrant knows that I missed my lunch having a talk with Mr. Sherborne."

"You have talks with him often?"

"He has a few issues that still bother him."

"Like his gambling with George Webberly?"

Farrell's gaze collided with Flick's smoldering one. He cleared his throat. "That. And nightmares. He hasn't really found a friend or a confidante among his colleagues here."

"He didn't call George Webberly a friend?"

"More of rival, I suppose."

"A rival for Mrs. Filmer's affections?"

"Look here. I said nothing of that!"

Flick glanced at the inspector. His sergeant was scribbling rapidly in a little notebook. He flipped a page and wrote more. The inspector looked calm—except for his dark eyes. *Why does he remind me of a falcon loosed to hunt?*

"Did anyone at Greavley consider Webberly a friend? I understand that he caused arguments."

Miles Farrell shifted, the *fauteuil* no longer comfortable. "He liked debates. Old Neville had it in for him. They always sniped at each other. Neville played tricks on Webby. At first, Webby blamed the boys, but then it was clear the person had access to the Lodgings. We narrowed it to Neville."

"*We* narrowed it? That's what you said. And you call him Webby."

"Look, that's what the boys call him. I fell into it from them. Have you questioned the boys? Some of them have it in for Webby."

Isabella made a sound in her throat.

Farrell looked at her and smirked. "You've heard it, haven't you? You spent a good part of today with one of them. Young Malvaise and his group. Chevington. A few others."

"A boy couldn't have done that damage," she retorted.

"Mad enough, a boy could do it," the Irishman retorted. "Chevington and his friends aren't boys. Big enough to be called men. That's names for you to question, Wainwright. Edward Malvaise. Bryce Chevington."

Callaway cleared his throat. "They were logged in for the Sunday service. They didn't leave."

Farrell looked startled by both the sergeant's input and his words. "Well then, you need to question the Old Guard. Webberly and I and Sherborne and Alexander, we were a force that stood for the boys against the Old Guard. They were petty, devious. Webby and I often talked about his problems with them, trying to narrow down who hated him. We eliminated who didn't fit. We put the clues together. But he's the one who caught Neville turning the ink bottle over his marked essays. We enjoyed stacking them up, like dominoes, then knocking them over, one by one. Filmer didn't guess."

"Did you know Webberly from before? On the front?"

"We did meet at a field hospital. Ran into him in London after we were demobbed. I was surprised he found employment here."

"Surprised?"

"He's not the class that Filmer wanted to fill positions. Hell, I'm not. Pardon me, ladies. Most of our generation were wiped out in the trenches. Webberly knew his Latin. None better."

"You were friends then?"

Farrell shrugged. "You can call it that. I wouldn't."

"Were you rivals for the affections of Mrs. Filmer?"

The glaring question shocked Flick. The sergeant paused and looked up, eyes on Farrell. Flick wondered if the man would admit it.

"Not rivals. Rivals implies that I have a hope. I didn't. Webberly got there first. He'd had his run with her, though. He'd already found a replacement. She didn't like it. Just yesterday—." He stopped. Drank the rest of the ale. Then he set the empty glass on the tea tray. He leaned back, unclenched his fist, and smoothed his hand down his trouser leg.

"Just yesterday?" Michael Wainwright prompted.

He bit his lips then shrugged. "You've talked to the vicar, haven't you? My keeping shut about it doesn't matter. She left the service. Is that what the Rev. Leverett told you?"

"We know that from two witnesses, yes. You're not betraying your potential paramour."

Flick glared at the inspector. His focus left Farrell and shifted to her. Those dark eyes didn't blink. His lean face remained expressionless. His square jaw was a rock, a boulder, immovable, unbreakable. He'd settled into his planned interrogation, and Isabella and she had to endure it.

He'd skipped over Chauncey, thank God.

"Mrs. Filmer left the service? Where did she go?" His gaze turned back to Farrell, and Flick realized her breath had frozen in her lungs.

Farrell ground his teeth then gritted, "She was to meet Webberly in the maze. He didn't show."

"They had planned to meet?"

"She told him, before the service. Demanded that he meet her there. She saw him, you see, with that maid from here."

"Nuala," Isabella murmured.

"That's the one."

"I thought," Flick said stonily, "that you called Mr. Webberly an unsavory character."

"He is. He was." Farrell cleared his throat. "I wouldn't introduce him to my sister."

"But you call him a friend."

"I don't introduce most of my friends to my sisters," he retorted. "I told Mrs. Filmer that, before she became involved with him. I should have held my breath. She was all the more eager to pursue him."

"Forbidden fruit is tastier," Isabella said quietly.

The three men looked at her, as if surprised by her insight into Verna Filmer. Flick wasn't surprised. Women understood women. Even though some wouldn't stoop to the baser levels, they understood those who wanted to dwell in dishonorable actions or immoral behavior.

Wainwright turned back to Farrell. "Did you have a taste of your own forbidden fruit? Did you relish her distress at Webberly's perfidy?"

Farrell shrugged.

"She expected it," Flick said. She didn't know Verna Filmer, but she knew her type. "It doesn't matter how lightly we may go into a relationship, our heart soon becomes involved."

Wainwright studied her, and she wished she'd bitten her tongue. *Does he think I'm talking from experience?* She remembered where she'd first seen him and who was escorting her. Alan Rettleston would be a man just like Webberly, a skirt-chaser, not happy unless he had two women on-stage and one waiting in the wings, eager for her debut. *Does Mr. Wainwright think I'm talking about Alan Rettleston?*

She wouldn't explain, not before Isabella or his sergeant.

Farrell had clenched his fists and thrust them between his legs and the chair. Wainwright studied him, no doubt seeing those clenched fists, no doubt reading the man's increased antagonism as Verna Filmer centered their conversation. "Tell me," he asked quietly, "what motivation do you have for serving as priest-confessor to Mrs. Filmer? To Chauncey Sherborne? To whomever else needs to talk and you're waiting, ready to listen? Eager to listen?"

The Irishman flushed. "Look here, that's a foul insinuation. I've answered your questions. I won't stand for comments like that."

"I insinuated nothing, Mr. Farrell."

"I have an alibi for the time of Webberly's death. I've told you what I know, more than I should have. You want to pen the blame on someone, you need to look around you, not at us who were at the service. There's plenty who thought worse of him, more than I did, plenty who hated him. Like Elwen here." He gestured behind him to the door.

They all looked, surprised he'd seen the figure with his hand on the door knob.

Only after did Flick realize that Miles Farrell had seen Kenneth Elwen's reflection in the mirror above the low bookcases on the far wall.

Kenneth Elwen looked like any young man in country tweeds. They were a little baggy on him, but until he took a step, no one would realize the war had crippled him.

Michael Wainwright stood. He stepped aside and gestured to the settee. "Please join us, Mr. Elwen."

The young man hobbled a few steps forward. He frowned. "What do you want to know?"

The sergeant had leaned back to survey the fisherman. Michael Wainwright continued to point to the settee. "I believe you'll be more comfortable here, sir. I believe you know Mrs. Tarrant and Miss Sherborne? Are you acquainted with Mr. Farrell? That's good."

"Who are you?"

"Detective Inspector Wainwright. My sergeant, Callaway." He accomplished the introductions with a nod. "We're talking about the murder of George Webberly. Mr. Farrell has just told us something very interesting. He says you had reason to hate Webberly."

Flick expected the young man to deny the comment. She would have. Kenneth Elwen shocked her by agreeing with Farrell. "I did hate him. I wasn't the only one. He came through unscathed, did you know? The men under his command died, as good as murdered by him. I despise him."

"Death in war isn't—."

He snorted. "I hear that more than I want to. I know Webberly murdered his men. Close to thirty men went over the top at dawn. By sunset, less than handful survived. Only three of us standing to this very day. He deserved to die. I'd like to shake the hand of the man with the courage to kill him."

"I know what happened," Wainwright said.

Elwen's head jerked back. "You do? You must have read the only report that wasn't manufactured to conceal his cowardice. You know what he did, but you're concerned about his death?"

"It's my job."

"Elwen was at the Abbey School on Sunday morning." Farrell jerked the words out, intent on having the inspector focus his questions on someone else.

"I was there," the young man admitted. He took a step sideways then leaned his slight frame against the sideboard beside the door. "I went to see Mr. Dodges."

"The butler at the manor?"

"That's right. His son was in my unit. Along with Robby Gilchrist. I didn't expect to see them Sunday morning. Mr. Dodges refused to let me into the house. Mr. Gilchrist at least let me sit down when I visited on Saturday."

Kenneth Elwen's appearance and his obvious hatred may have thrown the inspector, but he didn't stumble over the switched focus. "Did you talk with Robby Gilchrist? Where is he at Greavley?"

"Undergardener. He was intended for the law, did you know? Now he can't keep a single thought in his head. He's ruined here." He tapped his temple. Then he slapped his leg. "I'm ruined here. I didn't see him on Sunday, nor his father. Just Dodges. Who didn't want to talk to me. He thought talk was worthless. I proved him wrong. Didn't need a lot of words to say it, either."

"What did you say to him?"

"Not much. He said he'd be late to the service and asked me to come back. And I said, well, I said 'Webberly commanded your son.' Four words. That was enough. Then I left."

Flick remembered Dodges' waxy pale face, Gilchrist equally wan, both men looking sick. They would be sick, realizing who Webberly was.

"Is that all?" Wainwright asked.

"Damme, what more do you need?" He straightened from the sideboard. "Coming, Farrell? I could do with a pint."

"I need another one." Miles Farrell climbed to his feet and looked down at the inspector. "Are we finished here?"

Wainwright leaned back on the settee and crossed his hands over his stomach, looking at ease instead of sorting through Farrell's answers and slotting them into the other information he'd gleaned. "Keep yourself available, Mr. Farrell. Don't go on a tramp without notifying Constable Amsley."

The man snorted. "Ladies, our brief conversation was a pleasure." Then he edged around the sergeant's chair and headed out of the lounge.

Sgt. Callaway flipped closed his notebook. "More than I was expecting, sir." He shifted from the hard-bottomed chair to a *fauteuil*.

"Much more, including an unexpected suspect."

"Mrs. Filmer?" Isabella asked.

Wainwright didn't answer. He transferred the tea tray to the chair his sergeant had abandoned. He drew out the courier envelope that he'd slipped between the settee cushion and the upholstered arm. Looking at Flick, he unwrapped the string, and her stomach twisted into a knot. Wordlessly, he spilled the photo prints onto the table.

"Those are Flick's photos," Isabella said. "Did you find them helpful?"

"We would like to consult you ladies. My sergeant and I have a couple of things we don't understand." He spread out the photos, disarranging them from the neat stack that had slid out. He picked up one print by its corner and extended it to Flick. "What can you tell me about this photo?"

She glanced at it, not needing another inspection to remember her purpose in printing it. "I didn't have time to tinker with the exposure for the enlargement. Your photographer at headquarters may know a better technique to bring out the results. He'll find dark patches in the grass. Blood. From where something was set down in the grass over several steps. This photo shows that. If my film were capable of color, you would see the red in the grass."

"Murder weapon," Callaway said. "Set down repeatedly. How far apart would you say the patches are?"

"A foot. About a foot. Wouldn't you say that, Isabella?"

She nodded. The flames had her entire focus. She had no curiosity about the photos. Since several showed Webberly's bludgeoned head, Flick understood.

"And this?"

The body looked dropped onto the path like a rag doll. The bloody mess of his head was out of view. "Isabella and I guessed that the magistrate, Sir Robert Goodkind, and Constable Amsley would want to move the body. Rain was expected."

"Mrs. Tarrant?"

It ticked Flick that Michael Wainwright would confirm with Isabella. *Does he think I'm lying about the position of the body? The reason we took the photos?*

"That's correct, Mr. Wainwright." Her gaze flickered to the men then back to the flames. "I confess that we didn't have a strong belief in the local constabulary's ability to investigate this murder. As soon as we learned from Sir Robert that he'd called Scotland Yard, I was relieved. We told you that, didn't we?"

He was sorting through the photos, hunting the next one. "What were you doing while Miss Sherborne took her photographs?"

"I held the blanket and refused to look. I am certain I told you *that*."

He picked up another photo. "And this?"

Isabella looked away. Flick leaned forward. "It's his pocket.

Nothing bad," and Isabella looked then.

"That's right," she said. "He had a crumpled paper in his pocket."

"What was on it?"

"We don't know."

"We didn't touch it," Flick added.

"Not even to read it and put it back?"

"We didn't touch it," she repeated.

"We wouldn't," Isabella added. "That would be disturbing evidence. The whole reason that Flick took photographs was because the scene was going to be disturbed."

Wainwright looked at his sergeant who promptly said, "A crumpled paper is not on the list of items with the body."

Isabella's brow crinkled. "We didn't touch it."

"It must have fallen out when they moved the body," Flick added.

"Constable Amsley searched the scene afterward, a twenty-five foot grid, and he collected and listed everything he found. We have that list. No crumpled paper."

Since Isabella still puzzled it over, Flick had to answer. "I don't know what to say. It was in his pocket when we covered him again with the blanket."

Wainwright's gaze searched Flick, not Isabella. Did he think she'd somehow stolen the crumpled paper from under Isabella's eyes?

"We were together the entire time," she defended. "Once we covered him back up, we stepped away. He was in our view. No one could have crept over and touched anything."

"That's right. Flick is right."

"It would be foolish, don't you think," Flick pointed out, "to give a photograph of evidence that's now gone missing? I do bear a brain, Inspector."

His mouth twisted. He lifted another photo, this one displaying Webberly's hand. "What is he holding?" He looked directly at her.

Isabella leaned forward. "It's a gold chain in his hand. We couldn't see anything expect that little bit. He was gripping it tightly."

"No gold chain." The sergeant didn't bother to flip back to his evidence list.

Flick stared at Wainwright. She didn't think he was accusing her for no reason. The paper was missing. The chain was missing. Neither she nor Isabella had taken it. Chauncey wouldn't. Would he? The ambulance men must have lost it, somehow, somewhere, when they picked up the body onto the board then transferred him to the gurney.

"It was there," Isabella defended, "just like the crumpled paper was in his pocket. Since the paper and the chain are gone, then Flick was smart to take photos. Somewhere between our leaving the body and its transport to … I don't suppose they have a morgue in Upper Wellsford, do they? But somewhere between there and here, those items must have been jostled out and lost. They might have fallen into the grass or under leaves. Have you searched the ambulance?"

"We will." Wainwright finally looked away from Flick. With his focus removed, she drew a slow deep breath.

"And ask your constable more questions, specifically about the paper and the gold chain."

"The problem is that Constable Amsley, under the direction and the eye of Sir Robert, emptied Webberly's pockets at the scene. We have the list of Webberly's possessions. Amsley also described both hands as open and empty. Rigor didn't set in until later. Miss Sherborne, your brother was alone with Webberly's body, wasn't he?"

Flick's body seized up. She had a sudden memory of Chauncey at Christmas, asking for money when she dropped him at the train station for his ride back to Greavley Abbey. And Webberly had pushed for money, on Saturday. Chauncey promised him a paper and a surety. That gold medallion on its gold chain, a gift from Great-Uncle Tristan Allworthy, that would have fit in a closed fist. The medallion had diamonds inset and an engraving on the back to Chauncey. Gold and diamonds, good enough to pawn or sell and raise money to pay debts.

George Webberly may have held that in his hand.

The crumpled paper would have been Chauncey's IOU.

"My brother wouldn't take evidence," she claimed. "Even though he was alone with the body, he wouldn't touch it. Besides, we covered Webberly with the blanket. How would he have known the gold chain and the paper were there?"

"He wouldn't know. Unless he had given them to Webberly that very morning. And he decided to take them back."

Wainwright didn't say it, but five words hung heavier than smoke.

After he killed the man.

Chapter 19

Monday, Late Afternoon

"No." Flick's denial was automatic. "My brother didn't commit murder. He didn't steal evidence."

Yet even as she spoke, she remembered thinking how much the war had changed him. In those first week after being demobilized, when he slept on the couch in her flat, Chauncey had spoken wildly about wasted years, his broken plans, his dreams lost forever. He'd had a reckless disregard for his life and others. She'd let him drive the Calcott only once. He'd scared her so badly around pedestrians, gunning the engine to pass lorries and slower autos, that she didn't allow him behind the wheel until last Christmas.

"Not Chauncey." She crossed her arms, determined to do battle. "Are you accusing my brother now, Inspector?" Her mind revved up. The Masters' Lodging had no telephone. The Prior's House did, as did Greavley Manor, but she doubted anyone would take a message to Chauncey until morning.

DI Wainwright had aimed his sights at her brother. She had to warn him.

"You don't think he would remove evidence that might incriminate him?"

She didn't dare answer that. "You are accusing him," she snapped. "Chauncey would not commit murder. He's had enough of killing."

"You need to focus on someone else," Isabella chimed in. "Chauncey Sherborne is no fool. He would know that he would be blamed for taking evidence."

"Did your brother know that you took photographs of the scene, Miss Sherborne?"

Curses. There was the weakness. "No, he did not." *Oh God, it could be true.*

"We also have a statement from the vicar." The sergeant's flat tone revealed the words would be damning. "He says your brother, the young dark-haired teaching master, wearing a dark robe, the one serving as beadle for the service, left during the singing. He returned after communion had started, a few minutes after, before everyone came up for the bread and wine. That description only fits Mr.

Sherborne."

"Oh God," she breathed then stood up. The inspector was building a case against Chauncey. She shouldn't sit here and let him.

"Where are you going, Miss Sherborne? To ring your brother? Warn him?"

"I'm going to be sick," she lied. Clamping a hand over her mouth, she rushed from the lounge and hurried upstairs.

In her room, she looked wildly around. *What to do? What to do?* Then she seized her coat and her tote. Her hand dove deep, searching for the key that would unlock the ignition.

Can I warn him?

I must.

Flick knew Inspector Wainwright wouldn't approve of what she was going to do. *He might arrest me. Obstructing his investigation. Accessory after the fact.*

She didn't care. It was Chauncey. He didn't do it.

He couldn't have.

.~.~.~.

Callaway glanced at the door. "You want me to watch her, sir?"

Michael chose to consult Isabella. "Will she warn her brother?"

"They are very close. I don't know if she will."

"How well do you know Felicity Sherborne?"

"We met Saturday evening, before dinner."

"You don't know what she's capable of, then. And her brother?"

"I met him less than an hour after I met Flick. She can't ring him. The only telephones at Greavley are in the manor and in the Prior's House. Do you really believe Chauncey Sherborne killed George Webberly?"

Michael shrugged. "Evidence is missing."

Yet Isabella knew that the vague gesture hid his actual interest in Chauncey Sherborne as a chief suspect.

Would Chauncey have a good reason for leaving the service? For taking evidence? Without a credible explanation, Michael would arrest him.

"Have you determined—?" She stopped, for Sibby came in, to prepare the tables for dinner.

Callaway stood abruptly. The maid halted mid-step, but he only returned the straight-backed chair to the table from which it must have come.

The maid came to their semi-circle. "No more tea, Mrs. Tarrant, I'm sorry to say. And Mrs. Eccles, our cook, says no more biscuits or savories." She pressed down her apron as she stared at the two men, then she became brave enough to ask "Are you the men from Scotland Yard? The ones what Nuala checked in 'round noon? Mrs. Eccles wants to know if you'll be wanting anything more than the cottage pie. She's time to make a dried fruit sweet. You'll be wishing you'd come when Mrs. Halsey was here."

Michael frowned at the question, but Sgt. Callaway gave a little cough. "The local constable spoke highly of Mrs. Halsey's hot cross buns. Soft as pillows, he said."

"Mrs. Halsey's off on Monday and Tuesday. Mrs. Eccles can put together a soda bread or scones. I'll have her do that, shall I? Anything for you, Mrs. Tarrant?"

"I think I'll pass on the bread, so I won't feel guilty about indulging when Mrs. Halsey returns."

"And Miss Sherborne?"

"I dare not guess. She went up to her room."

"I'll ask her in a bit then." She glanced over the tables. "Half-past seven is dinner this evening."

As soon as the lounge door swung closed, Michael pinned her with the question Sibby had interrupted. "Have we determined—what? The murder weapon? You know we shouldn't talk of any specifics with you."

"Well, I like that," she said huffily. "It's not like I'm a suspect. Or am I?"

"No, you aren't."

"And I've given you lots of information. *Quid pro quo*, Michael. Do you know anything about the weapon? I'll be all around Abbey School with a legitimate reason. I might spot something out of place."

"A weighted stick," Callaway told her then grinned at Michael's obvious displeasure. "You just said she's not a suspect, boss. She might have ideas that we wouldn't."

"A weighted stick. Like a garden tool," she murmured, much as she and Flick had speculated. Nothing swam up from her unconscious. "Do you think Miles Farrell was pointing you to a culprit?"

"Those boys? Edward Malvaise and—who was the other?"

"Bryce Chevington," the sergeant said, without looking.

"Malvaise is the subject of your portrait, isn't he? Has he said anything?"

"Mr. Farrell would have us believe," she spoke carefully, not wanting any word to sound accusing, "that he and Webberly and Sherborne and—I don't remember the other man—that they formed a hedge around the boys, protecting them from the petty tyranny of the Old Guard. Edward Malvaise didn't say that, not at all."

"What did he say?"

"Can you use my words as fact? I thought they were hearsay."

"Not as evidence in court. We'd have to hear them from him, then he would have to testify to them. You can report it to us for investigative purposes, though."

"Well, Edward didn't talk about the four men. He didn't seem to think highly of any of the masters."

"Us versus them?" Callaway hazarded.

"There's this," Michael added. "Farrell pointed us to this Malvaise and to another boy. He wanted us to blame them."

"Chevington."

"Bryce Chevington, boss."

"Edward talked of Chevington. He said he didn't like Webberly, but that he took it out on the rugby field."

"Classic misdirection," Michael murmured. "Look at the boys, don't look at an adult. We need to talk with this Edward Malvaise. And with Bryce Chevington. Tomorrow. Perhaps."

Isabella didn't like that added *perhaps*. Michael didn't look like a bulldog; he was too lean. But once he snagged a bit of evidence, he grabbed it and shook until he'd worked everything out of it. "Edward said he would tell me about his classmate Chevington tomorrow."

"You want she should ask anything specific of Malvaise?"

"I don't see how either of the boys will help your murder investigation," she protested. "I saw Edward at the Sunday service. He didn't leave."

"Did this Chevington leave?"

"I don't know who he is, but I can tell you that none of the boys left."

"The vicar confirms that, boss. Only two people left. Chauncey Sherborne, back for communion. Verna Filmer, absent for the whole of communion. None of the other masters. None of the employees who attend Abbey Church. Not Mrs. Tarrant here or Miss Sherborne. That Dunley gave us the list of the boys who logged in, matched it to the roster of those in the school; all there."

"Dean Filmer takes attendance for Sunday service?"

"Any boy absent must make up with an extra chapel, Mrs. Tarrant. Makes our life easy, but as a boy I wouldn't like my time regimented like that."

"You never liked check-in at headquarters either, did you, Callaway?"

His grin this time was wide and impish. "No, boss, that's truth. I like working with you. You want I should put those boys on the list for tomorrow? And a new interview with Farrell?"

"I think we'll see what happens."

Isabella cringed inwardly. Michael did sound as if he'd made up his mind. On Chauncey, she feared. *What can I do to distract him?* To save Flick's brother, she had to sacrifice someone. "You must interview Verna Filmer, too." She wasn't certain she was making the right decision. Madoc would know, but he wasn't here. He was sailing to the southern hemisphere. She had to act as she thought best—and she didn't think Chauncey Sherborne had committed murder. At dinner Webberly had only annoyed him. "After the service, Flick and I heard Mr. Farrell trying to calm down Mrs. Filmer. They were in the maze, talking loudly. We heard them quite clearly. She'd apparently discovered that Mr. Webberly was involved with—." *In for a penny, in for a pound.* "With Nuala."

"With Nuala?"

"The maid who checked you in. Sibby said Nuala did."

"The maid just now is Sibby?" Callaway had drawn out his notebook and pencil. "How do you spell Nuala? Like it sounds? What's her last name? Rice?"

"I don't know her last name. Sibby will have to tell you."

"What else?"

She hoped she'd upset Michael's neat apple cart of facts against Chauncey. Isabella looked forward to mixing in some green apples with his ripe russets. "Nuala was in danger of losing her job because of her involvement with George Webberly. Mrs. Pollard was jealous. Apparently, their *affaire* had just started."

Michael thumped back in his chair.

"Skirt-chaser." Callaway shook his head. "That's real trouble."

Isabella primmed her mouth and threw more apples. "I do not know if Mr. Pollard and Dean Filmer were aware of their wives' connections with Mr. Webberly."

"Constable mentioned something like, boss."

His mouth twisted. "Yes, I remember."

"Have I thrown you sideways?" She knew she had. She just didn't know if she'd said enough to convince Michael to look away from Chauncey.

"Not quite. More than I'd like," he admitted. "At least we have other directions to look if we need to. I would like to talk more with Miss Sherborne before we make any firm direction. Do you think she's recovered?"

"I suppose you want a more in-depth interview? Were the statements we gave Constable Amsley not enough?"

"Very basic, Mrs. Tarrant. You should know that."

"I do. Shouldn't you interview me first? I mean, here I sit."

"I may confirm a few of her statements with you, if you don't mind."

In the guise of being amenable, Isabella assented. Then she trudged upstairs.

How can I delay Flick's interview without it seeming like a delay?

She liked Michael Wainwright and Sgt. Callaway. Madoc owed loyalty to his former colonel. He wouldn't want her to interfere with any investigation. She also liked Flick. They'd quickly formed a friendship. She liked Chauncey Sherborne.

But someone likeable could be a murderer.

Chauncey, though, didn't seem the type to hold grudges.

She'd met two murderers, on Crete and at the Malvaise estate of Emberly. She'd disliked both of them. Every person she disliked, though, wasn't a murderer. The law of averages was such that, if she encountered another murderer—and she had—then two out of three, the next murderer had to be someone she liked.

Isabella tapped on Flick's door. While she waited, she convinced herself that a different law of averages was at work.

Flick didn't come to the door. Isabella couldn't hear anyone moving around in the room. Flick wasn't in the water closet; that door down the hall was partly ajar.

She tapped again. Still no answer. Isabella tried the knob. It turned, and the door opened on its well-oiled hinges.

Flick wasn't in the room.

Chapter 20

Monday Evening

The Calcott's wheels skidded on the gravel. The auto stopped with a slide then a jerk. Flick flung open the door and slid out, barely remembering to grab her purse. Then she ran down the road behind the Prior's House and to the Master's Lodgings beyond the teaching hall.

Her open coat swung, admitting freezing air. She didn't feel it. She hadn't felt the cold at all as she drove. A greater fear chilled her. She prayed Chauncey had merely been an idiot. She prayed that, while the war had scarred him, it hadn't completely changed him.

She didn't fear that he had killed George Webberly.

She did fear that he had helped the person who did.

.~.~.~.

"Flick isn't in her room," Isabella reported.

Michael Wainwright leaped to his feet. "Where is she?"

"I don't know." She didn't like admitting that. She didn't like thinking that Flick had fled rather than help the investigation. She feared Flick had gone to her brother. *Did Chauncey need his sister's protection?*

Callaway looked up from the notes he'd been scanning. "She the one that owns that green Calcott? I'll see if it's in the garage, boss."

"I'll come with you."

"She wouldn't help her brother escape," she protested. *Would she?*

Michael glanced her way as he circled the seating to reach the door. "That you find the need to say that, Mrs. Tarrant, adds to the doubts in my mind. Let's go, Callaway."

After they left, Isabella collapsed onto the settee. Where Sibby found her, many minutes later.

"Those policemen off? I didn't find Miss Sherborne. Didn't you say she went to her room?"

Isabella struggled to answer. There wasn't a good answer to either question.

"Mrs. Eccles won't like having to keep their dinners warm. Ruins them, she says. Can save them scones, no trouble, but the cottage pie— it will dry out if it's left warming."

"I don't know when the inspector and his sergeant will return." *If they arrested Chauncey—.* "It may be hours."

"Then Mrs. Eccles best set by sandwiches for them and serve the rest. Will Miss Sherborne want dinner kept for her?"

"I believe she may have gone to speak to her brother." Isabella hoped that was all Flick intended to do.

.~.~.~.

Chauncey came down the stairs. "What's happened?" Yet he didn't meet her eyes.

He knew.

The Masters' Lodgings had a wide entrance hall with a common room on one side and a work room with scattered tables on the other. Both rooms had several masters, three members of the Old Guard in armchairs before the fire, a couple of men marking papers at separate tables. While she'd waited for the porter to take her message up to Chauncey, Flick realized that no one should overhear their conversation.

Her first words became "You need a coat. Do you have one down here?"

His mouth twisted. He stepped off the stair and passed her to take a coat from a hook near the door. Several coats crowded those hooks as well as the coat stand. Flick buttoned her own coat as Chauncey shrugged into the thick overcoat.

"Sir." The porter had followed him down. "Should I log you in as away from the Abbey School?"

Chauncey looked at Flick, silently waiting for her to answer.

Putting the burden on me. In his first months back he'd ducked any obligation until she confronted him.

He'd left Owl stranded in a pub, she recalled. They three had planned to have dinner together, converging at the pub from their various locations in London. The two young women had had doubts, but he assured them he would be early. Delayed by Alan Rettleston, Flick had rang the pub. Owl had been in tears. Chauncey wasn't there; men kept bothering her; she wanted to leave. Flick sent her home, promising to reimburse her for the taxi. When she confronted Chauncey, he'd shrugged. She lost her temper then. After that, he didn't let her or Owl down.

"We'll be outside. Having a smoke," she told the porter even though neither of them smoked. Then she followed her brother out into the cold.

She had no trouble dredging up that old simmer of anger. If she confronted Chauncey without it, she would cry—and this was too important for distracting tears.

He walked only a few feet from the steps, until they stepped outside the sphere cast by the exterior light at the entrance. "What is it, Young Thing?"

"I think you know."

"How could I?"

"Oh, you know."

He grimaced then tried to blank his expression. "It could be a half-dozen things."

"You've never been a good actor, Old Thing."

"You're angry. I don't know the reason. How could I? You've said nothing to give me a clue."

"Clue." That word was choice. "Let's start with the hardest. Did you kill George Webberly? In the bit of time you were gone from the service, did you kill him?"

"No. How could you ask that? You know I would never murder anyone."

"I don't know that. I know what I think and what I hope, but how can I *know*, Chauncey? How can I *know*?" She flung out her hands. The darkness around them was fitting. It obscured unless a light shone out. Her ignorance of so much obscured her certainty. "I don't want you to have killed him. The brother I knew before the war would never have contemplated it. But you've changed."

Not able to look at her shadowed form, he flung around, giving her his back. "Don't tell me war changes people. God! I've heard that so much, too much." He ground the words.

"You *have* changed. Before—well, you would never have let Owl sit in that pub alone. You would never have drunk to extremes. You would never have needed money for gambling; you never used to gamble. You never used to duck obligations, like visiting Grandfather Allworthy and Great-Uncle Tristan on Boxing Day. They were expecting you. You have *changed*, Chauncey."

"How do you know that's not just growing older? I was a half-formed university lad before."

"No, you weren't. You weren't before you enlisted. You would never have missed time with Grandfather."

He whirled around. "You accuse me of killing George Webberly because I refused to sit around at Grandfather's? Damned boring, listening to him and Great-Uncle Tristan prose on, agog for war stories, disappointed when I won't talk."

His words thrust her back. "I shouldn't have used that as an example."

"You're saying I drink to excess. You're saying I gamble past my means. I lay that to Webberly; I think he fuzzed the cards."

"Lord, Chauncey, don't say that to the inspector. That will give you a better motive."

"I didn't kill him, Flick. I haven't gone off the rails. I was unsteady last spring and summer. I admit it. I wanted to—I felt guilty—." He gave a cutting gesture. "No. No excuses, only facts. Look, Flick, my work here is always done on time. I'm never late with anything. I drank too much last summer. Not here. I don't have the time or the opportunity here. Webberly rooked me into poker, but I was working my way out, I promise you. I wouldn't kill him. After watching men die around me—god, Flick, why accuse me of that?"

Her anger crawled away. She wanted to crawl into a similar dark hole. "Inspector Wainwright questioned me."

"About what? You have an alibi. We all do."

"You left the service."

Four words, but they struck hard. His head came up, the faint light casting a sheen on his dark hair. "Has the time Webberly died changed?"

"The vicar said you absented yourself for a quarter-hour. That's time enough."

"*If* I'd known where Webberly was. *If* I'd had a bludgeon at hand. *If* I wanted to kill him. Even then, I would need more than fifteen minutes. I was gone less than ten."

"*Did* you want to kill him?"

"No! God, Flick, what's come over you? I would never—."

"The old Chauncey wouldn't have, that I know. Just as I know the old Chauncey wouldn't have disturbed Webberly's body. Wouldn't have removed evidence."

"Oh."

"I took photos of the scene. You didn't know that, did you?"

"Why would—?" He shook his head. "You had your camera. I suppose you took photos for the newspapers."

"No. Of the crime scene. In case they moved the body. Which they did."

He pressed the heel of his palms to his eyes. "That inspector knows, doesn't he?"

"That you took a gold chain out of Webberly's hand. That you took a paper from his pocket. He thinks you were hiding evidence."

His hands dropped and hung uselessly at his sides. "I was."

"Chauncey!"

"I *didn't* kill him, Flick. It was my medallion, you know, and my vowels. Two bits of evidence that would be a distraction from the real killer."

"That's not what Inspector Wainwright thinks."

"Obviously."

"If only you hadn't left the service—."

"I needed a breath of air. Just a little. I'm telling the truth! I didn't go more than ten feet from the door."

"Did anyone see you?" His mouth twisted. He shook his head. Flick gave a frustrated huff. "I know you have your medallion. Do you still have the paper? Maybe it could clear you."

"Not likely. I owed Webberly over £500."

"£500! Chauncey!"

"He wanted it immediately. I suppose he wanted it before I accused him of fuzzing the cards. I needed proof first. I thought Alexander or Farrell would back me up. They were in the same game. He pestered me about it on the drive to the pub."

"Saturday evening?"

He nodded. He kicked an uplifted corner of a flagstone, staring at it rather than meeting her gaze. "He demanded it when I came in after our drive. I put him off until Sunday morning. I gave him the medallion and the paper before the service. I didn't have the funds, not anywhere near that amount." He gave a short, humorless laugh. "I thought getting back my medallion and my vowels was a gift from God. But it's payback, for racking up that debt in the first place."

"I don't think you should play poker with cheaters like Webberly. Or at least not play so deep that you have to give up your medallion and write IOUs. Or take evidence from a murder victim's pockets."

"I didn't want to be suspected of Webberly's murder."

"Were you blotto, then? Look where you are now."

. ~ . ~ . ~ .

"She's not going to like it," Callaway advised as he set the parking brake.

"Then she won't," Michael said firmly. "I can't let that sway me from the facts."

How had Callaway leaped to the knowledge that Michael was interested in Felicity Sherborne? Flick, as Isabella Tarrant had called her.

Despair flooded him. The gravel crunching under his feet was like the rubble of a half-dream demolished, the building blocks destroyed before they formed a foundation.

This was not the first time his work had conflicted with his personal life. It happened twice before the war, when he first became an inspector and Callaway kept him from tripping over his own feet. A couple of friends had removed themselves from his life. The girl who had his eye stopped accepting his invitations. He had shrugged and moved on. He hadn't had time to miss them before he was jerked out of England and into battle.

Chauncey Sherborne's arrest would infuriate his sister. Michael had barely conceived an interest in her. That blossom would shrivel and die before it bloomed.

He had to follow where the evidence led. He had to reach a result— the right result. The longer the delay in reaching that result, the worse it looked to his chief.

That shouldn't be a consideration. Flick Sherborne's fury shouldn't be one. Chauncey Sherborne had shot to the top of the suspect list because he removed evidence and he had motive and opportunity for murder.

Where would I be if Sherborne hadn't removed evidence?

Sifting evidence. Conducting more interviews. Pinning suspects down.

Mrs. Filmer, missing for a half-hour.

Mrs. Pollard—not her, though. She'd gone to London on the early train.

Nuala Rice.

Herbert Pollard, the cuckolded husband. Not Dean Filmer, his alibi held up.

The boys that Miles Farrell had mentioned. Also with alibis.

Could the time of the murder be wrong?

No, he didn't think so. People had seen Webberly alive before the service. After, he was dead.

Who else?

Gilchrist had hovered. What had the major domo hesitated to say?

Michael and Callaway still had interviews to conduct. Dodges the butler. The head gardener.

Normally, he spent the first days gathering information. Yet he was moving to arrest Chauncey Sherborne. *Too fast?* The case had come together.

He recalled Constable Amsley's list. Not for the first time he wondered if the murderer was on that list.

They emerged from the Crossing and passed the Prior's House, darkened for the night. Voices reached them. Beyond the teaching hall was the faint glow cast by a light—and two people standing at the edge of that yellow puddle. A man and a woman.

She cried, "Chauncey!"

Flick Sherborne. She hadn't gone to her room. She'd come here, as he had anticipated. Where had she parked?

Flick and her brother were arguing, not escaping.

Callaway grunted. "Straight on, boss, or should I go around the side?"

"Straight on, sergeant."

They heard her clearly say "blotto" and "look where you are now". Then sister and brother became aware of their advance and swung to face them.

Flick stepped in front of her brother. "He didn't do it. He admits taking the chain and the paper, but he didn't kill George Webberly."

Michael refused to speak. She'd handed them answers to half their questions.

Callaway didn't hesitate. "We'll have to determine that, Miss. Chauncey Sherborne, will you come with us?"

"No!" Flick spread her arms wide. "He didn't do it. Chauncey—!"

"Leave off, Flick." Her brother stepped around her. His chin lifted, like a boxer confronting his opponent. "I muddled the deal, and now I'll have to straighten it out."

"Don't arrest him." She tried to block Callaway. "Inspector, you can't arrest him!"

"Callaway, take him into custody." Michael seized the opportunity that Flick's admission had given. "We'll hold him on perverting the course of justice."

The sergeant placed a hand on Chauncey Sherborne's arm. "Do I need handcuffs, Mr. Sherborne?"

"No. I'll come quietly. Flick, don't interfere."

Her glare at Callaway vanished as she looked at her brother. Agony aged her fine features. When her gaze swiveled to Michael, the glare returned. "At least it's not murder. They didn't step that far into idiocy. Chauncey, I'll call our solicitor. He'll have someone here tomorrow, I promise."

"Miss Sherborne—." Michael stopped. He had nothing to say. Without more proof, he wouldn't arrest Sherborne for murder. Perversion of justice by disposing of evidence was a serious charge. He couldn't give her any hope.

"You!" She breathed the word with fire. She brushed past him, following her brother and Callaway until they passed the Masters' Lodgings. Then she took the path to the gravel road that ran behind the buildings.

Michael watched her dark form disappear, and his hopes disappeared with her.

Chapter 21

Tuesday Morning

Michael woke several times. Memory of Flick Sherborne's wrath and Chauncey Sherborne's devastated expression when the cell door shut haunted him. At dawn, he abandoned sleep and started his day.

The tiny size of Upper Wellsford's gaol, a converted closet with a barred door, didn't help. Any occupant wouldn't be able to stretch his legs. Sherborne, as tall as his sister, would be especially cramped.

The young man had maintained his innocence in Webberly's

murder even as he confessed to destroying the paper. The chain and medallion he'd turned over with his possessions for Constable Amsley to log. A gift, he'd said, and seeing the inset diamonds that emphasized the points of the engraved sun along with the engraving on the medallion's back, Michael believed him. That didn't make Sherborne's situation any better, especially when he explained his growing gambling debts.

"Ever think Webberly had fuzzed the cards?" Callaway had asked as he poured Sherborne's possessions into an envelope.

The young man's silence answered them. He must think it, but since he was square in the frame, he was keeping quiet.

Michael cleaned up and dressed then paced in his room until he heard others stirring. He encountered an older man dressed for fishing when he emerged. In the lounge below, the maid Nuala brought him a pot of coffee. It tasted burnt, but Michael drank it.

He was finishing his second cup when Callaway came. The other maid was arranging a spread on the sideboard, sausage and rashers, scrambled eggs, crumpets and dry toast, cream and marmalade. His sergeant filled his plate, but Michael ate only enough to get him through the morning. Callaway knew better than to comment—although he did cough a good bit while drinking his first coffee.

Michael wanted to see Flick, but he didn't want her recriminations. Holding her brother for destruction of evidence was just. It wasn't a charge of murder although everyone would assume that.

Not for the first time he wished for more experience. He'd barely settled into the job when the war started, and his lack of experience meant he wasn't the best asset for the Metropolitan Police. Demobbed, he'd gone hat in hand to his old chief, not really expecting a position but hoping the chief's friendship with his grandfather would give him another opportunity. Hired back, he stumbled to solve his first case. Callaway's return was more than timely; it was fortuitous. The sergeant had the experience that Michael lacked. Paired up again, they began to solve cases. The MacBride case was their only failure. By then, though, Michael's results made up for his sole failure, and his chief had thawed.

He hadn't solved the murder at Emberly. It solved itself when the woman tried to kill her niece, Cecilia Arkwright, and Isabella Tarrant.

He needed to solve this case. He wouldn't jump on the charge of murder against Sherborne, not yet, not until they had finished their interviews. A good barrister would show the jury all the holes in the case. That trouble Michael didn't want. He wanted all the holes filled in, a clean ride through the case.

They entered the gaol. Amsley rose from behind his desk and stretched. Sherborne rose to a sitting position on his bunk. He rubbed his scruffy chin and pushed his hair back.

"Sir, may I have an hour?" the constable asked. "I need to clean up, eat breakfast. I'll order a tray for Sherborne while I'm at the pub."

"Do that." He pretended to sort through Amsley's files until the constable had left, then Michael drug a chair over to the barred door. "Tell me about Webberly."

The young man lifted his head. He eyed Michael then Callaway behind him, his arms crossed as he leaned on the desk. "What do you want to know, Inspector? I didn't kill him. How many times do I have to repeat that?"

"What kind of man was George Webberly? We've heard he chased skirts. I suspect he cheated at cards."

Sherborne shrugged. "He taught Latin. Liked to rile the Old Guard whenever he caught them in the wrong. He liked to argue just to have an argument."

"And?"

"What else do you want to know?"

"He had an automobile. Did he have wealth?"

"Family didn't. Titus Bellamy twigged him about that more than once. I was surprised Filmer hired him. He wasn't gentry. Sometimes that was obvious. He must have impressed him with his knowledge of Latin."

"How did he have an auto if he had no wealth?"

"He won it off someone over Christmas. Webberly bragged about that. That's how he had his fob watch and his diamond cufflinks, that money clip. Won those."

"We have those, sir," Callaway put in then read from his evidence list. "Pocket watch. Cuff links. Tie pin with blue stone. Money clip with £317 and odd change. No diamond cuff links. These were silver, carved with R.G."

"Who's R.G.?"

Sherborne's head had sunk to his chest. He raised it a little. "Maybe Robby Gilchrist. He's an undergardener here."

"His father the major domo at the Prior's House?"

He opened his mouth to say something, hesitated, then his mouth twisted slightly. "Gilchrist Younger and Webberly knew each other before this term. From the war. Same regiment, I think."

Michael thought of his War Office source. "Now that is an interesting connection. Where do you think those diamond cuff links are?"

"His room. He usually wore them with his tuxedo, kept the silver for day. He was wearing tweed that morning. Usually—." He stopped abruptly. Michael prompted him. Sherborne's brow contracted. "I don't know this, not for a fact, although Webberly laughed about it once. He had a girl he met on Saturday and Sunday mornings, early, down at the Rowing Shed."

"A girl? Not a lady? Not a woman? He said 'girl'?"

"He did. Before we left the school on Saturday evening, he told me dinner was fine, but I wasn't going to convince him to spend the evening with my sister while I hared off with another lady. He had 'hay to make'," he grimaced again, "then a bit of sleep before he had his girl to meet. 'Up early for that, you know.' More than I wanted to hear."

"He didn't like your sister?"

"They met last October. Flick disliked him from the start. Webberly gave up at Christmas."

"Webberly saw your sister at Christmas?"

"In passing. Flick picked me up at the station. He and I rode the same train to London."

"Together?"

"Not planned. We discovered it on the station platform. Then, once we reached London, Flick was there with her auto. She snubbed him, quite obviously, and he had words to say about that, when we came back from holiday."

"You rode the train together? I thought you said he had an auto."

"He came back from holiday with it. I think he won it off someone. He didn't say so, but he said enough."

Callaway sucked air. "A person beyond Upper Wellsford, sir. This would have been good to know before, Sherborne."

The young man's head came up. "You didn't ask."

Michael's shoulder raised, his head tilted over, a sign his sergeant should know. "Later for that. Tell me, did you like Webberly?"

"He was a colleague."

"Nothing more? You played poker together. You didn't call him Webby?"

He received a hard look from those blue eyes.

"Miles Farrell called him Webby. Called you Sherby."

"That was him and Webberly. Webby called him Farry; he called him Webby. They tried to call me Sherby. I didn't like it. Still don't. If anyone was friends with Webberly, Farrell was. They knew each other."

"In the war?"

"Must be. I don't know specifics. I know Farrell was stationed in a field hospital. I was never wounded that badly."

"Farrell mentioned that occasionally he was placed with units preparing for an assault." Sherborne didn't respond to that, just looked at Michael through those eyes so like his sister's. "Did you ever hear anything unsavory about Webberly's service?" He heard Callaway shift behind him.

"Unsavory? What do you mean?"

Michael didn't elaborate. He and Callaway had to rework the case, this time without a blue-eyed, dark-haired lady blinding him. He'd bent so far away from favoritism to any Sherborne that he wondered how many wrong threads he'd picked up. The threads would knot, all right, but the knot would easily unravel. Sherborne wasn't the murderer. Michael needed a tight case, especially with the blot from Christmastide staining his record. He'd missed clues. He hadn't pushed hard enough, and two—no, three more people had nearly died. The chief inspector had claimed not to hold it against him, but he held it against himself. He wanted no reputation as the detective inspector who could only solve open and shut cases.

"What else can you tell me about Webberly? Who was the girl he was meeting?"

"Some maid at the hotel. Worked mornings, he said, and had to leave when he wanted to lie up in bed. He planned to throw their relationship up to Mrs. Pollard, make her jealous."

"And Mrs. Filmer?"

Sherborne looked up again. "I heard that rumor. I didn't give it credence."

Yet Mrs. Tarrant had. Constable Amsley had.

Michael had shoved his chair under the constable's desk when Amsley returned, holding the door open for a maid from the pub. Her hands were full of a tray with covered dishes.

"For the prisoner, sir. May I?"

"Of course. Who's this?"

"Nuala Rice. From the pub, sir."

Callaway's head came up, dog catching a scent.

"Sergeant, why don't you escort this young lady back to the pub?"

"Right-O."

Michael waited until the door shut. "That the one Webberly was to meet?"

Sherborne's "yes" was echoed quickly by Amsley.

"Should I question her, sir?"

"The sergeant is doing it."

"She couldn't have done it, sir. She's on duty at the pub every morning but Wednesdays. And I don't think she can hit that hard."

"Let's narrow our current list by determining who cannot provide a solid alibi, constable, rather than who we think cannot wield a weighted bludgeon." He turned to Sherborne. "The vicar said you left the service."

"So, it wasn't just the missing evidence."

Michael controlled his flinch, keeping it internal. "Where did you go?"

"Outside. For a smoke. Don't tell Flick. She thinks I gave that up."

"How long were you outside?"

"Six or seven minutes. Nowhere close to fifteen. Ten at the most."

That tallied with Rev. Leverett's account. "Did you see Webberly?"

"Saw him that morning, I told you. At breakfast. I was coming in from my run. We met in the dining room. He was in a hurry to avoid the headmaster. That's how I wound up as beadle. I didn't duck out fast enough. Filmer caught me when I asked the cooks for a picnic lunch."

"Anyone see you smoking?"

"Maybe MacAlphin. I see him when I run. He usually walks the grounds after he has his morning tea, planning what's to be done for the day. He was late that morning for some reason. When I ground out my cigarette, I saw him coming from the woods on the other side of the drive. I did think I saw him earlier, before the service, behind the manor. I must have been mistaken."

"MacAlphin is the head gardener. I thought the servants were required to attend the service."

He shrugged. "Couldn't say. I know Gilchrist the Older and Dodges were there. Looking sick, the both of them. Occasionally I see the maids and the porter. Not the cooks, though. Never the gardeners. I don't know about the manor staff."

Amsley began rattling off names, which Michael could only assume were staff at Greavley School and at the manor. "None of them attended, sir."

"Who are they? What would they have been doing Sunday morning?"

"Cooks, maids, porter for the Lodgings. They would have been working. They get half-day on Sunday and alternate a full-day during the week."

"Who are the grooms? Is there a stable?"

"No. Grooms—I'd guess you would say chauffeur now. Luther, though he calls himself a jobber. He drives for the dean and Mrs. Filmer, occasionally for the masters. He's usually hauling goods from the station to the school."

"Would anyone else have seen you, Mr. Sherborne?"

"The only person I saw was MacAlphin."

Michael picked up his hat.

"Heading out, sir?" The constable quickly stood, as stiff as if he'd been called to attention. "If I receive a message, where will I find you?"

"My sergeant will let you know."

Michael waited outside the tiny four-square building that served the village as constabulary and gaol. He stared sightlessly at the common as he drew on his gloves. He had three directions to pursue.

Callaway came from the side road that led to the pub and thence to Greavley Abbey. He kept an eye on the clouding sky as he walked across the common to join Michael. "Snow expected. What's to do, boss."

Michael considered everything before them. They weren't at the start line, but they had a lot of ground to re-cross. "This morning I want you here in the village."

"New witnesses?"

"Ones we need to question. I want you to re-interview the vicar. See if you can get him to narrow the time for Sherborne's absence. And talk to that photographer. Roberts, is that right?"

Callaway had withdrawn his notebook and was making checks on a list. "What do you want from the photographer?"

"Did he watch Miss Sherborne make her photographic prints? Did he see any negatives that we haven't seen? What was his impression of her? Find out whomever he knows from the Abbey School. You know the kind of things."

"Anyone else?"

"Do you remember Amsley's list? Interview whoever's left that's in the village."

"And the other people on the list?"

"I'll interview them."

"You're heading to the Abbey?" He tore out a paper from his notebook and handed it over to Michael. "Here they are, boss. What's your first direction?"

"I think it's time I spoke to the gardener, especially an undergardener named Gilchrist."

"You going to question Mrs. Filmer? There's that missing half-hour."

"Before the gardeners."

"Right-O. And when I see Miss Sherborne and Mrs. Tarrant?"

Michael winced. "Give Mrs. Tarrant my regards. I doubt Miss Sherborne will want to hear anything from me as long as her brother is locked up."

"I'd say that's mild, boss."

Chapter 22

Tuesday Morning

Flick spied Sgt. Callaway across the common on a definite angle for the church. Michael Wainwright had driven away before she could tackle him. He'd taken the road to Greavley Abbey. No doubt he looked for more evidence against Chauncey.

He won't find it!

Without knocking she barged into the gaol, letting the door thud shut behind her entrance.

The tiny room held a large desk, commanded by Constable Amsley, chairs, a barred door, and a door to the back. Through stout bars she saw Chauncey sitting on a half-size bunk. A little hearth on the same wall barely heated the room. She wanted to demand that her brother be released. Instead, she tore off her scarf and unbuttoned her coat. "Have you had breakfast?" she demanded.

The constable had stopped as she entered, but he resumed his hunt and peck at the typewriter keys. "Miss Sherborne. Good morning to you."

"Sausage, eggs, toast and marmalade," Chauncey said. He came to the doorway. Resting his wrists on a crossbar, he let his hands dangle outside the narrow confines of that cell. "Burnt coffee," he added and grinned at the constable.

He may have eaten, but he hadn't shaved. *How can he grin when he's locked up?*

The pecking stopped. "Burnt coffee's your punishment for not sticking to good English tea. The marmalade should have made up for it."

"It did, believe me."

She looked from her brother to the constable and back. "I don't— what?"

"I've finally tasted Mrs. Halsey's marmalade," Chauncey said, as if a barred door wasn't between them. "I usually eat the school breakfast. Now I will definitely have the occasional Saturday morning at the pub. Sit down, Flick. You look a little shocky."

"Here." The constable leaped to his feet and carried a chair closer to the cell. "Sit here, Miss Sherborne. You've come to visit your brother. You shouldn't have to talk across the room. Now you have a good visit, and I'll get back to my reports."

She could have commented that *across the room* was no distance at all. She hesitated, trying to read upside-down the papers on his desk. "Which report are you working on?"

"Now Miss Sherborne, you know I'm not supposed to tell you anything."

"Not even when the inquest will be?"

"Sir Robert hasn't set it yet with the coroner. The inspector hasn't wrapped up the case."

"But Chauncey—."

"He's merely being held," the constable said, and her brother added, "Removal of evidence from the crime scene. I did do that, Flick. Our constable is likely typing up my statement of that."

"You shouldn't have given any statement! Not until our solicitor is here."

"You don't need to worry, miss, not with the inspector on the case. He's several theories of the crime. He needs evidence, different evidence, to narrow down to the real perpetrator." He rolled the paper out. "And I haven't typed up your brother's statement about the evidence, not yet."

Chauncey's not charged with murder. Flick held on to that bit of information. She took a deep breath as she sank onto the seat. "What—? Where has the inspector and his sergeant gone?"

"Now, miss."

"More interviews," Chauncey said, still sounding cheerful. "Wainwright does have a murder to solve, more alibis to check, that sort of thing. I'm not police. Now that I'm not in the frame, I'm willing to wear blinders."

"He's not—you aren't—?" She cast a glance at the constable who had rolled in another paper and had resumed his slow peck. Chauncey's cheerful grin unbalanced her. She settled on asking "Did you pass a good night?"

He glanced over his shoulder at the cot against the far wall. The blankets were still rumpled, a pillow smashed against the wall. "Not the most comfortable night. But I'm used to cots." His mouth twisted. "Haven't always had them. The constable here gave me a good pillow. Almost made it better than my rooms. Better than your sofa, I'll say that." He grinned again.

Is his cheerfulness a mask so I won't worry? But, no, the constable seems to think Inspector Wainwright is looking for someone else. She leaned close to the bars and whispered, "Wainwright is looking for a different person as his murderer?"

"Seems his conscience bothered him all night." He didn't bother to lower his voice.

"Good. Yet you're still sitting in gaol. Even with the inspector changing his mind. Or has he? He could be gathering more evidence to use against you. Have you considered that? You may regret whatever statement you gave."

"I told the truth, Flick. I didn't kill Webberly. Telling the truth shouldn't convict me."

"You have a lot of faith in the courts. How can you? After everything you railed against last summer. About bobbies stopping you on the street."

"I was disorderly—."

"How many times have you railed against useless officers? Worse, you railed against stupid officers who can spout regulations and nothing more. Bad equipment. Sickness in the trenches." Her voice rose as she remembered his tirades, nearly one every day that he stayed at her flat.

"Hold up, Flick. That was the war. Don't lose your temper."

"It's not right! You shouldn't be in there. You didn't kill Webberly."

"I'm not happy behind these bars," he gripped one and gave it a shake, "but it could be worse. Wainwright could have picked the easiest person to accuse. That would be me because I removed evidence. He's a good sort. Not taking the easy road."

"I don't care if you think he's a good sort. I will not be happy as long as you are behind those bars. Until you're free, I will not trust that he will free you. His sergeant is off to the vicar, you know. Rev. Leverett doesn't know you, the kind of man you are, your citations for bravery, the way you help others." Salty tears choked her throat.

He reached down. "Don't cry, Sissy."

Sissy. He'd called her that when they were in the nursery together and Maman had forbidden his use of *Flisty* for Felicity. Her tears flowed fast. She sniffed and dabbed with her handkerchief. It would be sodden if she didn't shut off the waterworks.

Chauncey and she were close. They'd always been close. Their three older brothers had always seemed more like cousins come to visit than siblings.

Part of it was their close ages, only four years apart. The heir Warren was already in his late thirties. Darton, had he lived, would be past that decade. Worthy, their name for their nearest brother, had just edged over it.

Another part was Warren himself, proudly a solicitor. Working with their father had turned him into an old prosy—maybe he'd always been an old prosy.

The third part was all the kerfuffles they'd caused after their brothers enrolled in public school. Three governesses in three years was a badge of honor—until Miss Pynchon came. Nothing had frightened Miss Pynchon.

She'd had a mind to call Warren last evening—but his area was civil law, not criminal. Allworthy was in finance, commerce. He'd worry about his firm's reputation before he'd worry about Chauncey.

"Did you ring the pater?"

"This morning. *After* I rang Gresham and Gresham."

"You didn't think the pater's firm could handle it? You didn't consider Warren?"

"What do contracts have to do with crime? If you aren't cleared, you'll need a barrister. Giles Gresham can help with that. He said he'd send someone this morning."

"That will be noon. I could be freed by then."

"You have that much faith in Wainwright?"

The typewriter carriage returned. The sound seemed very loud. The first peck resumed.

"He listened to me this morning. Really listened, Flick. I misjudged him. How did the pater take the news?"

Their father had controlled his reaction, as always. He would have told Maman after he rang off. He wouldn't want the operator to hear any comment. Servants didn't matter; they didn't exist for Cedric Sherborne. Their father would hold his censure of his youngest son and only daughter until they stood before him. Chauncey's refusal to enter the clergy meant months of cold stares and curt words. His choice of school master, even at the well-known Greavley Abbey School, had not ended the freeze.

She bit her lip then shrugged, off-hand. "You know."

Chauncey paled. He gripped two bars. "That bad, huh? He'll tell Warren as soon as he reaches the firm, and Warren will come on the same train as Gresham's man."

"We don't need Warren here."

"No, we don't, but you'd better be at the station, ready to greet him."

"I won't. I won't leave you in here, not alone. Besides, the pater won't send him. I told him I had contacted Giles Gresham."

"He wouldn't like that."

"No, he didn't. But I didn't apologize. He won't send Warren. He won't."

"Flick." That single word had a five-stone weight.

She raised her eyebrows, daring Chauncey to censure her when there were bars between them. He had been an idiot. He had removed evidence. He let fear grab him.

When he winced, she knew he'd correctly read her expression. "You can't stay in here all day, Flick."

"I can if the constable allows it." She twisted on her chair. "Will you allow it, Constable?"

"Now, miss—," he started, which proved that he'd been listening to them.

"You won't, Flick," her brother ordered, adamant even though the iron bars meant he couldn't enforce his edict. "What did you plan to do while I had classes?"

"A garden article."

"Then work on that."

"How can I concentrate on that when you're—?" Unable to say the word, she waved at the bars.

"I will soon be released."

"You hope."

"Now, Miss, I do think Mr. Sherborne has the right of it." He returned the carriage and continued typing.

"Don't give me false hope, Constable Amsley."

"I would never," he said fervently. Then he sighed and reached for his eraser.

The door opened. Sgt. Callaway stopped on the threshold when he saw Flick, then he came in.

Flick shifted her chair so the sergeant stayed in her view. "Constable Amsley tells us the inspector has a new theory of the crime and that he doesn't believe my brother did it."

Callaway frowned, and the young constable looked embarrassed. "Now, miss, I didn't say those exact words."

"Well, Sergeant?"

That frown turned to her. "We're pursuing several theories."

"Why is my brother not yet released?"

"Flick—."

"Tampering with evidence at a crime scene is the reason we're holding Mr. Sherborne."

"So he says."

"That's perversion of justice, miss."

"Wouldn't do," the constable chimed in, "to let people think we don't care about evidence at the crime scene."

Flick wasn't placated. "What people think is that you've arrested my brother for George Webberly's murder. That isn't correct. He could lose his position. His reputation will suffer."

"I'm sure, Miss Sherborne, that you will not let anyone think the wrong thing about your brother. Amsley, what time does the train run on Sunday?"

The switch of topic didn't throw the constable off beat. "Two train times, sergeant, to reach the connector to London. Train to London stops at nine in the morning and three in the afternoon."

"Are those the only times?"

"On Sunday, yes. For the rest of the week, another train arrives nine o'clock each night. We're on a spur that runs from the connector to the end of the line and back, and it repeats twice more. The spur runs several districts over. That's all the spur does, runs up and down the line. Late train to the connector arrives there at eleven. Meets the night train to London. Old steam engine. Treat to see it, sir."

"Do you have a timetable?"

"Never bothered with one, but I'll look." He scrabbled through the desk drawer then started through the top side drawer, jamming his hand to the back. "There's a schedule. Yes. Right here." Amsley withdrew a yellowed pamphlet, London-Haverly printed in large letters at the top. The edges were curled and ragged.

Callaway stared at it. "Nothing more recent?"

"It's been the same schedule for years, sergeant, even before I came. Nothing more recent than this. The station master himself will give this to you."

The sergeant opened it, turned pages to find the Upper Wellsford station times. He muttered.

"Something I can help you with, sergeant?"

The burly man looked at Flick and Chauncey, both watching with interest. "Your report on our interested parties' locations on Sunday. You cited Mrs. Pollard as leaving on the first London-bound train. Who told you that she left then?"

"Her husband. The station master what sold her the ticket."

"Mrs. Leverett said that Mrs. Pollard lunched with her and the vicar, after they returned from the Abbey Church service. Mrs. Pollard didn't take the nine o'clock train."

Flick glanced at Chauncey. He shrugged, unconcerned.

But she immediately knew that Mrs. Pollard had re-entered the lists as a suspect. Well out of suspicion just a few minutes ago, now the woman had time enough to kill George Webberly. No one would have been looking for her. No one would have noted where she was and when. She'd been gone from Upper Wellsford since Sunday afternoon, two nights and a day and more if she had wanted to abscond. She had the motive of jealousy. Since Webberly had died on the path behind Greavley Manor and since Mrs. Filmer had quarreled with Webberly, then Mrs. Pollard could have heard the argument, become enraged, killed Webberly, then carefully restored her emotions and her clothing before anyone saw her again.

"The vicar's wife said that Mrs. Pollard intended to take the later train." Callaway fixed his stare on the constable, who twisted uneasily in his chair. "Why did the stationmaster not tell you that she was on the later train?"

"Well, sir. He had a gastric upset on Sunday. The conductor handles the boarding. He sold Mrs. Pollard the ticket and expected her to be on the train."

Flick folded her arms and leaned back, watching the men's tennis rally of words.

"We don't know if Mrs. Pollard took the later train or if she missed the train entirely."

"Mr. Pollard said that his wife rang him briefly to say she'd arrived. She didn't talk long, he said."

"Because the woman would have arrived in London well after midnight," Flick murmured.

Callaway glanced at her but addressed Amsley, "Do we know where she was staying?"

"London."

"Where in London, Constable?"

Amsley's eyes dropped to the report he'd been typing. He looked as if he wanted to return to that laborious and tedious task rather than deal with answering the sergeant. "I don't know, sir."

Callaway dropped the train schedule on top of the scattered interviews, typed and handwritten, and spread-out files. "Get on to her husband. See if he knows her hotel. Then ring wherever she stayed and confirm she was there, when she arrived, if she left."

"Her husband did say, sir, that she was expected back today. I did learn that from him."

"When, today? On the one p.m. train or the one at seven? The inspector will want to talk with her, constable. We hadn't added Mrs. Pollard to our inquiries. Now we discover that we should have. We also do not know where she is or if she's missing because she met with an incapacitating problem or she fled or something else. Did Herbert Pollard confirm that she'd reached her destination?"

"I didn't ask him," the constable exclaimed while Flick mouthed *murdered* to Chauncey.

"Ask him now, then ring where she was intended to be. One question and one telephone call will straighten this out. The inspector will appreciate it."

"I never thought, sir. I never did. I didn't think a woman could have done it."

"That was rage," Sgt. Callaway said. "I don't think we can eliminate anyone based on normal strength to swing a bludgeon."

Chapter 23

Tuesday, Mid-Morning

Not having found Mr. Gilchrist at the Prior's House, Michael approached the manor. As he climbed the entrance steps, the door opened. The butler who stood, stiff and formal in a drab livery, was unknown to him.

He, though, was not unknown to the butler. "Inspector Wainwright." He came down a step and closed the door behind him. "Mrs. Filmer remains indisposed, sir. I am ordered by the dean to have you direct any inquiries of her to the Prior's House."

"Ordered?"

"Yes, sir."

Ralston Filmer might be headmaster of the well-known school, but he wasn't master of Michael Wainwright. "Mr. Dodges, correct?"

"Just Dodges, sir."

"Well, you've done your duty. Now tell me if Mrs. Filmer is truly indisposed."

"The death of Mr. Webberly on manor grounds grieves her."

He recalled more than one person hinting or outright stating the relationship between Webberly and the married woman. Servants could be extremely loyal. Some, though, were mere employees. How loyal would Dodges be to his mistress? "At Webberly's death? Or murder on the grounds?"

No flicker of an eyelid betrayed Dodges' emotions. "At the death, sir."

"Was she involved with Webberly?"

"An intimate association existed between them since the autumn."

Those careful words told Michael no more than Amsley had reported the first day. "What do you call *intimate*, Dodges? Was her marriage in jeopardy?"

Now the butler's eyelids flared open. He hesitated then said, "The dean did not know the extent of their intimacy."

And good servant that you are, you don't provide information unless specifically asked. Gilchrist was the same, he remembered. He needed the specific question to break the unspoken rules of butlerdom.

Since Ralston Filmer knew nothing, he would have had no reason to confront Webberly about the *affaire*.

He doubted Dodges' rules of butlerdom would bend to specific details about intimate encounters. "Where did they meet? Here in the house?"

"Sir, I do not believe—."

"Tell me what you know, Dodges. Where did they meet?"

"The Rowing Shed, sir, in the beginning. When the weather turned chilly, they visited an unused cottage near the other gate."

"There's another gate?" He had a sudden wish for Isabella Tarrant's skill with a map.

"One used by the manor staff, sir."

"Not near the river, then?"

"No, sir. Quite the other way. Around the curve of the road."

Webberly wouldn't have been heading to an assignation with Mrs. Filmer when he was struck down.

Or he had, but not with Mrs. Filmer. Had she followed him and struck him from behind? She had a half-hour. Did that give her enough time to stalk behind him, discover that he wasn't going to meet her, locate a weapon, and do the deed? No. Although he and Callaway might time it out later, if things became desperate.

Webberly had a reason to be on the woods path to the river. Either he planned to meet someone, or he used the route to reach another trysting spot.

"Does the woods path go to the Rowing Shed?"

"No, sir. One uses the gravel drive behind the Abbey School buildings for that. The woods path connects the manor to the river path. From there, one can reach the Rowing Shed or venture along the path to the Hook and Line Pub."

"Where does it go in the other direction?"

"Nowhere, sir. At least, the old manor dock, but it's in disrepair. Fishermen are known to use that part of the river path. The boys who row for the school occasionally carry their sculls along the path to the old dock, but that is rare, I believe."

Chevington and Malvaise, entering the case again. "Where is the normal location to float their sculls?"

"The Rowing Shed, unless the school sponsors a race."

"Tell me what happens at a race. Starting point and finish line."

"Those are past the pub, sir. The village provides the best viewing for spectators. The sculls are placed in the water at the Rowing Shed then floated down to the village. The starting point is just past the willows, and the bridge provides the finish line. Why are you inquiring about the races, sir? There will not be a race until next month."

"Following a rabbit's trail, Dodges. I never know what will be pertinent to a case."

"I understand, sir, that Master Sherborne was arrested last evening in connection with the case."

"Sherborne is not the murderer. We're holding him on a different charge. Not an arrest. Nothing to do with Webberly. I came here specifically this morning to question your mistress. Mrs. Filmer left the Sunday service for a half-hour. I'd like to know the reason. I need to speak with her for that, notwithstanding Mr. Filmer's orders."

"She came here, sir. She had a gastric upset."

"You were at the service, Dodges. How do you know that answer?"

"A maid admitted her to the house and assisted her, sir. They were upstairs together until Mrs. Filmer left. As the maid was upstairs cleaning, the cook can confirm for you when Mrs. Filmer left the house. The cook spoke with me upon my return. I left the service a little in advance of the benediction, sir, and a good thing, for the cook had a problem which had to be addressed before the dean and Mrs. Filmer came for luncheon."

Michael felt his wind sigh away. Mrs. Filmer was now accounted for. He hadn't really expected any result that would help his investigation. "Is that all you have to tell me, Dodges? Nothing more about Webberly and Mrs. Filmer?"

The man's mouth compressed, a good butler refusing to speak about his employer.

"Who else knew of their *affaire*?" He expected a strict *I could not say*. Dodges' answer surprised him.

"Mr. Farrell, sir. And young Gilchrist, who informed his father who spoke of it with me."

Now those were two definite lines of inquiry. How would Farrell know? Mrs. Filmer confided in him, just as school boys and masters confided in the man. And young Gilchrist? *Gilchrist the Younger*. He remembered hearing that.

And Gilchrist the Older had hovered, wanting to share something but needing the right question to enable him to break those unwritten rules of butlerdom, the same guide for major domos.

"What did young Gilchrist say?"

"He spotted them, sir. In the cottage."

"How do you know this?"

"I was there when he informed his father."

"Where can I find young Gilchrist?"

"He's an undergardener. Mr. MacAlphin, the head gardener, will know his assignment for the day."

No rabbit trail this but a direct path to where he needed to reach. "Where can I find Mr. MacAlphin?"

"I would try the maze, sir."

The maze. Michael headed round the manor and spotted the tall hedge in the distance, past the ornate garden. The maze kept surfacing, but was it a rabbit's trail, like the boys and their races, or a definite need of inquiry?

One step forward: Mrs. Filmer could be wiped from the suspect list.

He hoped Callaway was making headway.

. ~ . ~ . ~ .

Tuesday Late Morning

Flick had used the public call box then dashed to the gaol. Isabella rang the Prior's house. The major domo answered, and she gave him the message for Edward Malvaise that their next meeting would be Wednesday morning. She stayed in her room, sketching, improving the illustration of the garden, thinking about colors for the portrait. When she could not stand the silence any longer, she ventured downstairs again. *Maybe a spot of tea*, she thought and ventured to the lounge.

Nuala sat tucked into the settee. She cried into her handkerchief, tears flowing and breath catching, signs of her broken heart. With a day of grief behind her, no wonder Sibby had covered for Nuala yesterday. The young woman cried now as if the news of Webberly's death was recent. What had set her off?

"Nuala." Isabella risked a comforting hand on the maid's shoulder. "What is wrong?"

"I—shouldn't tell. I shouldn't." A fresh sob sent her back into her sodden handkerchief.

"Is it about Mr. Webberly's death?"

A sound from the hall made her turn around. Had the open door shut? She hadn't shut it. With Nuala's weeping, she could understand people avoiding the lounge.

She turned back to the maid. "Tell me what is wrong."

Nuala lifted her head. "I don't know what to do," she wailed.

Isabella winced. *That* would have been heard clearly all the way into the pub. She lowered her voice, hoping the maid would imitate her. "Do about what?" she asked ungrammatically.

"I know who killed him." Nuala had lowered her voice, just not enough for words that should be whispered. "Oh, what should I do?" That returned to a carrying wail.

"You know—?" Isabella stared. How could Nuala know such a thing? Common sense kicked her. "You must tell that nice Constable Amsley, the one that Sibby is seeing."

"He won't believe me. No one will. They think George is dead because of money or because he broke Mrs. Filmer's heart. That's not true. That's not the reason."

"It's not? What *is* the reason? Nuala, you can tell me."

"Nuala!" That distant shout was Mr. Pollard. "Get out here now! Where are you?"

The maid jumped to her feet. "I have to go."

Isabella blocked her. "You cannot leave without telling me. At least tell Sibby when she comes to work."

"Nuala!" Mr. Pollard yelled. His voice was much louder. He must have opened the door to the hall.

The young woman hesitated, then she reached under her enveloping apron. She tugged from a pocket a folded and crumpled envelope, the flap open. "You keep it," she whispered and sniffed. "You show that constable. I can't." Wiping her eyes, she hurried from the room.

Isabella unfolded the envelope. The address read *George Webberly, Greavley School, Upper Wellsford.* Printed in block letters. With a London postmark. Feeling like she tampered with evidence, she drew out the single sheet.

More block letters. Seven words. *You killed them. Now you will die.*

A threat against Webberly. Reality, now.

.~.~.~.

Tuesday Noon

Flick followed Callaway to the station to wait for the arrival of the one o'clock train. They had an hour to wait. She intended to pester him with her presence. She knew better than to harass a policeman with comments. She'd taken enough photos of suffragettes arrested for that very reason. She hoped, though, that he would answer a few questions.

He glared at her, but she didn't falter.

"Don't be interfering with my investigation," he warned.

"Of course not. I want my brother freed before the inquest. When will the inquest be?"

"That's up to the magistrate once he hears we've charged someone."

"Is my brother charged? He said only that you were holding him."

"That's up to the inspector, Miss Sherborne."

"Then he hasn't been charged?"

Callaway groaned. "Don't you be getting your hopes up."

That groan sounded promising. "What do you want to ask Mrs. Pollard? Do you think she killed Webberly then went to lunch, cool as you please, with the Rev. and Mrs. Leverett? I don't. She would have needed to know where Webberly was. She would have taken a weapon. That's premeditation. On Saturday night, it certainly didn't look as if Mrs. Pollard was considering Mr. Webberly's murder."

"What happened Saturday night?"

"They were kissing in the hallway."

He grunted.

"Could she have killed him?"

"Why do you sound like a newshound?" he retorted.

"Why do you think she did it? Jealousy? A lover's quarrel? That seems a curious way to kill your lover. Especially since I've heard no rumors that she's wildly emotional. Wouldn't she need to be? To kiss him Saturday night and kill him Sunday morning? Maybe obsession … but I've never thought she was the obsessive type. Pleased with herself, of course, and very much the lady of the manor air with her help, but obsessive? Emotional? No."

"You've got it all worked out."

She couldn't decipher the meaning of Callaway's comment. He sounded neither pleased nor perturbed. "Why *are* you questioning her?"

"Right-O, Miss Sherborne, I'll let you know something. We ask a lot of questions that don't seem connected to any crime. Why are you still angry with me?"

"I'm not angry."

"You're pestering me, for certain. You wouldn't do that if you weren't angry."

"I'm not angry at *you*. I'm pestering you because His Highness Detective Inspector Michael Wainwright is not available. *You* didn't decide to arrest Chauncey. My apologies, *hold* him in gaol. And you didn't answer my question. Why are you questioning Mrs. Pollard?"

She didn't hear what he grumbled. "Look. I've things to do more important than answer your questions."

"You're going to be standing on this platform with nothing to do until the train comes in. *In an hour.* Answering my questions can be easily done while you wait."

"A sergeant doesn't talk to reporters out of school."

"I'm not a reporter."

He grumbled again. This time she caught "sounds like".

"Who did Wainwright go to interview? I expect that's what he is doing. Did he go to the school? He drove that way. Is he going to interview Mrs. Filmer? You should talk to Nuala before Mrs. Pollard. I think Mrs. Pollard was a new interest for Mr. Webberly, but Nuala had been with him for *weeks*. I saw them, you know. Early Sunday morning. He was escorting her back to the pub from wherever their tryst was. My window overlooks the back garden. He helped her climb over the wall."

"You know it was him and her?"

"See, you're getting valuable information about the victim's movements prior to his death. Yes, it was them. I saw them clearly. He had a torch. Did the inspector ever discover the reason that Webberly was on the path to the river? I would have taken the drive to the Rowing Shed and then to gone to the path along the river." When she paused, Callaway merely grunted, so she answered her own question. "He was meeting someone. But who? I would think he and Mrs. Filmer would meet in the maze. If it was anyone from the school—well, he couldn't talk to them in the Lodgings or in the Prior's House."

"How do you know that?"

Flick hid a triumphant smile. Callaway was opening up to her. Maybe she would get a line to track the killer. "The Lodgings aren't private. He could hardly meet someone there. Was it blackmail? Have you found any evidence of that? I know he had money to burn."

"How do you know that?"

"His automobile. It takes money to run it. *That* I do know. I have a Calcott. The traffic makes it nearly impossible to drive in London, and the garage fees eat up money I don't have."

"You could sell it. Hire a cab. Travel by train."

"I invested in an auto because I kept running into places where cabs and trains do not run. For my articles, you know. Garden features for *Modern Woman*."

"Is that a magazine?"

"Yes. Hmm. Webberly had an auto which means he needed ready funds to pay for it. More than what a school master brings in once a month." She'd seen Chauncey's pay chit. He didn't make nearly enough.

"No garage fees at the school," the sergeant pointed out.

That sentence deflated her musing. "No, that's true. But he would need petrol and the like. Still, was he blackmailing someone? One of the women he was involved with? Now that would be a reason to kill. Is the inspector asking questions about blackmail?"

Callaway didn't answer that. He paced a little on the platform then stopped in front of her. "Why wouldn't Webberly have met someone at the Prior's House?"

"It's locked on Sunday. I believe only Dean Filmer and Gilchrist have the keys."

"How do you know that?"

"This isn't my first visit to Upper Wellsford, sergeant. Anyone who has visited the school on a Sunday and wishes to use the telephone is out of luck. The only available one is at the manor, and the butler refuses to let anyone use it unless they have specific permission from the Filmers."

He twinkled at her. *Twinkled.* "Tried to call your editor, did you?"

Didn't sergeants have rules about *twinkling*? "Yes," she admitted baldly.

The station master emerged. He walked toward them. Sergeant Callaway lifted a hand. "Sir. I'm with with Metropolitan Police. I've some questions about the Sunday trains."

Flick backed off then turned to hurry back to the inn. *If the sergeant won't talk to Nuala, then I will.*

Nuala had been with Webberly early Sunday. They'd used the path behind the pub that led to the river. He died on a path to the river, this one behind the manor. Was that a coincidence? *Am I clutching at straws?*

Or did the river point to his killer?

Chapter 24

Tuesday

"Mr. MacAlphin." Michael stopped several paces behind the gardener raking twigs and leaves from under dormant bushes.

The rangy man paused in mid-stretch and turned, his back too stiff to twist and look over his shoulder. Seeing Michael, he doffed the battered hat he wore, revealing a thatch of grey hair cut short and an ancient face with watery eyes. He said nothing, just looked Michael up and down.

"You are Mr. MacAlphin?" He needed that confirmed before he started with questions. The man nodded, his weathered face expressionless. "I am Michael Wainwright, a detective inspector with the Metropolitan Police. Sir Robert Goodkind enlisted our aid with the investigation into George Webberly's death."

The man still said nothing.

"Would you help with that, sir?" Then he waited. While a gardener should be enured to silence, no one could long leave a question unanswered.

Those pale blue eyes scrunched a little. He pulled the rake back then rested his arm on the top of it. "Can't tell you naught. Don't have naught to do with them over at the school, just the boys they send for workin'."

"I understand you attended the Abbey Church service."

He didn't move, not a twitch of his body, not a flicker of his eyelids, as planted as one of the bushes around them. "What of it?"

"I am actually looking for Mr. Gilchrist?"

"He were there, too, the Sunday."

"Yes. I have a few questions for him. About Mr. Webberly. They crossed paths in their work."

"All the masters did. Naught to do with me." He reached out the rake to clear under a bush, using quick flicks to remove the winter-accumulated leaves.

"Mr. Gilchrist is not at the Prior's House. I believe his son works for you." He paused. When Mr. MacAlphin didn't look up, Michael added, "Mr. Dodges sent me in this direction."

The weathered man stopped his work. He straightened and once more pulled the rake in. "Dodges did?" He hefted the rake in one hand. "Best you come this way."

The path ran beside the manor, the ground held back by a retaining wall. MacAlphin walked along it at a slow pace, moving with the speed of the season. A perpendicular path ran away from the side passage and into the trees, and the gardener turned onto it. Once they passed under the old oaks, the air was colder, not warmed by the sun glimpsed through vagrant clouds. Michael's breath fogged. The old man's didn't.

They emerged from the narrow woods to a cluster of buildings. None were as large as the school buildings. A barn and an old stable with a carriage house athwart matched the size of the manor but not its quality of construction. Sheds, a greenhouse toward the river, storage buildings. Behind those buildings were fallow fields, a pasture with grazing cows, and another for sheep.

MacAlphin angled across browned grass to the carriage house, bypassing the stable and barn. Narrow windows marched along the first floor, wood construction above the stone foundation. Dormer windows in the second story also overlooked the graveled forecourt. Following the curving line of the drive, Michael saw a distant stone wall, much like the main entrance.

The carriage house had four sets of double doors, centered by a small single door with a glass pane set into its top. One set of double doors stood open, revealing an automobile, the hood buffed by a man in shirtsleeves. When they neared, the man straightened. He rubbed a rag in a can of wax then applied it to the auto, but his gaze remained on Michael and MacAlphin, not on his work.

"Luther," the gardener said.

The man's response was equally brief. "MacAlphin."

MacAlphin leaned his rake against the stone wall then opened the single door, revealing a stair to the first floor. He climbed, Michael behind him, at the same speed of his walking. The stair opened onto a hall running the length of the carriage house, with several doors opening to it on each side.

MacAlphin passed two doors then stopped at the third. On the side that overlooked the fields. MacAlphin tapped a quick staccato. His head bent, listening.

Michael hadn't realized that he heard the murmur of conversation until it stopped. The door opened. Gilchrist the Senior looked out.

The gardener jerked a thumb at Michael. "Inspector's here."

Gilchrist stepped back. "Come in, Inspector Wainwright."

MacAlphin entered behind Michael and shut the door.

They were in a bedsit, with room for a table and two chairs, a burner with its kettle and a cup beside it, cabinetry along the interior wall, and a narrow bed, unmade, on which perched a young man with his head in his hands. He wore a loose shirt and baggy trousers, but he'd only socks on his feet, one with a hole in the toe. An uncorked bottle of whisky stood on the table, the amber liquid half-gone. An empty glass stood beside the bottle. The cork had rolled to the table's edge.

"Inspector." Gilchrist had moved closer to his son. "You have us at a disadvantage."

"Your son?" Michael nodded at the young man who hadn't lifted his head.

"Robby had a difficult night. I am certain you understand a former soldier's difficulties."

"I do. Actually, I have questions for you both, Mr. Gilchrist. Robby." The young man dropped his hands but didn't raise his head. His shoulders hunched a little. *Dreading questions*, Michael judged. "About George Webberly," he clarified, as if it needed saying.

Robby Gilchrist jerked upright and shot to his feet. He pushed aside his father's out-stretched hand. He stationed himself at the window, bracing his hands on the frame.

"Inspector, I regret to inform you that the events of these past days have reawakened the horrors that my son was beginning to set aside. Specifics—."

"I'll answer anything he asks," Gilchrist the Younger said hoarsely. He continued to look out the window, but Michael saw that his knuckles, where he gripped the frame, shone white. "Webberly was a regular shite. I'm glad he's gone. I didn't have to remove him. I'm a coward." The last was a fading statement, the strength ebbing from his words.

"You wanted him gone, Robby?" Michael asked, inspector to the bones of him, although his gut cringed at the need for the question. When the father started to speak, Michael held up his hand for silence.

"I did." His elbows bent. He leaned close to the window, his breath fogging the cold glass that he continued to stare out. "I don't know anyone who would want him walking this green earth, not after what he did."

"What did Webberly do?"

"He killed us."

MacAlphin grunted. Gilchrist the Older aborted his movement to his son.

Michael knew what Robby Gilchrist meant. His War Office source had talked around the record, but he'd detailed enough to understand what had happened. Yet he wanted this young man to explain it. "Tell me."

"We just wanted another day to breathe. Not live, not in those trenches. Just … exist. We had a clear spate. You do, you know. A couple of days before the shelling and the shooting starts back. Time to think about what you've survived. Time to wonder if you'll still survive. Rumor—." His voice cracked. "Rumor was that the Germans had fallen back. And Webberly—."

When he didn't pick up after that abrupt stop, Michael prompted, "Webberly was in charge? What was he? Field captain?"

"Acting lieutenant." His voice went flat, emotionless. "Not a full lieutenant. He wanted the rank. I see that now. Not then. Couldn't see anything clear then."

Another pause, stretching uncomfortably. MacAlphin and Gilchrist the Older had frozen when the young man began his account. Michael glanced at them, but their gazes were on Robby Gilchrist's back.

"Did it happen at night?" he asked.

"Dawn. Fog lifting. Cold and wet and mucky, but the rain had stopped in the night. Webberly came along the line, telling us to get our trench knives ready, telling us the Germans had pulled back. Only sentries before us, not a full line. Nobody in their trenches, we can take them. Then he blew his whistle. We went up and—. The machine guns cut us down."

"Not you?" Michael asked softly.

"I slid in the mud. Couldn't see. Couldn't get up. I heard, though. God, I heard—." His head bent, his shoulders hunched, and he sobbed once, deep, aching.

Gilchrist the Older stepped between Michael and his son. "Enough."

Michael nodded.

Then came more words, thick, hoarse. "I didn't get a scratch. All around me, my friends were dead. Dying. I didn't get a scratch."

His father rested a hand on his shoulder. "Stop, Robby. Stop. It's enough."

He jerked away from his father, staggered a step. "I need a drink."

Gilchrist the Older blocked him, putting a hand on his son's chest. "That makes it worse."

He stared over his father's shoulder, at the open bottle on the table. "Makes me forget. I need to forget."

"No."

His hands fisted. He glared at his father.

"When did you know—" and Michael's words broke that stand-off, claiming the attention of son and father, "that Webberly had come to work here?"

Robby Gilchrist stepped back from his father. He scrubbed his face with both hands, then he wavered to the bed and dropped onto it. His head fell into his hands again. "God," he groaned. "Not for some weeks. I'm in the greenhouse and the orchard. Mac gets me up early, I come in late. I eat with the others at the manor, off the kitchen. I don't come into the common areas in the Lodgings except to sleep."

"My son rarely visits the school-side, sir. He shared rooms with me in the Masters' Lodgings, but we have—had a small efficiency on the ground floor, at the back. Robby does not venture into the areas common to the school employees."

"When did he discover Webberly worked here?"

"It was 10th October, sir, before he ran into Mr. Webberly, walking about the grounds."

That answer was specific. He turned to the younger man. "Did you confront him?"

"Me? No. I'm a coward. I couldn't—couldn't face him."

"You've not seen him? Not talked to him?"

"No. Seen him from a distance only. Once I knew he was here, working here—."

"We left our efficiency and moved here. I have the room beside." Gilchrist the Older nodded to the rooms next door.

"What happened when you saw him, on October 10?"

"Nothing. I left."

"He came back here, to MacAlphin, and started drinking," his father said.

"No interaction with Webberly at all?"

"No."

"He had no reason to interact with him," Gilchrist the Older said firmly. "They didn't meet in their work. They were far from friends. Robby attended service with me—."

"No. Don't lie for me, Father. I was here. Sleeping off a drunk."

"I can vouch for that," MacAlphin said gruffly.

Michael swung around. "You said you were at the service?"

"He weren't in fit shape to leave the bed. Ask Luther."

"Downstairs? With the auto?"

"That's him. Jobber he is. Drives it for the Filmers. Has a truck for the heavy."

Michael turned back to Robby Gilchrist. "You had no reason to meet with Webberly on Sunday morning? No reason to run into him? Maybe with a garden tool in your hands? He came on you, surprised you. He walked past, and you swung around and struck him?"

"I wish. I *wish*. I wanted to be the one to wipe him off this earth. But I wasn't." Muffled words. Then he lifted his face out of his hands. "I'll regret that for the rest of my days."

"How many in your unit survived?"

"Three. If you can call it surviving."

"Do you ever see them?"

"Why would I want to? It brings it all back. God, I need—."

Michael stopped that thought. "Who else survived?"

"Harvey Crabtree. He's in a sanitarium outside London. Kenneth Elwen. They released him from hospital last autumn."

Michael whirled and pushed past MacAlphin.

"Inspector."

He stopped mid-stride and looked back at Gilchrist the Older. "You knew, didn't you? You wanted to tell me—but it would betray your son."

The major domo nodded. "I suspected only. I hoped him and not—. I wasn't certain."

"Did *he* know Webberly worked here?"

"He came to Upper Wellsford to see my son in December. It may have come out."

"We talked—." His son shook his head and retreated to his hands. "I wished—."

His father looked at him then rested a hand on his bowed head. "Yes. I know." Then he turned to Michael. "Elwen came here on Sunday morning to see Dodges."

"Dodges? The butler at the manor?"

"Dodges' son died that day. He and my son were in the same unit."

Michael hesitated, wanting his facts straight. At the time of the murder, Dodges was accounted for, at the service with Gilchrist the Older. "Elwen saw Webberly, didn't he? That very morning?"

"I do not know that, sir."

It *had* to be. If Elwen shared an nth of Robby Gilchrist's grief and guilt, then he would be consumed with hate when he saw Webberly. They *had* to have met. Elwen was a fisherman. He came from the river to see Dodges, for the river path was the short way from the pub to the abbey. He met Webberly in the woods.

But what weapon had he used?

"Keep him off the drink," he ordered. Then he strode for the door. He had to reach the village. He had to question Elwen.

But he knew—*knew* that Elwen was the murderer.

He only needed a few more details before he arrested the young man.

MacAlphin had said "can't say naught about that". *Can't* as not able? Or as having no idea?

Outside the efficiency, he turned to the gardener. "MacAlphin. A word." He jerked his head to indicate they should move farther along the hallway.

The old man walked unhurriedly to the head of the stairs. He waited patiently while Michael shoved together puzzle pieces to build the whole scene. MacAlphin had given Robby Gilchrist an easy job where he had no reason to encounter anyone who would cause him stress. He had other men working for him as well as the scholarship boys. He didn't have to employ young Gilchrist. Yet he had. As a favor to the older Gilchrist? They were of an age, MacAlphin weathered by his work, Gilchrist smooth with his position—but both obviously long-term employees of Greavley Abbey, one for the manor, the other for the school.

Dodges fit in there as well.

And Gilchrist and MacAlphin and Dodges would shield their family and friends, long before they felt a need for a murderer to see justice.

"Did you see Kenneth Elwen on Greavley Abbey property on Sunday morning?"

The old Scot gave a curt nod. "Made it specific, didn't you?" he groused. "Here's this, Inspector, sir. We don't let the fishermen on the river use the grounds."

"That's not what I asked. And Elwen's already been on the grounds, in December and on Sunday. He obviously visited the manor to talk to Dodges. Didn't he?"

"Aye. About his son."

"And that upset Dodges?"

"Dodges were at the service."

Michael crossed his arms, prepared to ask every specific question that he needed to. "Your answer?"

"He were here. I saw him when I walked over to the church. Came round the back of the manor, I did. He was at the entrance to the maze, listening like."

"Listening. To whom?"

"That Webberly and Mrs. Filmer. They were having a row. I could hear them, even with my old ears."

"What was Elwen carrying?"

"What d'ya think a fisherman would have with him?"

"And what else?"

MacAlphin grunted. "I need a whiskey." He glared at Michael then gave again that curt nod. "He walks with a stick. You probably know he's got a bum leg."

"What kind of stick?"

"I ain't doing your work for you."

"I want to know what you saw."

MacAlphin scowled. "I saw him leaning on a stick. Had his rod and reel in his other hand. He were listening to `em. I don't know more than that."

"What kind of stick?" Michael asked again.

Those bleary eyes closed briefly then opened. "One of them golf clubs. He used it when he walked."

"This was Sunday morning. Before the service? How much before?"

"I was late. Bells were ringing. Mrs. Filmer came running out as I crossed the garden."

"Thank you, Mr. MacAlphin." And he ran down the stairs.

Luther still buffed the auto. Michael paused, and the man straightened. He stuck his rag into the can of wax and slipped it around.

"One question, Mr. Luther?"

"Just Luther. I'll answer what I can."

"Where was Robby Gilchrist on Sunday morning during the church service?"

He applied the rag to the fender. "Getting drunker."

"You saw him?"

"Took the whiskey away from him when he spilled it."

"You know this for a fact."

The man straightened. "I sat with him. His father asked it. Don't usually, but boy was in a bad way."

Michael ran for his auto, re-tracing the path through the woods, crossing before the manor, skidding on the gravel as he grabbed the door handle. He prayed Elwen hadn't left on the day train.

Chapter 25

Tuesday

Isabella had started up the steps. The train had left minutes ago, heading for the end of the spur. She wondered if Mrs. Pollard had taken that train or the later one from London. The outer door opened on that thought, and she paused and looked down. Flick came in with the cold wind. She dragged off her scarf.

"One would never know we planned a picnic on Sunday. I do

believe it's colder than it was this morning. That wind! Did you not go the school today?"

She came down three steps. "I rang and left a message that today would be inconvenient. I worked on your illustrations. How is your brother?"

"I think—*think*—that they will release him. Soon. I'm not certain what they're waiting for. They re-questioned the vicar, and he said Chauncey wasn't absent from the service long enough to track George Webberly down, let alone kill him, not in that amount of time."

Isabella didn't question it. Flick didn't need anyone siding against her brother. "That's good, then, isn't it?"

"I don't understand the reason they still want him behind bars." She wrapped her arms around herself, fighting an inner chill worse than the icy wind outside.

"Inspector Wainwright will want more information, more witnesses. He will not hold your brother unnecessarily."

"You have a lot of faith, Isabella. I worry that Chauncey is that inspector's best suspect. He may just decide he has enough to convict and close the case."

"Michael Wainwright wouldn't do that."

"You say that, but you do not *know*."

"No, I do not. I *do* know my husband. Madoc thinks Mr. Wainwright is honorable. Sgt. Callaway is not a bully. I believe they want the right resolution to Mr. Webberly's murder, not any solution. Look, you're shivering." She came down the last steps. "Let's have a pot of tea."

"I want Chauncey free."

"Yes. I know. Let's go into the lounge, and I'll see if Mrs. Eccles keeps the kettle going, as Mrs. Halsey did. What did you do after you left the gaol?"

"Followed Sgt. Callaway to the train station. He's going to wait there for Mrs. Pollard's train."

"Does he think she has evidence? I thought she took the early train."

"Apparently not." Flick let Isabella usher her through the pub, empty even though it was after noon. "She had luncheon with the Rev. and Mrs. Leverett and took the second train to London, not the early train."

"Oh. That puts her in the time frame for the murder."

.~.~.~.

"Faster," Michael muttered.

The trees flashed past. The engine rumbled, straining at the speed his foot on the accelerator demanded.

Elwen was at the pub, but he might not stay there. How had he arrived in Upper Wellsford? Had he driven? Or taken the train?

The train from London would soon arrive. Elwen could take it. His destination didn't matter. Eluding arrest did. The spur line headed into the countryside. Other villages. Farm land. A boat on the river. Once away, he would make his way to London or one of the other cities where he could disappear. Let him reach a port, and Elwen was gone.

That wouldn't happen.

.~.~.~.

A man exited the hall to the lounge. He drew up short when he saw the young women. Mr. Elwen glanced back at the lounge, then he limped toward them. "I need to go upstairs."

"Of course." They stepped out of his way. Isabella watched him limp heavily for the stairs. Those halting steps rang a strident note.

"What is it?" Flick hissed.

"I don't know. Something—. No. It won't come."

Mr. Elwen's halting steps climbed the stair.

"Flick, do you think Mr. Pollard knows about Mrs. Pollard and Webberly?"

"No. And that's another line of inquiry that your so-honorable inspector should pursue."

"He's not my inspector. He's my husband's former colonel."

"You know him, though. And his sergeant."

"I met them at Christmastide."

They entered the hall, dim without the lights switched on.

"While he didn't solve the murder at Emberly, he would have. In hindsight, there were a lot of clues to the actual murderer. Murderess. He didn't try to pin it on anyone either—which is the reason I am not worried about your brother. Mr. Wainwright will not make the evidence fit a convenient suspect. He'll look for a suspect who fits the evidence, if you see what I mean. Here." Isabella held open the swinging door. "Go in. Hopefully, Nuala has kept the fire going. I'll speak to Mrs. Eccles about our tea."

Flick went in, rubbing her arms.

Isabella hadn't taken two steps to the kitchen when Flick cried out. She rushed into the lounge. "What is it? What happened?" Then she saw Flick crouched beside a body on the floor.

Nuala.

"Is she—?"

"No." Flick tapped the maid's cheeks. "Wake up, Nuala! Wake up. Oh, wake up!"

"Was she struck?" She hovered, wanting to do something *but what*?

Nuala stirred then coughed. Then she moaned. Her hands flew to her throat. "Help," she croaked.

"We're here, Nuala. You're safe." Flick helped her sit up and kept an arm around her. "You're with us. Safe. Safe, Nuala. Can you tell me who did this?"

"He—tried—strangle—."

"Don't talk."

"I'll call the gaol." Isabella whirled to leave.

"Wait—wai—." The maid coughed and coughed. "Is there—water?"

She hastened to the sideboard and splashed water into a glass. Then she brought it and knelt, steadying it in Nuala's hands. The water shook and sloshed, but the bar maid managed a sip only to begin coughing again.

"Call the train station," Flick ordered. "Sgt. Callaway is there."

"He—."

"Don't talk," Flick urged.

Nuala looked past her, to Isabella. "Letter—do—?"

"I still have it." Isabella patted her skirt pocket.

"What letter?"

"A letter George Webberly received from London. Threatening his life."

"Good Lord."

Nuala sipped more water then croaked, "He wanted—it."

"He knew you had the letter?"

"Thought—I did." She touched her throat. The skin was reddened. It would bruise.

"Was it Mr. Elwen?" Flick asked.

Nuala nodded.

"I'll tell Sgt. Callaway."

Isabella ran for the call box in the entrance. She clicked the receiver to signal the operator then demanded a connection to the train station.

Thumps on the stairs drew her attention.

Kenneth Elwen had started down. He had a duffle in one hand. The other touched the wall, steadying his descent. He took the stairs one at a time, the same as he'd gone up them. His balance seemed off.

And Isabella realized what the missing something was. Elwen didn't have the driver that he'd used as his walking stick.

A golf club that had a metal head with which to strike the balls. And Webberly's head.

"Who's there?" The tinny voice crackled on the line.

Isabella turned away from the stairs, hoping Elwen's descent muffled her voice. "Is Sgt. Callaway there?" she whispered. "On the platform?"

"What? I cannot hear you. Operator, this connection is bad. Speak up, Miss."

She dared not. She tried to speak distinctly. "Is Sgt. Callaway there?"

The pub door opened. She glanced up.

A burly form filled the doorway. Sgt. Callaway. "Hello, Mrs. Tarrant."

"Sergeant." *How do I let him know?*

Then a revving motor reached them. Callaway looked over his shoulder as the auto roared close.

Elwen reached the foot of the stairs. He stopped, steadying his balance.

"Hello, hello," sounded in her ear. "Who's this?"

Isabella slowly replaced the receiver.

Elwen stared at the sergeant, still in the doorway but his attention outside, on the automobile. He held the door partly open, and the cold wind whisked in, driving away all warmth.

"Nuala didn't die, you know," she told him.

He jerked and stared at her. Callaway whirled around.

"We found her in the lounge," she added, her tone conversational. "Where you tried to strangle her. She can testify against you. About the letter you sent to Mr. Webberly."

He grimaced. "He deserved to die!"

"Judgment and execution are not up to you, Mr. Elwen."

"Here. What's this?" Callaway sounded slow on the uptake.

Elwen groaned, then he hefted his duffle and flung it at the sergeant. Callaway stumbled back. He fell into the door, an elbow crashing into the door's frosted glass pane. The glass shattered.

Elwen thrust past Isabella, hobbling into the pub, heading for the hall and the back door into the garden. And the path to the river.

She started to tackle him—then Callaway cursed. She looked and saw blood pouring from his head and his hand. She dove for him. Elwen could wait. That blood had to be stanched.

She was pressing on Callaway's hand when a shadow loomed over them.

"What happened?" Michael Wainwright demanded.

"He's getting away, boss. Elwen." Callaway greeted his teeth as he pressed a handkerchief to his temple. "He did it."

"Keep pressing that cloth," Isabella ordered.

"You're hurt, Sergeant."

"Mrs. Tarrant's got it, boss. Get after him."

"Here. Use this." A scarf dropped over Callaway's bent legs. "Lean down, Mrs. Tarrant." Then Wainwright climbed over her, and Michael ran for the bar.

"The back hall," she called once she'd straightened. "He tried to kill Nuala!"

.~.~.~.

Thumps and breaking glass alerted Flick.

"Stay here, Nuala." She had maneuvered the maid into a *fauteuil*.

"What—? Where—?"

"I'm not leaving you." She seized a poker from the fire stand. Raising it above her head, she tiptoed to the swinging door and eased it open. Movement. She hastily shut it. Then she cursed herself and opened it again.

Elwen hobbled past, heading for the door beside the kitchen, reaching it. He flung it open. As he half-fell down the doorstep, he looked back.

Flick brandished the poker—then heard the pub door open. Someone rushed through. When she peeked, she saw a rushing form, a scary determination. Then Michael Wainwright was passing her. He paused. "Ring the gaol," he ordered. "Callaway's bleeding badly. We need an ambulance."

"Here! Use this!" She thrust the poker at him.

"Don't need it." Then he ran on, plunging into the garden.

.~.~.~.

Michael caught Elwen before he reached the wall. The man turned and offered his fists. He took a swing as Michael came close, so he tackled the young man around the waist and bore him to the ground.

He jerked cuffs out of his coat pocket. "Kenneth Elwen, you are under arrest for the murder of George Webberly." He snapped the cuffs then grabbed the man's arm and hauled him to his feet. He had to steady him before they marched back to the pub.

Why Elwen tried to run Michael didn't know. The man had a severe limp. He shoved him along the hall and into the pub. Flick had disappeared, but he heard her on the telephone, demanding Amsley "help Inspector Wainwright with his suspect."

Callaway looked up when Michael loomed over him. The cut on his forehead still dripped blood which he dabbed away with a stained handkerchief. Isabella was tying off his hand, with Michael's scarf. "That will hold, I think. No, don't get up, Sergeant. You lost a lot of blood."

"I didn't hurt him," Elwen said sullenly. "Your officer. I didn't hurt him."

"No," Flick said into the telephone. "I won't tell you. I have to call for an ambulance. Do hurry!" She replaced the receiver then picked it up and clicked for the operator. "The doctor. It's an emergency. Then an ambulance."

Blood covered Isabella's skirt, but she ignored it as Michael lifted her up. She glared at Elwen for several moments filled by Flick's precise explanation to the doctor. "Bleeding badly" and "injured" were words she kept repeating.

"How did you know?" Isabella asked him.

"Robby Gilchrist gave me the motive. Gilchrist the Older saw him on Sunday morning, as did MacAlphin who also saw Elwen listening to the argument between Webberly and Mrs. Filmer. That's opportunity. As for method, he had a golf club with him then."

"Yes. He used it for a walking stick. I didn't remember that, not until just now."

The clangor of an ambulance reached them.

Michael steered Elwen to a booth just as Mr. Pollard came down the stairs. He stopped and stared. "What's all this? Shut that door. The cold's coming in."

"Pollard, I want you to watch Elwen for a few minutes."

"He's—why, he's cuffed."

"Yes. He killed George Webberly."

"And—Mrs. Tarrant, are you hurt? You're covered with blood."

"No. This is the sergeant's blood."

He stared at the sergeant still sitting on the threshold. The door stood open, cold air rushing in with every gust. Then he saw the door. "The door, it's broken."

"Just the glass," Isabella said.

"It must be replaced. I'll have to ring—."

"That must wait."

The man turned to Michael. "My wife will be arriving at the station. I am to meet her."

"You can leave when the constable arrives."

They heard crunching gravel. Michael saw Amsley coming across the forecourt. An ambulance appeared, rolling to a stop before the pub as the constable gaped at Callaway's blood. The siren switched off.

As Amsley bent to help Callaway, Michael snapped, "Constable. I have Kenneth Elwen in custody. We need to secure him and release Chauncey Sherborne."

"Thank God," Flick breathed.

Then the doctor was there, shoving Amsley out of his way as he knelt to tend to Callaway.

And the adrenaline drained out of Michael, leaving him propped up only by will.

Chapter 26

Tuesday into Wednesday

After an hour in the doctor's surgery, Callaway looked pale around the gills, but he was steady on his feet. His left hand had a massive bandage. Sticking plaster covered the cut high on his brow, hiding the three stitches needed to close the skin. Dr. Woolsey prescribed a fortnight without using the hand then ordered a nurse to visit night and morning to ensure the bandages stayed in place. Then he rang the London doctor that the sergeant had grudgingly allowed as someone to check the wound's progress. Finally, he ordered Callaway to the pub, "bed rest and beef tea."

"I can work, boss, never think I can't," Callaway protested.

"Not today." Dr. Woolsey peered over his spectacles. "Not if you want that hand to heal. Bed and beef tea. I'll ring Mrs. Halsey and send her over to the pub to make the broth. You, Sergeant, take to your bed."

"What can I do, Doc?"

"No driving," he ordered, and Callaway shrugged. "No typing or writing," and Callaway grinned. The doctor's last order of "No use of that hand at all" won a frown.

"I'm not planning on fisticuffs!"

"Nor should you," the doctor ordered. "He needs bedrest and beef tea this evening," and though Callaway complained, Michael saw to it.

When they left the surgery, Callaway pressed to join Michael at the goal, but Michael refused. Callaway had missed Kenneth Elwen's confession, and Constable Amsley had had the onerous task of typing it up, with a carbon copy for Michael's chief inspector.

Once his sergeant was pinned to his bed by a bossy nurse, Michael returned to the gaol. Three automobiles were parked before the constabulary. When he entered, three men stood to greet him. Sir Robert introduced the local Crown prosecutor Mr. Debbenham and the shire's coroner, a man named Jefferson.

Then the tedious decisions about Elwen began. Michael protested driving the young man to London only to return him for the inquest. Amsley, glad to break away from his typing, said he would enlist a constable in the next town for the night shifts at the gaol. Elwen would stay in Upper Wellsford for the inquest and for his plea. Since he'd confessed, he would soon be transported to prison. Then the wheels of justice would spin out the rest of his life.

Apathetic, Elwen had lain on the bunk, arm over his eyes. "I don't care" was his only comment, even with Debbenham offering to contact an attorney to represent him. "With this leg, I don't have a life." He hadn't moved, even when the sharp-featured maid from the pub brought his supper on a tray.

The afternoon was nearly gone when Sir Robert considered all decisions made, Mr. Debbenham agreed that they were, and Mr. Jefferson had the necessary files to begin his review of the case prior to the inquest. Constable Amsley returned to his typing.

Callaway also missed Michael's return to Greavley Abbey. Twilight was falling as he drove past the main gates to the graveled entrance that seemed to go nowhere. It tracked alongside the woods with an old cottage tucked under the branches. Then the road turned around the edge of the woods and Greavley's fields and work buildings stretched before him. Michael found two of the men he needed at the carriage house: Gilchrist the Younger, now sober, and MacAlphin. Neither reacted when he told them Elwen had confessed. They signed their statements, typed by Amsley while Michael dealt with bureaucracy.

Gilchrist the Older he found walking back from the Prior's House. He stopped on the path through the oaks. "Sir. I did not expect your return."

"I need your signature, Mr. Gilchrist. Read it first."

He stared at the paper. "The man is in custody?"

"He confessed."

"What will happen to him?"

"Inquest. A judge will take his plea. Then prison."

"Tragic, tragic all around."

Michael held out a fountain pen.

The major domo removed spectacles from an inner pocket. He tilted the paper to the light and scanned it. Then he took the pen. Holding the paper on his hand, he signed then capped the pen and returned it.

Michael checked the legibility of the signature.

"You have the statement from my son?"

"Already signed." He folded the document and slipped it into his coat pocket. "Thank you, Mr. Gilchrist."

They heard a motor rev then gravel crunching. Both looked at the entrance gates. A green Calcott rolled over the forecourt, the opposite way around the conifer feature, then it stopped smoothly. A young man climbed out, bent to say something to the driver, then slammed the door.

"Mr. Sherborne has returned," Gilchrist said unnecessarily. "I suppose the dean will allow him to resume work tomorrow."

Michael bit back the strong retort he wanted to make, that Sherborne should have no threat to his position. "There shouldn't be a problem with that. No charges have been filed against him."

"Elwen's confession would clear any question about him for Dean Filmer."

"As it should," he gritted. "Thank you, Gilchrist. You should not need to see me or the constable again." He didn't watch the green Calcott begin its return to the village. He turned his back on the major domo and headed for his own automobile, parked at the carriage house.

At the pub, he saw the Calcott being driven into the old barn. No sign of Flick Sherborne, not outside in the icy wind and not inside, when he entered the pub. The smell of cooked beef filled the building, and his mouth watered. He didn't remember lunch. He rang his chief again, wishing the pub's telephone was a true call box with a door, offering a modicum of privacy. He identified himself then updated his chief on the case and Callaway's injuries.

"When do you expect to return?"

"Another day, sir, to clear everything for the prosecutor, a Mr. Debbenham. Then we'll return to London. Callaway is under orders of bed rest."

"Tell me about the case."

"I would rather not, sir. Public call box."

"I see. Tell Callaway that he will have through the weekend for his bed rest."

"I will do that, sir. The doctor has ordered no desk work. No typing, no writing, no filing. A fortnight of restricted work, at minimum."

"That must have been a nasty cut. Tell the sergeant not to worry. We'll find something for him to do. Liaison, perhaps, with constabularies close to London. That will keep him busy. We'll need to find you a bag man."

"Only as a stand-in, sir. Callaway and I work well together."

"We'll see, we'll see. Did you ring his wife?"

Michael inwardly sighed at the chief inspector's consistent memory lapse. "Not yet, sir."

"Congratulations on solving this case. Sir Robert gave me to understand there were great difficulties in discovering motives and suspects."

"A few, sir. We arrived at the correct result, though."

"That's good, that's good. You're making a name for solved cases,

Wainwright. That shows to your favor."

He thought of mentioning that last night the wrong man had sat in Upper Wellsford's gaol. The young man had happily turned over his cell to Kenneth Elwen and agreed to hold himself available for any inquest. Sir Robert had agreed that a charge against Sherborne would unnecessarily confuse the case.

He slid onto a booth and ordered meat and bread. The maid with the pinched face waited on him, but he didn't bother to look at her. He endured villagers who came to congratulate him on solving the case, a silver-haired man bought him a pint, and Herbert Pollard arranged a toast. Then Michael escaped upstairs. He would have talked briefly with Callaway, but the nurse shushed him and sent him on his way. He didn't see Isabella Tarrant or Flick Sherborne. He wanted to. He wanted to explain. Maybe it was better that he said nothing.

He had nightmares, though.

Callaway didn't look as if he'd slept any better when they joined in the morning. "Anything more to do, boss? Interviews? Statements?" And so their day was spent, the morning in interviews, the afternoon writing up the reports for the constable to type, Callaway hampered by the sling that the nurse had demanded he wear for the day.

As the late afternoon headed toward twilight, they trudged back to the Hook and Line. Callaway stopped outside the boarded-over front door of the pub. The wind had died. It was cold but not the freezing temperatures of the morning. They could clearly hear the buzz of talk inside the pub. "You want to drive back tonight, boss?"

"Tomorrow. Early start. I'll drive."

Callaway smirked. "Right-O." He headed in, stopping beside the call box. "We still need a statement from Mrs. Pollard, boss. I guess that would be her behind the bar."

"I don't see a need for her statement now, do you? She doesn't enter the case we have. If Elwen hadn't confessed, then yes, I'd want all the ins and outs covered. As it is …."

"Then we're finished for the day, boss?"

"We are. Get your pint. Be prepared to regale the whole pub with your injuries and the arrest."

Callaway grinned and headed for the bar.

Michael went up, packed what he could, then sat in a chair, staring into the darkness outside the window. *Lucky, that's what I am.* He didn't feel lucky.

When he couldn't stand his thoughts anymore, he decided to share a pint with Callaway and any admirers still clustered around the sergeant. Then dinner. Maybe a walk around the village after.

Isabella Tarrant was passing as he opened his door. "Inspector. Join us for dinner."

Us could only be Flick Sherborne, perhaps her brother. "I don't think—."

"Nonsense. No one will bear a grudge. Chauncey admits that removing evidence was foolish, even if his IOU and medallion had nothing to do with Kenneth Elwen." She reached forward and took his arm, drawing him out of his room. "Service is early tonight, anyway. Come. I'll smooth the way. Unless you would rather have dinner in the pub. With everyone goggling at you."

He repressed a shudder and tried not to let his hopes rise.

Men slapped his back as he followed Mrs. Tarrant through the pub. Callaway held court at one end of the bar, an amber-filled pint at his elbow, another emptied beside it. Then they were through, in the hall, and entering the lounge.

One man had claimed the table before the hearth. He sipped a glass of wine. A newspaper was propped up before him. No one else was there. An iced cake had pride of place on the sideboard.

No Flick Sherborne.

He didn't know what he would say to Mrs. Tarrant. He had settled on asking her about her upcoming voyage when she veered to join the single man.

"Mr. Allister, I want you to meet Inspector Wainwright. Michael, this is Mr. Allister, the barrister that Flick's solicitor sent to help Chauncey. He arrived on the day train from London and decided to take the evening here before returning to London."

"Mr. Allister."

"Inspector Wainwright." He smiled slightly and reached up to remove the newspaper. "We are often on the opposite sides, are we not? I am pleased that this time we do not have to be. I spent an hour with Sir Robert Goodkind, my first stop, even before coming here to secure a room. I have also visited the Constabulary as well, to review the evidence against Mr. Sherborne. I understand that he is not to be charged."

Isabella's eyes opened wide. "Are you not to represent Mr. Elwen, sir?"

"He refused the offer of an attorney," Michael explained. "Mr. Debbenham, the Crown prosecutor, asked several times."

"Yes. He refused my offer as well. I will remain until the inquest, I think, to ensure all goes well. I wish to say, Inspector, that I appreciate that you requested of Sir Robert Goodkind that no charges be brought against young Mr. Sherborne."

"That's excellent news," Isabella said. "Flick, did you hear? The inspector has asked that no charges are filed against your brother."

Michael hurriedly stood as Flick slid onto the empty chair at their table. Allister made only a half-attempt to stand. She smiled a greeting at the barrister. She didn't look at Michael, not once.

He had a long road to regain any consideration from her.

She draped the napkin over her lap. "Chauncey should not have been taken into custody at all."

"Chauncey shouldn't have removed evidence," Isabella defended the action. "He admitted his error."

Flick shrugged. "That's not the important thing, though. Chauncey had nothing to do with George Webberly's murder."

Allister cleared his throat.

Michael wondered how much more uncomfortable this evening could become. "Will your brother be coming to dinner?"

Flick looked at him then, hostility in her blue eyes. "No. He said he'd spent too much time away from his work."

"I saw you drop him at the school."

"Did you?" She shifted a little, angling her body away from him. "Chauncey is worried about his position at the school. He didn't know if the dean welcomed his return. Apparently, the contract he signed has an ethics clause, and any arrest would nullify the contract."

"He wasn't arrested," Michael said.

"Indeed not," Allister said. "Merely held in custody. I confirmed that with Constable Amsley. Should the dean wish to enforce the clause, then I will happily speak with him, to set him straight about actions that he may and may not take against your brother. As a matter of fact, I will visit this dean tomorrow, to inform him of that fact."

"His name's Filmer, Ralston Filmer." Michael gave the name with relish. Here was someone for Flick to direct her anger toward, not him.

Sibby came in with bowls of pea soup, a welcome interruption. "Ham and colewort to come," she informed them.

"Have Mr. Sandhurst or Mr. Nelson said anything?" Isabella asked, her voice quiet.

"No," Flick mouthed.

"Will they have anything to say about Elwen?" Michael asked. "Were they good friends?"

"They were fishermen together," Isabella said, "but I do not know if they were good friends. I do know that Mr. Nelson ensured Mr. Elwen had more protein with his dinners. He shared his catch," she explained.

"That's interesting," Mr. Allister said. "Perhaps I should inquire. They are staying here?"

"It is called the Hook and Line," Flick said. "Fishermen always stay here. The pubs in Lower Wellsford are too far from the river. Why would you speak to Mr. Nelson?"

"About Mr. Elwen."

"Mr. Allister has kindly offered to remain until the inquest," Isabella said, her words intended to drive the barrister in the direction she wanted, "to help Mr. Elwen. He may change his mind about legal representation."

"Indeed," the lawyer said and sipped his soup.

The soup had been removed, they were well into their ham and greens, when Flick suddenly sat back. "It's constantly on my tongue. I won't avoid it any longer. Inspector, can you tell us *anything* about the case?" And she looked at him, full on, the hostility no longer in her eyes.

Flick's use of his name should not please him so much. He was farther gone than he realized—with no hope of going further with her—but his spirits lifted out of their abyss. "A little."

"Can you tell us his motive?"

"Elwen served in Webberly's unit in the war."

"Oh." Isabella's fork clattered onto her plate."That's not good, is it? Mr. Farrell intimated that Webberly had done something very bad, something that should have had him up on charges."

Michael remembered how his War Office source had refused to speak in specifics. Yet he had talked around and around until enough details emerged to build a picture. "I have no proof and Elwen hasn't said." He shot a direct look at the barrister. "My understanding is that those higher up didn't want any accusations brought against Webberly. He didn't receive the field commission that he apparently hoped for. They relocated him to another regiment and a different field of action to stop rumors."

"What happened in the war?"

"This is a rough description, understand. Webberly ordered his men to charge across the battlefield to take a German trench. He told them that the Germans had withdrawn and they would face opposition only from a few sentries. Machine guns cut his unit apart. Only three survived." That he'd learned from Robby Gilchrist as well as "Webberly didn't go over with his men but stayed in shelter."

"Elwen didn't tell you that, did he?" Flick's question pre-empted Allister's. "Who told you?"

"Two different sources." He hid a smile at her frustrated look.

"So, Elwen recovers as much as he can from his wounds and tracks down Webberly."

"No. He didn't know Webberly was here. He saw him in December. I think his need for revenge built from then. I don't know. He didn't speak of that. He visited Greavley Abbey on Sunday morning to see Dodges, who lost his son in that charge."

"Is Dodges a source?" Allister asked.

"No." He didn't mention Robby Gilchrist. Let Elwen tell the lawyer that. Gilchrist the Younger deserved to bury those events, not keep dragging them out.

"Dodges' son and Webberly and Elwen, all together," Isabella marveled. "It's a small world."

"Recruitment from a single area means that men who are acquainted will serve together," Allister said pedantically. "The belief is that they will provide moral support for each other."

"The actual result," the hard note had returned to Flick's voice, "is that whole districts lost every young man. So, Elwen sees Dodges then sees Webberly and decides to kill him?"

"I don't think that was his plan, no. Nothing he said sounded premeditated. That may prevent his execution. Elwen had returned to Greavley to see Dodges, heard Webberly arguing—."

"With Mrs. Filmer," Isabella inserted.

"Yes. He saw her leave. He waited, and Webberly appeared."

"But … we found Webberly on the path to the river." Isabella sounded confused. "Did he follow him? Did he strike him from behind? How could he keep up with Webberly? His leg is crippled."

"Mr. Allister, do stop me if I say anything I shouldn't."

The barrister shrugged at Michael's request. "He's not my client."

Flick gave the man another glare then turned to Michael. "Did he only intend to confront him? I doubt he had premeditated the murder."

Michael leaned back. This next was from Elwen himself. He needed to be exact with Elwen's confession. Allister had said the young man wasn't his client. That could change. Would change, he supposed, if Flick convinced the man to take the case. Lawyers could be tricky, sliding around words' meanings to get the result they wanted. "Whatever Elwen was thinking, he led the way to the river path. Webberly became impatient at his slow pace. At some point, they argued, and Elwen struck him over the head with the golf club. He said, when he surfaced—by which I understand Elwen to be in a rage— Webberly was dead. The church bells began ringing. He knew people might soon come onto the path. He left."

"Leaving the splotches of blood because he used the club as a walking stick. What did he do with it?"

"I would have flung it in the river," Flick said sturdily.

"He did."

Isabella turned over her plate knife, again and again. "He expected to—well, get away with it?"

"He said nothing about that, Mrs. Tarrant."

"How is he doing?" Flick asked.

"Not good. Which is the reason that a visit from an attorney interested in helping him may change his mind."

"It's not premeditated?" she asked.

"Not as he described. Not as he's charged."

Allister smirked. "Are you building a case for the defendant, Inspector?"

"Why should he not?" Flick cried. "And it would be a good case. Every jury would hesitate to convict a man who merely wanted revenge for the dozens upon dozens of men that Webberly killed when he sent them on that assault. An assault he himself didn't go on. Isn't that correct, Inspector?"

The barrister shrugged. "Juries can be capricious. I would take him for client, but I doubt he can pay my fee."

"We were going to pay you to represent Chauncey. We can pay you to represent Elwen."

He bent his head in acknowledgment. "Very well. I will remain for the inquest and his sentencing. I may even convince him to allow my representation."

"There, that is done," said Isabella, "now for cake," and she determinedly turned the conversation to Mr. Allister's background, asking about his experience, his firm, and his family. From there she tugged out his favorite restaurants in London and his perspective on the best places for gatherings.

Michael gave one last check on Callaway, still holding court in the pub, then he headed upstairs.

He was yawning as he climbed between the bedcoverings. He lay back, hands behind his head, and considered the evening.

Flick Sherborne no longer actively hated him, yet she still grasped at a grudge. She had refused to shake his hand in farewell and added no well wishes behind Isabella's for his journey to London in the early morning. She didn't even say goodbye, remaining silent as Isabella promised to send his message to Madoc in her next wire.

He would see Flick in London. He hoped time would work its magic.

Yet time hadn't worked for Kenneth Elwen.

He turned to his side, thumped his pillow, switched off the lamp, and stared into darkness.

Epilogue

End of March

Owl loved the photos and article about the topiary garden. She also snapped up all of Flick's photos of public school boys, running along a cloister walk for the next class, strolling across a green, laughing together outside a building. "Greavley?" She held aloft a photo of the Saturday games day, boys scrumming in a rugby match against the masters.

"That one, yes. You'll find Eton and Harrow and Godolphin for girls. That was yours, wasn't it?" Flick had gathered the photos from Greavley with a collection that she had taken over the past couple of years, whenever she'd swung past one of the schools. When she'd begun the series, she had had only the glimmer of an idea for a feature.

Flick hadn't mentioned the murder, and Owl didn't know to ask. The murder hadn't interested London newspapers.

"The mamas who subscribe to *Modern Woman* will love them," Owl crowed, and that was the easiest pay chit that Flick had earned. "We'll take them all. When you have those other gardening articles ready, we'll take them as well." She slid toward herself the photo of Chauncey and a master of the Old Guard, laughing. "How is your brother?"

"Doing well." Thank God that was true. "He gained weight in the three weeks that I was there."

"Were you bored? Village life can be pure tedium."

Actually, Flick's return to London was filled with tedium. Stepha and Milla had each found a beau and were out most nights. The flat stood empty, lonely.

She spent her first week at the London Library, the Tate, or another museum, researching ideas for new articles and writing letters to the sources MacAlphin had given her. She needed to branch out from obscure gardens like Greavley.

She wandered the streets with her camera ready, taking photos of an aged couple on a park bench and rowdy men clustered outside a pub, a young couple perusing a movie poster and a queue at a soup kitchen. She didn't offer the street scenes to Owl. She took them straight to the *London Daily*. Alan Rettleston barely looked at them before committing to buy. Then he buzzed his secretary and asked if old Pickwick was in.

"Another photo narrative? I can find more photos of returned soldiers and men out-of-work."

He grinned but didn't comment, lighting another cigarette. Then he stubbed out the one he'd finished. "Know anything about that murder in Upper Wellsford? That's where you were, wasn't it?"

Flick's breath caught. She laughed. "I know it happened, but I wasn't involved."

"Doing anything tonight?"

"Are you offering dinner again?"

"Dinner. Dancing. A party after."

"Where's the party?" She ran her finger along the side of his desk and started to breathe again. She'd escaped discussing the murder. She didn't want any of her comments in a news story: *Eyewitness Tells All.*

"Bloomsbury. Stephen Pettigrew. Know him? Artist. Connections in theatre."

Art and theatre. Her flatmate Millie worked in theatre, but more connections never hurt. Especially theatre directors, actors and actresses wanting publicity shots, and newbies and wannabees looking for a way to stand out before their stars flickered and faded.

"Sounds fun. I may find some business there. Dinner at the Fitzwilliam Victoria, please."

"God, why do you like that place? Filled with frumps and grumps."

"The chef is extraordinary."

Flick didn't mention the person she hoped to see. Their paths hadn't crossed elsewhere.

She wore a beaded gown borrowed from Stepha, a fan spandelle loaned by Millie, and her own Spanish shawl, tied around her waist this time. The *maître d'* smiled upon her but still led them to a table behind a column, blocking her view of the dance floor and the orchestra.

She had no obstruction to her view of Michael Wainwright.

The woman draped around him in the foxtrot was the woman of before. Flick envied her embroidered dress in the new style.

Halfway through the dinner with Rettleston, a waiter called him to the telephone. "An emergency with the presses, sir."

Rettleston swore words that ladies weren't supposed to hear, flung down his napkin, and stalked away with never a word to her.

Flick propped her chin on her hands and played speculation about the other diners.

Michael Wainwright's group—only four this time—were leaving. He murmured to the older man then crossed through the dancers to her side of the floor. He moved slowly, not speaking, and couples shifted out of his way, his aura alone clearing his path.

Then he reached her. He extended his hand, and when she placed hers in his, he bowed and kissed her fingertips. "Good evening, Miss

Sherborne."

"Is that your chief and his wife? Who is the lady?"

"Margot Pomphrey, widow. How is your brother?"

"Chauncey is very well, thank you." Expected pleasantries. *Have we nothing else to say to each other?*

Then he said, "I saw your photos in the *London Daily*. Women In and Out of Work. F. Sherborne. That's you, isn't it? They're good, very good. Important."

She swallowed her surprise. "I didn't think the *Daily* would be a newspaper you normally read."

"Callaway brought it in to me."

"How is Sergeant Callaway? How is his hand?"

"He's using it without trouble. He hated his two weeks working with local constabularies, though. He's back with me now."

"Oh. Um. I have an article about topiaries in *Modern Woman* in June and a photo spread in September."

His mouth quirked. "That's not a magazine that either I or Callaway will see."

"I can send them to you. Advance copies."

That half-smile broadened. "I would like that, Miss Sherborne. A break from the norm. Like tonight's dinner. It's hard to turn down the chief inspector when he's feeling benevolent to the lower orders."

"When I saw you here, in mid-February, before—all that, you were with Miss Pomphrey then."

"It's Mrs. She's a widow and a friend of the chief's wife. I'm Spare Man," he explained, "called upon when no other escort is available."

Rettleston appeared, trying to loom beside Michael and failing. While their heights were equal, Michael's shoulders were broader, and he held himself straighter. "Excuse me, sir."

Michael shifted over. "I have to leave. Have a good evening, Miss Sherborne. Sir."

Since she didn't want to raise Rettleston's ire—he looked harassed—Flick didn't watch Michael leave.

"How do you know Michael Wainwright?" he asked as he slid onto his seat.

"In passing," she lied smoothly. "How do you know a rather obscure detective inspector of the Met?"

"Business," he said, which explained nothing. Tit for tat, Flick supposed. "I've a problem with the presses, Felicity. I must return soon. We can finish our dinner, but I don't have time for the party. I'll make it up to you. If not a party at Pettigrew's, then somewhere else."

"Right-O," she said and wondered where she'd picked that up.

.~.~.~.

10 April 1920

Isabella tossed a blanket over her legs then opened her sketchbook. Shipboard life offered endless possibilities for drawing. Tony Carstairs had a source who promised to use every illustration of life aboard a cruise ship. Posters, brochures, postcards: the uses for illustrations were endless.

Tony had snapped up her six watercolors of Greavley Abbey's gardens. The pen-and-ink drawings of London sites had pleased him; those had given him the idea for the shipboard illustrations. He promised to send her a tourism contact in Australia. "Your watercolors come to me. Always. And anything in oils. I hear Lady Malvaise is very pleased, but no portraits, if you will, Izzy. Your letter box may be filled with offers of portrait commissions. Please do not distract ourself with those. Ocean. India. Australia. An exotic interest for the gallery. Now the war is definitely over, everyone's looking around for possibilities. Freight will be less expensive when you send the shipment in groups."

"Yes, sir," she said meekly, happy to bask in Edward Malvaise's pleasure with the portrait rather than take another commission. The youth had promised to hang the portrait in public rooms as long as he was at Emberly.

He laughed. "I'm being a dictator, aren't I? You know me well. I have an eye for the new and different as long as it's *good*."

"Would you be interested in photographs?"

"No, no, Izzy darling. Don't convert to photography."

"Not me, Tony, my friend. She works for magazines and newspapers, but she will be branching into art photography. You might try three or five, see how the public likes them."

"Who is she?"

She gave him Flick's name and direction and a telephone where she could be reached.

"No guarantees," he warned.

"I only said to her that I would mention it. Nothing more."

Tony nodded and tucked the paper in an inner pocket of his bright plaid jacket. "When do you leave?"

"A week," she said and shivered with delight.

Isabella had thought a week would give her sufficient time to finish packing. She only had clothes to pack, those to take and those to store. In addition to two large suitcases, she'd had to buy a trunk. She comforted herself with the knowledge that she was sailing into the southern hemisphere. The *SS Sophocles* of the Aberdeen Line had given her a cozy berth with no room for anything beyond one suitcase. She consigned her heaviest coat and clothes to Cecilia's boxroom then packed two jackets and other warm clothes in a trunk now stowed in the bowels of the ship. Warm weather was only a guarantee around the equator, but that would be the greater part of the voyage.

A steward came along the deck. "Mrs. Tarrant? Mrs. Tarrant?" he called.

Isabella lifted her hand, and he brought a sealed envelope to her. "A letter?" *Who is writing to me?*

"Waiting for you in port, ma'am. We sorted the mail bag, and I recalled that you had booked a deck chair for the afternoon."

"Adonis, isn't it? Thank you for remembering."

"Have you everything you need, ma'am? Would you care for tea?"

"Not yet, thank you."

He bowed a little then sauntered away.

The handwriting was sloped block letters. She didn't recognize it. Isabella closed her sketchbook, tucked her pencil in her bun, then peeled open the envelope's flap. She drew out the folded papers. Three pages!

She flipped to the last page for the signature. Madoc!

Sighing happily, she began to read.

Thanks!

Thank you for reading *Portrait with Death,* the conclusion to Isabella Newcombe Tarrant's **Into Death** series and the introduction to a new series with Flick Sherborne.

When I conceived the idea for Isabella Newcombe and an archaeological dig on Crete—the story that became *Digging into Death*—I fully intended it to be a stand-alone. Imagine my surprise when *Christmas with Death* started clamoring to reach the page. Then I never expected to write a third. Isabella would have a duology; I could live with that. So I thought! Lo and behold, the idea for the third book happened last summer as I finished *The Hazard with Hearts,* my 12th Regency mystery. Here it is July of 2021, and the third **Into Death** is hitting bookshelves.

Flick Sherborne wasn't in my mind when I first set pen to paper on *Portrait with Death*. She came fully formed, though, as Isabella met Dean Filmer and Edward Malvaise. Once she introduced herself to Isabella before their Saturday evening dinner at the Hook and Line, I knew she would be the second protagonist in the novel. At that point, the story's victim and the murderer were not yet decided. Characters just appeared in their roles. Once Flick demanded a dominant role, I jumped back to the beginning to insert her into the story. As the novel took shape, Flick offered many opportunities for a series. I have only the barest glimmer of ideas, but that will occur—after a couple of other story ideas reach paper. Letting Flick's story percolate will create a richer novel.

Last year, as I finished the Hearts in Hazard series, sadness at leaving Regency England filled me. Now we've reached the final novel in the **Into Death** series. Maybe I shouldn't say 'final'. I could think up something else: Isabella on ship, in India, in Australia, returned to Britain. Oops.

I'm always glad to hear from people who enjoy reading my Regency mysteries and the Into Death series.

Free Novella

Set in the 1920s, *The Lion's Den* is a mystery novella with Filly Malvaise and Jack Portman. The novella is available free when you sign up for my newsletter. It's also available for 99 cents at Amazon.

The Lion's Den

Escaping the lion's den needs more than a warrior angel.

Jack Portman had never forgotten Filly Malvaise. Then she walked into his local pub and into the clutches of a loan shark. Can he rescue her before she falls victim to evil?

Here's the link: https://dl.bookfunnel.com/wc84divkre

For any questions, comments, and speculations, contact us direct at winkbooks@aol.com.You can find my books on my website ~~ www.writersinkbooks.com. Look for all my books at online distributors both nationally and internationally.

One more thing:

Indie writers thrive on reviews. I'm small beans, without the advertising budget of the big peeps. You can help with a short review at the retailer from which you purchased this book.

And with *any* book that you enjoy, please share with other readers looking for escape from the dark stresses of life.

Dream it. Believe it. Do it.
~~ M.A. Lee

Hearts in Hazard by M.A. Lee

Mysteries with a dash of romance, set during the Regency Era of England

1 ~ *A Game of Secrets* ~ Smugglers, secrets and spies: Kate tries to hide in plain sight; Tony tries to catch a spy. First they fall in love, then they fall into trouble with smugglers. Will they survive?

2 ~ *A Game of Spies* ~ Salons and soirées, flirtation and dancing, gambling and spies: Josette and Giles fall in love over a deck of cards—and try not to die.

Spymaster Giles Hargreaves was introduced in *A Game of Secrets*.

3 ~ *A Game of Hearts* ~ **Two couples** :: One titled widow, one wealthy businessman: two hearts shadowed by their past. One bright young flirt, one hard-edged young man: two hearts crossed by circumstance. Mix in a courtesan and two rakes, all out for mischief, and murder bloody and foul.

4 ~ *The Danger of Secrets* ~ Deep in the wintry countryside, a house warmed by relatives and friends: secrets of family, secrets of hearts, secrets of blood and pain. Match a daughter to an unknown father; match a spinster to an earl; match a serial killer to his next victim.

Gordon Musgrove was introduced in *A Game of Spies*.

5 ~ *The Danger for Spies* ~ Impossibilities? Rakes don't lose their hearts. Spies don't give up the game. No one hides in plain sight. Codes are unbreakable. A man can't hold onto revenge for years and years. Impossibilities are designed to be shattered.

Toby Kennitt was introduced in *A Game of Spies*.

6 ~ *The Danger to Hearts* ~ A country manor in early Spring: older woman and younger man. Horses, cats, needlework, roses and afternoon teas ~ What could possibly go wrong in an idyll? Trouble in the past, trouble now, and murder.

The character Jess Carter was introduced in *A Game of Secrets*.

7 ~ *The Key to Secrets* ~ Debutantes should snare fiancés, not murder them. Constable Hector Evans must solve three murders. Is his former love guilty, of is she a convenient scapegoat?

Constable Hector Evans was introduced in *The Danger to Hearts*.

8 ~ *The Key for Spies* ~ Spies and traitors. Lies and treachery. Unexpected love where bullets fly. One traitor destroys loyalty. What

will two traitors destroy?

9 ~ *The Key with Hearts* ~ A convenient marriage inconveniently causes murder.

10 ~ *The Hazard of Secrets*. Two hearts with dangerous pasts— Can they keep their secrets, or will murder force them to reveal all?

11 ~ *The Hazard for Spies* ~ Disguised to spy. Will murder destroy their chance for love?

12 ~ *The Hazard for Hearts* ~ Two wives haunt the castle. Will she be the third to die?

Isabella Newcombe's Into Death Series

Digging into Death ~ Has the love of her life beguiled her straight into death?

A governess seeking refuge, a handsome young man, an archaeological dig: romance is inevitable; murder is not. Suspicions escalate, artifacts are stolen, and then a second murder.

Has Isabella found true love only to lose her life?

Christmas with Death ~ Christmas is for miracles, merriment, and murder.

A holiday party with the uppercrust of English society: gifts and feasts, games and romance, and people with motives for murder … including Isabella's friend.

Will Isabella discover the truth? Or will she be the next victim?

Set in 1919 at an English country manor for a party throughout Christmastide. Available in paperback and e-book.

Portrait with Death ~ A British public school. Former soldiers haunted by the trenches of the Great War. Ladies who only act like ladies. A photographer. Three fishermen. A headmaster. A medic. A pub owner and his wife. And more.

Who committed the murder? Can Isabella find the answer? Or will a murderer paint with more blood?

Nonfiction by M.A. Lee

Think like a Pro Writer series

1] *Think like a Pro: New Advent for Writers* ~ Seven lessons to guide your growth from newbie writer to "thinking like a pro writer". Now available in paperback and e-book.

2] *Think / Pro: A Planner for Writers* ~ An undated planner with daily word counts, progress meters, project planning, and goals analysis. Paperback only. How else will you record your goals and progress?

3] *Old Geeky Greeks: Write Stories with Ancient Techniques* ~ Storytelling has its roots in the strong foundations of classical antiquity. Avoid the re-packaged "exclusive insights" and "wham-pow webinars" and return to the source, organized as a seminar in book form.

4] *Discovering Your Novel* ~ a 52-week course for new writers, offering guidance from original idea to publication and marketing.

5] *Discovering Characters* ~ Delving deeply into your primary characters is more than just templates and character interviews. You also need to know your secondary characters. Focus on more than appearance, more than personality types, and explore your characters hearts and souls. Discover them!

6] *Discovering Your Plot* ~ What writers need and want for plot structures and genre expectations. Control pacing, tension, and suspense with a stronger comprehension of the major sections of a novel.

7] *Discovering your Author Brand* ~ The greatest secret to catch the attention of fly-by readers? Branding. Writers need to brand their books, their series, and themselves as the author. Packed with examples and explanations from past successful marketing efforts.

8] *Discovering Sentence Craft* ~ Zeug-what? Chiasmus? Auxesis? Are those spelled correctly? Well, yes. For centuries the best writers have used these are literary devices to make their works memorable. Writers are artists, seeking ideas from the creative muse. We're also crafters, looking for the best ways to present those creative ideas. *DiscS~Craft* presents techniques for using figurative & interpretive concepts as well as the structures of inversions, repetitions, oppositions, and sequencings.

Just Start Writing :: Inspiration 4 Writers, book 1 ~Writing can be a dizzy whirl of a carousel, all colors and mirrors with unicorns and griffins and dragons to ride. How do you get your ticket, climb on the carousel, and join the writing ride? If you want to pursue your writing dream, open up *Just Start Writing*.

. ~ . ~ . ~ .

2 * 0 * 4 Lifestyle: A Planner for Living ~ *Intermittent fasting. Bible Journaling. Keto Diet. 7-Minute Workout. Five minutes with God.* If the newest fads to follow are leaving you cold and edgy, time to re-think your daily plan. Return to Luke 10:27 to involve the whole self—heart, soul, mind & body. 2 * 0 * 4 offers an undated planner to help you muse and move, feast and fast, and live and love. Paperback only. How else will you write in it? Available in the Meadow and the Mountain River editions.

Pen Names of M.A. Lee

Remi Black ~ Fae Mark'd

Fae Mark'd Wizard
Weave a Wizardry Web
Dream a Deadly Dream
Sing a Graveyard Song

Fae Mark'd World
To Wield the Wind : Spells of Air 1
To Charm the Air: Spells of Air 2
To Curse the Wyre: Spells of Air 3

Edie Roones ~ Seasons in Sansward

Summer Sieges
Autumn Spells
Winter Sorcery
Spring Magicks (in the sketching stage)

All books from Writers' Ink are available at online distributors.

For any comments, questions, and speculations, contact winkbooks@aol.com. Use the subject line to direct your email to a specific book or series.